GW00362796

Pra

'Like a weird mix of Dickens and Martin

but
and

s he
the
ctly
ing

e of

DORKING LIBRA...
www.surreycc.gov.uk/libraries

- - MAY 2014

9/12

28/4

SURREY
COUNTY COUNCIL

Overdue items may incur charges
as published in the current
Schedule of Charges.

L21

lish

you

at is

his
iday

ing.

ark,
like

Also by Joseph Connolly

Fiction

POOR SOULS

THIS IS IT

SUMMER THINGS

WINTER BREAKS

IT CAN'T GO ON

S.O.S.

THE WORKS

LOVE IS STRANGE

JACK THE LAD AND BLOODY MARY

ENGLAND'S LANE

BOYS AND GIRLS

Non-fiction

COLLECTING MODERN FIRST EDITIONS

P. G. WODEHOUSE

JEROME K. JEROME: A CRITICAL BIOGRAPHY

MODERN FIRST EDITIONS: THEIR VALUE TO COLLECTORS

THE PENGUIN BOOK QUIZ BOOK

CHILDREN'S MODERN FIRST EDITIONS

BESIDE THE SEASIDE

ALL SHOOK UP: A FLASH OF THE FIFTIES

CHRISTMAS

WODEHOUSE

FABER AND FABER: EIGHTY YEARS OF BOOK COVER DESIGN

THE A–Z OF EATING OUT

STUFF

JOSEPH CONNOLLY

Quercus

First published in Great Britain in 1997
by Faber and Faber Limited

This paperback edition published in 2014 by

Quercus Editions Ltd
55 Baker Street
7th Floor, South Block
London
W1U 8EW

Copyright © 1997 Joseph Connolly

The moral right of Joseph Connolly to be
identified as the author of this work has been
asserted in accordance with the Copyright,
Designs and Patents Act, 1988.

All rights reserved. No part of this publication
may be reproduced or transmitted in any form
or by any means, electronic or mechanical,
including photocopy, recording, or any
information storage and retrieval system,
without permission in writing from the publisher.

A CIP catalogue record for this book is available
from the British Library

ISBN 978 1 78206 703 0
EBOOK ISBN 978 1 78206 713 9

This book is a work of fiction. Names, characters,
businesses, organizations, places and events are
either the product of the author's imagination
or are used fictitiously. Any resemblance to
actual persons, living or dead, events or
locales is entirely coincidental.

10 9 8 7 6 5 4 3 2 1

Printed and bound in Great Britain by Clays Ltd, St Ives plc

Typeset by Ellipsis Books Limited, Glasgow

To A.N. (and no Other)

SURREY LIBRARIES	
Askews & Holts	13-May-2014
FIC	£8.99

CHAPTER ONE

Emily hit Kevin with a coffee table – just upped and did it. And was she now content with leaving the man writhing around on the ground (his eyes quite dulled yet lit with surprise, all overlaid by a thick and dripping, big brown slice of fear)? She was not – of course not: this was Emily, after all. She couldn't have told you why her imbecile husband maddened her so, why sometimes the very sight of that large and moonlike face of his should move her to passionate violence.

'Don't do anything you might regret!' implored Kevin, from amid the debris, as Emily bore down upon him, waving above her head a dense and mighty pair of tassels on a rope.

'I *won't* regret it, Kevin,' insisted Emily. 'I have never regretted hurting you in my life, not ever.'

'Look!' tried Kevin, struggling upwards none too steadily (hadn't seen the table coming, of course – was hardly aware that Emily had even been in the room). 'Look!' he went again – seeing full well that there existed here more chance of halting a shield-thumping and fully-fledged Zulu attack by means of extending an imperious arm than there ever could be of diverting the fury of a wild and hurtling Emily.

'Glag!' was the noise Kevin was making now, because Emily seemed newly intent upon choking the man. One of the huge and much-swagged tassels had been forced into his mouth, and with each downward thrust of her bunched-up fists, Emily intoned a mantra in tune:

'Why – are – you – always – so – bloody – damn – bloody – *annoying* – Kevin?' to which Kevin could only reply *glaaaaaarg* – and even Emily could see that a fair deal of his cheeks was tinting over nicely into quite a palette of warm and festive colour. She stopped, then; Emily prided herself on always knowing just when the time had come to stop (often some years later than anyone else on this planet, and sometimes right on up to the point of death – but there you go: that's Emily for you).

She looked down at Kevin as he coped with dribble – which, when you are in the business of extricating a colossal tassel from halfway down your throat, tends to be a by-product of the whole endeavour: just another part of the deal.

'You're just not *worth* it, are you, Kevin? Just not worth the bother.'

Kevin knew better than to reply: was anyway feeling none too chatty, if he was being honest.

'Just get all this mess cleared up,' sighed Emily. 'At least you can do *that*. I'm going out.'

It was bliss when the front door clanged shut: Kevin could breathe again – a thing that just a short while back had seemed very much touch-and-go. He rubbed his back and half-heartedly patted down a clump or so of hair as he rose now and cast a glance around him. One of the legs of the coffee table (cabriole, in point of fact – sturdy, you would have felt safe in thinking) had cracked (amazing it hadn't been his bones) and no prizes were to be doled out for guessing – once Emily had settled back down again into as normal as she was ever going to get – just who it was to be well on the receiving end of any sundry portions of blame going begging.

Kevin smiled really rather ruefully as he left the room to its own devices. God – that Emily! She was really quite a one, was she not? Yes indeedy – quite a one, our Emily: no mistake about it.

2

'It's not so much the sensation of having a tassel in your mouth,' reasoned Kevin, quite mildly, his wide eyes urging Raymond to listen and understand. 'Although neither is the sensation one to be ignored, I have to say. Some of the tassels on those great big tie-backs – you know the type of thing, for curtains: *drapes*, Emily calls them – they're pretty sizeable, I can tell you. Quite a mouthful.'

Raymond looked at the man before him; Kevin, as ever, sat slumped and scruffy with a lopsided haircut, the oldest child in the world. What was he now? Forty-five? Yeah, must be about that: three or four years younger than Raymond. But never mind all that – the point now was, what could Raymond say next? What on earth could he say? Whenever Kevin talked like this – and, let's face it, this was Kevin's usual way of talking – Raymond was always struck dumb: every single time. I mean, this time the man was talking about having a tassel in his mouth, right? A tassel.

'No,' went on Kevin, 'it's not so much how it actually feels when it's inside your mouth – along with quite a fair deal of the attached, er – you know, rope sort of affair, I have to say – no, it's more the *insight*, the thoughts, the way it has of making you reconsider the manner, the style, the instincts of the person who stuffed it there. You follow?'

Maybe for once Raymond vaguely did.

'You mean Emily? Emily put this, this tassel in your mouth? Why in God's name would she do that?' Christ – that woman.

Kevin shrugged, smiling sort of fondly. 'Why does Emily do anything? She's a funny girl, you know that. But she's a diamond, though – a real gem. The business would be nothing without her. She's the brains – she's the talent. And the drive. Emily gets things done, all right – no fears on that score. Did I say? We've got two separate commissions on at

3

the moment – one enormous flat and a bit of a hotel, small hotel. And they both want the works: redecoration, carpets – right down to the pictures and knick-knacks in the hotel. Tell you, Raymond – even the big-name designers are fighting for jobs like that, these days – and she got both of them, just went out and got them. She's a dream, like that.'

'I'm sure,' said Raymond.

'Yes,' agreed Kevin, rather airily. 'Sorry – what were we talking about?'

'Emily. Being a dream. Stuffing a tassel in your mouth.'

'Oh right, the tassel, yeah. Well, that's Emily for you. I expect I was being tedious. Am, sometimes. Probably asked for it.'

Good Lord, thought Kevin – I think Raymond's a wee bit shocked by this. Wouldn't have told him, wouldn't have thought to mention it if . . . well, I never imagined he'd be shocked. Better not go into that business of the other day, then. Now I don't know if you have ever undergone the experience of a Mies van der Rohe Barcelona chair very narrowly missing your head (I very much doubt it) having been dropped from a considerable height – actually from the minstrel gallery affair we got from a chapel that we were going to install in some club or other – but from that moment on, let me tell you, your day can only improve. And the Barcelona, I have to tell you, is not the cantilevered tubular one, the curvy one – although that would have been plenty bad enough; no, the Barcelona is a bleeding heavy solid steel job – elegant, very elegant in its way, and covered in buttoned leather upholstery. Emily has strong views about modern furniture. Hates it. It's not *all* bad, I'd say.' Tis, she says: hate it. Not that the Barcelona *is* that modern – nineteen-twenties: that's not modern, is it? Not really. Anyway, it's worth a bomb – we could have sold it; not now we couldn't – all the legs are buckled up and the joint at the back's gone. She acts before she thinks, that's Emily's

4

trouble. Acts before she thinks. The Thinker, I told her, Always Drinks Last. She just looked at me: I think she understood. *I* didn't understand; I never understand half of these little homilies I come out with, but they obviously have considerable impact with others because they never say anything back. They just look at me. Anyway, not a word about the chair – not to Raymond. Best leave well alone.

'It's just that Emily can be rather, I don't know – touchy.'

Raymond nodded slowly. 'Touchy,' he repeated. More like fucking demented, you mean.

Kevin for his part was nodding energetically, as if swiftly to verify that all parts of the neck and vertebrae were in full working order.

'It's no more than that,' he allowed. 'And to be fair, I suppose I must be absolute hell to live with, on the whole. So sometimes she just – you know, lets off steam. Understandable, really.'

'Like the time she tipped the gravy all over you.'

'Ha ha. Yes. We laughed about that, after.'

God oh God, what was Raymond to make of the man? He'd known him for years but it was always as if they had only just met. They'd talked for hours on end on countless occasions but nothing had ever been said, not a single idea exchanged. What Raymond could never understand – and Kevin would never tell him – was why the man had walked out of a perfectly decent job, when? Two years ago? Well-paid job doing something or other Raymond couldn't recall, not very interesting, and then the next minute he was suddenly employed by his wife in the interior decoration business – something that Kevin knew bugger all about, a state that was to continue. I mean – this is *Emily*, for God's sake. Well that was the end of Kevin, so far as Raymond could see. Emily's contempt rapidly became palpable, and now she treated him – well, it was perfectly obvious just how she treated him. And Kevin seemed to lap it up – sucked the punishment into him: gloried in the humiliation. Sickening, Raymond thought. Quite sickening.

'Any chance of another drink?' he said. Didn't really want another drink, but he had nowhere to go and it was something to say.

'Of course, Raymond. But natch. It's not bad, this stuff, is it? Some sort of Spanish stuff Emily got from somewhere. She's got a good nose. She's got a good eye.'

She's also got a bloody nice arse, thought Raymond; which made him smile a bit. 'So what's your part in all this prettification of the house beautiful?'

'Mm? Oh the jobs, you mean. Well – you know me, Raymond, I'm just the dogsbody. Fetch and carry. Actually, I've got to meet the lighting contractor at the flat this afternoon, and I'm not too happy, to tell the truth. I said to Emily – Emily, I said, it'd be much better if *you* meet this lighting person because you know what you're talking about and I haven't a clue. I mean, I don't know if you know, Raymond, but lighting's not *like* lighting any more. I mean, in the old days you had a light, central sort of light thing hanging from the ceiling, couple of wall brackets, maybe – that's how it was in my house – and the rest you just plugged in – Anglepoise, maybe. Christ, that's all gone now – it's all about uplit this and downlit the other and window washers – wall washers, is it? And special funny bulbs that do this and that and the *awful* thing is – well, *he's* the bloody lighting expert, but he'll expect *me* to know all about it and I *don't*. I mean, when it comes to lighting, Raymond, I'm completely in the dark, quite frankly.'

'So why doesn't Emily meet him?'

'She won't. She says – ' Kevin smirked, even blushed a bit, Raymond was disgusted to observe ' – she says I have to grow up some time. Grow up a bit. Do me good, she says, to get out there and get things done. But I tell you frankly,

Raymond, I *hate* out there, can't bear the thought of it. And it's *she* who gets things done.'

Raymond looked at the floor: couldn't look at Kevin any more.

'It's only lighting,' he said quietly. 'You've only got to talk about lights.'

'Easy for *you* to say,' Kevin said miserably. 'And God help me if I get it wrong. Christ, if I specify the wrong fittings she'll absolutely kill me.'

He wasn't exaggerating much, thought Raymond.

'Of course,' Kevin went on, now quite chattily, 'if I get it *right* – ah, that's a whole different story. She's wonderful, then, when you get something right. She says "Good for you" and "Well done – that was *brilliant*." She actually says "brilliant",' grinned Kevin, the delightful memory yanking at the corners of his mouth. 'She can be very. Nice.'

I've never noticed, thought Raymond.

'You maybe have never noticed that,' continued Kevin, 'but I *know* her, you see. You have to know the woman. Knowledge is all.'

Crap, thought Raymond. Another of Kevin's crappy little sayings. Knowledge isn't all, is it? It's a lot, it's a good deal – it's *important*, granted – but it's not fucking all, is it? And he *doesn't* know the woman, does he? Of course he bloody doesn't. Doesn't know me either. Kevin knows absolutely bugger all about anything or anybody. Raymond – *he* knew about Emily, good Christ yes; he knew more about her than Kevin ever would in a million years, and nice she most certainly wasn't. Wouldn't Kevin just love to be party to this reservoir of knowledge? Yes he bloody would. But he's not going to. Not yet, anyway. Not for a good while yet. Raymond would sense the moment – and then he'd let him have it.

❧

7

Kevin had gone to the lavatory, now. He had actually said, much to Raymond's wondering disbelief, that the time had come for a man to do what a man had to do. No arch or roguish smile, no John Wayne accent, not even the merest trace of an incipient inverted comma: just said it – said it as if no one in the world had ever said it before.

Raymond poured more of the Spanish stuff (which he actually considered to be perfectly filthy, but what can you do?) and glanced around Kevin and Emily's living-room. He had tried to like it – or at least see the point of it – many times in the past: tried and failed. Couldn't quite put a finger on why he found it quite so offensive, which ludicrous flourish the most noisome of all. The swagged pelmets? The way they looped the loop and displayed custard-coloured interlinings as in the slashings on a grenadier's pea-jacket? They were certainly strong contenders. But right up there too was the pair of rock-hard sofas (one of which Raymond had just vacated, as the massaging of his rump sorely testified) in some sort of apricoty, peachy, nectariney – anyway pretty damned repellent crinkly sort of stuff, each flanked by round little identical sofa tables with bloody silly curtains on them and even bloody sillier lacy cloth-type things on top of *those* and then a couple of table-lamps made from ginger jars that had never seen ginger, matey, each bearing a cream drum shade, pleated and actually quite all right in itself, if only one hadn't seen so fucking many of them in every single hotel room in the country.

Raymond didn't know quite why he let Kevin and Emily's interiors get to him like this, he really shouldn't let them bother him – but just look at that! Look at that bloody obelisk! What's a bloody *faux lapis*, he shouldn't wonder, obelisk doing just stuck there next to four leather-bound books resting on their sides, all surmounted by a cloisonné bowl full of silver chocolate dragees? Hey? I mean it's not *real*, is it? It's just *unreal*. Raymond supposed that it was the fact that the pair of them did this sort of nonsense for a living that really turned his mind (well, Emily did anyway – Kevin couldn't decorate the inside of a cereal packet) and presumably that meant that people actually *paid* them to make their houses look like this. Crazy. I mean, it's just got to be *crazy*, hasn't it? Raymond's own house had evolved over the years, and he used to quite like it that way; a few of his father's pieces, a couple of modern bits – and now all the terrible jumble and debris because of Maureen, of course. OK, sure – it wouldn't ever be featured (ha!) in one of those shiny house magazines – and *look*, will you just for one moment look at all the shiny house magazines over there: all fanned out, and just the one curlingly ajar; why hadn't they placed a Montblanc pen in the gutter and be done with it? The odd thing was, in Raymond's game (he had a PR company, nothing remotely grand) this was exactly the sort of room he was expected to have. Not that he ever entertained at home (of course not). The house might once have been described as 'comfortable' (dowdy dumps in which it was well nigh impossible to live often were) but it was always absolutely filthy, that was the trouble. Down to his wife, Maureen. Why don't you ever bloody *clean* the place, he'd go. Don't want to, was all she said: don't *feel* like it. And she couldn't cook to save her life: Christ she was the most godawful cook in Christendom. Why did he put up with it? Hey? That's what he'd like to know. Once or twice now, quite recently, he'd said look, look – just *look*, will you? I'm not any longer prepared – I *refuse* to put up with this. Nothing changed, nothing had remotely changed, and so now he went on putting up with it and repeating over and over again that he *wouldn't* – did she hear him? Are you listening, Maureen? That he *wouldn't*, no longer, not for a single *day*.

And damn! Was that the . . . ? Oh God, it was – that was the front door clanging shut – and yes, that was a fob of keys being clunked into that disgusting brass Indian incense-burner (that had never seen incense, matey) which loomed so large in the hall. Emily was home, then. Damn. Raymond had very much wanted to be off and away by the time Emily came home. Too late now.

'Emily,' he said. 'Pleasant surprise.'

'Raymond,' sighed Emily in a rather busy, somewhat distracted and generally Christ-I-hope-you-don't-think-I've-got-either-the-time-or-the-interest-to-be-fucking-*polite*-do-you sort of a way. 'What are you doing here? Don't you ever work? God, are you actually *drinking* that filthy Spanish stuff? Good. I thought we'd never get rid of it.'

'It is pretty filthy,' Raymond conceded, grimly.

'It is,' concluded Emily, 'but you're not getting anything else. Where is the tragedy that is Kevin?'

'Loo.'

'Well then that's the end of *him* for the day. He gets completely hooked on those back issues of *Exchange & Mart* – loses all track of time. I tell him to comb them for fascinating *objets*, overlooked trifles, but he just reads about limited-edition Dinky Toys, mint and *boxed*, God help us, and then he goes on to the animals and birds section and says things like Emily, don't you think it would be interesting to own an iguana? The man is in a world of his own – a world, unfortunately, that I am forced to inhabit. Are you going, Raymond? I rather wish you would, actually, if only because I simply *have* to talk to Kevin about this lighting contractor business and explain to him quite patiently that if he cocks this up I'll fry him alive. More to put the dear lamb's mind at rest than anything.'

'You're a bitch, Emily,' Raymond said, the semi-wry grin not quite making it. 'But then you already know that.'

'And there's something I wanted to say to you too, dear sweet Raymond. Now what was it?' Emily passed a hand through her quite blonde hair and peered into the middle distance. 'It's clean gone out of my mind. Oh no – *I* remember: fuck *off*, Raymond. That was it.'

Raymond shook his head slowly – not in anger, certainly not in disbelief, Christ he'd heard a lot bloody worse than this from Emily – and took another hateful swig of the filthy Spanish stuff.

'I think,' he said, 'I'd better be going. The thought has just occurred to me. I was just saying,' he tacked on to Kevin, who had wandered back into the room, wearing his usual air of moderate distress, face expressing his determination to remember something, anything (if only his name), 'that I have to be off. Work to do.'

'Oh *Christ*, Raymond,' spat out Emily, before Kevin could even open his mouth. 'When did you last do any work? You don't *work*.'

'Oh don't go,' protested Kevin. 'Stay. I'll open another bottle. Didn't hear you come in, Emily. You're looking well.'

'Kevin, dear heart,' explained Emily, acid-sweetly, 'that's the sort of thing, you say that sort of thing, "you're looking well", to comparative strangers in the street, or people recuperating in a hospital, do you see?' And now the blood rose up to her neck – Raymond saw it even if Kevin didn't. 'Or someone you haven't seen for fucking *years*. You don't – nobody does – you simply *don't* say it to someone who left the house barely an hour ago – particularly *me.*'

'Sorry,' smiled Kevin, wryly. 'You're right – of course you're right. I tend to do that. Sorry.'

'I'm off,' said Raymond, making for the hall. Jesus God Almighty, he was thinking, I've just got to be out of here; I simply can't *stand* it when these two do all this. And *now* what? More keys rattling in the lock – Jesus *damn* why didn't I leave when I said I would? *More* bloody people to talk to. But it was Raymond who spoke out first:

'Oh it's *you* two,' he said, quite genuinely surprised by the sight of his son Gideon (and pretty relieved it wasn't anyone

11

he'd have to smile at), and there hanging on to his arm (as per usual) was Shelley, Emily's girl – and of course they were both laughing and snorting and hooting (as per usual) as if the funniest joke in the world had just that minute been cracked, but of course there never ever *was* a joke, and Raymond had long since ceased to search for it: this maddeningly youthful bloody laughter was just their usual state. And wasn't it odd a while back there the way he mentally registered Shelley as being *Emily's* girl? Of course, strictly speaking, she was the daughter of both Kevin *and* Emily, but somehow, somehow – no, this gorgeous young thing (well she was, she was really – you just have to look at her legs if nothing else) was very much, and quite exclusively, Emily's girl.

'I thought you were going to see a film?' said Kevin. 'Shall I open another bottle of wine? You're looking well, Shelley.' And then the panicked and anguished glance at Emily – just caught her, just got it in time before another torpedo was launched at his face. 'Sorry, Emily, sorry. Stupid thing to say – you're quite right. Stupid.'

'Not that filthy Spanish stuff!' protested Shelley – which set the pair of them off into another snuffling collapse of the giggles.

It was all very juvenile, all very bloody *silly*, in Raymond's opinion. Christ – they were both twenty-two, near enough, it's not as if they were children, is it? I mean, please tell him if he's wrong, but the point here is that there's never anything actually *funny*, is there? It's not *funny*, is it? So why the fuck are they always bloody *laughing*? (Of course, once he'd even wasted breath on the business of *asking* Gideon and Gideon had assumed a rare straight face and told him to lighten up: no surprise there. Raymond just turned away before all the blood in his body coursed up into his neck and blasted right out of his nostrils.)

'You don't have to drink that,' said Emily. 'Kevin – open

something decent if anyone wants it – but we've got to talk soon about the lighting man, Kevin – and also Portobello. You've got to go there as well. Raymond – weren't you leaving?'

'I don't have to go,' said Raymond, throwing himself far too energetically into one of the concrete sofas and damn nearly cracking his spine. Anything that annoys Emily, he thought, is perfectly fine by me.

'*Is* there anything decent?' piped up Gideon. 'I wouldn't mind a glass of wine, actually.'

'So what happened to the film?' asked Kevin. 'I could open some of that Marks & Spencer stuff if anyone's game.'

'Oh, thicko Gideon got the *times* wrong, didn't he?' grinned Shelley – and Raymond turned his back on the inevitable storm of hilarity that this perfectly banal non-bloody-statement evoked from the two of them.

'Don't open the red one, Kevin,' ordered Emily. 'We need the –'

'Not the red one?'

'– I'm *speaking*, Kevin. I can't *stand* it when you do that. I simply can't *bear* it when you cut in when it's utterly plain that I haven't finished *speaking*.'

'I just thought –'

'Very *humorous,* Kevin. You – thinking. Now just run along and open the white one because we need the reds for next –'

'Oh *I'll* do it,' interjected Shelley.

Emily smiled. 'Oh I wish you would, Shelley my sweet. If we wait for your father we'll all die of thirst.'

Kevin brightened. 'It's A Noble Thirst That Awaits To Be Quenched,' he announced, and everyone just stopped dead and stared right at him – and I don't know, can't explain it, this always made Kevin feel just so good: putting one's finger on the nub – it certainly made people sit up and think.

In point of fact, Emily was thinking The Works, The Works – as soon as I've got everything straight in pratty

13

Kevin's mind about lighting and Portobello, I've got to get down to The Works and Shelley was thinking that she'd love to touch Gideon right now somewhere really rude just for the hell of it and the look on everyone's face and Gideon was thinking God in heaven what does one actually have to go through to get just one simple glass of wine in this bloody asylum and Raymond was thinking Noble Thirst! Noble *Thirst*! Where does he bloody get all this bloody garbage? Reader's bleeding *Digest*? Christmas fucking *crackers*?

Shelley wandered back with an open bottle of Pouilly Fumé, the fingers of her other hand stiff into the mouths of a bunch of glasses. Kevin was mumbling now that there were some other whites, actually, quite a few other ones, didn't have to open a posh one, it's not as if they were celebrating anything or anything and Shelley had said Oh Dad and Emily had glared at him and Kevin had said sorry, I thought I'd just say, I'm not making a point – it's no big deal.

'Lovely,' said Gideon, damn near downing his in one. 'Mm. I quite feel like getting pissed.'

'You *always* quite feel like getting pissed!' roared out Raymond, that fat self-satisfied smirk of youth enraging him more than anything. And then more quietly, 'That's the trouble. That's half the trouble. Thank you, Shelley,' smiling quickly and collaring his. 'Very nice indeed, my dear.' Christ, he thought now – a fresh wave of fury empurpling his cheeks – why in a world that makes any pretence at all at justice does my son bloody Gideon get to put his hands all over this adorable girl? Just look, oh God just *look* at the strength and the curve on that long, lean, denim thigh.

'Oh for God's sake leave him alone,' scolded Emily. 'God's sake – he's *young*, Raymond, he's *young*.'

'I know he's young. I *know* he's bloody young.'

'Well why *shouldn't* he get pissed if he wants to? Bloody good idea if you ask me.'

'Hey!' protested Gideon in mock indignation. 'I am *here*,

you know. I can actually speak for myself. I'm not a *total* idiot, I'll have you know.'

Shelley squawked like a dying macaw. 'You are when it comes to cinema times! Everyone knows that 1500 is three o'clock.'

Gideon grinned, almost proudly. 'Yeah well – I thought it was five.'

'Prat,' muttered Raymond.

'*Isn't* it five?' queried Kevin. 'Oh no of course because 1200 is twelve so yes of course 1300 is –'

'Oh Jesus spare us, Kevin,' exhaled Emily, her arms up before her in defence against any further mudslide of tedium.

Gideon and Shelley were now apparently demonstrating the results of having inhaled the better part of a cylinder of nitrous oxide and Raymond thought now, right now, if I had a bren-gun handy right this minute I'd bloody well blast away the lot of them. Gideon was wiping his eyes and making hoo-hoo noises, it was all so hysterically *funny*, and now wasn't he as bold as brass pouring himself more wine – *himself*, mind you, just for himself – and stroking the little golden hairs on Shelley's forearm while he was doing it. Christ, that boy. That boy. Sometimes he really asks for it, that boy of mine, and one day soon I'll let him have it.

'So how's the world of publishing, Gideon?' asked Kevin, amiably. 'Has the end of the fixed book pricing policy had any noticeable –'

'Oh Kevin I could just scream!' screamed Emily. 'Nobody gives a flying fuck, do they, about bloody book prices, do they? It's just a boring, boring subject.'

'Well I'm sorry, I just thought –'

'Well clearly you *didn't*, did you? Who on earth do you think in the world gives a damn about –'

15

'I just thought as Gideon works for a publisher –'

'Yeh,' chipped in Gideon, 'but to be honest I don't know the first thing about it. I'm really at the shit end of –'

'Kevin,' intoned Emily, darkly. 'You cut in on me.'

'Sorry. Did I? Sorry.'

'*Again.*'

'No,' went on Gideon, gaily, 'I mean they barely entrust me with making the coffee. That's more or less what I seem to do all day, make coffee. That and the slush pile.'

'The slush *what*, I'm sorry, Gideon?' checked Emily.

'The slush –'

'I've never been much of a one for coffee, myself,' mused Kevin.

'Oh for Christ's *sake*, Kevin!'

'Oh why don't you all let Gideon *speak*,' squeaked Shelley.

When does he bloody stop, thought Raymond.

'The slush pile,' ploughed on Gideon. 'It's what publishers call the unsolicited manuscripts – well, they're not, of course, manuscripts these days, they're all print-outs, but we still call them manuscripts for some unfathomable reason – like Fleet Street, I suppose.'

'I'm very sorry, Gideon,' interjected Emily, curtly, betraying not a jot of repentance. 'I appreciate that I must be quite the densest person on earth but I am not understanding a single word you are saying.'

'Um, um,' stuttered Gideon, much to his alarm – and then he started to babble a bit: Emily, let's face it, could be a very unsettling woman, and never mind all that guff Shelley kept saying about her being really not too bad and you just had to get to know her. It often seemed to Gideon – and God, he'd been trying to get to know Emily for nearly a year now – that she was just one of those unget-to-knowable people. She *could* be friendly, of course – Gideon well remembered the occasions – but here was a friendliness of a sort that Gideon didn't welcome; or, he was forced to qualify, he

16

didn't *think* he did, anyway: pretty sure not. He never spoke to Shelley about any of this.

'No, I just mean,' said Gideon – a semi-tone too high, breathing in the wrong place, wheezing badly towards the end – 'that none of the newspapers are *in* Fleet Street any more but we still call it –'

'Yes but what has Fleet Street got to do with your publishing place?' insisted Emily, now growing rather impatient.

'Nothing!' screeched Gideon, as if in answer to a prefect who had asked him just what he imagined he was doing lurking in the corridor when the rest of the school was watching the match. 'I just meant *manuscripts*, you know – the old term –'

'Oh *can* it, Gideon,' growled Raymond. 'No one's interested.'

'*I'm* interested!' pouted Shelley, in her hands-off-my-man voice – the one voice more than any likely to induce in Raymond a state of bug-eyed apoplexy.

'Interest Thrives On Disinterest,' chimed Kevin, his index finger aloft.

'Sorry?' blinked Gideon.

Raymond had had just about enough. He swivelled fully in his godawful Christ-my-back-is-breaking sofa and said right up close into Kevin's face:

'Crap. Fucking, fucking *crap*.'

'Oh *God*, Raymond,' drawled Emily, 'you're not *drunk*, are you?'

'Sorry?' queried Kevin. Best make light of it, he thought.

Raymond drained the last of his Pouilly Fumé, brought his face even closer to Kevin's so that his eyes reminded Kevin of nothing so much as gooseberries, but these, it had to be said, were infinitely pinker.

'I said,' said Raymond, slowly, and with a good deal of menace, 'crap. Sodding crappy sodding fucking crappy *crap*.

17

Everything you say, all these stupid bloody things you say, all of them are just the most total, utter, total *crap*.'

Kevin nodded, put a finger to his lips, narrowed his eyes into understanding

'Right,' he said. 'Got you.'

Raymond nodded too, apparently satisfied. 'Good,' he said, banging down his glass. 'Gideon, I'm off back to your loving mother – you coming? Or do you want to hear some more of these pearls from Confucius here?'

'Oh stop being beastly to Daddy,' giggled Shelley.

'How *is* the lovely Maureen?' smiled Emily, suddenly pleased to be rather enjoying herself.

Raymond seemed genuinely off his guard – that, and trying to suppress a coronary as a result of the gales of laughter billowing around Shelley and Gideon.

'Maureen?' he queried with suspicion, even an under-current of true bewilderment. 'How *is* she? Christ I've no idea. Last bloody person. Gideon? Coming?'

'Yeah, I wouldn't mind a lift actually, Dad. I'll call you, OK Shelley? God,' he added, apparently adjusting his cheek-bones, '*that* was funny.'

Raymond turned to face him, and there was pleading in his eyes.

'But it *wasn't*, was it?' He shook his head. 'No it wasn't. It never bloody is.'

In the hall, Emily managed to whisper to Gideon You never call me, you say you will but you never do, so why don't you call me, hm? The clatter of goodbyes took over all that but when Kevin and Shelley had vanished inside and Gideon was waiting in the car (awash with fresh and living turmoil) Raymond squeezed hard Emily's large left breast and she said Not now and he said I'll call you and she said They'll hear you and he said I need you, I need you soon. But right now is what he meant: after all of this, he'd really like to let her have it.

CHAPTER TWO

'Is this light never going to go green, or what?' muttered Raymond, the pads of his fingers beating an increasingly frenzied tattoo on the rim of the steering-wheel. 'Bloody lights.'

'It's only just gone red,' yawned Gideon, with more than a hint of his oh-God-Dad's-off-again voice – a more potent way of rolling up his eyes to heaven. He wasn't laughing now. What? Laugh when he was alone with Dad? Now that really *was* a joke.

'Always got an answer. Haven't you. Ah – about bloody time.'

The snout of the BMW flared its nostrils and leapt, as Raymond put his foot down. Though why he was in such a bloody hurry to get back to Maureen and his mother-in-law and his bleeding tip of a hugely mortgaged house he could not have told you in words of one syllable. He'd go to the office, later. Yeah. Go to the office. Nothing for him to actually do when he got there (he employed the sorts of people who quietly got on with things, which was, if you knew what he knew, just as well) but he supposed he ought to put his head round the door. Get him out of the house, anyway. Couldn't stay at home, could he? Couldn't hang around there – not with Maureen all over the place. And he'd already dropped in on Kevin and look how *that* turned out. He'd phone Emily from the office. Yeah. Maybe she could slip out later.

Gideon said You're going pretty fast, Dad, but Raymond didn't hear him (wouldn't have responded if he had) because Raymond now needed to be well down the velvet path of thinking hard about just one element of Emily. He'd hardly begun, though, when Gideon said something else: Gran's ill, is what he said, and although once again Raymond had failed to make out the words he was this time at least aware of the sound of them and so he had to say irritably to Gideon Oh do for the love of God be quiet, Gideon, can't you, and could easily have tacked on Because I want to think erotically of Emily if only for the reason that he talked to himself so bloody much nowadays it would have seemed perfectly natural to him and sometimes, just sometimes, he had to look around, check who was there, because sometimes he couldn't remember whether he was alone or not and if he wasn't talking to himself then who, then?

'I was only saying,' said Gideon.

Got that. 'Yes. Well don't.'

Now then: Emily. God how he loathed that woman, and God he needed her badly. Was this normal? Couldn't be normal, surely? Anyway, normal or not, these days it was an absolutely vital and integral part of his life. Couldn't, of course, stand her company: that was the trouble. That was half the trouble. (Well look – you know Emily.) Could just as easily kill her as fuck her and one day, good Christ, he might just do it. It was about, what – year ago? Nearer two now, he should think. Raymond had been round there – trying not to be sick at the sight of a pair of huge and dumb ceramic leopards, he seemed to recall. Kevin was out. Where's Kevin, Raymond had asked, and Emily – yes, he remembered this – Emily had said Kevin? Oh, on some fool's errand and Raymond had looked up at her and was on the point of uttering something on the lines of Oh for the love of Christ, Emily, and it was then, it was then – oh *God*, he remembered this bit, all right – it was right *then* that his eyes had fused with the deep-down glittering coals in hers and Jesus they just impacted and he practically raped her on the floor, right

20

on the floor – right there on the floor, playing all sorts of merry hell with the kilims and the dhurries, and Emily's nails were gouging trenches in his back and Jesus at one point he could have sworn he was smelling his blood. And that's how it had been ever since – often at first, less so lately – and even right now he was so excited by the very thought of just any of all this that he forgot, he forgot for, ooh, too long a while that he was even at the wheel of a car and it took a long and nasal honking of a horn on a juggernaut and the sight of Gideon's blanching knuckles to make him remember and to haul him back.

'You OK, Dad?' checked Gideon – anxious for his life if not for his father.

'Mm?' offered back Raymond, distractedly. 'You're not OK?'

'No, are *you* OK, I said.'

'Mm?'

'I *said* are *you* – oh, forget it.'

Raymond swung the car onto his crunchy forecourt and cut dead the engine.

'Of course I'm OK,' he said briskly. 'Why on earth shouldn't I be?'

'Why on earth shouldn't I be nervous?' Kevin was mewling. 'Nervous isn't even the word – I'm just completely out of my – I mean God, Emily, it's always been you who meets all these people.'

'You really are, aren't you? You really are the most unutterably pathetic creature on the whole of God's earth.'

Kevin looked grave. 'You may well have a point,' he conceded. 'But nevertheless.'

He was only going through the motions, if he was honest. He knew he was slated to meet the lighting contractor come hell or high water and the writing had been on the wall right from the moment that Emily had decided the matter. And afterwards, she wanted him to go to that funny little shop in Portobello Road – no not *that* shop Kevin, not the one at that end, the one at the *near* end, the one with the red-striped awning, oh you *do* know the one Kevin, you stupid little man – Christ, you've been there often enough. And do you know why he had to go there? Kevin could hardly bring himself to tell you. To buy *objets* – well, fair enough, but get this: in the words of Emily, oh God save me, he was to *use his own judgement*. Believe it? No guidelines, no hints, no suggestions – worst of all: no explicit instructions. Well it was damn nigh unthinkable, right? First the lighting, now this. Wasn't fair, was it? To his way of thinking, it just wasn't turning out to be Kevin's day.

'OK, OK,' he said, wagging his head in mute and impotent acceptance of the message that doomsday had finally dawned. And do you know he would have . . . well no, he wouldn't have: couldn't have, could he? It's just that the thought had briefly crossed his mind that he just *might* have added on But if I get it all wrong don't blame me, but that was a silly thought, wasn't it? A thought so frighteningly silly as almost to make him titter so he jettisoned that one, that one had to walk the plank all right – if only for reasons of self-preservation: rather than say that to Emily, why not save time all round and quickly slash his wrists and be done with it?

'Do you think maybe Shelley'd like to come along?' Kevin enquired, without much hope.

It was unlikely, most unlikely, that Shelley would even consider it – God, the two of them hadn't been out anywhere together since she was at school. 'It's not that there's anything *wrong* with you, Daddy,' she had once explained to him – he blinking back at her and thinking no, no, I haven't until this moment imagined that you thought there might be – 'I mean, I love you dearly but it's just that, well, we do rather go for different things, don't we? I think frankly my presence anywhere would bore you.' Translation? Kevin is risibly old, has no taste and could render comatose anyone of spirit just as soon as look at them. Kevin didn't press it: never mentioned it again. Along with much else.

'You only want Shelley along so that you can say what do *you* think, Shelley? Is *this* the right thing, Shelley? Isn't that right?' demanded Emily. 'Anyway, it's not her job, is it? It's yours. But do *ask* her, Kevin. Ask her by all means. I think she's in the kitchen, destroying something with Adam.'

Ah, Adam. Adam is Kevin and Emily's other great mistake: a seventeen-year-old afterthought that Emily decided would on balance be a good idea and Kevin had demurred because at that time Shelley was already about five but the only bits of her he was aware of were her rawly vibrating tonsils because she still bawled her head off day and night to the point where Kevin was walking into walls and cackling hysterically and so to his mind *she* certainly can't have been a good idea, can she? So why should another one be such a stroke of brilliance, then – hey? I'm not really *sure*, Kevin had said at the time – to which Emily replied (I know – you could have seen and heard it coming like a train) Well *I Am* – and so that, not for the first time, was that. She didn't go quite so far as to chain him to the bed over the next few months (yes, remembered Kevin with shock and pain, it took *months*, all that – set to the background of Shelley's pitiless shrieking) but by God he could barely walk by the end of it. Anyway, Adam was eventually born and it became perfectly clear from day one that this little innocent was hell-bent on becoming a shit of the highest order and so Emily blamed Kevin for having subjected her to this endless double dose of drudgery ('It's all right for the *man*') and seventeen years on, not a lot had

23

changed: the seasons had changed, but most else stayed the same.

But back to now: both Emily and Kevin knew that Shelley wouldn't take him up on his offer to have a fun-packed afternoon with a lighting contractor and then on to a dingy little hole awash with curios (this being the reason, of course, why Emily had been so magnanimous in her insistence that Kevin should, by all means, *ask* her) but Kevin was now damned if he was even going to bother because if Adam was in there (where had he been earlier, actually? He wasn't here earlier, was he? Kevin had not the slightest idea where he was most of the time, now) he'd only start talking about sex, or something, because Adam had divined soon after his sixteenth birthday that such things reduced his already quivering father to the status of a homeless snail and Kevin at this very moment and with fairly good reason did not on the whole suspect he could bear it.

But, as it turned out, Kevin had no say in the matter because Adam had now loped in – Kevin had noticed the lope before, it was almost like a sloppy version of guardsmen when they did that thing, with each pace half broken – his face around most of a loaf, a hand cupped beneath to catch God knows what awful things were oozing out of it.

'Low, Flad,' spluttered Adam.

'Hello, Adam,' returned Kevin. 'You're looking well. Oh Christ, I do keep saying that, don't I?'

'Kevin,' said Emily crisply, 'don't you think you should just go? Half the afternoon's gone already. Just go and *do* it, why can't you? Now – I've got to get down to The Works for those bergère chairs – they're for The Grange – and oh yes, the dresser, Jim said – he *promised* – will be ready by the end of the week: Friday. You'll have to collect that because I'm going to be absolutely up to my eyes.'

Oh yeah: The Grange – that was the hotel Emily had taken on. Kevin wished *he* was going to The Works; it was always

24

Emily who went to The Works and that as far as Kevin could see was the easy bit. Mind you, she did specify exactly what she wanted which was more, Kevin acknowledged, than he could ever have done, even if threatened with torture. It was nice down at The Works, though – a series of sort of workshops and old garages, couple of offices, run by Jim since forever – tucked behind Tottenham Court Road, quite close to Heal's bed factory. They did all sorts of stuff there for the trade – special mouldings, panelling, weird-type furniture, repro Chinese fretwork, marbling, upholstery: the most extraordinary great tasselated tie-backs, but the least said about those the better.

'Where are you off to, Dad?' asked Adam, leerily, wiping his hands on his trousers (had he really eaten all that disgusting stuff so quickly?). 'A den of vice? A tryst with a top French model requiring urgent discipline?'

'Christ where does he *get* it all from?' gasped Kevin, thinking don't blush, don't – it's silly to blush, so don't: it's only Adam doing his usual so don't give him the satisfaction and don't whatever you do start blushing but oh God it was no good, no good at all, because now he could sense the warm and unwelcome surge in his neck and his cheeks began to feel pin-pricked and the sudden awareness of his own blood's fresh betrayal of himself saw all resistance vanquished as the whole of his skull flushed scarlet.

'Those cards in phone boxes,' said Shelley, now sitting cross-legged on a rug and sucking forcefully on a long Silk Cut. 'They're amazing.'

Kevin nodded. He had once got a terrible, really terrible look from a woman because he had just hung up the phone in one of those plastered little cubicles and he was going to just walk out, smile at her pleasantly, but then on impulse paused to unpeel a card and the woman outside – oh God that look, that *look*, Kevin would never forget that look – and he yearned to run out and tell her that the only reason he had done it was that he had just this morning noticed that he was running seriously low on Blu-Tack at home and the johnnies who stuck up these cards really threw all caution to the winds as far as economy was concerned and it just occurred to him that it seemed a shame to waste it all but what good would any of that have done? Oh God, oh God – that *look*. He crammed the card with its two blue, soft, sticky cushions into his raincoat and bustled away, only to be perfectly disgusted later on to discover that they had both latched on to a single stray Strepsil and the whole point of the exercise was lost. It wasn't easy, you know – just getting through the day was by no means easy.

'Dad's blushing,' joshed Adam. 'Look at Dad – he's blushing.'

'Anyway,' said Emily conclusively, 'I'm leaving right now, and so are you. Where are the pyramids?'

Kevin looked up quickly. Oh God, what was this, now? Test, was it? Some sort of snap intelligence test, could it be? Where are the pyramids. Trick question, is it? Is it a trick? I mean, if I say Egypt I'll be wrong – right? Can't be that, can it? Too easy. So what do I say? What do I say?

Emily exhaled through two hard nostrils. 'The *pyramids*, Kevin – the onyx and malachite pyramids that I keep by the ruined columns. Oh the *pyramids*, God blast you, Kevin!' she bellowed, maddened more than she could say by Kevin's blank and startled expression. 'On the mantelpiece! On the mantelpiece! The ones I bought in Bath with that rosewood knife-box you unutterable moron, Kevin!'

Kevin had it now: two little semi-precious stone pyramids – yes, he remembered. He had picked one up, once – weighed it in his hand: Christ you should have heard Emily when he put it back in the wrong place. Well he didn't, he didn't – he put it back in the only place free on the mantelpiece but Emily went crazy and bounded up and shifted it so fractionally you wouldn't believe and Kevin for one couldn't see any difference at all in the change and he even would have said so but, hey – let it go, right?

'I don't know,' he said. 'I haven't moved them.' Wouldn't dare.

'Well that's very odd because they were definitely there on Sunday when I dusted.' Emily had a woman who came in, of course, but largely for floors and baths and brass and dishes: the *stuff*, in theory, was her personal province. 'Anyway, I'm off. Now Kevin, tonight I'll thaw something from Marks and you can tell me in detail exactly what you've done.'

Emily was gone like a tornado, and Kevin too was on his way to the door, head hung low not just now because of his brace of appalling appointments, but also as a result of the prospect of the coming evening when Emily would thaw something from Marks, whereupon Kevin would tell her in detail exactly what he'd done. Oh God. But hey – try this for size: We Are What We Do And We Do What We Are – right? So where was the comfort? Kevin shook his head sadly: he was damned if he could find any because, I don't know – maybe philosophy of this order works better on strangers.

Now that Raymond was sitting in his own living-room – just sitting there, no purpose in his head, just sitting on the bloody chair by the bookcase thing that was such a wreck – Kevin and Emily's suddenly didn't seem so bad. I mean, granted it was all goosed up to be fake English country house and, as we have seen, it drove Raymond close to distraction, but at least by Jesus it was *clean*. At least it was *ordered*; OK – too ordered, yes, no argument there – it looked more like a shop window than even a shop window had any right to – but there is a middle road here, surely; I mean, look around him, will you? Has this room been recently ransacked? Hard to say. And the dust – the grey, ages old, felt-like dust: the house was abandoned a year ago, yes? And now Raymond has just burst open the council padlocks and prised from the windows the thick, oak shutters to let in the thinning afternoon light. No, not a bit of it. This room, this house, has been lived in constantly for what seems to Raymond like centuries by Maureen and himself, Gideon of course, and, more recently, Maureen's mother – who Raymond, at this precise moment (in common with all other moments, if the truth be faced), chooses not to think about.

So what was it about Maureen, hey? I mean, what was *wrong* with the bloody woman, *hey*? Don't ask Raymond – search him: last person in the world. And although he should be used to it by now – I mean, if he came down in the morning and found a clean cup, if in order to fill the kettle he didn't have to negotiate a pile of unspeakably greasy plates and glasses and Christ don't even ask what the bits floating around might be – then this, *this* would be truly astonishing: God Almighty, he'd probably drop dead on the spot. But it was the usual, wearing squalor that amazed and astounded him. Every single day of his life. Was this normal? Couldn't be normal, surely? Normal or not, these days it was an absolutely vital and integral part of his life. And he hated, oh God oh God how he hated it. Yeah. Raymond couldn't think of anything he *didn't* hate, if the facts were known, and that was the trouble: that was half the trouble.

So he might as well go out again, yes? He was always doing this: driving home, dumping his coat on the pile of coats, not caring two hoots when it slid onto the floor taking half a dozen others with it, not looking at his hard set face in the mirror, whose heavy film of dust was broken only by Gideon's initials, and thinking I might – shall I? Just might have a drink, oh Christ look at this, no clean bloody glasses. Oh shit, I might as well go out again, yes? But where to go?

Office? Didn't really want to go to the office. Could talk to Amanda, he supposed – Amanda at the office. She'd tell him what in Christ's name his company was up to, because he as sure as hell hadn't the vaguest idea. Quite an attractive woman, actually, Amanda. Not a bad-looking woman at all. Came from an awfully rich family: Christ knew why she was working for Raymond. But then what? Then he'd just put his bloody coat back on and go where? He could phone Emily. Yeah, he *would* phone Emily – but then he'd have to see her, then he'd have to hear her when all he wanted to do was fuck her blind; Christ oh Christ if only he didn't have to *know* her.

'I didn't hear you come in.'

Raymond sighed: bleeding Maureen. 'I didn't blow any trumpets. Didn't bang any drums.'

'What?' said Maureen – slurred would be clearer.

Raymond glanced up at her strained and papery face. She was a year older than him: forty-nine. She looked bloody ancient from Raymond's standpoint. He remembered distantly that when she smiled she could look just as young as when they'd first met Christ knows when, but she didn't do that any more; for Raymond and Maureen, smiling wasn't really on the agenda. She *could* look better, of course, if only she'd take the trouble, but the awful truth is that she fitted this pig of a house to appalling perfection. Look at that housecoat, flowery affair – well, she called it a housecoat but to Raymond's eyes it was a dressing-gown, plain as a pikestaff, no bones about it. Christ, he could barely remember when she'd worn anything else. Oh yes he could – Christmas office party, Quaglino's; she wore some sort of dress-type thing – bleeding similar flowers – and as a result of God knows how many vodkas (she said later that she had, just as he had told her to, been keeping a tab on her drinks, it was just that when they climbed to double figures she had simply lost count) Maureen was magnificently sick

29

into her ratatouille and Raymond was left praying that no one would notice.

'Mummy's not well.'

Raymond gagged: always did. How can a forty-nine-year-old bring herself to call an eighty-four-year-old *Mummy*? It was nothing short of plain disgusting.

' "Mummy", as you so nauseatingly address her,' intoned Raymond, just as he always did, always did with Maureen, 'has not been "well", as you choose to put it, for nearly five bloody years. She is *mental*, Maureen. She is completely round the bloody *bend*.'

'Don't be unkind. I think I have to sit down. Have you seen that bottle of vodka? The new one?'

'If you can find anywhere to sit,' grunted Raymond. 'Why don't you sweep all those papers and books off the sofa and pray there aren't any dead cats underneath and then maybe sit there? I'm *not* being unkind. Unkind doesn't enter into it. I'm simply stating –'

'Where's the vodka?'

'– I'm simply stating a perfectly obvious – yes I *have*, actually, since you ask, seen the vodka. It is now an *empty* bottle of vodka nestling within the upturned contents of a packet of cornflakes because you finished it, if you remember, at what we may jokingly refer to as breakfast. Around noon.'

Raymond grabbed a packet of Marlboro and lit one furiously. The smoke in turn grabbed his throat and he felt he just had to let out a spluttering cough but didn't trouble giving in to it – couldn't be bloody bothered, if you really want to know.

'I thought you'd given up,' quavered Maureen.

'I *have* given up, of course I've given up. I give up every day.' Raymond didn't want to dwell on that, so he swerved onto another hopeless tack. 'I don't suppose there's the remotest chance of anything to *eat* in this place? You know –

food? Managed to get to the shops this year, have you? I know it's a trial when you're trying desperately to fit in bugger all every day of your life.'

'There's – I think there's some pasta in the fridge. Think so.'

'Pasta? Have you cooked pasta, then, Maureen?'

'You know I did. You remember –'

'Oh *that* pasta, oh yes – I remember that very well. It's become something of an old friend, that particular pasta. You cooked that, Maureen, two weekends ago and it was unspeakable. You then heated it up three days later and no one ate it that time either. Are you seriously contemplating offering it to anyone *again*? And anyway, why disturb the happy home of a colony of bacteria? God, germs must just love you, Maureen; I should think they've formed a fan club.'

Difficult to know if Maureen ever heard any of this: she never seemed to listen – but who knew, who could tell? Raymond himself didn't take in much of it, he just did it, spewed it out, reflexively. It's just what he did with Maureen. Maybe she's going gaga (there's a thought) like her bloody mother. Christ, it wouldn't surprise him – she drinks enough to annihilate the renal capabilities of the Territorial Army, so Christ knows what it must do to what's left of her brain.

Oh to hell with it – can't stand any more of this. Go to the office, will I? Have to – have to get out of here; don't *want* to go to the bloody office, that's the trouble. Don't really want to go anywhere, that's half the trouble – but Christ alone knows I bloody can't stay *here*. And here's the clincher: Gideon has just come in, and who do you think he's billing and cooing at like he always does? Yes, got it in one – his dear old Gran: *Mummy*, in a word. Rosie's her actual name – pretty bloody silly name for an archaic, washed-up nutcase, isn't it? They don't think of that, parents, do they? When they christen their chubby little offspring. They don't think how it'll suit them, once they come to resemble driftwood. Anyway, no one ever called her Rosie because anyone who ever might have done was safely dead; Maureen and Gideon were happy with 'Mummy' and 'Gran' respectively, and Raymond for his part was damned if he'd ever call her anything – not to her face, anyway.

And would the woman *die*? Would she buggery. Christ, she'd only come here in the first place because she couldn't manage the stairs at her old place and *listen*, Raymond, be *kind* – we never use that other front room, do we? And honestly, Raymond, she's very frail, she's very weak – the poor love isn't going to be with us for very much longer. Hah! Five fucking years! And now the old cow looked fitter than he did!

The real bugger of it was – oh God, he really didn't want to think about this one, couldn't do this one on top of everything else, could he? Not right now. But *got* to, really. Well go on then, say it: money. Yeah, that old thing. Raymond was . . . um, how could he put this? Raymond had seen better times. How's that? Not quite it, is it, Raymond, old lad? No it bloody isn't. The truth is – oh God oh God, please don't let it be true – he was damn nearly, oh Christ help him, broke. Yeah. Said it. Finally got it out. So now you have it. In fact in real terms, there was no damn nearly about it – it was just that nobody knew: no one knew yet. Is this why Raymond is always so worked up? Expression of fear, could it possibly be?

Quite why he should be broke was something of a mystery to him – he used to be quite OK, once. Spent money like water, of course. On what? Where did all the money go, in point of fact? Difficult to say. Clothes – Raymond liked the best clothes: Savile Row, Jermyn Street, all of that – neglected them terribly now, of course. Restaurants and clubs (couldn't eat at home, could he?).

The drink bill. Everyone at the office got rises every year, bonuses of course – quite unrelated to performance; this was because he was terrified of losing them – particularly Amanda, Christ if he lost Amanda it would really be curtains – for the simple reason that it was now so long since he had even *pretended* to do any work that he had damn nearly lost track of even the *nature* of his business and he couldn't, simply couldn't contemplate working it all up again – Christ, all the pressure had very nearly killed him the first time round. And then there was Maureen – she didn't *work* or anything (let's face it, she barely functions), and Gideon has only just got his first job after university (tea boy in some crap publishers, is what Raymond tells everyone, hauling down ten bob a week) and what with that and Maureen's vodka and the mortgages – Jesus don't even *think* about the mortgages – and the overdraft, oh God, all right – the three overdrafts – and yes, well, there you are: not such a mystery after all, is it, Raymond? Plain as day when you look at the thing.

So here was the point in old looney tunes Rosie coming to stay: she'd just sold her house in Hampstead for a tearmaking sum, but would she part with a penny of it? No chance. Give something away? Rosie? Forget it. 'It'll all come to you when I've gone,' she sometimes said, during the course of one of her increasingly sporadic and actually rather unnerving lucid moments. Yeah? thought Raymond. Yeah? Well what's bloody keeping you, then? I mean, don't feel you have to hang around on *my* account. *Go*, why don't you – huh? I mean just for once, just for once in your life, why don't you do the decent thing and *die*?

Raymond crushed out the Marlboro into a plate that had the residue of almost anything all over it (fudge? Worse?) and was surprised to see a stub already there and still smouldering: good Christ, he didn't even remember lighting the second one, and now here he was reaching for a third.

Well it didn't really matter, did it? I mean, look at it: if it killed him, so bloody what?

'What time is the train to Doncaster?'

Oh yes, oh no: here we bloody go!

'There's no train to Doncaster, Gran,' said Gideon placatingly – in that horribly oily way, as Raymond saw it – there was no other word for it: decidedly oily. 'We're not going to Doncaster. Not today.'

'Not any day,' said Raymond, testily. 'We've never been, have we? Not going, either. Why's she always banging on about bleeding Doncaster?'

'She knew people there once,' said Maureen. 'When she was little.'

'Well they're not going to be bloody there now, are they? Still though, why not? Why not pack her off to Doncaster anyway? Why not let Doncaster have her for a while? Lucky old bleeding Doncaster.'

'He doesn't mean it, Mummy.'

'He bloody does,' growled Raymond.

Rosie narrowed her eyes and came up really close to Raymond, a thing he really hated and for at least two bloody good reasons: one, she was blindingly ugly and horrible white hairs stuck out of crevices like blighted grass on the most devastated plain – and two, he took hours, days to rid himself of that awful stench of stale violets that rose up from the very core of the woman: truly the odour of decay but not, alas, of death.

'Who *is* he?' she said.

'You know who he is, Mummy – it's Raymond. My husband Raymond. Gideon's Daddy.'

'I know *Gideon*,' said Rosie, with gradual suspicion.

'Of course you do, Mummy. And this is his Daddy!'

Maureen announced this as if awarding a prize to an imbecile – which was, in the circumstances, Raymond adjudged, fair enough, but inexplicably irritating anyway.

34

Oh God. Should he go to the office? Should he? Didn't *want* to go to the office, that was the trouble. Couldn't stay here, though, could he? I mean Christ – you can see what it's like.

The phone rang, which didn't particularly engage Raymond's interest as few, very few people ever phoned Raymond at home; few, come to think of it, ever phoned him at the office either – or maybe they did: he would never know because – well, let's be truthful – he was never there. But because his cherished mother-in-law was now instructing Maureen that she wanted a blood orange but it had to be *green*, Raymond decided on balance that he had very little to lose by wandering off and answering the phone, particularly in the light of the twin truths that Maureen, bloody Maureen, never seemed to register bells of any sort (or music, or doorknockers, or howling in the night) and Gideon was about as likely to answer the phone as he was to wipe that bloody grin off his face while putting his horrible hands all over the delectable Shelley and that's quite enough of all *that*.

So here was Raymond in the hall, picking up the phone, saying his hello, and who do you think it was at the other end? It was Emily. It was. Quite unusual, this, Emily phoning, and what with just about everything Raymond would, I suppose, have been very pleased indeed if only he didn't so deeply dislike talking to Emily, on the phone or otherwise.

'I can get to the office,' she said. 'One hour.'

Oh bliss. Oh no. 'An hour! An hour's no good – everyone'll still *be* there in an hour ! I can't –'

'An hour,' said Emily. And hung up.

Oh God oh Christ why was that bitching bitch so fucking *bitchy* all the time – oh *God* he loathed her. She knew, she knew no one went home until five-thirty and it was only three now and how in God's name was he expected to –? Well he couldn't, just couldn't, that's all. But he had to fuck her, didn't he? Just had to. So he picked his coat off the floor and shoved it around himself and went out to the car thinking How am I going to empty the office by four o'clock and why don't I suffocate my mental mother-in-law and he paused only at the bin to dump deep into its fetid depth an onyx and a malachite pyramid and don't ask him, don't even ask him *why* – it was just that they had been driving him crazy for bloody ages.

CHAPTER THREE

Kevin had felt unnaturally pleased with himself when he managed to get a taxi within just a minute. It had started to drizzle and Kevin had thought Oh God no, I'm no good at taxis at the best of times but if it was raining, forget it, please. And *that* means I'll get absolutely soaked because the tube is miles away and I'll turn up at this cursed little shop looking like a – oh God look at the time, look at the time, not only will I look as if I've just been dredged from a canal but I'll be late on top of it and with disadvantages like that stacked up against you before you even begin what bloody chance have you got of getting anything right?

And then out of the blue a taxi had sailed along, quite as if it had been ordered, cosy orange light aglow – and did it cruise on past Kevin, quite as he might have imagined it would, ignoring his frantically flapping arms and in its wake quite feasibly sending up a spray of water so as to make his trousers cling to his limbs as if they loved him? It did not. It came to a halt right beside Kevin and Kevin clambered in and said Portobello Road, please, and now Kevin had clambered out again and paid off the taxi and the rain was coming down in sheets, there was a wall of water all around him, and now the taxi was hissing away and just at that moment did Kevin think No, this is wrong isn't it? This isn't the end, is it? Oh God no of *course* this isn't the end – this is the slummy end with the fruit shops and the shop *he* meant, the shop Emily meant, the damn little shop with the red-striped awning was a thousand miles away at the other end and there was nothing for it but to splash on up there because if he didn't look lively the shop would be shut and the thought of saying to Emily Hah! You'll laugh at this – you won't believe it, but by the time I got there the shop was . . . well, the thought didn't bear thinking, not in the light of what had happened at the flat. With the lighting contractor. Whom he had just left. With him thinking God alone knows what, but if you had only seen the look on his face, I think it might have told you all you really needed to know.

At least Kevin had got there on time. It was a very smart little flat – or would be, as soon as Emily had waved the wand – in more or less Mayfair, as near as dammit, and although there were three bedrooms and all the rest you might expect, it was owned by a bachelor (lucky dog) who would only use it for a few weeks at a time – when he wasn't in one of his other smart little flats all over the world, Kevin assumed. Nice for some. He was in fashion, or something, whoever this bloke was, and had apparently heard about Emily by word of mouth: well, Emily surely did have plenty of mouth. Quite a coup, though – I mean, clearly there was money there. His only stipulations had been that he adored shades of brown and there had to be space and – dear God – sympathetic lighting for his collection of Piranesi etchings. How, thought Kevin with anguish as he mounted the single flight to the flat, do you sympathetically light a Piranesi etching? What, while we are about it and when it is at home *is*, in fact, a Piranesi etching? Oh God oh God – why wasn't it Emily meeting the blasted lighting man, hey? I mean it was Emily who was always out there. It was Emily who got things done.

The lighting man was standing outside the flat. Kevin thought of bolting back down the stairs (maybe he hasn't seen me?) but even Kevin had to reject that one as being altogether too absurd. No, no, he just had to be a (gulp) man about it.

'Ah,' he said, as jovially as he could manage (not too jovial, then). 'Mr Fear?'

'Fern,' replied the man.

'Fern, of course,' agreed Kevin with energy. 'Whatever could have made me think Fear? I'm sorry if I've kept you – it *was* three we said? Anyway, shall we go in?'

'You have the key.'

Had he? *Had* he? Yes – calm, Kevin: you do have the key, you know you do, because all the way here you have been forever clutching at your trouser pocket in order to check that very thing and thinking Oh God that would just finish it if I turned up without the key; so yes, no worries on the key front – here it comes now, with its brown card label, and yes it *is* the right key, as witness the fact that the two of them, Kevin and Mr Fern, were now safely inside the flat, and the door was shut behind them.

'Well,' said Mr Fern. 'Where do you want to start?'

Don't want to start. Want to go home. 'Oh, well, anywhere. Where do *you* want to start?'

'Might as well do the main room first. Do you mind if I smoke?'

'Smoke? No, I don't mind. Not a bit.'

I don't mind if you self-combust, thought Kevin; maybe one of us will have a heart attack and die, and I don't really mind too much which. Mr Fern was pointing upwards at a brass chandelier, a multi-branched thing that Kevin had heard Emily call Flemish.

'This is out, we presume?'

Kevin rather liked it. 'Oh God yes – out. Completely out.'

'And what, then? Track? Or we lose the ceiling?'

'Lose the *ceiling* – oh God no. We can't do that because of the people above. Or do you mean – ah, wait, I get you, you mean have no lights at all on the ceiling, yes? Well I don't know about that – make the place pretty dingy.'

Mr Fern shook his head. 'Nah. Room this size can take all forms of indirect.'

Kevin nodded. 'Yes,' he said slowly. 'I see what you mean. What, quite, do you, um, mean, exactly?'

39

'Well,' allowed Mr Fern expansively. 'I mean, off the top of my head I'd say we're looking at integral plaster halogen uplight wall washers here . . . and here, track – variable track – in the recesses and plenty of power for task, where needed. Central sunken points for your indirects. You wanna feature the cornice? Mini tungsten, indented.'

Kevin stroked an imaginary moustache. 'I see, I see. Yes, well, that about sums it up, I think.'

And so it went on; in the kitchen Mr Fern pointed to where there should be concealed strip lighting and Kevin asked what was the point of a light if you couldn't actually see it and now the funny looks were coming thick and fast and by the time they got to the bedrooms Kevin was specifying central pendants (very similar to the ones that are already there – in fact, why don't we leave the ones that are there?) and maybe a lamp next to wherever the beds might be going in case anyone wanted a bit of a read before they dropped off. The bathroom, Kevin knew, was to be more or less covered with bevelled mirror and now he was convinced that the positions he had determined for the spots would ensure that anyone flicking the switch would be rendered instantly blind but he couldn't possibly change his mind because interspersed with the funny looks there were now sliding smiles and Kevin was blowed if he would afford this man one jot more ho-ho amusement than was absolutely necessary. Nearly over, thank God – and then oh Lord! No! *Can't* have those plaster uplight wall things in the living-room, can we? That'll leave no room for the cowing Piranesis which have to be, dear God in heaven, sympathetically lit.

'What, so all the walls are going to be covered with these wossnames, are they? Bit of a collector this bloke, is he? Well what we want here, then, is vertical tracking with adjustable pop-in picture lights: might need dozens.'

Kevin nodded. 'And these popping picture lights –

reasonably sympathetic, are they? Shed a kindly light, yes?'

What a nightmare. So now it wasn't just the wind and the quite ludicrous rain that made Kevin shudder as he squelched on up to the bloody little gee-gaw shop: I mean, what a total fiasco, what a complete – I *told* Emily she should've done it herself, God knows *what* I've done and – hang on, is this it? Is this the –? Yes, think so, yes: red-striped awning, deplorable junk in the window, this must be – oh God it's *not* shut, is it? Oh please God don't let it be – ah no, someone's inside, light on, infernal little cracked and jangly bell when you shove open the door. Right – off we go: round two.

'They're back again, then, are they? These bergère chairs?' said Jim – maybe the last man in Britain who worked in a dung-coloured heavy drill workcoat, the breast pocket smeared with the royal blue traces of a hundred well-chewed Bics. He did not affect a cigarette or a pencil behind either ear, nor expanding armbands on his nylon shirt – and while it was true that no one had ever actually seen him in bicycle clips, somehow none of this on Jim would have seemed surprising. The joke was that the man was only early fifties, but – like The Works itself – had the air of having been around since time began. 'Used to knock out a lot of these for that fellow, what's his name, Hicks, David Hicks in the old days. He had a lot of time for your bergère chair.'

'They never went out, as far as I'm concerned,' replied Emily. 'They make a powerful statement. They're quite excellent to float over the perfect rug.'

'Well I daresay, Em. You're the one what knows.'

Emily twanged on a smile. 'Please don't, Jim – you know I can't stand you calling me that. So why do it? Hmm? It makes Emily extremely cross.'

'Oh I love it when you do that, Em. Illy. You're a very strong woman. I like that in a woman. I like a strong –'

'Enough, Jim. Now look – the dresser. You *faithfully* promise me it'll be ready by Friday? My neck's on the line on this one: I've absolutely given my word.'

'A promise is a promise. Don't worry – it'll be ready. It's practically ready now – just needs a bit of finishing. Don't suppose you've got time for a drink or anything, have you, Emily? Fancy a quick drink, do you?'

'I really have to rush, Jim – you know me: rush rush rush.'

Jim sniffed, looked a bit hurt. 'Always rushing away from *me*, that's for sure. I sometimes think you don't like me.'

'*Silly*, Jim – what a thing to say!' chided Emily. Pretty acute thing to say, actually. I find you perfectly loathsome, if you want to know the truth, Jim – and do you want to know why I find you so utterly repellent, dear Jim? How shall I count the ways? Is that haircream that keeps your skull gleaming like a sweating horse, or simply the coagulated result of years of neglect? Have you ever caught sight of your short and horny hands, with those spatula nails lined in grime? The hair in your ears resembles an outbreak of dry rot and your thin, thin mouth is permanently wet. And you will persist in calling me Em. Dear, dear Jim – if you and The Works weren't so terribly good at your job, I would lift this bergère chair now and smash it over your very horrible head.

'Anyway, I'll see you at the ball on Saturday, won't I?' sang Emily, as gaily as she could. 'You and the rest of the gang.'

'Wouldn't miss it,' nodded Jim. 'Not for worlds.'

No you wouldn't, worse bloody luck. For the nth year running the entire tone of the truly prestigious Annual Interior Decorators' Ball would be irremediably lowered by the presence of plebby old Jim and the rest of his simian team. But what could the committee do? Everyone tacitly agreed that without the efficiency, versatility and, let's face it, pretty low prices of Jim and all his Works, half the decorators in London would be out of business. Everyone had to be nice to Jim: fall out with Jim and you've had it.

Arnold sloped in then, carrying a mighty headboard all tricked out with pineapples and acanthus leaves, and Jim said Ah good lad, Arnold, good lad, we'll get that packed up and off. Arnold nodded from behind his lank curtain of hair – grown, he once confided to Emily, to hide his acne, his boils and his birthmark: Emily had practically passed out from sheer revulsion but managed some sort of smile and some sort of comment – something on the lines of Really? That's nice.

'Wanna cup tea?' offered Arnold, sounding, as was customary, as if he were slowly rousing himself from a deep, deep sleep.

'That'd be grand,' enthused Jim. 'Em? Illy?'

Yuk, thought Emily – just take one look at his fingers!

'I'd love to, Jim – really love to – but honestly I have to rush. Another time would be lovely. Arnold, do you think you could load the chairs into the car before you have your tea? Oh thanks, Arnold. Thanks.'

Bloody ape, she thought. Lifting is what Arnold did. She'd never seen him do anything but lift – oh, and make tea, of course: did a lot of that.

What was the time? Nearly four. Emily grinned maliciously – it had been quite delicious phoning that belligerent pig Raymond and hitting him with the 'one hour' thing (hee hee) and then just hanging up. Bliss. Of course, she wouldn't nearly make it by four, but who actually gave a flying fuck? Let him sweat. Let him stew. Let him suffer.

And Christ was he suffering! Raymond was in a real stew and sweating like a pig. Why did Amanda have to be so *difficult*?

'Look, Amanda,' he tried again, 'most people would be happy to get off an hour or so early. I mean, why are you making such a –'

'I'm not making such an anything, Raymond. I simply can't understand why you're going on about it. I told you I've got this release to get out and you can't just leave the phone ringing in office hours. I mean, we're meant to be PR, for God's sake – how's it going to look?'

'Look, Amanda.'

Raymond breathed out once, and shortly. Well look what? What? He'd already done the cheery, kind old boss bit. Everyone's been working far too hard – why don't you all scoot round to the pub and have a few on me? Charge it to the company (you see how the money goes, don't you?). Well most of them had gone like a shot – Johnny, he was first out of the door (would be) and Sarah and Sals weren't far behind. Rupert sloped off soon afterwards and now there was only bloody Amanda and she looked dug in for the night and – good Christ! That clock can't be right, can it? Christ it was, it was – it was just on four o'clock. Oh desperation. Oh panic. Oh my Lord.

'Look, Amanda – the phone won't have to be left ringing because *I'll* be here, you see. I'll answer it. You see?'

Amanda put down her pen. Good-looking woman, Amanda – not a bad-looking woman at all.

'*You'll* be here? Why, in fact, will you be here, Raymond? I'm confused.'

She's *confused* – Christ, Raymond was just about scrambled.

'Because,' he blustered, 'because there's something I just have to finish.' And he nodded wildly.

'Raymond,' said Amanda slowly. 'There's nothing you

have to finish because to my certain knowledge in the past two years there is absolutely nothing you have even started.'

'Look, Amanda.'

Couldn't think of a bleeding bloody other thing to say! What could he say? What could he say?

'If you want – OK, if you want the truth, I'm expecting an extremely important phone call. Can't go into it. Too important to, er, receive at home. Hush-hush. And it's not that I don't trust you, of course not, it's just that –'

'Well why didn't you say so?' said Amanda, lightly.

In almost one fluid movement, Amanda swept up her shoulder-bag and her legs, fine legs, very fine legs indeed, and was halfway out of the door saying she'd ring him in the morning, see if there had been any messages, and Raymond just stood there fizzing with relief and not quite believing that he had said hush-hush – couldn't have, could he? Did, though.

And so he sat down to wait; what was the time now? Just gone four: perfect. When Emily finally arrived at a quarter past six Raymond felt as if his spine had taken root in the little typist's chair in which he had been stranded. The feelings had deserted the ends of his fingers because while he had been sitting there for the last hundred and thirty-five minutes glaring at the holiday planner on the opposite wall his mind had been rebelling at the impossibility of what Emily had done. Everyone was always gone by a quarter past six – a quarter past six was the absolutely ideal time for Emily to arrive but not not not when she had said bloody four o'clock and what if Amanda had thought him strange? Don't make him laugh – Amanda had thought he was off his trolley: or worse, or worse – maybe she knew he was lying and would despise him for it and think I can't, I can't work for a man who would lie, a man who doesn't trust me, and God help me, then she'll give in her notice and she *runs* the place, and then it'll fall to pieces and everyone will suddenly

45

know that I'm broke, I'm broke, and then the banks will move in and the clients will go and all this will happen because that mad cunt Emily had said to him four o'clock and turned up at fucking quarter past six!

'Pleased to see me?' grinned Emily.

Raymond glanced up at her as if from the depths of a trance.

'Emily,' he said, dark and slowly, 'I could fucking kill you.'

Emily drew up her skirt until it was tight over her hips. No underwear: usual.

'Now's your chance,' she hissed.

All thoughts of everything left him as he rushed at her. He tore at his clothes as if they were burning him as he hauled her down to the floor and even Emily's mocking smile was knocked sideways now as she caught her breath and scrabbled among Raymond's fingers as they both fought with cloth and buttons and now he was on top of her and she had him by the hair and his face was deep into her neck and now he was deep into her and up her as far as he could go and screaming his hatred as she wailed out jaggedly like a broken evil angel and the thunder of Raymond's own body subsided now as he stemmed the fear of sudden death and rolled away to let the carpet scorch his cheek as he inhaled the deep-down stains of time gone by. *God* how he despised this woman: there could be no end to the depth of this feeling.

You would think that Kevin would be feeling none too bright as he sat on the Underground, his rank and clinging clothes quite beyond the pale after so much rain had saturated every fibre, provoking the most terrible odours. But that smile – fatuous, some might say, dreamy would be the verdict of others – betrayed something quite different. Okay, on the face of it we have a bit of a puzzle, here: this has not been a great day for Kevin, I think we are agreed, and within a very short time he is due to be confronted with a plate of something from Marks (newly thawed) and telling Emily in detail exactly what he's done. So what's with the beatific smile, then, Kevin? Escape into hallucination? The type of euphoria that can so easily tip over into serious derangement? What exactly is going on here?

The truth is that something really rather surprising had happened in the funny little shop, red-striped awning – something so frankly alien to Kevin that at that moment on the tube his fairly gaga expression was merely a reflection of his inner oscillations between sheer good feeling and the conviction that no, this couldn't really have happened, not really – could it? Let him just go over it one more time.

There had been a bit of trouble getting the door shut, but nothing Kevin wasn't used to; he didn't know if it was just him, but quite often doors on these funny little antique shops – and particularly those with infernal and cracked jangly bells – were a complete pushover as regards actually getting in but were the very devil when it came to shutting them behind you: always seemed to wedge on something entirely invisible. Anyway, the girl had come over and said Don't worry, not to worry, it's always doing that and she lammed into it in a secret place and that was it, it was shut in a jiffy. And then she smiled and said:

'We've met before, actually. My name's Milly.'

Well now look, it was no good her saying that to Kevin, and certainly the addition of her name shed no light on the matter because Kevin completely blanked out faces, even faces whose owners he had known for quite some time. As to names! Well – whenever a hostess reeled off half a dozen names and Kevin saw each one nod in recognition of their respective monikers his mind simply expanded into

47

brightness and colours and he smiled jerkily at each face in
turn, not so much forgetting every name instantly as failing
to take in a single syllable of even one of them. He wished he
had the weight – it was nothing to do with age, God knows
he had that all right – but he wished he possessed the sort of
confidence to address women as my dear (of course, they
could hang you for that, nowadays) and men as my dear
fellow. But it takes a certain easy style, even a sort of
glamour to carry off that sort of thing – at least to the degree
where people don't hit you each and every time you try it on
– and Kevin was under no illusions on that score: he might
have many talents (no *don't* ask him, don't – it's not fair, you
know it isn't) but style, he was forced to admit, simply
didn't enter into the picture. So although he could see with
his own eyes that what did she say her name was? Molly,
Milly did she say? was a very, gosh, attractive youngish
woman – the sort of woman any man worth his salt damn
well should remember – he had no recollection whatever of
any previous encounter in this time zone or in any other, so
he said what he always said at moments like this:

'Oh yes of *course*, of course. How lovely to see you again.'

But Milly wasn't having it.

'You don't remember, do you?' she said – but not in a
sulky way, no – much more matter-of-fact than that.

Now was the time for Kevin to capitulate, to know when
to throw in the towel: well, he should be saying, I have to
say, since you put me on the spot, I have to admit I can't
actually place . . .

'No no no of *course* I remember,' is what he said (wouldn't
he just?), 'it was in, um, it was, it was –' and then, inspiration
' – it was *here*, surely? I've been here lots of times.'

Milly shook her head: marmalade hair, straight and thick
– and did you spot that hint of a twinkle in the pale green
eyes? Kevin did.

'No – I only started here this week. It was actually at last year's Decorators' Ball – I don't blame you for not remembering, there were so many people. Are you going again this year?'

Oh God, the Annual Interior Decorators' Ball! Don't please talk to Kevin about *that*. Dread, in Kevin's world, was something of a way of life, but among the litany of people, jobs and events that most made his mind curdle along with his legs, the Decorators' Ball had to be right up there with the ritual of Emily's birthday. (What happened on Emily's birthday? Mm – maybe later.)

'Oh yes of *course*,' he now rejoined, thinking well OK, if you say so. 'Oh yes I'll probably toddle along again this year. Do most years. Every year, actually. Emily – that's my, er, wife – it's her business, really, the interior designing – I'm just really the dogsbody! Fetch and carry, that's me. But she likes it – she always says we have to go, have to be seen. Important to be seen, she says.'

Not for me it isn't, thought Kevin, who spent a good deal of the evening in hiding. He generally went to the lavatory about twenty times, and it had nothing to do with the state of his bowels. He actually found the attendants in the lavatory – well, the hotel was one of those lavish and very shiny ones, so they called it a cloakroom – but the chaps in there, the one who brushed away the shame-making detritus of scalp decay from the shoulders of one's look-I-know-it-doesn't-fit-but-I'm-damned-if-I'm-getting-another-one dinner-jacket, and the other fellow who ran the basin and handed you a towel – Kevin found these blokes far more congenial company than the designers and buyers and all the rest of the overdressed and braying crew that always came along to this terrible bash. It was the same at drinks things: the waitresses were always so friendly, but nobody else ever was. Kevin always kept an eye out for old Jim: at least he knew what he was talking about.

'Was there anything special?' asked Milly.

'Once there was,' sighed Kevin, suddenly elsewhere, far away.

'I'm sorry?' hesitated Milly.

'Oh got you, see what you mean.'

Of course he did. He was in this shop, right – he'd just striven through the Atlantic Ocean to get here, and why in fact was he here? To *use his own judgement*, of course. It was enough to make you swoon. Rivulets of water ran away from his shoes.

'Yes,' he went on, trying to sound vaguely in control of his future. 'I want to buy some, um, interesting things. We're doing a hotel, you know – small hotel – and I'm keen to acquire, I'm very much on the lookout for a selection of things that are. Interesting.'

Milly just looked at him. Well, what would you have done? But then she said the first of the surprising things that Kevin was destined to mull over and over for ever and ever, thinking she didn't say that, did she? Oh well yes, she might have said it – all right, *did* say it – but what exactly did she *mean* by it and if *that's* what she meant why didn't she say . . . ? Oh, on and on for days: a new and exciting pursuit for Kevin at the beginning, but God it wore you out, trying to second-guess the profound intention behind a throwaway remark from a perfect stranger.

'I like you,' is what Milly said. 'You're funny.'

Right, OK – I like you; well, not too much of a problem there: what she is saying is she likes you, right, as in she doesn't *dis*like you, but not as in you are the man of my dreams take me take me take me. Fair enough for now. But what about the next bit, hey? This had Kevin going all evening and beyond: *funny*. Right. Now we all know about the peculiar thing, but of course strictly speaking peculiar means unique – did she mean that Kevin was unique? Doubtful. Was she using the word, then, in its more popular rendering of strange, odd, decidedly weird? She can't, surely, have intended funny as in *humorous* because, as Emily often told him, Kevin couldn't crack a joke, be remotely amusing, not even to save his life. But all this had to be stored away for later, do you see, because Kevin had suddenly heard himself come out with:

'Do you? Am I?'

Witty, no? No, *no*, he chastised himself forever: not witty at all – why couldn't he have said something *witty*? Milly was talking again now, and Kevin was eager to hear it.

'Yes,' she said. 'You're different.'

Different! Oh God oh God: *different*. Different from what, now? Different from her? Well of *course* different from her, don't be stupid, I mean she's a . . . and you're a . . . but no no no she can't have meant that but on the other hand could she possibly have meant different from the human race as in freak, monster, lunatic, ape? Could have done, could have done – but hardly likely to say it, do we think, if this was in fact the basic thrust? It's the sort of thing you keep quiet about, no?

Kevin could have continued to plough long furrows through the loam of his mind, but just as he was thinking I think it's probably my turn to say something inane now, is it, the thought struck him as a blow that he found this Milly a very attractive woman indeed and from the way she was looking at him – amusedly, maybe, with that little twinkle in her pale green eyes going like the clappers – was it impossible (foolish, even) to imagine that she just might be attracted to him? Kevin almost laughed out loud at that: ridiculous. Why, Emily was telling him almost every day of his life that if he were the last man in the world surrounded by women he'd die all alone – and he believed her, he really did: why on earth wouldn't he?

'Are *you* going to the ball, Milly?' Remembered her name – yippee!

'Cinders,' she laughed.

Kevin was concerned, and his face began to work with regret. 'Oh God really? I could have sworn you said, I thought you said your name was – ah, no, got you: right. *Cinders* – very good. Yes. And will you be turning into a pumpkin and wearing glass slippers?'

Not bad, was it? Not too bad.

'Terribly uncomfortable, I should think,' smiled Milly. 'I expect they only wore glass slippers if they were being carried around in one of those things, chairs, what do they call them? *Some*thing chairs . . .'

'Yes, *I* know what you mean,' enthused Kevin. 'What in fact *do* they call them? I know exactly what you mean – those box affairs with two men on poles –'

And then both at once, followed by a great gust of snuffling laughter: '*sedan* chairs' and then colliding variations on that's it, yes, *sedan* chairs, of course.

'Oh dear,' sighed Kevin, fondly, touching the corner of his eye with the back of a finger: what a fun moment. He giggled again for a bit: no fresh prick of comedy, just a way of prolonging an unfamiliar and delicious feeling.

'Anyway,' said Milly. And she looked down as she said it which was at once demure and not a bit demure and Kevin was busy enjoying whatever he felt (analyse it later) but then when she brought her eyes back up to meet him he was pole-axed, gone, utterly transfixed.

'Gosh, Milly,' he said, quietly.

'It's Kevin, isn't it?' she asked.

Kevin nodded. 'It is indeed. It is indeed.'

Milly nodded too. 'I thought it was. Well – hello, Kevin!'

And the lights, the merry lights in her pale green eyes! It must have been the eyes on top of everything else because Kevin could barely believe he was hearing himself say, 'Hey look, Milly, I don't suppose you ever feel like slipping out, do you, for a drink sort of thing or lunch maybe or how about dinner – dinner would be nice.'

Milly's smile to Kevin was as a sunburst.

'Dinner would be *very* nice,' she agreed.

Kevin lightly touched her fingers as he turned to go.

'Well,' he said softly. 'Dinner it is.'

Nothing, nothing could spoil the sweetness and perfection of right this very second, thought Kevin. A shame, then, that he made a right pig's ear of getting out of the door, what with it opening abruptly and striking his nose and then refusing to budge any further and the bell clanking away for all the world as if school was finally out forever.

That's why Kevin was grinning on the train: this is the power of that sort of thing. He had all of it to hug to himself while Emily went on and on at him (at last he had something to hide behind), for he had remembered every single word that Milly had uttered. On the down side, he had completely forgotten to *use his own judgement* in purchasing a single interesting thing. Hm. On balance, Kevin thought he maybe wouldn't tell Emily in detail exactly what he'd done.

The moment he'd had her, the very second the volcano of abhorrence had subsided within him, then so Raymond's hatred for Emily flooded back with such full-blooded potency that sometimes it made him worry for the lives of both of them.

'God you look vile,' sneered Emily. 'Just take a look at you. Why don't you lose some weight, Raymond? About a ton.'

Raymond already had his mouth ajar, ready to spit back at her whatever spleen rose up within him, but now his hatred simply choked him and his eyes clouded over with malevolence.

'Just go, Emily,' he said – and it didn't really sound like Raymond's voice, not to Raymond.

'As you well know, dear Raymond, I go when I am ready to go – but you will be delighted to know that I am ready to go right now. One doesn't care to spend a second longer than is necessary in your vile and frankly rather vulgar little office – you need a *decorator*, Raymond, that's what you need. Know anyone?'

'You need a bullet in the head. That's what *you* bloody need.'

'*Temper*, Raymond,' chided Emily, in one of the most fury-inducing voices of all – fake headmistressy, with her face slashed across by a grimace of damn near salacious cruelty.

Why not kill her? thought Raymond. Why bother? he answered himself: she'd die one day anyway, along with everyone else. Except his mother-in-law: it's *her* he should be killing – then he could get his hands on her money and maybe stop this endless and pitiful crying that seeped forever behind his eyes.

Raymond walked down to the street with her – more to make sure she'd gone than for any other reason, and Emily had said I'd rather you didn't kiss me, Raymond, only I've just put on some lipstick – and she said it with such a complete and utter lack of irony that Raymond was again dumbfounded. *Kiss* her? *Kiss* her? He'd never kissed her in his life. *Kiss* her? The idea was too repellent even to contemplate.

Raymond lit a Marlboro as he stamped back upstairs – just two left in the packet, Christ. Lock up, answering machine, check the lights, bugger off back home. Home. No, the word just didn't fit: couldn't think of it as home – it was far too alien to be close to home. And what? Pick up another pack of cigarettes along the way? Or should he be strong and deliberately have none for the whole of the night? Nah – buy a carton and be done with it. Why inflict any more? There was enough, wasn't there? Without inflicting more?

The confusion Raymond felt when he saw Amanda sitting

54

in the little typist's chair he had himself so recently vacated was at first no more than that. Funny . . . How could . . . ? *Odd*, because Amanda had . . . Only when he saw an expression meander over Amanda's face, the like of which he had surely never seen there before, did the slow dawning of something quite sickening take firm hold on his belly and squeeze and then propel bad feelings right up into his throat.

'Well!' said Amanda, in amused and ironic triumph. 'Well!'

'Amanda!' Raymond hailed her lightly, with oh so little hope. An airy sort of well-well-fancy-meeting-you-here tone of voice just wasn't going to cut it, was it? Something bad had just happened in his life, this was plain to Raymond; no room, you might have thought – but there, that's life in a nutshell, isn't it? Yes yes, Raymond was sure now as he looked at Amanda – awash with knowledge and twirling the knot of office keys around her index finger – that something truly bad had just happened in his life but you can't even relax into that idea because worse – oh yes, worse – was surely coming.

'You perfectly disgusting person, Raymond,' zapped out Amanda, but the smile hovered between many things – a rapt disbelief, contempt and some sort of fat enjoyment. 'There's not a lot of love lost between you, is there?'

Try a smidgen of affront? Not going to work, is it? No, but it might delay. Bit of affront, then – yes? Well I'll try it, but I'm telling you, it hasn't got a chance of working.

'What the hell do you mean by – ? I thought you'd *gone*, Amanda – where the hell were – I mean, *Christ* Amanda how dare you –?'

'I was next door, if you want to know – went through the back way and into the sample room,' cut in Amanda, smug as smug. 'I thought – *hello*, Raymond's acting *very* strangely – what on earth is going on? I mean, I've known for ages that you come back here when we've all pushed off, we all know that – you leave *traces*, Raymond: *traces*. But this was a new one: why is Raymond so terribly eager to get rid of us? What in the world could be so very hush-hush?'

'I didn't *say* it was –'

'Oh but you *did*.'

Raymond was close to anguish. 'All right I *did*, but when I said it was – I mean, *Christ* Amanda it's really none of your affair *what* I –'

'I mean I can see why you find her attractive,' went on Amanda, now quite chattily. 'Good breasts. Into breasts, are you, Raymond? Bit of a tit man, are you, Raymond? She's not very *nice*, though, is she?'

Raymond shook his head. 'No,' was all he could say. But how could Amanda be *talking* like this? I mean, Amanda – best schools, rich family, classy clothes. Now Amanda was a good-looking woman, not a bad-looking woman at all, Amanda – but Raymond had never associated her with even *thinking* like – I mean, being a woman who was *aware*. She was so very cool about it all. That's how young women were, then, these days, was it? No idea – don't know. No good asking Raymond: last person in the world.

Well look – if she knew, she knew: can't undo it, can I? God – do you think she, you don't think she *watched*, do you? What *can* they have looked like? Whatever did Raymond and Emily ever look like when they were angrily grappling with each other, overtaken by spittle, sweat and frenzy? Still, at least it was, by its nature, mercifully brief. Right, OK – these are the facts: you've been caught by your PA (PA – that's good: she assists *you*, does she? No she bloody doesn't – she does the sodding lot) – caught in the act of, um, well – you know, with, in fact, Emily. Right – damage limitation: maybe this isn't so bad.

'Anyway, Amanda,' tried Raymond placatingly, 'I really think that when you said you were leaving you should have actually left, but now that what's –'

'I didn't actually say that I was leaving, Raymond. You simply assumed I was leaving – I didn't actually say so.'

Oh shut up, Amanda, Raymond thought – a good deal of bitterness rising: this was a deeply uneasy situation and she didn't have to make such bloody hard work of it.

'Anyway,' he tried again, in a reasonable tone that grated on his ears. 'What say we both go and have a bite to eat? It's been quite an evening and I think it would be much better for all concerned if we –'

'Not hungry actually, Raymond. I have after all been feasting my *eyes.*'

Raymond was slapped by shame. 'Christ, Amanda,' he muttered, the softness of his voice hurting him badly. 'Well look,' he tacked on brokenly – there was to be no salvaged dignity here, so go for shared conspiracy, yes? – 'look, Amanda – just keep it under your hat, OK?'

Amanda stopped twirling the keys – all this time she had been twirling the bloody keys and it was all Raymond could do to stop himself dashing them out of her hands. She turned two eyes on him as if to floodlight his soul.

'You're *joking*, Raymond! You really have to be *joking*!'

The shock, even asperity in her voice jolted Raymond back into dull incomprehension: what was she saying now? Had she misunderstood?

'No I simply meant,' he stumbled on, 'that we want to avoid, er, as it were, any of this getting out.'

'And *I* said,' countered Amanda, now rather shrill, rather shriller than she should be, 'that you must be bloody *joking*, Raymond! I'll have this all over London, into the ears of *everyone* by the morning. You can't just *do* these things and expect to get away with it.'

Raymond could barely believe what he was hearing.

'Now you just wait a bloody *minute*!'

I mean, was he *hearing* right? I mean OK, the girl had hung around and caught him fucking Emily – but who was

57

Amanda, then? His wife? His lover? His *mother*? She wasn't even his boss – he was *her* boss: this was *his* bloody office! What the fuck did she think she was playing at?!

'The consequence of your actions, Raymond,' said Amanda, warningly, actually wagging her finger at his face. 'That's what you've got to face up to.'

Raymond felt his eyes prickle with a hot and unaccustomed blurring.

'Why, Amanda – why? Why are you doing this to me?'

'Because it *matters*, Raymond. It matters to me.'

Raymond looked up imploringly, the first fat tear rolling away from him. The puzzlement, the beseeching in his wet and shiny eyes – it was almost as if he were a weak and doubting disciple, seeking some small sign from the Lord.

'But *why*, Amanda?' he could only repeat. 'I just don't get it.'

'You will, baby. Believe me – you will. Soon you're going to get the *lot*.'

Raymond took a step towards her – might have done heaven knows what at that moment because now the shock was beginning to vibrate into wildness, but then he checked himself as thoughts, more thoughts, other thoughts came.

'Well,' he said, quite ponderously, 'obviously you can't go on working here. For me.'

'Obviously,' agreed Amanda. 'Couldn't, could I? I'd like to leave right now, actually, Raymond. Can we finalize all this right here and now?'

Panic gripped his heart. 'But the *business*, Amanda – the company! I don't know the first thing –'

'No you don't,' said Amanda with vehemence. 'But you *do* know that it's on the point of bankruptcy, and you have known for ages. The company is about to go down the drain, and I'm not going down with it, Raymond, believe you me.' Then she looked up and grinned almost cheekily. 'You are, though.'

Raymond nodded as he turned over yet another thought; how did this one look as it slowly revolved? Would it catch light in the sun, or would it drop to earth like a burnt-out coal?

'OK, Amanda – you win. I don't know why you're doing all this, but if this is what you've made up your mind to do, then there's nothing I can do to stop you. Come home with me now, and we'll sort it all out. Then you can walk.'

'Why should we go to your house? Why can't we do it all here? I don't want to go to your house – it's ghastly there, it always is; and Maureen will be drunk, as usual.'

'I'm not issuing a social invitation, Amanda – I am simply saying that if you want out, here and now – if you're really committed to *doing* this – then all the stuff, all your – you know, the *stuff* you need – that's where it all is, in my desk, in my study. And there's some cash. Not much, but probably a month's salary.' And then suddenly: 'Why are you doing this, Amanda? Please don't do it, don't do it to me, Amanda!' Fresh fear and realization were suffusing his face. 'You must hate – you must really *hate* me. Why do you hate me, Amanda? I don't understand. I mean – I'm not a *bad* person!'

Amanda was flicking off lights, setting alarms, more or less pushing Raymond towards the door.

'Don't hate you,' she said quietly. 'Come on – let's go if we're going.'

As soon as Kevin got home, the second he got through the door (Is that *you*, Kevin? went up the Emily cry – Yes it is yes it is: wish it wasn't but it is), the first thing he wanted to do was to telephone Milly. He couldn't take his mind off – well, there was nothing to think of, really – he had only been with her for – but gosh, all these hundreds of snapshots were flicking in his mind – a still frame for practically every second he had spent in the shop. Couldn't have told you what was for sale in the shop – didn't notice – and you could hardly move in there for all the stuff: stuff piled up to the ceiling. But Kevin hadn't focused on a single thing: Kevin had concentrated solely upon Milly. So, he thought – before the inevitable barrage – wouldn't it be sweet to hear her voice? Sweet indeed, but not on the menu tonight. Had he obtained her phone number? He had not. Surname? Nope. Address? Forget it. No – somewhere in London (she would have left the shop now, would she? Did he have the name of the shop? Afraid not) there was an angel called Milly – out of reach, out of touch, sadly out of earshot, but nimbly clambering all over Kevin, inside and out – you bet your boots, you'd better believe it.

So can you imagine how his heart fluttered up to the back of his throat and damn near choked him at the first bright trill of the phone in the hall? For he had at least left his card with Milly (well – Emily's card) and goodness, bit risky, isn't it? Phoning here? I mean Christ – she doesn't know Emily, does she? Milly – Emily: quite similar names. Quite similar *names*, maybe. But was he going to answer the phone or what? It wasn't going to ring for ever, was it? Coming, my love, coming – but don't blame me if I whinny in fear and hang up immediately because it's Emily, you see, it's Emily – you don't know Emily, Milly, and believe me, you really don't want to.

Kevin snatched up the phone and tried to inhale her.

'Low. Zadam air?'

Kevin felt spent by disappointment. It was just one of those croaky, guttural and thoroughly ill-mannered friends of Adam.

'I don't know,' said Kevin, trying to hold back all audible signs of heartbreak. 'I've just got in. Adam! Adam!' he called, for some reason towards the ceiling. 'Are you in?!'

And then, back into the mouthpiece: 'I'm just trying to find out if he's in.'

Suddenly the whole house trembled with thunder which indicated that Adam was indeed in and was now coming downstairs. He whipped the phone from his father's hand quite as if it had been left somewhere foolish rather than being held out to him by a human being and commenced one of those extraordinary conversations that Kevin could surely never remember conducting when he was a lad. Conversation was a bit strong, actually – the exchange merely comprised hoarse and zombie-like deep-set mutterings that nonetheless contrived to sound as if some dark plot involving at the very least murder were under serious discussion, these semi-literate gruntings regularly broken by brief and jungle-like howls of hysteria and then a string of apparently random words uttered in awe, as if they were the benediction of the gods: respect, skill, wicked, well evil. Adam hung up now and noticed Kevin as if for the first time in years.

'Ben's coming over,' he said. 'Might bring his bleeding Dad. What a cunt.'

His eyes were now asking of Kevin what the man imagined he might be doing, hanging around the hall of his house. But better not get into it: be grateful for the bestowal of facts. Not many people round here ever considered it worthwhile to apprise Kevin of whatever might be going on, so at least he could assimilate the none too dramatic information that Ben (who's Ben?) was coming over, quite possibly accompanied by his father who was, word had it, a cunt. Well – we make do with what we get, don't we?

'Oh God!' snorted Shelley, wandering through with a large white towel around her head – reminded Kevin of a wasp's nest they had once found in the loft in the house, the old house. 'Not cross-eyed, greasy-face Ben! God, he's spooky. He keeps looking at my tits and he's really creepy. Urgh.'

61

'Good bloke,' Adam defended him. 'At least he's interesting – doesn't talk about bloody *clothes* all the time.'

Shelley became haughty. 'Well if *you* like him, fine. He's *your* friend.'

'Yes he bloody is. Better than bloody Gideon.'

'You leave Gideon alone!' screeched Shelley.

'Come on you two,' mollified Kevin, patting down the air with the palms of both hands. 'Cool it, why don't you?'

The two turned and screamed at him in unison 'Oh shut up, *Dad*!' and then simultaneously burst into laughter, all traces of enmity dissipated, Adam tacking on hootingly: 'Cool it! Cool it! Jesus *no one* says *cool* it any more!'

Kevin wasn't at all enjoying himself but now he was hearing Kevin! Kevin! Are you there?! Yes, Emily – still here, God help me, still here. Come into the kitchen! Now! We have to talk! Kevin traipsed off towards the kitchen thinking well so long, frying pan – hate to rush off but I have an urgent appointment with the fire.

'I can't believe it: the freezer's empty so I'm doing risotto – it's all I can cope with,' said Emily. 'How did you get on at the flat? Chop the onion, Kevin – there, on the board. Tiny pieces.'

'It always makes me cry,' said Kevin. Always makes me cry.

'Do it under water. Was everything all right at the flat?'

Years ago, many years ago, Kevin would have made a joke about that: OK, not a very good joke, but something on the lines of can't do it under water, can I? Haven't got my scuba gear; or and how do you expect me to breathe? And Emily wouldn't have laughed, exactly, but she might have grudgingly acknowledged at least the good intention behind so lightweight a frivolity, maybe even smirked her partial appreciation. But Kevin didn't joke, not these days. Why? Why on earth? He got told to close his mouth and not be stupid on a pretty regular basis as it was, so why

62

should he hand it to them on a plate?

'I think . . . that is to say – *yes*, the flat went fine. Mr Fern, is it, seemed to agree with what I thought.'

'You didn't forget the Piranesis?'

'God no.' How could he ever forget the Piranesis? 'They'll be sympathetically lit, all right: no fears on that score. Popping lights.'

'What?'

Was that right? Popping lights – wasn't that right? Was it? Better not get into it. Oh Christ, the whole flat was probably going to end up lit like a supermarket so there was little point in pre-empting the inevitable hell that would surely come.

'I'll do the onion,' said Kevin. I'll do the onion and think of Milly, and then I can smile while I am weeping.

'Well there's no more risotto but I've put some sausages under the grill and anyone who wants toast can make it,' announced Emily, none too pleased. 'It's all I can cope with.'

Why hadn't Adam thought to tell her that Ben was coming over? Was she supposed to be a mind-reader on top of everything else? And why on earth had Ben's *father* come along? What an extraordinary thing to do, just show up like that. His name was Julian and he really was, he really was a Julian to the depths of his being.

'Well I'm sorry, Ben,' he was saying, with the high-pitched self-righteousness of a highly strung nun, eyes arched into sincerity behind no-nonsense spectacles. 'I just don't happen to think it terribly clever to wave sparklers in somebody's face, that's all. I mean, if you think it's a *wise* thing to do, Ben, then I'm sorry, I'm really sorry, but I'd like you to think it through, because I think you'll find – I could be wrong, but I don't think so – I think you'll find when you give it a little

63

thought that it maybe wasn't the wisest thing in the world to do.'

'Christ, Dad, it was only a *sparkler*.'

'Could have been worse,' said Adam.

'Yeh,' agreed Ben, snorting like a truffle-hunting boar. 'Could've been a rocket up his arse!'

'Oh God you are *disgusting*, Ben,' said Shelley, her face actually averted.

'I think,' piped up Julian, 'that some sort of apology might be called for here, Ben. I don't want to preach and I'm not going to *tell* you to say anything, but I think if you consider the situation carefully in your mind –'

'Yeh OK – save the sermon. Sorry, Adam.'

Adam howled like a dying mammal. 'S'all right, Ben!'

'Ben you *know* I didn't mean Adam,' interjected Julian, still as patient as a helper, but the slight grit of the teeth demonstrating to anyone who was looking for signs (no one at all – you just had to glance at everyone's face) that although he was perfectly prepared to be giving and reasonable, it should be understood that there was a limit, a mark that should not really in all fairness be overstepped because there was such a thing as the straw that could finally break the back of a camel as I am sure you have heard say, and if only out of sheer good manners, if anyone remembers what *they* might be, then I feel that some sort of reflection is called for here and then we can all air our grievances man to man, discuss the real issues at stake here and at the end of the day arrive at an understanding that will meet the requirements of all parties concerned.

Gosh, Kevin was thinking: Adam was right – he really *is* that C-word.

'Did you *hear* me, Kevin?' bellowed Emily. 'Are you actually sitting at this table or are you a mirage?'

'Yes of course I heard you,' responded Kevin: knee-jerk reaction.

64

'Well?'

Oh dear. 'Well, when I said I *heard* you –'

'Does anyone want the last of the toast?' offered Adam. 'Or else I'll have it.'

'I don't mind some,' said Ben. 'Are there any more sausages? Have you got any Coke?'

'So you didn't hear a word, in fact, did you Kevin?'

'You've already had four,' accused Shelley, frankly disgusted.

'I didn't hear it all,' Kevin admitted.

'I should have thought,' said Julian, 'although I may be wrong, that four was more than enough.'

'Yeh but I didn't eat that rice thing,' Ben defended himself.

'I *said*, Kevin, that Jim has definitely promised the dresser for Friday, but you've also got to – you are listening this time, are you, Kevin?'

'But there's no gainsaying the fact, is there, Ben, that whichever way you look at it, there's no getting away from the fact that four sausages is four sausages.'

'I'm listening, I'm listening: all ears.'

'After that I want you to go down to Brighton. I'll tell you why later – it's some really excellent stuff that will be perfect for –'

'Is there any more bread, Mum? I can't find any more –'

'In the outside cupboard, Adam – use your eyes. Absolutely perfect for The Grange's little cocktail bar. Some bronzes and one or two other things – very cheap.'

'You sure that's enough, Ben?' enquired Shelley with heavy irony. 'We could slip out and get another couple of loaves if you'd like.'

'You *see*, Ben,' warned Julian. 'You *see* what people think of you if you don't just stop and take stock?'

'Brighton, OK, 'agreed Kevin. He'd been down there before – it was no special deal.

'Ad, let's get out of here, shall we?'

65

'What about your *toast*?' shot back Shelley.

'*You* can have it,' grinned Ben. 'Come on, Adam – let's out.'

The two boys picked up bomber jackets from where they had hurled them and left by the side-door in the manner of a startled herd.

'Now look, Shelley,' intoned Julian, 'far be it from me to speak on behalf of my son, but I would just like to say –'

'It's OK, Julian. It's not a problem.'

'Well that is generous spirited of you, Shelley, I do have to say, but nonetheless there is a fundamental principle at stake here that I think should –'

'Julian,' came Emily's blackest voice. 'Would you just please shut the fuck up? Hm? Just for me? I simply can't cope with any more '

'I'm terribly *sorry*, Emily,' replied Julian, in a tone that more suggested he was placing her under close arrest. 'I'm very sorry if anything I've said has contrived to –'

'Julian,' interjected Emily tightly, her mouth elongated into a hard and joyless smile, while her eyes remained veiled in deadness. 'Enough.'

'How can I go to Brighton *and* pick up the dresser?' Kevin wanted to know.

'I think,' said Julian, 'I had better go.'

'Is that toast cold, Dad?' asked Shelley. 'Chuck over a piece.'

'You can drive there in no time, Kevin. Bags of time. Goodbye, Julian. You can see yourself out, yes?'

'Ugh, it's *stone* cold,' spluttered Shelley, before scraping back her chair and leaving, without a further word.

Julian turned at the door and said, 'I do hope none of you runs away with the impression – that is to say, I'd like it on record here and now that any opinion I might express is my opinion and my opinion alone and in no way is it ever my intention to infer –'

'Good*bye* Julian,' interrupted Emily, quite firmly, for

which Kevin for one was profoundly grateful: God, this man could go on and on for ever and not actually say anything at all. Kevin thought *he* was boring, but good heavens – Julian surely took every biscuit going.

'*Christ*, what a *prick*!' was Emily's summing up, just as soon as Julian had finally backed and stammered his way out of the door, which she firmly shut behind him.

'I have to agree,' agreed Kevin, thinking well goodness me, this is a turn-up: me and Emily eye to eye and she with someone else to sweep the floor with: quite nice feeling, on the whole. Couldn't last two seconds, of course.

'*Now*,' launched in Emily, eagerly, 'tell me about everything you bought in Portobello.'

See: told you.

'Yes – quite an interesting selection, really: some small little knick-knack things – some larger, of course. Some –' What was that phrase Emily used? What was that property she sometimes invested in the blatantly inanimate? Oh yes '– some things that will make a *statement*.'

'Like what, exactly? What sort of things?'

'Hm? Oh, you'll see them when you see them. Difficult to put into words.'

'Well what was the absolutely utterly best thing in the shop?'

Oh no contest: Milly. Milly without a shadow of a doubt.

'Difficult to say, really: chalk and cheese, isn't it?'

'Well whatever you've bought make sure it blends in with the stuff in Brighton, Kevin, because I've decided that you'll be doing the final arrangement in the lounge and cocktail bar – pictures, ornaments, rugs, lamps, the lot. Furniture, of course.'

Kevin just stared at her.

'Don't *stare*, Kevin – you look like a gargoyle.'

'Emily,' he finally said. 'Now this time you really have *got* to be joking, I hope, because look – OK, look, buying a few things, fine – talking to Mr Fear, Fern: fine. But Jesus, Emily, I can't *arrange* – I mean you say so yourself, you've said it yourself: remember that time you put four things on a table? Ashtray, little statuette, forget what the other two things were, and you said, what did you say, arrange them into a pleasing and balanced – well *you* know, arrange them properly. How many goes at it did I have? How many times did I try to get it right? Good Christ. I was up half the night juggling these bits of junk around the table and every single time you said it was hopeless and it *was*, I expect, I expect it was – but the point is it didn't look hopeless to *me* and then when you did it, when you put them where you said they all should be, I didn't know if that was brilliant or hopeless either! It's just not *me*, Emily. It's just not *me*, that sort of thing, Emily!'

Emily looked at him, quite unperturbed. 'You'll just have to use your own judgement,' she said. And when it was clear he had nothing in the world to add to that old one she went on implacably, '*Look*, Kevin, you've really got to start pulling your weight. If you joined me in this business, then that's what you've got to learn to *do*. I mean, it was *you* who chose to leave your job, wasn't it, Kevin? I didn't ask you to, did I? It was *your* decision, wasn't it, Kevin?'

Oh no. Oh God. Not this.

'Well *wasn't* it, Kevin?'

Yes, yes it was. If you can call it a decision. It was really just an ill-thought-out reaction to a situation that had finally become intolerable. And as his mind turned slowly and reluctantly delved back into all that stuff of must be nearly two years ago, so the bright and flickering image of Milly that had been dancing behind his eyes throughout the afternoon and evening was instantly replaced by the dark and richly glowing face of Sophie: the one and only, the fabulous Sophie.

Kevin may revert to all this later, but for now all that

really needs to be said is that when he had been deputy marketing manager for a supplier of bathroom fittings (wasn't quite as deadly dull as it sounds; well, on balance, maybe was) Kevin had found that he had quite a good deal of time on his hands – and money, the money wasn't bad – partially because the products were so very good that they practically sold themselves, which was just as well as Kevin freely acknowledged to himself that he was incapable of marketing a parasol during a heatwave. So he hung around at home more than he maybe would have done if he had actually been earning the money he was being paid and before too long became chummy with Emily's assistant at the time and soon after really quite friendly and alarmingly quickly after that and almost before he realized he was capable of any such thing, Kevin had fallen deeply in love with her and was already telling her so: Sophie, oh Sophie: Sophie, I *love* you. The look on her spears him still: her entire face had become suffused with kindness, but there was just the dim light of compassion lurking within her eyes. She kissed him with true tenderness and told him that she liked him, she did, she truly liked him very much, and Kevin looked away as if he had been whipped and determined never ever again to even allude to the matter but he came back to her the very same day and pressed his love upon her as if its jostling urgency might inflame and infect her and then he came to haunt her for days and weeks and at nights his eyes were red and stung by tears so hot he felt they would surely burn him.

Eventually Sophie told him she already had a man, and shortly after left her job with Emily, didn't say why. Emily called her every name under the sun and kept imploring whatever forces there were around them to tell her how and why Sophie could *do* such a thing when they were in the middle of twenty million projects and Kevin like a fool felt he had to step in, had to be maybe a tourniquet around an open wound of his own creation, and so he left his job and pledged to Emily that he would be her right-hand man and that everything Sophie had done up to now, he would do thenceforward. Even to be close to Sophie's half-done work brought with it a sometimes vicious comfort but it soon became clear that Sophie's talents had failed to filter down to Kevin and Emily's continued undermining of what could no longer really be referred to as his character had put an end to all ideas of his actually applying for another job and on what Emily earned alone there was no question of her employing anyone else and so that was why they continued to pretend to work together and that was why he was no longer deputy marketing manager of the bathroom fittings supplier and that was further why any thoughts of those days gone by always ensured that the barriers of his mind crumbled and fell away and instantly he was invaded by all of Sophie as he was right now, as he was right now, and it hurt him, it hurt him still.

'So you do *see*, Kevin, don't you? You do under*stand*?'

And when Kevin continued to look at her but not really at her at all, Emily wagged her head and spread her fingers and in a voice more soft than usually she ever used on him she almost sighed out, 'Oh Kevin: sometimes I really do worry about you.'

Yes, thought Kevin. I used to worry about me too, a while ago. But as one by one the things that really matter cease to exist, so do worries shrivel to merely transient, distorted terrors and jagged irritation, as the whole of life becomes little more than conversation, and the avoidance of despair.

'Sorry about this,' said Raymond, as he and Amanda stumbled over four black plastic rubbish sacks in the hall, and then slushed through piles and piles of newspapers that no one had ever opened. 'Not always like this.'

'It's always been like this every time I've been here,' pouted Amanda. 'The place is a tip. You're always telling me what a complete and utter slob Maureen is – actually, Raymond, I never believed a word of all that until I saw it for myself. Still, never mind – you have other diversions, don't you? What's her name, by the way? I don't suppose for a minute there's any food here, is there?'

'I said I didn't want to say another word about any of that, Amanda. You've made your point, you're determined to screw up my company and then my entire life with your malicious little tongue and I'm buggered if I'm going to give you any more fuel to do it. As to *food*, forget it. Unless you go for vintage pasta. I wouldn't recommend it. There's drink, possibly.'

'No – don't feel like a drink. Let's just get to your study and do it. Then I'll go and that's it.'

'That's it. Just like that. You can really do this to me after all this time – I don't understand, Amanda.'

'No. You don't. Come on – let's just go upstairs, Raymond.'

'Who's *this*?' came a voice from the wilderness. 'Who's this woman?'

'Oh God,' moaned Raymond – and then in not really an undertone to Amanda, 'Sorry about this – my mother-in-law. Completely mental.'

'Where *are* you, Mummy?' came another groggy voice from somewhere nearish, and it was Amanda who groaned this time round, for she well knew Maureen's drunken drawl when she heard it. 'Oh it's Raymond,' slurred on Maureen, a good deal of vodka slopping out of the tumbler loosely connected to her arm. 'And a little friend. Have we met, little friend?'

'We have met, Maureen, on several occasions. And we have spoken on the phone countless times. Amanda. From the office. The one you narrowly missed when you were sick into your ratatouille last Christmas in Quag's.'

'Oh *that* Amanda, yes of course. Delighted. Have you come to dinner?'

Raymond snorted in derision. 'Dinner! Very bloody funny, Maureen. Even *I* don't come here for dinner.'

'Why's she staring at me?' hissed Amanda to Raymond, nudging his ribs with her elbow, and making like a hitch-hiker in Rosie's direction.

'She does that,' mumbled back Raymond. 'Oh God, I think she's going to talk.'

She was indeed. Rosie came right up close to Amanda, and Amanda didn't like it, not one bit. Quite without warning, Rosie bawled into her face:

'You do the Hokey-Cokey and you shake it all about!' this causing Amanda to flinch in alarm and instinctively clutch at Raymond's arm, a sensation he was surprised to find he enjoyed immensely and it was a shame, such a shame, that Amanda was behaving the way she was because in any other circumstances – well, she was a fine-looking woman, Amanda, let's face it: not a bad-looking woman at all.

Raymond and Amanda traipsed upstairs ('Just a bit of work to sort out – won't be long'), Amanda's shoulders hunching at Rosie's parting shot:

'Never mind the pricks!' she husked. 'Only women bleed!'

'Christ,' muttered Amanda, throwing herself into Raymond's swivel chair, 'you're right about *her* – she's completely out of it, isn't she? How do you *stand* it, Raymond?'

Could this be a chance? Could there have been sympathy there? Got to try, haven't I? Got to make a last-ditch effort otherwise I'll be forced into that other thing and I *know*, I *know* it's the craziest idea in the world but I can't, can I? I simply can't let all this happen.

'Well you *see*, you see better than anyone, Amanda, just how awful my life is! I mean – this is how I live every day of

72

my life. You don't *blame* me, do you, that I occasionally – I
mean you can't *blame* me for it? And the company, the
company – you're right about the company, of course you
are: we *are* nearly broke, it's true – completely broke, really,
and don't *ask* me, don't ask me – I don't *know* why, I really
don't – but it's *you* who holds it all together, it's *you* who
does it all. If you keep it going the banks will never suspect,
the clients won't have a clue – but if you walk, if you go – oh
please think about this, Amanda – if you talk – it's not just
my reputation, it's *everything* And think of Johnny and
Rupert and Sarah and Sals – their jobs are on the line too,
you know. Please don't do this thing, Amanda, *please*. Stay
with me, Amanda. Don't leave. Please.'

Amanda turned and looked him full in the face.

'You really don't get it, do you?'

Raymond wagged his head sottishly like a bull after the
picador has been and gone.

'I'm not out to destroy the company or put people out of
work. If I hadn't seen what I saw this afternoon I would
have worked for you for ever, Raymond.'

Raymond now looked as if he were fighting to remember
the name of a film star – you know the one, the one who was
in that mini-series with that other one's wife.

'Well, then – why? Oh God – I didn't get any cigarettes.'

Amanda hissed her impatience. 'Because, Raymond, you
total fucking creep – I *love* you.'

Raymond just goggled at her. Amazing. Astounding. He
simply couldn't believe it: Amanda saying *fucking*. And
what was that she had said about love? Hang on – there was
more to come:

'Why else would I be running your tin pot bloody
company, Raymond? Christ, I could get twice what you
pay me just about *anywhere*. Of course you never noticed –
you can't even see it now, can you? I feel like that stupid
actress in that stupid film –'

73

'But if you *love* me, Amanda . . .?' quavered Raymond.

'What's the name of that stupid film?' demanded Amanda. 'That film with Richard Burton and Elizabeth Taylor? You know the one.'

Raymond now looked as if he were fighting to remember the name of a film – you know the one, the one with Richard Burton and Elizabeth Taylor in it.

'*Cleopatra*?' he hazarded.

Amanda let out a gust of scorn. '*Cleopatra*! Don't be so stupid, Raymond – how could there have been an airport in *Cleopatra*?!'

'Ah,' conceded Raymond, thinking this conversation, this conversation – what are we actually now talking about here?

'*V.I.Ps*!' roared Amanda, causing Raymond to wince, and then half smile in sympathy with the radiance of her triumph. 'That was it, that was the one – and that dopey secretary who was in love with her boss, what was his name, Rod somebody, and the actress was – oh Christ, who was the actress?'

'Um – Elizabeth Taylor?'

'*Taylor*, that's it – it was Rod Taylor and who was the woman? Who was the woman? Anyway – he didn't notice, didn't see it, it was right under his nose for years and he didn't even smell it. But that's *men*, isn't it?'

Now let's just get this straight. thought Raymond. She loves me? *Really*? Bloody funny way of showing it.

But if – just let's assume that this is in fact the case, then all this show is just a fit of jealousy, yes? Because of that brief and ugly little rut with Emily. Well then surely this can be turned to Raymond's advantage in all sorts of ways, no? Women in love could be persuaded into anything – all he had to do was talk her round. Also, Raymond, I know that you have been pretending that the subtext here hasn't yet crossed your mind (which nobody will believe for a single second) but if Amanda's feelings for you are indeed in

74

accordance with her really rather surprising announcement – and taking into account that she is, at this very moment, alone with you in your study at the top of the house with only a drunk and a lunatic lurking three floors below, then all in all it would, one feels, be a grossly wasted opportunity were one not to . . . well, not to beat about the, um, bush – Amanda is, not to put too fine a point on it, a fine-looking woman: not a bad-looking woman at all, Amanda, as it happens.

Raymond wandered over.

'Amanda,' he said. 'Darling.'

'Maggie Smith! That was her. It was Maggie Smith, the secretary.'

'Darling,' repeated Raymond, in what he seemed to remember was his closest to seductive, and as he did so he slid a hand onto her shiny black nylon knee and under her skirt as it turned out just a fraction because now the hand was back out and up to his face and clutching at where she had slugged him and this was no joke in truth because Amanda was famous for the big rings she habitually wore and Raymond could now swear that at least one of them was forever embedded into his cheekbone.

'What in Christ's name do you think you are *doing*?' shrieked Amanda, as she got to her feet. 'What makes you think you can lay so much as a *finger* on me?!'

'Christ I think you've broken my skull!' roared back Raymond, just the movement in his face causing him fresh rounds of red-hot pain. 'You *said*, you said you *loved* me – !'

'Not in that *way*. Not in *that* way, Raymond! Of course I don't love you in *that* way. You must be crazy if you think I could love you in *that* way!'

'Well what bloody other way *is* there to love somebody you raving fucking madwoman!'stormed back Raymond – and as the sound of what he had just said struck his ears he was hit too with the thought Well I'm buggered if *I* know, I don't know – just take one look at them all: Emily, Rosie, Maureen, Amanda – this is maybe just the way women *are*, then, is it? I mean, what – maybe they're all born a bit doolally and as the years progress – through periods of instability and paranoia they all end up as terminally deranged to finish their days in designer straitjackets and idly strumming their lips; well, if that *is* the case, then I really think we should be told.

'All right, all right,' attempted Raymond now – as far in the direction of soothing as he could go in the light of the fact that his face was killing him, but very necessary because Amanda still had that look in her eye and was all set to bash him again, he could tell. 'Look, OK. You said before, when we came in, that you were hungry. Let's drive back into town, grab a bite, and you can tell me all about it – forget this ghastly day, and then tomorrow everything can be back to normal.'

Oh, thought Raymond – *normal*: what a blissful, lovely word is *normal*.

'Raymond,' said Amanda – fairly calmly as far as he could judge: she'd unbunched her fingers, anyway. 'Raymond – listen with your ears. I am leaving the company. I am going to tell everyone I meet the *state* of the company and I am further going to tell them exactly how the chairman sees fit to spend his leisure time, and where. Clear? Now – give me all my insurance stuff, give me as much money as you've got – pitifully little, I should think – and then I shall be away.'

'Amanda, tell me – did I get this wrong? I mean, was there some acoustical trick being played on me here, or did I in fact hear you saying that you loved me?'

'I did say that. I did say I loved you. I do love you.'

'Good, right, fine: just wanted to be clear on that point. Now, my experience of life is, I admit, on the narrow side, but I was firmly under the impression that when people love someone they tend not to destroy that person's life and then swan off into the unknown. I mean, I'm open to correction here, but surely if you love me you should want to *help* me, not tear me into bits.'

Amanda shook her head, and whether the quiet smile hovering over her lips was one of sadness or malice, Raymond could not have told you.

'I'm not going to be a Maggie Smith,' she said. 'I saw what I saw, and I will never forget it. Nor,' she added, 'will anyone else.'

Right. Desperate remedies. And no, since you ask – of *course* he hadn't thought through to any logical conclusion exactly what would be the consequence of what he now, so far as he was any judge, simply had to do – but in the light of all she had just said he really could see nothing that even remotely presented itself as a saner alternative. He'd try one more time, though: a compromise. Not too happy about compromise, but let's try it anyway.

'Look, Amanda – be *reasonable*, won't you? Look, OK – leave the company if you must, leave the job – but keep your mouth shut, yes?'

'No, Raymond. No. I sing. I sing like that little bird – what do they call them, those birds that sing?'

'Songbirds?' returned Raymond. 'Please be reasonable, Amanda.'

'Not songbirds, no – well yes they *are* songbirds, of course they are, but there's one in particular . . .'

'Nightingale? Don't do this, Amanda.'

'It's too late, Raymond. It's done.'

'Right then, Amanda. In that case – 'and Raymond took a deep breath, because there was really no backing out of it now '– then I am afraid you cannot leave.'

'Big joke, Raymond.'

'No joke, Amanda. If you absolutely insist on doing all this, then I just have to prevent you. And the only way I can do that is by keeping you here.'

'I see. You're going to lock me in a dungeon, is that it, Raymond? And when I die of old age you'll chuck my bones in the moat. Come on – grow up, Raymond! Why are men so utterly pathetic? Just give me my stuff and I'm out of here. Ha!' she then burst out. 'The thought of you doing anything like that is just *funny*, Raymond: there's a thick yellow streak that runs right through you.'

'You are not leaving this room, Amanda.'

'*Canary* – that's the thing that sings.'

'I'll send out for your food, your laundry – you can have anything you need, but you stay here until you agree to keep your mouth shut. I mean business, Amanda.'

Amanda looked at him. 'You're not serious,' she said, without enquiry. 'You are, aren't you?'

Raymond nodded 'Very,' he said 'Have to be. Want to change your mind? I wish you would.'

'Never,' said Amanda, flatly.

'Then,' said Raymond, as he walked to the door. He was through it and had it locked on the outside before he could believe what it was in Christ's name he was doing. He felt the weight and jarring of Amanda's fists on the door and she was repeating his name tunelessly again and again like a mantra. Of *course* he considered coming to his senses and turning back the key in the lock: didn't do it, though. Couldn't. Not now.

Later on, when he had ceased to shiver, he ordered some Chinese food, enough for the two of them – but by the time he'd got the lids off all the little boxes he couldn't bring himself to even taste any. He carried it all up to Amanda on a tray and there was a tremendous tussle as she made for the door and Raymond was forced to be a little bit rough which he hadn't enjoyed but if you make your bed, well then yes, you just *have* to, don't you, knuckle down to lying in it? That's the way it is. Just before he squirmed out of the door, she threw all the food at him and spat that she'd get him, she'd get him for this, so all in all the well-meaning meal merely amounted to just one more mess and another lump of money scattered to the winds. Along with all the rest.

Later still, he listened at the door. The radio was on – some phone-in programme, it sounded like to Raymond. Yes, Raymond *had* disconnected the phone – did it from down-stairs, because she probably would, she was quite capable of having the police round, she wouldn't think twice about that. He slipped a note under the door: 'Tell me what clothes you need and I will buy them. Anything else as well. Sorry.'

He tried to wash a bit in the bathroom without actually touching anything: God. the bathroom must be *the* most vile spot in this whole horrible house: or the kitchen, maybe – yes, just had to be the kitchen, but the bathroom came a damn close second. Every crevice was grouted with grime and overlaid by sticky excrescences in really any colour you've a mind to – the residue of not just such as Night Nurse, but conditioners, shampoo, lotions, you name it: *cleansers.* The floor was generally damp, and so always were the towels, though one of the lights was usually working. Mirrors were impenetrable, which was fine by Raymond. God, what would Emily have made of it all? She'd have a seizure. It must be nice to live in a clean and ordered home, with a woman who was earning money: Kevin really didn't have it at all badly, Raymond supposed. Except, of course – and we keep coming back to this, don't we? – that Raymond would rather share a sauna with a leper than a single hour with Emily.

Raymond eased himself into his unmade bed (Maureen slept somewhere else, oh God yes, not really sure quite where) and thought that what with one thing and another, it had really been quite a day. Emily's irritating little pyramids had yet again prompted him into thieving a short while before his ritual bout of fornication with their rightful owner and then a bit later the contemplated rape of his ex-personal assistant (who loves him) before in the end plumping for a spell of good old-fashioned kidnapping.

Raymond snapped out the light, just this sending eddies of dust scurrying around his face. He closed his eyes, and then he closed them tighter. Tomorrow soon.

CHAPTER FOUR

Shelley had really been quite sweet about Gideon landing his first job in publishing: how marvellous, she had said, how wonderful to be an actual editor when all she was was a lousy shopgirl. Joke, really; Shelley earned just as much as he did (little) and of *course* he wasn't an editor – an editor? Don't make him laugh. OK, he had played it up a bit – all I do is make the coffee and try to read the unreadable – but goodness knew there was a good deal of truth in it. His official title (title!) was editorial assistant, but it had never been made clear quite who it was he was meant to assist; whoever wanted a pile of manuscripts off his floor right now, right this minute, I can't stand the sight of them for another second – or else anyone who had a yen for a cup of coffee: this is how it seemed to Gideon.

He'd taken the day off yesterday – that's why he and Shelley had been going to see a film except *didn't* of course because of the stupid times. Shouldn't really have taken a day off at this early stage of the game (he had only been there three, getting on for four now, weeks) but Shelley wasn't going in to work for some reason or another and she had said how about it and he had said yeh, OK, why not. He fell in with most things that Shelley suggested – everything, really. She was always full of ideas – really good fun, Shelley – and Gideon just let her get on with it. Sometimes she didn't like it, or said she didn't like it, always coming up with schemes and places to go and at times like that she'd say Why don't *you* ever think of a surprise, why don't *you* plan anything and book it and Gideon had gone along with that as well saying OK, fine, I'll buy that, and Shelley would say

81

Well? And Gideon would say Well what? And Shelley would come close to stamping her foot and came back with What do you mean well *what* – where are we *going*? And Gideon could only reply Well – where would you *like* to go? So it didn't really work, all that, it never really came off, any of that, and so most (all) decisions tended to remain in Shelley's domain. Gideon justified it to himself by thinking well look, all this male–female role playing is really no more than that, when you come down to it, and all the domination and submission thing, well – it's hardly more than a game. One should stick to one's last: if you're good at cooking, cook – it doesn't matter surely to goodness what *gender* you are; and if you're into decisions and plans, *make* them for heaven's sake: this was Shelley's line of country, so just let her get on with it.

Which rather begged the question, of course – and it nagged at Gideon, this, gnawed away at him – what in practice was *his* line of country, then – hmm? Tricky; tricky one. He was never going to be a mover, that was for sure – nor a shaker, either: as well as being perfectly happy to let others take the reins, he sympathized far too much with the underdog (can't think why) to ever dream of furthering himself at anyone else's expense. A case in point: he didn't at all care for the state of the house – at times the dirt and the clutter were beyond belief – but he wouldn't have contemplated giving his mother any sort of a hard time about it: I mean, *look* at her, for heaven's sake – she's not up to it, is she? So why go on and on? Damned if he'd actually clear up any of it himself, though – this was surely not his line of country – so he just relegated all the domestic upheaval to the ever-expanding container packed full of things he had decided he could do nothing whatever about. And Gran – she was another one. Maybe not so bats as she loves making out, but nonetheless without a doubt one prawn short of a seafood platter, I think we are all in agreement. But where was the sense in exploding at these two helpless women like Dad did? Didn't do any good, did it? It just made Dad look vile which, Gideon reflected, he probably was, all things considered: never could stand Dad, even when he was little. Now, of course, the main reason he came very close to hating his father was that Raymond so openly held Gideon in such utter contempt that it seemed the only possible reaction available. Another thing he could do nothing about.

And Emily had rung him again last night. She did it quite regularly now, always beginning her hushed-up monologue by gently admonishing him for not having rung her, as he had promised to do. Which was fair enough in its way, Gideon allowed, because he did promise, it's true – every time she whispered to him (Christ – sometimes when Shelley was just a few feet away) ring me, Gideon, why don't you ring me, hmm? Promise you'll ring me, she always said, and Gideon hushed back yes, OK, I will – I promise. Never did, never did – well how *could* he? I mean, Emily had never left him in any doubt about her intentions – or had Gideon, oh dear God: here was a thought – had Gideon got it all spectacularly wrong? No – not possible. What else *could* she mean? Actually, in some ways, Gideon did now admit, he was quite in favour of whatever it was she had in mind: might cure him of one or two, um, problems he was encountering of late. Emily was very much the sort of woman to take charge – believe it – and maybe that was what Gideon needed, maybe?

Well it looked like Gideon was about to find out because last night, last night when she had rung, Emily had been even more insistent than usual and kept pressing him to come over, why don't you, come over when there's nobody here, and Gideon had said (as he did) that actually he wasn't quite sure of his movements, not this week, but this time Emily clearly wasn't having it and so Gideon had agreed to come over the following evening because the following evening was good, Emily had assured him, because Shelley as he knew was going to a hen party and Kevin she would simply dismiss. Gideon maybe agreed too rapidly because he had been distracted by quite a lot of banging going on upstairs – sounded like someone trying to break down a door, God knew what Dad and his secretary were doing up there (none of his business, thank God) – but after a good deal of thought he had come down later from his room to phone Emily back and say Look, I'm awfully sorry but I clean forgot I have an urgent appointment with just about anyone in the world tomorrow evening but for some reason the phone wasn't working, completely dead, and although now he was safely ensconced in the little partitioned-off section of corridor that it pleased his employers to refer to as his office, he didn't really think he could decently telephone her now and put her off because so much time had elapsed since he had agreed to her, er, proposition, and he didn't want to give Emily any sort of a hard time or anything or make her feel bad or anything and so it really did seem that this evening it was quite on the cards that Emily and he would be alone but together in Emily's designer house and what on earth was going to happen then, then? Hey?

'Gideon, my dear chap – I fear I come with bad tidings.'

Gideon's feet clattered down from the desk drawer where he had perched them, his swivel chair bucking so violently he thought for one not blissful second that he might be pitched over and on to the floor. It was just the sudden sound of a voice in the room: God, he had been absolutely miles away.

'Hi, Sam,' said Gideon, recovering himself.

Sam was quite high up in marketing, Gideon had divined, and a fairly decent bloke as far as he could tell. Sam still wore red braces and his main contribution to the world of publishing seemed to be the commissioning of increasingly highly-coloured and elaborately expensive fibreboard dump-bins which were rapid-expressed to all the major bookselling chains who equally promptly dumped them. No doubt he did other things too. But what was all this about bad tidings, though? Sam was grinning fit to bust, so presumably he was being ironic, yes?

'Mrs Milligan is sadly indisposed,' went on Sam, 'and I regret to say that a hastily convened forum comprising anyone who happened to be around has elected *you*, dear Gideon –'

'Oh no. Don't say it.'

'Alas, alas – it must be said, dear lad: you are to be the proud custodian of the trolley for the day.'

Oh good God, how shaming. Now he really *was* the teaboy, then. Mrs Milligan, it might be mentioned, was a large and foul-mouthed Irishwoman whose wild and pinkish hair always suggested to Gideon that she had recently fought her way through a tempest, her face – permanently set into an angry scowl of challenge – the colour and texture of prosciutto. But never mind that – the point was that she was the woman who twice daily manhandled a huge industrial trolley around the corridors (none of the conglomerates still did all this – but this was, wouldn't it be, one of the few independents that did) dispensing tea from a steaming urn, along with a blinding selection of technicolour cakes and fancies. Gideon surely wasn't expected to . . . I mean, everyone – *everyone* on the entire floor would see the new editorial assistant doling out tea – even to the temps and typists, oh God no. Wall-to-wall funny remarks and sneers-a-plenty.

'No chance of a temp or typist doing it, Sam?'

' 'Fraid not, old chum – all rather busy, you see.'

Yes, thought Gideon: point taken. Right, then: Tea Time.

And if Gideon really thought he had braced himself for the very worst – oh dear, oh dear: never mind all those gags about supermarket trolleys being pre-programmed by fiends to veer and crash like drunken dodgems – this great brute was wholly unmanageable, pure and simple. The weight of the thing alone was astounding and not a single one of the massive and rubber-tyred wheels could make up its mind just what it was about; Gideon was not so much pushing this trolley as frantically restraining it as one would a runaway Rottweiler, wild and hell-bent on gore and mayhem.

First stop – and the only way he could stop the thing was by jamming it in the doorway – was the Sales department, and wouldn't there just be a clutch of reps there, loitering, all of whom Gideon just knew were determined to have a field day: *well*, Mrs Milligan, you're looking fit and trim today – had a sex-change, Mrs Milligan? They just don't make tea ladies like they used to – fancy coming to a motel, darling? Got a licence to drive that thing? Make mine a Scotch – has he got one lump or two? On and on. Gideon was scarlet – not just as a result of the hot sweep of humiliation that rushed all over him, but also for the reason that when finally he had worked out which way to twist the vicious little tap at the base of the urn, a hissing blast of scalding steam rose up into his face and practically flayed him and it sure explained Mrs Milligan's dark raw ham complexion (maybe the frenzy of hair as well) – and Gideon now became deeply concerned that by the end of the round, if ever there could be so heaven-sent a thing, he could end up permanently scarred and doomed to walk the earth as the living incarnation of the last of the bloody Mohicans.

In Contracts, some woman he had never seen before warned Gideon gravely that he must on no account, whatever happened, part with his éclair. Gideon's hair now hung in coils, his shirt a limp and sodden thing, and so maybe he looked at her a little wildly as yet again he failed to get his fingers out of the way of the jet of hot, oh Christ – so tearmakingly molten white-hot tea, and alarmed either by

86

his expression or his evident ignorance of the importance of what she was saying, the woman explained quite rapidly that the only chocolate éclair ever on the trolley was the sole and exclusive preserve of that nice Martin Pilley in Editorial, and if Gideon did not know that fact before, then he surely was aware of it now.

Gideon ploughed on grimly – resigned now to his fingers for the remainder of his life being stiff and brittle things, little more than burned-out sticks of charcoal – while uncomplainingly fishing out from the increasingly deepening sea of tea in the trolley's upper tier whatever little multi-hued tooth-breaker the punters required. It was only when he had actually reached Editorial that he acknowledged by way of a bout of lowing the inevitable ding-dong that would surely result from the unignorable fact that nice Martin Pilley's chocolate éclair was by now evidently well down the throat of someone else.

'Who *are* you?' he growled. 'Where is Mrs Milligan? More to the point, whoever you are – where in blazes is my chocolate éclair?'

'Yes,' apologized Gideon. 'I'm sorry about that – it was definitely there in Contracts, so somewhere between there and here someone must have –'

Nice Martin Pilley stared at Gideon as his eyes glazed over.

'You don't seem to understand,' he said, really very thickly.

'It's OK, Martin,' said some girl or other – sounding reasonably scared to Gideon's ears. 'I'll pop out and get you one.'

'That is not the *point*,' averred Mr Pilley. '*Everyone* knows that the éclair is mine – *everyone*. It is an established tradition. Now this clearly means, we have clear evidence here, that someone, someone taking advantage of the absence of Mrs Milligan, has deliberately – *in cold blood* – stolen my éclair!'

He was joking, yes? No – take one look at him: serious, very.

'*So,*' he went on, in the manner of a headmaster on the verge of meting out harsh but rightful punishment for a catalogue of crime, 'it must either have been Gwen in the Art department – who has always envied me my éclair, I know this for a fact – or else that bloody Sam person, is it, in Marketing. Yes – it's him, it's him: it's *got* to be him.'

Nice Mr Pilley strode towards the door, and on his mind was no idle stroll – believe me, you could tell. 'Right!' he barked. And no one in the room was left in any doubt at all that Martin Pilley meant business all right – fists were clenched, for starters.

At least Gideon wasn't getting the blame: something, he supposed. He stepped aside sharply to make way for Mr Pilley and thought oh God I can't believe that so-called grown-up people . . . anyway, the round is over, the round is over – Editorial was the last. Haul the trolley back, should I? To hell with it – leave the trolley to rot: Gideon never wanted to see the bloody thing again. And if they expected him to wheel it round again this afternoon, well – he'd simply chuck in the job (didn't like the job anyway), get some other job, a job with dignity, a job with prospects: stacking shelves, cleaning the streets – nothing to do with *publishing*, anyway. Hmm. Might as well slope along and see how Sam and Mr Pilley were getting on.

Sam was over by the window – gosh look, what an enormous Swiss cheese plant, almost blocked out all the light – and snorting dismissively. 'Oh for Christ's sake, Martin – it's only a bloody *cake.*'

Gideon went over and stood by Richard's desk, Richard, whom Gideon had noticed before once or twice – Richard had smiled at him once or twice – was a nice-looking, fair-haired fellow maybe three years older than Gideon, and hugely enjoying what was proving to be quite a show. Nice-

88

looking? Subjective, of course – but, yes: Gideon would have said so.

'It is not just a bloody *cake*, as you choose to put it, Sam,' said Mr Pilley slowly, and seemingly without moving his lips. 'It is by way of being something of a *tradition* – a tradition, I might say, that Mrs Milligan was more than happy to uphold. If Mrs *Milligan* had been here –'

'Oh *God*, Martin – I've really heard enough. I've eaten your bloody cake, end of story. Here – here's fifty pence: run out and buy yourself another.'

Woof. Bad move, on the whole: *big* mistake.

Sam was now making the most awful noises because nice Martin Pilley had him by the throat and was apparently attempting to smash his head through the wall and if Sam hadn't swiftly punched Mr Pilley twice in the stomach, then maybe Sam wouldn't have been alive to tell the tale with uproarious and quite untrue detail which, of course, he subsequently did – for years and years. Sam now straightened his clothes (the red braces had got into an awful twist) while Martin Pilley was left bent in half and goggling at the floor as if he could hardly believe it was there, with eyes that could well plop out and he was clutching the middle of him as if to counter the eruption of an alien.

Extraordinary. Quite extraordinary. But to Gideon's mind, something even more extraordinary had happened while all this was going on – was still happening, in point of fact: yes indeed – right this very minute. At first he hadn't been at all sure, but then he was sure, no doubt about it: the back of Richard's hand was gently stroking the back of Gideon's thigh, Richard all the while snuffling with pleasure at the fisticuffs before him. Gideon froze, but quickly unfroze and had to admit to enjoying the feeling of warmth, while his heartbeat rose to the audible and he felt terrified and yet quite safe to stay just like that, just as he was. And even more extraordinary, when Richard boldly transferred the caress to the open flat of his hand, which he let more firmly travel upwards, Gideon stayed stock-still. While helplessly acknowledging his blatant arousal, Gideon was thinking well look, I'm seeing Emily tonight, Shelley's mother: maybe she will help me. Sort out one or two things.

Well. Tea Time over.

Kevin was striding on up the Portobello Road, which shouldn't surprise anyone unduly; grinning like a juvenile, of course – oh yes, but naturally. And why not? As Kevin earnestly demanded of himself: it wasn't often, was it, that Kevin had something to grin about? No, answered Kevin – indeed it wasn't.

Milly Milly, Milly Milly – Milly Milly Milly! That's how Kevin was going, roughly in time with one of those old steam trains – and he had to keep it up for what seemed like miles because although Kevin dimly acknowledged the possibility that one of these fine days he would finally assimilate the information that the little shop with the red-striped awning was practically at the top of the other end of the road, clearly that day had yet to dawn.

He thought of not stepping on the cracks in the pavement but on balance he decided no – that would only make the endless journey longer. Actually, when he was a boy, some of his mates did that for a lark and Kevin became aware that one or two of them went on to habitually avoiding all those cracks, really quite obsessively, purely as a result of some new-found and deep-seated superstition. This had made Kevin feel rather sorry for the cracks: poor little cracks, he thought – why shouldn't they get walked on too? It wasn't fair, he reasoned, to marginalize the cracks. Kevin sighed at himself, now – Christ what a crazy kid: is it any wonder I turned out such a mess?

All the little things of childhood had always been oddly perceived by Kevin's dancing mind. Daisy chains. Let's just look at daisy chains: Kevin could hardly bring himself to pick the daisies, but when it came to splitting their thin and barely sappy stems – well, he simply wasn't up to the raw emotion that such a thing would entail. See what I mean? *Silly*, Kevin – don't be so *silly*, Kevin, hissed his peers and parents; yes but there we have it – silly or not, that was little Kevin for you, better to just face up to it. His mother – oh yes, he remembered this well (why? Couldn't tell you; it's amazing the things you remember and the things you forget) – his mother, yes, she called him into the kitchen, where the pan was fizzing and popping fat. *Look* Kevin, she said, holding out for him a creamy porcelain bowl. Look Kevin, *look* – a double yolk! Kevin recoiled and looked up to his mother's face with new light and a curdling horror: here and now is my sweet mother gaily murdering yellow twins. Weird? You got it in one. And talking of yellow, that reminds him of the buttercup; after he had fled from the awful prospect of the wholesale daisy killings, so some child would do the buttercup thing: there would Kevin be, the fresh and young (newly slaughtered) petals tickling the underside of his sensitive chin – and yes! With glee the child would affirm that Kevin loved his butter. But he didn't, did he? Loathed it. And for years and years choked it down, just so as not to prove the buttercup wrong, to let the buttercup not have died in vain. Sad, really. Ah well.

Milly Milly, Milly Milly – Milly Milly Milly! Nearly there now, must be. Kevin could hardly wait, as well you know. But oh no – what if she wasn't there? Oh horrors. Possible, though, isn't it? It is a possibility. She might not work there all the time – maybe she went out buying, or something (does she go out buying?), or maybe it was just a part-time thing, or maybe she had been there *just that day*, helping out a friend! Or what if – no, forget them, Kevin, forget your fears and terrors, put them all back in the box for later: just have a look at that vision in the window, Kevin my dear old lad: is that the loveliest thing or what? Yes it is, yes it is – and goodness: that's my Milly!

Kevin barged in, panting like a horse (it was in fact a bloody long walk, let him tell you) and flapping his hand as if to detach from it something sticky and vile, but actually for the reason that he had badly jarred his wrist by slamming into the door of the shop and then getting caught out by that old gag of its plain refusing to go all the way, as if reluctant to admit anyone at all of regular girth.

'Hello, Milly,' beamed Kevin. 'I was just passing and so I thought well, you know, why not? You're looking well, Milly. Oh no, sorry, I'm not meant to say that – but you are, Milly, you are: you're looking very well indeed. Can I please have your telephone number? Or maybe some other time if you're busy.'

Milly covered her nose with two straight fingers and let out a seriously girly laugh of, yes, real amusement and pleasure.

'How lovely to see you again, Kevin. I'm very glad you were passing. Where are you on your way to?'

Kevin looked down. 'Well . . . oh gosh, Milly, if the truth be known, I'm not *actually*, I'm not really on my way anywhere – I came to see you, really – *and*, oh yes – please don't let me forget this time, my life depends on it, I've got to buy some interesting things. Use my own judgement. Maybe you can help – I'd be grateful if you would, Milly. What here is interesting, would you say, and what is so dull it would put you to sleep? Oh yes, and can I please have your telephone number, Milly? Sorry to be so . . . um. You know.'

'Probably easiest if you ring me here,' smiled Milly, and she slid across to him a card with all the details of the shop printed in blue and red. This N'That it was called, apparently: This N' That. Would Kevin remember this name, maybe? It's quite catchy, This N' That. No – inconceivable. Kevin knew well that the second he ceased to stare down at the card, the name would be lost for ever.

'Better, maybe,' mumbled Kevin, 'if you don't probably actually ring me at all, maybe, what with one thing and the – that is to say, better maybe if I ring you here, yes? Think that's best.'

'Fine, Kevin. That's fine. Now, what would Sir be interested in purchasing from this wondrous establishment?'

Well, thought Kevin, peering around the heaps of what to Kevin was simply so much *stuff*: just piles and piles of old and useless *stuff*. That's a very good question.

'I suppose,' he said, glancing back at the card, 'a bit of this, maybe followed by a bit of that! Bad joke. Sorry.'

Milly smiled and touched his hand briefly and Kevin thought blimey O'Reilly, she's plugged in to the mains! That shot straight to the heart and back.

'Milly,' he said. 'You know when I was in yesterday? You remember? When I came in yesterday?'

'*Think* I can cast my mind back that far, yes, Kevin. Think I can just about manage that.'

'Yes, right, silly of me – of course you remember. Well, remember we touched on this dinner thing? You know, you and me, having dinner, as it were?' And then when she nodded – probably had no energy for a repeat of all her ironical memory whimsies – Kevin went on: 'Right. Well I was sort of wondering whether tonight, this evening, would be any good, in fact, because it just so happens it's very good for me and so I sort of thought, you know, if it happens to be good for *you*, then maybe we could –'

'Tonight's great, Kevin. Tonight's fine. When and where?'

And Kevin thought oh wow – not just for the obvious reason (Tonight's Great! Yes it is! Yes it will be!) but also because he was heartrendingly grateful that she had shown the kindness of heart to finally interrupt him, for there was no way in the world he could ever have foreseen an ending to what would surely have become the longest invitation since Come All Ye Faithful. But now there was something else: what time and where? Ha. Had he thought about it? Planned it out? No chance. He had only suggested tonight because just before he left the house Emily had informed him that he would be out all evening until late, and Kevin had said right ho, fine, and although it may or may not have crossed his mind to wonder quite why this should be so, it didn't do to meddle: just leave well alone, and hope to keep her sweet. Less sour.

'I actually live quite close to here,' Milly was now chattering, 'so maybe somewhere round here would be good. If that's OK for you.'

'Yes yes,' agreed Kevin. 'Fine for me.'

Of course in truth if Milly had suggested they dine halfway up a Himalaya Kevin would have eagerly professed his total commitment to the sheer convenience of such an idea, but in actual fact he did happen to know a couple of places in Notting Hill Gate – a little Italian, very comfortable, good grub, pretty cheap, and Kevin always felt at home there (more so, anyway, than he ever did at home), and then there was that larger French place which could easily be called Chez Nous but needn't, of course, be called anything remotely approximating to that, which Kevin on one occasion had not actually entered because he deemed it rather too starchily formal and bloody overpriced.

'Do you somewhere called Chez Nous, at all? *Think* it's called Chez Nous.'

'Don't, actually, Kevin. Where is it?'

'Well, you know the tube? Notting Hill tube? Well you come out of there and you turn right and then it's just near the corner on the left.'

'Oh *I* know that place – the French place. I've never been – I've heard it's frightfully expensive. But that's not called Chez Nous!'

'No?' said Kevin, thinking *frightfully* expensive, oh lumme.

'No – that's Les Quat' Chats Au Pot.'

'Doesn't sound too appetizing,' demurred Kevin.

Milly laughed – oo*wee*, Kevin just loved that laugh: keep it coming Milly!

'It's meant to be marvellous,' she said.

'Well let's go there, then,' decided Kevin magnanimously, thinking (one) God, I've made a decision, and (two) I wonder if Emily could be persuaded to give me an advance on next week's sub or not?

'I'll meet you there, then,' said Milly happily. 'Seven? Eight?'

'Seven-thirty,' said Kevin, thinking wow, another decision, what's got into me? But then he said no actually let's make it seven, yes, seven's best, because after all, who knew? Emily might want him out of the house quite early. You never knew with Emily, did you? And it was best for all concerned to play it safe.

And now, folks, we come to that part in the programme that we call Use Your Own Judgement Time! Yo! So Kevin, tell me Kevin – it is Kevin, isn't it? Just stand on that mark right there, my friend, just there, well done Kevin – and a nice big smile for all the good people at home. Well Kevin, so tell me – what prizes would you like to take home to your lovely wife tonight?! He settled for all sorts of things in the end – a what might be termed eclectic selection: yeah, just about as varied as he could make it: *something* here had to be OK, surely to God?

Initially he debated with Milly the relative merits of each and every bit of stuff – the slightly rusty helmet from a sort of suit of armour particularly engaged them – but with the

95

best will in the world Kevin simply couldn't see eye to eye with Milly vis-à-vis the intrinsic beauty of an immensely heavy steel and leather horse-collar – at least Milly was pretty sure it was a horse-collar, couldn't think what else it might be – but they both agreed on the must-haveability of a brass sort of, well, difficult to say quite *what* it was, really: kind of table or stool affair, Kevin supposed, but with little shelves and other bits and bobs poking out of it which Kevin had no reason to believe rendered the whole thing anything less than consummately *interesting*. I'm telling you – dump this thing in the cocktail bar of the small hotel and it would fascinate the pants off anyone so much as glancing in its direction: it would keep you up talking half the night, so desperate would it be to make the sort of statement you ain't never before heard in your entire life, baby, you bet your life. Well, you can maybe tell that Kevin was becoming slightly hysterical by this time (is *this* a nice piece? Don't know. This *isn't* nice, is it? Don't know: could be) and Milly was now just leafing through a magazine and leaving him to it, laughing ringingly from time to time as Kevin confronted some new and awful lump of stuff with the expressions on his face flickering all the way between sheer childlike incredulity that such a thing could ever have been manu-factured in the first place to open-mouthed horror at the sight of its price.

'Right, that's it,' he said finally. 'I just can't *look* any more.' And then, glancing down at Milly's open magazine, 'Oh I know him, I like him – I like his films, particularly the what are they, spaghetti Westerns; I like them, yeah.'

'Clint Eastwood,' said Milly. 'Yeah – I like him best like that: all that sexy, manly stubbly beard all over his face – and his eyes as he looks up at the sun.'

'Oh yeah, that's him,' said Kevin.

Milly nodded. 'The Man With No Name.'

'Yes,' agreed Kevin. 'Well of course they're all like that to me.' And then the index finger was up and pointing: 'A Beard Can Conceal, A Beard Can Reveal.'

Milly stared at him – well, you expect that – and Kevin adjudged that he could hardly leave on a loftier note.

'I'll pick up all this stuff tomorrow, Milly, if that's all right.' (Yippee! Another reason to come back and see Milly again!) 'So, then. À bientôt, dear Milly. Till seven, at Chez Nous. I can't wait.'

'Les Quat' Chats Au Pot!' laughed Milly.

Kevin nodded. 'That,' he said.

He squeezed through the door (how are you supposed to make an unforgettable exit sideways, pray?) and he felt good, better than for a very long time. Kevin screwed up his eyes to look in the direction of where the sun could well have been under all that black and filthy cloud but a little of that went a very long way and he narrowly avoided slamming into a lamppost – Christ, just missed it, that'd be a fine thing: very romantic – a broken bloody nose, lit by candles. Stupid thing to do – won't do that again. Kevin passed a hand over his face. Change for dinner – what should he wear? That black thing, probably: the restaurant suit. Have a bath. Maybe wouldn't shave: maybe not bother tonight. Maybe even leave it for a couple of days – week, possibly. Couldn't do any harm, could it? Nope, there was no harm there that Kevin could see.

Milly Milly, Milly Milly – Milly Milly Milly!

Amanda was wolfing her breakfast and castigating Raymond in one fell swoop, small but telling rivulets of milk and the odd Rice Krispie spluttering out from the side of her mouth as she continued to lay into the man with gusto:

'You're show stupib, Raymum! I mean what on *earth* do you think you're up tomb ? I've been kept here against my

97

will all bloody night without any food – *that's* a criminal offence for a start, so when you finally do come to your senses and let me out of here, not only am I going to cry from the rooftops all your sordid secrets but I'll be round to the police as fast as I can bloody well go, let me tell you *that*. You're *sick* doing this, Raymond. Totally sick.'

'You weren't without food,' said Raymond, quietly – on his knees by the door of his study, energetically doing what people generally do with a stiff-bristled brush and a dustpan. 'I brought you a very large and probably tasty Chinese meal,' he reminded her, as he proceeded to sweep up the last of it. But she's right, of course: she's right. 'What on earth *do* I think I'm up to?' He had been asking and asking himself all night long and of course now in the morning it all seemed more impossible than ever. He must, he supposed, have eventually dozed off some time towards dawn, and then soon after through the creamy dreaminess of waking half-sleep came a shard of something cold and rancid – the sourness of his dark and tossing hours of blackness was seeping into him again and that meant that all the bleak and scary visions must be true, for Raymond well knew that it was only the beautiful dreams that were never ever more than lustrous imagining. But *listen* to her, can't you? Just listen to the way Amanda was talking. I mean now it wasn't just Raymond's company and his solvency and his (don't laugh) reputation or his big and dirty horrible house – no no no, that was barely enough: now she was going to see to it that he spent some years banged up in a jail as a new and added bonus to her cocktail of destruction. So you see, *yes* there was no point in keeping her here (of course there wasn't, how could there be?) but he couldn't let her go, now, could he? Not now he couldn't – could he? That was the trouble: that was half the trouble.

'Well,' said Amanda, pushing away her cereal bowl. 'Come on, Raymond: what are you going to do? It's make-your-mind-up time. God I'm starving – isn't there anything else?'

Raymond got to his feet and emptied the last of the dustpan into a rubbish sack. He felt rather sick, among very many other things.

'No,' he replied. And he wouldn't tell her that half of her Rice Krispies he had shovelled up from the kitchen floor – God knows how long they had been there: there wouldn't have been enough even for a bowlful, not if he relied upon what was still in the packet. 'I'll get some food in later.'

'You won't *have* to get some food in later, Raymond, because I'm out of here right *now*. You can't keep me here, Raymond.' And then, in a fit of pique and exasperation: 'Oh Christ, you *know* you can't do this Raymond! Just unlock the door and stop being such a bloody *child*!'

Raymond shook his head. Felt, in truth, a bit more than queasy; felt something that could easily and maybe quite soon approach the makings of ill. 'Can't,' he said.

Amanda sat back and sighed – sighed as if to say well, we're getting nowhere and even what I am about to say will signally fail to further the position but I suppose I could do worse than humour the man.

'*Right*, Raymond.' This was not Amanda's accusatory voice, nor was it the prologue to an ultimatum. This was the practical voice, the voice of quite stern reason, the tone Amanda assumed in the office when there was a pile of proposals to see to, a stack of releases for release, a litany of messages – all to be answered – and just *looking* at it wasn't going to get it done, now – was it? Talking about it was no good to man nor beast – was she right or was she right? So let's make a start on it, why don't we, plough on till the end – a good day's work and then we can all go home. Or in this instance, maybe not.

'Well, Raymond – you tell *me*. You tell me just how you want to play it. I mean – is there a game plan, here?

99

Knowing *you*, I severely doubt it. Have you thought any part of this through? How do you think we're going to go about this, Raymond? Hm? Raymond?'

Raymond was not aware of cranking up whatever processes it took to begin the shake of one's head, and on balance decided that he had not yet stopped it wagging to and fro since the last time Amanda had so deftly highlighted his helplessness.

'Don't know,' he said, really quite piteously. 'Don't *know*, Amanda. Really can't think.'

'Well let's look at it,' suggested Amanda, quite briskly – and Raymond straightaway perked up a tinge: he was always quite excited by her let's-get-to-business voice, not only because the bare thought of Amanda achieving always moved him on a fairly basic level, but also because it generally meant that Amanda could almost certainly be depended upon to take over the whole damn thing and get results – sort stuff out – yes and *then* Raymond could slope off nowhere much in order to concentrate as hard as he dared upon nothing at all and (oh yes) this was fine by Raymond.

'Firstly, how do we explain my absence at the office?'

We. Raymond clutched at least that bit to him. 'Sick?' he hazarded, not enjoying the word.

Amanda nodded slowly, turning it over. 'Sick . . . OK . . . and when they phone me at the flat? And they always *do* phone, you know that Raymond – even if I'm off for a single morning you can depend on it that someone will phone about something.'

'Staying with your parents?'

Amanda shook her head. 'They're the very next people they'd call. And why didn't I *say* I was taking off somewhere, hey? Why would I just leave the office one night and vanish? They'll call the police, that's what they'll do – and they'll call *you*, Raymond. Either way, you're finished.'

'Oh Christ,' muttered Raymond. Kidnap – like other things – required a bit of thought, then – yes?

Amanda was striding around the room, tapping one front tooth with a fingernail whose varnish was – for the very first time in Raymond's experience – rather badly chipped. Well, he allowed, it's not as if she'd had time to pack, or anything. Didn't have about her all the things she needed. Poor Amanda. Poor Amanda. What a position to find herself in. If only there was something he could do.

'Look – we *could* say I had to dash off on some last-minute press trip thing –'

'Yes!' agreed Raymond with a bucket of alacrity, something approaching light just beginning to worry the mud of his eyes.

'*No*,' returned Amanda, with adamance. 'I'd be expected to phone in – and they'd want a contact number.'

'You could give them this number,' suggested Raymond, brightly.

Amanda smiled. 'They *know* this number, Raymond,' she explained, as if to a retard. 'You're the *boss* – it's your *company*.'

'Ah . . . yes.'

'Plus,' tacked on Amanda, 'if you reconnect the phone I'll call the police. You're sunk, Raymond.'

'Christ.'

'Un*less* – how about this? You tell them I've been kidnapped.'

'Funny, Amanda. Very funny.'

'No listen – it makes sense,' enthused Amanda, now quite warming to the thing. 'Tell them you have received a letter from the kidnappers informing you of the snatch.'

Raymond looked up. 'Snatch?'

Amanda nodded impatiently. 'They call it a snatch. No one is going to connect *you* with it, are they? No one's going to think of *you*. Of course, you'll have to show the letter to the police, there's always that. You're over, Raymond.'

'Christ.'

'*But* – if the letter was posted from out of London, they would concentrate all their enquiries on wherever it was postmarked. Is there *really* nothing to eat, Raymond? I'm absolutely ravenous.'

'There might be a Kit-Kat; I'll slip out in a bit. But this letter, Amanda – oh, by the way: did you want a bath or anything? It's pretty awful in there, I have to say. Or there's that shower thing in *my* loo – I could clean that up a bit if you'd like.'

Raymond's study – the place he went to silently scream – had an en suite loo and shower thing (master bedroom once? Who knew or cared?) which was just perfect if you've kidnapped someone because otherwise how could you play it?

'We'll think about all that later. What *about* the letter?'

'Hm? Oh yeah – yeah, the letter. What's this letter supposed to *say*, exactly?'

'Say? Well how should I know what it's supposed to *say*? What they all say, I suppose: We Have Got The Girl – Pay Half A Million If You Ever Want To See Her Alive Again. That sort of thing.'

Something there sounded nice. Half a million – grief!

'But hang on – why would they send that to *me*? I haven't got half a million. I haven't got half a *crown*.'

'But they might *think* you have – you do own the company, after all: the company does *look* successful.'

'Well they're pretty thick, these people, that's all I can say. Why don't they ask your parents – that's more to the point. They're the ones who've got the money, not me.'

And Raymond and Amanda looked at each other. Don't know why they did, but once they had done, there was no mistaking what either saw there.

'That's quite a good point,' agreed Amanda. And then,

after the briefest pause: 'Let's send the letter to Daddy. He'd *never* tell the police.'

'Yeah?' queried Raymond, doubt soon shading into icy fear. 'But Christ this is pretty deep water, isn't it? I mean, Christ – if the law *did* get a whiff of this . . .'

'Worth it, though, isn't it?' challenged Amanda. 'For a quarter of a million?'

Raymond looked at her unblinkingly.

'Each,' she concluded. And what a cat-like, sideways smile: Raymond had surely never seen *that* one before. 'Where's this Kit-Kat, then?'

It was later, rather later, and Amanda now said it was time to get down to the nits and the grits. She was lying on a sofa-bed that Raymond had bleeding nearly ruptured himself hauling in to his study from the spare room which just had to be off the landing and four stairs up. Even when he had got it to the door his troubles weren't nearly over because almost unbelievably to Raymond's way of thinking Amanda was climbing over the sofa when it was halfway through the door and hitting Raymond wildly about the head and there was he trying to shove in the bloody sofa-bed while preventing himself from being brained as with his fourth pair of arms he fought off Amanda's attempts to scramble through the door while using his face as a foothold. Eventually she had him by the hair and was screaming venom right into his ear and if Raymond's mother-in-law had not at that selfsame moment been one floor down and bawling out the chorus of 'Danny Boy' while beating the blue blazes out of a derelict old banjo then Maureen might well have heard the fantastic battle and could even have investigated and the fear of this too assailed Raymond as he finally got the door shut and locked behind him as Amanda still scrabbled on the floor biting at his ankles and so it would at least have helped him to know that Maureen had by now passed out head first into the fridge anyway having found herself finally unable to cope with the concluding stages of her quest for a fistful of ice-cubes to tinklingly drop into the last of the latest litre of hooch.

'Jesus Jesus Jesus!' babbled Raymond, really bloody annoyed, and now he was rubbing his ears and one hell of a bump on his head and there was a really dull and glowing purple pain spreading across his thigh and if that didn't manifest itself into a deep blueberry stain bleeding its way out into custard-skin edges then Raymond was a monkey's – but God Almighty look at her now! Just look at this bloody cow now! There was Amanda, calm as you like, stretched out on this damned sofa that Christ he'd only thought of dragging down for her own personal comfort, about to smoothly guide Raymond into the softly intriguing corridors of what Amanda had now christened 'Our Plan'.

'It was my *duty*,' was all he could get out of her by way of explanation as to why she had been prepared to leave him broken and bleeding in her furious bid for freedom. 'I saw it in that film, what was that film when Robert Redford leapt over that barbed wire on his motorbike at the end and the Germans were shooting and then they – no, not Robert Redford, it wasn't *Redford* it was Paul Newman, wasn't it?'

'Is this Colditz we're talking about?' asked Raymond dully. 'I don't know whether you care, Amanda, but my head feels as if it's been used for a –'

'Steve McQueen! That's it, Steve McQueen – dead now, I think, or maybe that's the other one, the one with the wig. And they all had a duty to escape – *Great Escape*, of course, of course, *Great Escape*.'

'Oh yes, I remember *The Great Escape*. They keep putting that one on, don't they? It's always on, that one. Good, though. And Donald Pleasence was blind.'

'The point is – do you want any of this ham, Raymond? It's pretty good, actually.'

'I got it in Sainsbury. There's olives there too, if you want. Oh *Christ* I didn't get any cigarettes again.'

'The point is they had to *try* to escape, and so do I. But now you've locked me in again there's nothing I can do, so of course we can resume our talk.'

'But Amanda, if you're really serious about demanding this, oh my God, *ransom* – it's not going to carry much weight if you're *not* kidnapped, is it? I mean if you go swanning back to the office –'

'To tell everyone,' interjected Amanda.

'If you go back to the *office*,' repeated Raymond with emphasis (I did not *hear* that last remark, *thank* you Amanda).

'*And* the police.'

'Look – Amanda: you've got to *decide*. Are you going to be kidnapped or are you not?'

'Well I *am*, aren't I? You won't let me go.'

'Yes but I mean *officially*. Actually, you're right – this is good ham, very nice indeed.'

Amanda nodded. 'And that bit where they're getting on the bus, d'you remember, and the Gestapo guy says in English "Good Luck" and one of them, who was it, answers back "Thank You" and you think oh *Gaaaad*! And then they're running all over the place – Christ it's *ghastly*, that bit.'

'Do you want another glass of wine?'

'That was that Scottish one with David Attenborough.'

'No wine? Spot more?'

'*Richard* Attenborough, I mean. Richard. No I won't have any more, thanks, Raymond – maybe later. Let's get to work.'

'Do you *really* love me, Amanda? You *can't* do.'

'Of course I do, you sap. Now write this down.'

'Well why don't you let me –?'

'Raymond – take away your hand *now*. Now, Raymond.'

'But I only want to – ow! *Jesus*, you are a mad and crazy woman, Amanda! You're another of the mad and crazy women. That bloody *hurt*, Amanda – Christ you've practically destroyed my entire body this bloody afternoon.'

'And the rest of you comes later. Don't *bleat*, Raymond, and write this down. I think I will have another glass now, actually, if there's any going. Gordon Jackson.'

'There's not much in here, actually – I can open another one. I'll open another one. It's not bad, is it, for five ninety-nine. Gordon who?'

'Never mind: listen – write this. Your personal assistant Amanda is safe and will come to no harm. You must give half a million pounds to get her back. Details will follow. One word to the police and we will slit her throat and throw her like a dog into a ditch where she will be eaten by –'

'Christ, Amanda!' protested Raymond. 'I mean – *Jesus*.'

'Yeah, OK,' conceded Amanda, 'scrub all that last bit. Just say, and you will never see her again. That should do it. Then you show this to darling Daddikins and he coughs up the loot – he won't have any trouble with half a mill.'

'And then?' Wish to God I had a bloody cigarette.

'And then you keep it. Say you took it to wherever you were meant to take it to, and then I turn up the following day, tanned and fit. When I say you *keep* it – you *don't*, of course.'

Raymond nodded. 'You mean I keep *half* of it.'

'We-ell,' drawled Amanda, 'yeah – that was the *first* plan, I agree, but we were both forgetting something.'

'We were? What were we forgetting, Amanda?' enquired Raymond rather slowly, not caring for the sound of it, not one little bit.

'Well – if we split the money . . .'

'Ye-es?'

'I'll still have to tell everyone everything, won't I? Plus the fact that you raped me.'

'That I –! You haven't let me so much as –!'

'I know, Raymond, I know – but that has nothing to do with what I *say*.' And then, quite pityingly: 'Do *think*, Raymond.'

Raymond gazed into the eyes of the woman who loved him. With plodding voice and features devoid of any expression, Raymond buckled down to embracing an awesome inevitability.

'OK, Amanda. What's the deal?'

'You get the money – you give it to me. Simple.'

'And then?'

'And then I go back to running your company.'

'But you'll be rich!'

'Well I already am, quite. But it has nothing to do with that – I quite like my job, actually, Raymond. And anyway, I have to keep the company going, don't I?'

Raymond nodded as if from the depths of a hypnotic state. 'Because you love me.'

'Yes! And of course I wouldn't dream of telling anyone *then* about your horrid little goings-on with Amazon Woman –'

'That's not kind, Amanda,' said Raymond, thinking actually – It's *too* bloody kind.

'And nor will I go to the police. See? It's easy.'

'I see, yes. I risk prosecution and prison for extortion, whereupon I lose everything and you gain a fortune – *or*, if all goes well, you *still* gain a fortune and my life reverts to its status of twenty-four hours ago. I don't really go for it, Amanda.'

'Don't have a choice, Raymond. Either way.'

'Blackmail, Amanda.'

'Ugly word, Raymond,' laughed Amanda. 'Mind you – so's kidnap. So what do you say? I want you to have a piece of this fruit-cake, Raymond, because it is absolutely divine. Get some more wine, Raymond, there's a dear. Oh – and lots of old newspapers as well: have you got any?'

'Oh yes. The old newspapers in this house date back to the seventies: collectors' items, most of them. Catching up on the news, Amanda?'

'Silly! Got to cut out the letters for the ransom note, haven't we? Don't you watch *any* films?'

It was as if she did this sort of thing every day of her life, Raymond marvelled. He backed towards the door (it was the only way to avoid a crazed attack from the rear) and then he checked himself.

'Amanda?'

'Hmm?'

'What would you do if I *really* raped you?'

Amanda did not hesitate: 'Kill you with a knife.'

Raymond pursed his lips. 'I'll get some wine,' he said. 'Get some more wine.'

Felt sick again. Felt a bit sick. Christ I wish I had a cigarette.

Amanda looked up – even smiled reassuringly, her eyes held wide.

'I'd do it for love,' she told him.

CHAPTER FIVE

Shelley was bending low and squinting at as many of her features as could be reflected in the bright brass fingerplate on the living-room door. She was brushing mascara upwards into her eyelashes and so her mouth was agape into an 'O' of surprise – and of *course* she knew it was a stupid place to apply her make-up: hell on the back for a start, only one eye visible at a time and her complexion overlaid with the pallor of jaundice. It was just a habit, a habit she had got into years ago when make-up was a new and illicit thing, and maybe the peep-show element of such a rigmarole in some way had enhanced her daring. Once Adam had twigged to this singular ritual, he had taken to barging through the door at every opportunity – once nearly had her eye out – but that very soon got boring (also, Shelley had threatened to cover his face with lipstick) and now no one even noticed Shelley, doubled up and daubing away: it was just another part of living at home.

Emily was watching her, though – a sly smile hovering like a butterfly at just one corner of her mouth, hesitant to land lest Shelley look round and catch her gaze; Shelley would have been alerted to something, then: there was some sort of understanding between the two of them, Emily knew, though quite on what level it operated she could never decide. Neither understood what the other was about, Emily was perfectly sure of that, but sometimes there was the twanging of intuition, and whatever was mutually gleaned from the activation of so fleeting a spark would then hang in the air accusingly, like an unsubstantiated rumour.

'How late do you think this thing will go on?' asked

Emily, which certainly surprised her: she had intended to say no such thing, for it wasn't the sort of thing Emily would ever say. If Shelley wanted to go out with a heaving cluster of girls from that silly little shop in which she chose to fritter her life, then Emily for one could care neither where they went or when they returned, and nor would it remotely bother her as to whatever went on in between. And here was an instance of that subconscious tightrope, taut between their respective poles, for Shelley had stiffened slightly at the unfamiliarity of even the nature of the words that had maybe not been uttered so casually at all?

'I don't know,' said Shelley, quite as non-committally as the slickest politician. 'Why?'

Could Emily really reply 'Oh, no reason'? Couldn't, could she? As well to paper the walls with the word Suspicion and wait not too long for Shelley's offhand announcement that on balance she didn't really think she would go out after all, since you ask me – not really in the mood, now I come to think about it: maybe a quiet night in. But Emily's insides rebelled at that. Shelley could have a night anything between mute and out-and-out deafening, but *in* was decidedly *out*. Because, you see, Gideon was coming over for Emily, ha ha – *not* for little Shelley, this time – and Shelley did not know that. Somewhere upstairs at that very moment, Kevin was thinking I don't know what Emily is up to tonight and I don't frankly care (so long as I don't get the blame if it all goes wrong). *I'm* going out with Milly, hee hee, and Emily must not know that.

It glanced into Shelley's mind now that maybe Emily had divined that she wasn't in truth going anywhere at all with the girls at work – the girls at work were not in the picture – and so maybe her mother assumed that she would be with Gideon and so why, then, an alternative story? Shelley's actual destination should not be known to either Emily or Kevin, Shelley had decided, because then it might get back to Gideon and he would only be upset. Would he be upset? Do you know, Shelley wasn't even *sure*? He was such a strange boy, Gideon – their faces always ached with laughter, when they were together, and Shelley could rarely work out why. Maybe because this blanket of mirth swathed him, got him out of other things; Shelley had not thought of it like that for long – at first all his reasons had been more or less plausible, but now the jokes, the apparently unrestrained hysteria on his part (increasingly forced on hers), had become a soiled and raucous mask for something quiet and vivid lurking beneath, and Shelley had to admit if only to herself that between them now had been slung a thick and dusty curtain of heavy evasion.

Adam lumbered into the room in that way he had, a slow and final approach to the shoot-out in a Tarantino, the clump of his boots forcing Emily's collection of miniature enamel boxes to shiver with worry atop a slim and curvaceous Plexiglass table. And wasn't Shelley just enthralled by the sight of Ben the Ape close behind him, his attitude being more that of an armoured hero shouldering his way through a gaggle of minions. Shelley flattened her mouth and deadened her eyes, the better to stonewall the coming double assault of genitally driven jeering and croaked-out platitudes, rich in elision and stuck with edited highlights from the finals of this year's glottal stop competition, brought to you live in the comfort of your very own designer home.

'Oh God, here's Shelley – trying to cover up her injuries with paint: won't work, Shell. You're too far gone.'

'Oh do shut up, Adam,' sighed Shelley – though whether she was heard through the guttural gurgling of Adam or Ben she couldn't have told you, couldn't have cared.

'I thought you were out tonight,' said Emily.

'Yeh – we're going out now. Man, we are going to get *blitzed* – totally out of it.'

'Oh come off it, Adam,' sneered Shelley. 'You've only just graduated to alcoholic lemonade and you're too bloody broke to buy *that*. Why don't you ever just grow up or shut up?'

'What do *you* know about it, *slag*?'

'Mummy!' Shelley appealed, in a higher pitch than usual; didn't often call her Mummy, these days, but she was caught off guard. She was used to Adam's idiot banter, but this was too much.

'Don't say that to your sister,' said Emily, 'you horrible little shit.' Say *anything* to your sister – just get *out*, won't you?

'Oh I'm getting out of here,' huffed Shelley – and then to Adam and Ben – Ben and Adam in order – 'You know, you two are quite the most repellent little children on earth, and my heart goes out to whatever blind woman you eventually succeed in drugging and tying up just so you can *fail* with her.'

'She's in a temper,' grinned Ben.

Adam nodded. 'Ought to be in an asylum,' he said.

Shelley made for the door after her glare of contempt had gone unseen and Emily thought Good, about time – that's one down, anyway; now, what's next? Bribe Adam into going, then just throw out Kevin and get things ready.

'Have you got money, Adam?' threw out Emily, as coolly as cool; no – didn't sound cool at all, did it? It just wasn't Emily, all this sort of thing. And didn't Adam know it! Gazed at Emily with a look of wonder fast being overtaken by hope, both now annihilated by out-and-out greed: Emily never, ever, offered him money on top of his piddling allowance – *ever* – and Adam sure as fuck never got anything from his *father*: Christ, Kevin was more likely to cadge off *him*.

'Well, Mum – since you ask, I am a bit . . .'

'Here,' said Emily, crumpling a twenty-pound note into his hand.

Now this truly would have amazed Adam if he could be bothered to let it; as it was, all thoughts about everything were immediately supplanted by – Hey, never mind *why*. Who gives a fuck *why*? Just take it before the mad old seacow changes her mind.

'*Nice* one,' approved Ben.

'Great, Mum,' chimed in Adam. 'OK, city – get ready! OK, Ben? Let's drift. We're outta here. See you, Mum.'

Emily just nodded curtly; *would've* said and don't hurry back but that really would've been too out of character to even contemplate; it wasn't that usually she insisted that Adam – or, indeed, anyone at all who lived here – be back *early*, or anything – it was just that during the normal course of events Emily was unaware and careless of where anyone was at all at any given time – even whether they were in the house or out of it. Just didn't matter. But tonight, well – tonight it did.

What was the time? Just after six; a little under an hour, then: where the bloody hell was the millstone Kevin? What was he *doing* up there? Well whatever it was he wasn't going to be doing it for much longer because he was leaving *now*, *that's* for sure, and I might as well go up and haul him down the stairs by his bloody hair because there is no way on earth I am going to wait the ages it takes for *him* to saunter down quite simply because the likes of Kevin should never be allowed to interfere with *anything*, nothing at all – even simple things – and certainly not with *this*; so, right, Kevin my lad – ah, so he *has* finally appeared, has he? Well that's just as well for Kevin then, isn't it? Just avoided a nasty incident. Even now as he stood before her, the nearest the poor sap would ever get to being 'dressed', Emily had to stifle a near-unconquerable urge to pick up that rather beautifully arranged bouquet of freesias, poppies and gypsophila and scatter the flowers to the four winds immediately prior to dashing the water into his face and cracking the rather pleasing blue-and-white Spode vase across the centre of his skull; there was just something *about* Kevin – there was just something *about* the man that always made Emily want to . . . anyway, forget all that, can't tonight. What – and have him traipse back upstairs again to change? Put together some other nightmare combination of obsolete rags? I don't think so. But this clothes thing had reminded her:

'Tomorrow, Kevin – shopping. Clothes. For you.'

Kevin – hitherto quite sprightly (and we know why, don't we?) – suddenly froze as if in a photo, his mouth really quite comically turned down at the corners in the manner of a clown. *Not* comically, as it turned out – he wasn't laughing was he?

'I don't need any *clothes*, do I, Emily? Got piles of clothes.'

'Oh don't be *stupid*, Kevin. I'm not going into it. The main thing we need is a new dinner-suit – you simply cannot wear that ghastly old thing *again*, this year.'

Oh God. The Ball: dread upon dread.

'But that's *ages* away . . .'

'It's this *Saturday*, Kevin. What's wrong with you? Why can you never grasp the really very simple concept that time's *passing*, Kevin? It's this *Saturday*.'

'Oh God it's not, is it?' Oh God it's *not*, is it?

'Anyway – just go on out. We'll talk tomorrow.'

'Right,' agreed Kevin eagerly. 'Um – Emily, you couldn't see your way to . . .? I mean, I wasn't *planning* tonight, and –'

Emily exhaled hugely and produced with slow and heavy gestures a fifty-pound note from the same wallet as the twenty with which she had bought off Adam.

'You children,' she sighed. 'You're all just children, aren't you?'

Kevin simpered in a way that could, one supposes, be construed as childlike.

Yes OK, granted – *now* he was sitting down with Milly – nice corner table, cloth the colour of his mother's rouge, carnation and fern (buttonhole-like) bobbing atop a slender silver vase affair that Emily might or might not have pronounced interesting, Kevin would never know – but it hadn't been all that simple, oh Lordy no. Why wasn't it simple, actually, Kevin? I mean – you walk in, you sit down, yes? No. In Kevin's case, no.

The first problem (and it was *finding* the place that Kevin had worried about, only for the entire duration of the journey – just locating the corner he meant – but that did not turn out to be the problem because he saw it straight away: Les Quat' Chats and so on: there it is). No, that was OK – the problem was: two doors. Two glass doors with chunky brass handles diagonally spanning bevelled glass panes with pleated and sort of lacy curtains behind them – the sort of doors that defy you to push, the sort of doors that whisper snidely that maybe on the other side of them you possibly do not belong? Hm. Which one, then? On balance – this one. Wrong, might be wrong: certainly it wasn't opening. Should I be pulling, maybe? A pull door, yes? Nuh; wasn't having it either way. Not one of those 'In Case Of Emergency Break Glass' kind of doors, surely? Oh for Christ's sake, Kevin, get a grip: don't for the love of Jesus become hysterical at this stage of the game – there *are* no doors like that, are there? (Of course there are not, of course not.) That's other things – fire things, they do that.

Right. So. Wrong door: only explanation. Correct, as it happened, because the other one opened like a breeze and Kevin was in and broiled by hot air and that passed briefly and now he was aware only of candles and glistening surfaces and a moustache half over a mouth held firm in maybe indecision as to just what degree of contempt on a

115

scale of infinite calibration ought soon to be unleashed.

Kevin muttered his name to the moustache, which now served to nearly conceal half a sneer while black eyes to the north of it lazily subdued a darkening glare into at least the beginnings of the cold light of a semi-greeting. The restaurant was deserted, but Kevin had booked. Kevin had phoned again to check that his booking had been noted, and then a third time to confirm that the booking was, in fact – yes, booked. His guest, he made out after three or four goes, was already here. (Oh Christ I'm not late, am I? Can't be *late*, can I? No – not late, early actually, therefore Milly even earlier, OK, good sign, good sign; good sign? God knows.) Then there was some sort of mumbling about 'down there' – either that or Dan Dare but that would be unlikely, wouldn't it? Not likely, is it? That a head waiter with the air of an oil-rich sultan should on first and slight acquaintance start debating the joys of ancient *Eagles*? (Of *course* not, of *course* not – keep a hold, Kevin, there's a good lad.) So on balance 'down there' seemed about the mark, and Kevin dutifully stumbled down darkish and decidedly winding stairs thinking Well I don't know – nice big empty restaurant, candle-lit as if for Easter Day in the Vatican, and I have to get a table in this damn hole – and now someone was shouting down the stairs after him and Jesus it was pitch-black down here and only when his foot had repeatedly clanged into a succession of galvanized buckets did Kevin think Hey, no, this can't be right, can it?

Oh God what a business; barked his shin on the way back up – wasn't going to yelp, though, because the owner of the moustache was looking positively murderous as he beckoned him along and it had clean left Kevin's mind that he had actually come here to eat with Milly and maybe even have a good time because he had rarely felt so under threat in his life and if only Emily had been here she could have sorted it out in a jiffy in all probability by way of a killer blow to the throat just some way below this really serious moustache that was looming forever nearer and nearer as Kevin tramped back up these bleeding stairs and now weren't there *teeth* involved and a fair deal of smirking snarl seemed now to be the order of the day and from the rasping grunts emanating from this dangerous man Kevin gleaned only that Milly was to be found down there at the *back* and not down there in the bloody *cellar* and by the time he finally got to the table he was flustered, yes, very much so, but Milly was not to know that, of course not, why should she, and didn't she look – oh look, oh look: forget all about everything, Kevin, and gaze on this. Sweet or what? Hm? The sweetest thing that ever walked. On two legs, he meant: the sweetest thing on two legs that ever walked, not the face itself – because faces unaided, obviously, are incapable *per se* – *actually*, Kevin, I really do think it's time to smother all the babble, snuff the volcano of nonsense, sit down, sit down – smile, and enjoy: I think so, yes – the time has come.

'You're looking well, Milly!'

'Hello, Kevin. What's that on your chin?'

'My chin?' My *chin* – oh God oh God, my chin, my chin! What's on my *chin*? A glaze of saliva or a leprous boil?

'Looks like that bit on the side of a Swan Vestas box!'

'Ah!' Kevin was all comprehension, much good it did him. She didn't compare whatever his name was, what was his name, The Man With No Name, yes, that was his name – she didn't compare him with a box of bleeding matches, did she? Oh no. *He* was – what did she say? – manly and sexy and all sorts of other good things while Kevin came across as no more than a strip of sandpapered cardboard.

'Didn't shave,' said Kevin, passing a hand over the very chin under discussion, wishing he could whip if off, lose it in his napkin, and then – under cover of an avuncular chuckle – subtly slap in place another, preferably one with forceful-ness, a cleft, and maybe even chiselled, to boot.

'Were you in a hurry, then?' Milly wanted to know. 'You get some kiwi fruits looking a bit like that too.'

Kevin nearly smiled. Memo: shave. Shave tomorrow and then twice a day for the remainder of your life.

'I'm starving,' he said. 'Have you had a chance to look at the menu, yet? I haven't eaten a thing all day.'

A waiter came up just then (another waiter – not Mephistopheles, thank Christ) and his smile seemed quite unrestrained as he nodded to each of them in turn and then proceeded to indicate one or two things on the menu that were not, it distressed him beyond endurance to confide, this evening available – and then, by way of huge and elaborate compensation, he began to gabble a list of specials that was so long and detailed that Kevin's eyes became as glass – maybe like those marbles, those old-style marbles that looked like they had been prised from the skulls of your more belligerent tabby – and Kevin could have told the man (who was now using all of his arms, the better to convey the gloss on some grand sauce whose name was lost) that all this was to him as a cascade over boulders – and do you know it was just at that moment, as the waiter's mouth was working away even more vigorously, that Kevin heard no noise as he recalled within a halo of light the one and only time he had lunched with Sophie – ah Sophie, dear Sophie – and she had read out for him everything chalked up on the blackboard, for he surely couldn't make out a word of it from a distance such as that, and despite his gazing at the loveliness of every scrap of her he had nonetheless made such a damn fine effort to listen, to hear, to *absorb*, but not one word of one single dish even so much as entered and he had grinned and ordered a steak and chips and Sophie had smiled and said You know you're a strange boy, Kevin – sometimes you're absolutely miles away: and it was true, of course – of course it was true; and sometimes, when he was miles away, miles away from Sophie and yearning only to be near her, then he wanted the other thing – to be further away still, further by worlds. Sophie, Sophie. Ah dear yes – little Sophie, that was not to be.

'All *sorts* of good things here,' enthused Milly – and Kevin crawled back from where he'd been: not that far at all – not too far, this time. 'What do you think you want?'

Kevin looked up. The waiter had gone and Milly's eyes gleamed, the candles lending to each of them a soft and golden lozenge of feline eagerness. Kevin shrugged in a small way, and batted away the approach of shyness.

'Hard to say,' he said.

Emily had forgotten the feeling of pure and utter peace when the house was completely devoid of all human presence save her own. That was how rooms – proper rooms, designed rooms, rooms designed by *her* – were meant to look. You didn't, did you – in the magazines, the glossies – you didn't see *people* hanging around the rooms, did you? You did not. Or sitting in chairs. Or cooking. Or bathing. You did not. That is because people *mess things up* – not just because of their shape, not solely because you cannot colour-coordinate people nor arrange them in such a way that they can be depended upon to stay as you leave them – no. It's not just that – it's a lot of it, but there's more: it's the horror they leave behind. They want a drink – which means what? It means that the glistening Baccarat decanter, amber and full, will soon be covered with dribbles, the stopper left by its side and the level of spirit within not at all in accordance with the inherent proportions of its very beautiful container. Then they will choose to set their glasses down, yes? Yes. And so they move the ashtray, but of course, as they crush themselves into cushions and annoy the fringes on rugs with their hideous shoes that have tramped the streets of London. Eccchhh. No no no: on this point Emily was clear: people and rooms simply don't mix; it is as plain as day to anyone with half an eye.

Anyway, everything looked wonderful now; twenty hectic minutes clearing away the debris of, oh, just *everyone*; you'd think at least Shelley wouldn't be so desperately untidy, but she was the worst, if anything. Why she didn't move out, Emily could not tell you; admittedly, with what she earned in that stupid little shop (and did Shelley wish to better herself, get a better job – help Emily in the business, even? Shelley did not) the sort of place she would get would be, well, not to put too fine a point on it, small and vile – but at least then Shelley would have the freedom to render foul her very own poxy little space and leave her mother to enjoy the out-and-out stylishness of hers. Except, of course, with Kevin around, the mirage of stylish living only shivered hotly in the distance and – as is the way of mirages – vanished and then laughed at you, whenever grabbed at.

Emily sprayed room deodorant over most things, on the whole, all the while stroking down the dark pink silk gown she had chosen to wear. She had wondered many times whether tonight would ever come. Maybe it had begun merely as a teasing game: why shouldn't she make some sort of a play for her daughter's boyfriend? It was just a bit of fun, wasn't it? Hardly more. But then it had become something of a challenge, and the more Gideon resisted (why did he resist, actually? Fear almost certainly: he was *male*, after all) the sharper the challenge. When those terrible interludes with Raymond began, of course, Gideon became quite vital: *had* to have him now – just had to. Strange, her couplings with Raymond – Emily well knew how strange they were, acknowledged completely the depth of their mutual loathing without altogether understanding it; but nonetheless, those periodic bouts were now a brief and yes, she supposed also, rather brutal little truth that she needed,

needed, just as he did. How sad that each of them had to be there before and after, and not just maybe die during the during.

That wasn't the doorbell, was it? Fifteen minutes early, how very odd: Emily had felt sure – would have put money on it – that Gideon would have been wilfully late, blushing and shamefaced, reluctant to enter, but now that he was here, entering anyway. But no: fifteen minutes early. Well.

Emily had not decided which expression to wear as she opened the door; she'd thought of several, even tried on one or two, but even as her hand went out to release the lock, indecision had her. Better look down – knowing and demure – then look up and see whatever there is to be seen there and react maybe even in a genuine manner, if nothing more convincing was to hand. So Emily did that – looked down, looked up – and what was there was Raymond.

Emily – and this didn't happen often with Emily (with Emily this was a rare thing) – was now momentarily silenced by surprise, and that took just long enough for Raymond to step smartly inside and get the door shut behind him, for he knew the risks, he was well aware of the appalling dangers.

'Emily, Emily – I know, I know I shouldn't just turn up but I've been sitting in the car for ages, don't know why, nowhere to go, and I just saw everyone leave and I thought – oh, I don't know what I thought, I just – thought.'

'Raymond –' and oh God, this was cold: this was as cold as cold; this was the very worst voice of all. 'Leave. Immediately. Now.'

'Emily, I –'

'*Now*, Raymond, or I will break your legs.'

'Emily – a drink, just a quick drink, I swear I –'

Emily came towards him now, and he flinched, he felt it, he felt his whole body urging him to take it elsewhere, to be free of the danger, but then he allowed his eyes to open fully (hadn't been aware they were otherwise) because although he had been dreading the infliction of such pain as only Emily could deliver he craved it too because then it could be done with and he could invade her horribly and then just leave the bitch lying there. She had stopped, though – stopped; she was looking at him now, just looking at him, and though her lips moved that time, a flicker in the eyes told him no, words not ready yet, but now the lips were moving again and, yes – here came the sound, and no no no, it wasn't what he expected at all.

'One drink, Raymond. In the living-room. Then leave.'

Now why had Emily said that? Why had she acceded to this? Because it was quicker. He didn't want a drink – he knew that, she knew that – but that is what he had asked for and that's all, then, that had to be supplied.

Raymond went into the living-room and poured his drink – taking huge care with the decanter – and then he swallowed it briefly. He came back into the hall, and Emily had not moved: her eyes were fixed on the door. Raymond walked up behind her and placed the palms of his hands on her shoulders and she did not turn round and punch him in the face although every muscle there was braced for just such an action but she did sink down to her knees and then lie fully just before Raymond collapsed on top of her and then the dark pink silken wings of the gown were away from her and Raymond's breathing came heavily amid grunting and though she twisted her face away from the wetness of his her body arched up to meet him as the two throbbed away like a clock gone crazy until Raymond roared his fury and Emily cried out at each fresh wounding before they were apart and he was heaving as if for the last time ever and Emily was up and pulling at his coat and pushing, kicking, kicking, really *kicking* him out of the door as he tried to keep together his chest and his clothes and now the door was shut in his face and Emily was thinking drive, drive – get into your car and *drive*, Raymond, because now I have to rid the sweetness of my body of every stinking trace of you before I can give myself up to the dream of savagely fucking your son until he begs me to stop – and then going on until it bloody well kills him.

'Are you going to get us in another glass of wine, Julian, or are we just going to sit here and look at the wall?'

So said Shelley, in her very flattest voice. Had to in fact shout it because this bloody wine bar (God – she didn't think wine bars still *existed*) was crammed to the dadoes with the oldest and most boring people in the world, all of whom seemed to be avid contestants vying for a coveted place in the final of the Shouting Your Fucking Head Off About Bugger All competition. The two of them would be out of here, soon – get the other thing done, oh yuk, and then she could sod off back home. Oh God. Home. But not for much longer, I hope.

'Well – you're very welcome to another glass, of course you are, Shelley – although I have to say that as Riojas go, I find it disappointing – but speaking for myself I have to confess to being well up to quota. Sensitive stomach lining – bane of my life, but I do well know that we are not put on this earth to complain!' yelled back Julian.

It's not *that* Julian, is it? Not the father of odious little Ben who Shelley would love to nail to the wall? It *is*, you know – the very same: recognize his self-satisfied manifesto anywhere.

'Another glass of the Rioja, Daphne please, when you have the time,' apologized Julian. 'And can I furnish *you* with something?'

'Kind, Julian,' replied Daphne (they shouldn't, thought Shelley, let people with bad teeth serve behind a bar because it put you off your peanuts). 'I'll have a spritzer.'

'A spritzer is yours, Daphne,' expanded Julian. 'And I'll just have a glass of still water, if I may – no ice or lemon, and preferably Evian or Volvic. Or Spa would do as well.'

'The one we've got is from somewhere in the Mendips.'

Julian's face assumed an expression of intense concentration. 'Mendips, you say. Hm. Could I just skim over the label, would you mind? You see it's the *calcium* question –'

'Oh *Christ*, Julian,' hissed Shelley (oh God oh God what a person – can I really go through with all of this?). 'Just drink the fucking water, can't you?' No wonder Ben is such a bleeding prat.

Up went the eyebrows. Yep, there they were, poking above his bloody stupid spectacles – here we bloody go:

'I'm very *sorry*, Shelley, I'm very sorry if this in any way antagonizes you, but I just happen to feel that it is very important to know just what it is one is putting into one's body – I mean, we do only have *one* life, you know, and if I happen to want to live a long and healthy one then I'm very very sorry if this displeases you, but in my view –'

'Julian. Drink the water – don't drink the water. Either way, shut the fuck up. I don't want this wine. Let's just go and get it done with, shall we? *Now*, Julian.'

Shelley didn't wait for any sort of response (quite like her mother, in this respect – and not just in this respect, either); simply ground out her – oh God – *nth* Silk Cut and began to press her way through the braying throng, now very eager to be absolutely anywhere else, even if it had to mean being there with Julian. Which it did. She glanced back once, and there he was with a bloody bottle of mineral water pressed right up close to his eyes, the glasses now aloft across his forehead. Stupid shit. Wouldn't get stronger lenses, he said, because he could see everything perfectly well. That's why his eyes were permanently screwed up as if he had just been sucking on limes and also why the last time he had told her this he had slammed face first into a wall that he hadn't seen coming, and Shelley had enjoyed the moment for all it was worth. Now he caught her eye – or more likely the vague and disappearing flurry of her hair – and was suddenly all activity: maybe hadn't noticed her leaving – but here he was now, lolloping behind her, eager for the next bit.

'Your car again, I suppose,' said Shelley. Outside, now; bit of a wind – chilly after the throttling fug down there. Pleased to be out, though – despite the looming prospect of the back seat of Julian's bloody Volvo.

'Yes, well,' allowed Julian, 'we're working to change all that, aren't we? Few days it'll all be different, if all goes well – and I must say I see no reason at this juncture why all should not.'

To which Shelley could only nod; wanted to hit him, of course – would've just loved to kick and hack and kick at his legs until he caved in brokenly and collapsed into a screaming and chaotic heap on the ground whereupon she would see no good reason not to just go on kicking – but then she felt that more or less every single time he opened his mouth. Well. So what's the *deal*, then? Why *doesn't* she give him a good kicking and then just run? Here's why:

It's clear, isn't it, that Shelley is – shall we say – less than happy with her domestic arrangements? No no – you're right, you're right, let's cut the crap and get down to it: Shelley hates living at home – *fact*. Adam irritates her intensely, as we have seen, her father is just a joke, and Emily – well, difficult to say what Shelley really feels about her mother, but there is always this air of *scrutiny* that Shelley now shrinks away from – cannot bear to be under her gaze. So what's the problem, then? She's twenty-two, she's not a kid – a job of sorts (although yes, we have received the message loud and clear, I think, that it is a pretty cruddy little job. What is it, exactly? Not stacking shelves, surely? I mean, Shelley seems a fairly educated sort of person – she's not stupid, certainly. No, OK, not stacking shelves – but not very much better: she works in Boots, but not as any sort of pharmacist; all she dispenses are cosmetics to women who are cared for, and to girls who have better jobs than she does). Why not go for a better job? Can't be bothered. And why not move out? Could only run to a nasty room somewhere vile: doesn't want that. She wants a studio flat in Hampstead, Chelsea, Kensington – somewhere you've heard of. Uh-huh. Uh-huh. And . . . Julian? Yes, Julian. She had been sounding off about it all, one time – Adam and Ben had buggered off, and Julian had just been hanging around, as he does, jangling his bloody car keys.

'Maybe I could help,' he had suggested.

Shelley twanged on her thinnest smile. 'I don't *think* so, Julian.'

'*Might* be able to. Sometimes solutions to problems present themselves from the most unlikely quarter.'

'Well the only *problem*, Julian, is a lack of money – and unless you happen to be a millionaire desperate to shed himself of the burdens of wealth, I really don't see that you can do anything about it. Anyway, it's not your problem.'

'I quite see that it is not my problem, Shelley – I was merely contemplating ways whereby I might be of assistance. It is true that I am not a millionaire – life has not seen fit to bless me –'

'Oh Julian – why don't you just go? I mean – *thanks*, and all that, I know you're trying to be nice, but really –'

'But I *could* help, Shelley,' insisted Julian, now rather more intense. 'Let me help. With the rent.'

Shelley looked at him. Looked at him a bit longer.

'With the rent,' she said, dully.

Julian nodded. 'Indeed,' he said. 'With the rent.'

Shelley nodded too, but more slowly. 'And why would you want to do that, Julian?'

'Well,' said Julian, looking down – looking up again quite

quickly, now. 'It's nice, isn't it? When people can help each other out?'

Well – Shelley could have gone on poking around the thing, but there didn't seem to be a lot of point. Once a situation like this is firmly grasped, there are only two ways around it – outrage or quasi-reluctant compliance, loaded down with all manner of provision and qualification. Shelley went for the latter (why not? Well why not? Means to an end – that was all) and soon and really rather coldly, the whole thing was worked out. After the third time (tonight, actually – the stuff that's coming soon) she would have enough for the deposit on a rather super place she'd seen in Belsize Park, and then the rent would get seen to – well, quite as regularly as Julian did, really.

Ah, but it wasn't quite that straightforward. *Yes* they had twice met before, and *yes* Julian had given her money – the agreed amount – on each of these occasions. But what – you mean it wasn't straightforward in the back of the Volvo? Well why, then? What was the nature of these activities (soon, am I right, to be transferred to the more spacious surroundings of a rather super place in Belsize Park)? Well, it's delicate – but since you press me, anything that went on in those first two meetings was repeated almost exactly during the third.

'It's not going to work, is it, Julian? It never does.'

'Gah!' is the noise that Julian expelled. 'Try a bit . . . try a bit harder. Bit more. Bit more.'

Shelley was rummaging around with both her hands quite deeply inside Julian's trousers and she was currently thinking a couple of things: firstly, isn't it odd that at times like these Julian talks only in tight little monosyllables and isn't it also a terrific relief? And secondly, my bloody fingers are already rubbed raw so quite how Julian's feeling is anyone's guess. The trouble was, you see – oh dear – he was putty in her hands.

'I can't understand it! I just can't understand it!' wheezed Julian. 'I mean – what's *wrong* with me?!'

Shelley sighed and gave up, and Julian didn't object: there is a limit, after all. He pulled together his clothes, and placed neatly folded money into her hand.

'I'm sorry,' he mumbled. 'Something of a waste of time.'

'I don't mind,' said Shelley. And it was true – she didn't: not one bit. Actually much preferred it. Except . . .

'I just,' started up Julian again, 'I just don't know what's *wrong* with me.'

Except . . . except, yes – that: maybe there's nothing wrong with you at all, Shelley now thought, as Julian kicked the car into life; maybe it's *me* there's something wrong with. Could well be. And do you know why she thought that? Because it's just like this with Gideon, too.

If Amanda didn't get out of this bloody room soon she would surely go absolutely mental! It wasn't so bad when Raymond was actually in there with her – when they were gluing together all those letters and words from old newspapers it had actually been pretty good fun – but just banging around these four damn walls was sending her utterly spare! When she computed that in fact she had been there less than twenty-four hours she could barely believe it was true – how do people in prisons cope? How do people in those horrible tiny cells *manage* it at all, knowing they are there for years and years? She would rather kill herself – or whoever it took.

Of course, if she was to be an official kidnappee – which she must be, as Raymond was more or less at this very moment handing over the hastily cobbled together ransom note to Amanda's father (serve the old goat right) – then she did allow that she had to be *somewhere*, and here, she supposed, was as good as any other place. Except it was so *boring*! OK, yes – Raymond had brought in a stack of magazines, but Amanda never read words unless she absolutely had to and so turning the pages and looking at the clothes had barely filled in an hour. She had been through all the drawers and cupboards, of course (*God* it was filthy in this place), and had found absolutely nothing of any interest at all: with Raymond, what you saw must very much be all you got – he certainly wasn't a one for squirrelling away secrets. One good thing she did come across, though – almost definitely useful later – was a long and gently tapering letter-opener (hallmarked silver, very elegant) whose point was not remotely blunt, as some of them were; that she had slid down the side of her boot. Well – you never know what might happen, do you? If Raymond ever really did take it into his head to sully the purity of her love for him – well, then, *something* would have to be done: surely that was clear?

It had been great fun too when Raymond had phoned the office to tell them about Amanda's abduction (didn't mention the letter, though) and then swear everyone to secrecy: fat chance, of course, but it had to be said anyway. Amanda had insisted on listening in; it was Rupert who had taken the call:

'Rupert? Is that you? Raymond, here. Yes. No, fine. Yup. Look, Rupert – rather disturbing news, I'm afraid: sounds rather, well, I don't know *what* it sounds, to tell you the truth, but it rather seems as if Amanda's been, um, kidnapped . . . I know . . . well, can't tell you much, I'm afraid – and you mustn't breathe a word of this to anyone, Rupert, because Amanda's parents want all this kept very quiet . . . yes . . . yes, a letter was sent to her parents, apparently . . . oh, usual thing – money, of course . . . no no, she's quite *well*, quite unharmed . . . shouldn't be surprised if she's back with us in a day or so because certainly Amanda's father has made it plain that he wants to play it their way . . . yes . . . yes well I *know* – it's quite a shock for *all* of us . . . yes of course I will, as soon as I hear anything. Yes of course. I know, I know – not the sort of call you expect, first thing in the morning. Anyway, Rupert, it looks like I'm the sort of go-between in all of this, so I'd better be – yes, yes – well of *course* it is, of course. So look – keep everything chugging along and don't breathe a word, OK Rupert? And yes, as I say, as soon as I hear . . . yup . . . yup . . . OK, then, Rupert – bye. Yup. Bye.'

And then Raymond had unplugged the phone and taken it away: had only just occurred to him that he didn't have to cut off the phone, of course he didn't: all he had to do was remove the extension from the study – simple. All that stuff about Amanda's father had been absolute guff, of course – hadn't even spoken to the man: that was what he was about to do, right this second. Didn't want to, though – was hardly relishing the thought.

'But won't he be terribly *upset*, Amanda?' he had pleaded. 'I mean – he might go to pieces. And what about your mother? What will she think? It could kill her.'

'Daddy won't go to pieces – he isn't the going to pieces sort: he'll approach it as a piece of business, like everything else. And he won't tell Mummy. Never tells her anything.'

So that was that. Raymond had left thinking I have simply got to got to got to get some cigarettes and Christ wouldn't it be great to fuck Emily and then have a cigarette afterwards? The cigarette would take much longer, of course. Maybe he would just drop by.

And as soon as Raymond had left the room (bit of a tussle at the door, more for form's sake than anything else) that awful feeling of being utterly confined washed all over Amanda with a really quite surprising force – and when she heard the key turning in the lock – well, that had just about done it. Only an hour or so had passed since then (seemed like years) and so you can imagine Amanda's surprise when she heard again that very sound; Raymond couldn't possibly be back yet – it was quite a drive to Amanda's parents – so possibly it had just been wishful thinking on her part, yes? Wanting the door to be unlocked, and hearing the noise that this would make? Yes? No; look – the door is opening: open now – and who was this rather nice-looking man just standing there? Looking at her? Very nice-looking young man indeed. Seemed rather distraught, though – as if he was not quite, you know: *with* it.

'Hello,' said Amanda, sweetly. 'My name's Amanda.'

Gideon looked even more confused than ever – he was still shivering and more agitated than he could say from the quite awful experience of the *last* thing and now here was some woman in the middle of Dad's study. And the door had been locked.

'I knew I'd be rescued soon,' said Amanda with manu-factured gaiety. 'I'm your father's PA – you must be Gideon.'

'Ah . . .' said Gideon, uncertainly. Well, that at least made a sort of sense. 'I'm sorry if I'm . . . I just came in to . . .'

'You're not interrupting *anything*, as you can see. No, it was the *stupidest* thing,' rattled on Amanda, thinking faster than she was talking. 'Raymond and I were working on a project here, and then he drove off to the office for some papers – and for some reason he locked the *door*! I can't imagine why he did that. Anyway, I have to be off myself, now, Gideon – but tell Raymond I'll call him in the morning. Good to meet you at last, Gideon – I've heard so much about you. Funny we never met before.'

'Right!' responded Gideon, having a go at a smile. 'Well – hello and goodbye, then!'

He stepped aside and Amanda slipped past him, wearing what may or may not have been an extremely attractive smile – Gideon just simply didn't *know* any more.

'Bye, Gideon,' Amanda called from the stairs.

Yes!

❦

Kevin was roaming the streets, alone, with no purpose in his head whatever. But had he had a good evening? How did the dinner with Milly go? Well? The food must have been good, anyway (at those prices, you'd hope so), and Milly did appear to be pretty good company: certainly she had seemed pleased to see him. Well yes, it had been a perfectly pleasant evening – more than that, much more than that, Kevin was convinced, right up until the end. Something happen to spoil it? Yes and no: nothing at all actually happened, you see – and although Kevin was even now uncertain as to what exactly he might have expected to happen, the fact that absolutely nothing did has left him feeling . . . left him feeling . . . well, not much, really. Bit hurt, maybe. Maybe a bit hurt. No – silly to be hurt; Milly meant nothing by it. By what? What did she say? *Nothing*: she said nothing, that's the point. Oh look – all right, all right – what is bothering Kevin if he is honest is that when Milly had suggested a restaurant around Notting Hill Gate because that's where she lived, he had thought that maybe afterwards – and it was still quite early – he might have, I don't know, walked her home, sort of style. Coffee? Yes – coffee. Didn't want coffee, though, did he? They had drunk enough coffee in the restaurant to launch a battleship. Conversation, then. But they had been gassing away to each other for well over two hours. Well just the *gesture*, then: it would have been nice if she had *asked*, that's all. That's all he meant. I mean, he wouldn't have . . . could barely remember *how* to . . . but a kiss would've been nice. What – she didn't kiss him? Didn't, no. Odd that, really. Still.

Gosh, though – the time they had actually spent together was truly magical, to Kevin's mind – a memory for ever, as far as he was concerned. And there was going to be more on Friday, you bet your life. Really – Friday? Isn't Kevin rather booked up on Friday? Isn't there some recollection of Obergrüppenführer Emily having instructed him to pick up a dresser from The Works, and then go on down to . . . oh hey, he *didn't*, did he? Well – good old Kevin! He's asked her to go down to Brighton with him, hasn't he, the little devil? Yes – there's happy nodding in the air, you can feel it. Well – women don't just swan off to Brighton with a bloke because they're at a loose end and fancy a blast of sea breezes, you know. Friday, it would seem then, is it. But lots of other stuff was said first, of course. They started off talking about the food; as you do:

'This pen is awfully good,' enthused Kevin.

'So's the soup,' said Milly. 'I think it's penn*ay*, actually.'

'Really? Well – it's awfully good. Odd, though, serving pasta in a French restaurant, isn't it?'

'I think pasta's rather gone the way of rice,' said Milly. 'International, now.'

'I expect you're right. Have some more wine, Milly.'

Kevin pointed the bottle at her glass but then Milly lifted the glass up to meet the bottle just as Kevin was swooping downwards so there was a bit of a collision, nothing serious, just a clink with very little wine lost – but didn't a lackey appear almost immediately with a huge white linen cloth – really huge, size of a tablecloth, could've *been* a tablecloth – and start mopping up a truly non-existent spillage and although the whole thing rather got on Kevin's nerves he was nonetheless apologizing for England and flicking up nervous eyes to the mopper almost as if pleading to be let off a cuff round the ear.

It took ages to restore any sort of normality after that – the glasses and bits and bobs were all in the wrong place and so Kevin played a quick game of chess with them while mumming all sorts of gaping and rueful expressions at Milly – who was sitting there calmly, smiling her smile, and Kevin was grateful for that.

'So what sort of week have you got on, Milly? I'm fairly busy, myself, what with one thing and another.'

Yes, he really did have quite a lot to do – didn't want to do a single bit of it, but there you go. As he well knew (said it before) he was just the dogsbody: fetch and carry, that's him.

'I love balls,' said Milly.

Kevin looked up, uncertain sort of smile came into play.

'Really?' he said, hesitantly.

Milly nodded, putting a fair deal of gusto into it.

'Can't *wait* till Saturday – you are going, aren't you?'

Kevin was covered in comprehension. 'Ah yes, right, got you – oh yes, I'm going, I'm going. I don't normally enjoy it at all, this ball, I have to be frank, Milly – but it will be different this year: it'll be wonderful to see you there.'

Christ though, he thought, I hope she won't want to *dance*, or anything; Kevin was never much of a one for dancing – just you canvass Emily's views on the subject – didn't really go in for anything at all like that. And Christ *again* – hadn't he also to go out and buy a new bloody penguin suit just for the occasion? With *Emily*. Well, he hoped she had the money to pay for it, because Kevin certainly didn't. Yes – she would have; she always paid for Kevin's clothes – chose them, mostly. Emily paid for everything, let's face it; well, it was her company, wasn't it? As she kept on telling him.

'I don't actually think I'll be able to pick up all that stuff from you tomorrow, Milly – I've decided to do a bit of clothes shopping. Get a few new things. But on Friday I've got to collect something from The Works, so I could maybe fit it in after that. Going to be a bit tight, though, because I'm going down to Brighton around lunchtime. *More* stuff.'

'You *are* busy, Kevin. I love Brighton. Just love it. It's so near to London but it's just so different – I love it. Even its name, I love. You don't fancy some company, do you?'

Yes I *thought* it was a bit rich – this suggestion that Kevin had asked her along: he did nothing of the sort, did he? Now we know the truth. Probably hadn't even so much as occurred to him. It was Milly doing the asking here – which not only makes a lot more sense, but is altogether more promising from Kevin's point of view, I should have said. Anyway – they're going, that's the main thing – and once Kevin had gabbled out his absolute approval of the scheme, the sight of Milly's glinting candlelit eyes on top of the arrival of the most sensually scented carré d'agneau was just too much heaven to handle.

Kevin and Milly gave themselves over to going mmm and ah-ing a good deal: the lamb truly was – *mwah*! Delicate rosemary, not too pink and almost indecently tender. Oh but aaargh! Oh God – the villainous and piratical head waiter was coming over now and at least some of his teeth were bared under that terrible moustache and Kevin set up a-munching and a-crunching as if under pain of death because he knew, he just *knew*, Kevin, that this man was going to ask if everything was all right and Kevin's mouth was simply crammed to the rafters with not just the wonderful lamb but sauté potato and mangetout and some sort of sauce affair and if he didn't get that lot down him in double quick time and certainly within the next two milliseconds well then he really was in for it because he wouldn't be able to answer the man and I don't know he might just pull out a cleaver and there and then whip off his head without so much as a polite excuse-me.

'Everything all right, sir? Madame?'

'Mmphlurgh!' enthused Kevin, with energy.

'Lovely,' said Milly.

'Mm*gurten*!' tacked on Kevin, eager for the man to be left in no doubt whatever on the matter.

Milly wasn't looking at him oddly, was she? Don't think so. Captain Blood had shoved off, anyway, so that was one anxiety over. Milly was smiling, now – fondly, if Kevin was any judge.

'You're a strange man, Kevin,' is what she said.

And Kevin could only give his famous half-simper by way of reply because, well, yes, it had as we know been said before – mostly when he was a lad, it is true, but not a lot would appear to have changed. But a thought has occurred – yes, here comes one of Kevin's little crackers, by the looks of things: certainly that forefinger was stabbing upwards into the air.

'Strangeness Is Normal Among Strangers!' he said.

Milly assumed the sort of face you might expect someone to pull upon opening the fridge and being confronted by a trussed-up and naked bank manager, or maybe a deep-fried border collie – something on those lines. Yes indeedy, these periodic insights of Kevin's surely did make people ponder.

Kevin had the most fabulous warm and cold crème brûlée – couldn't bear the thought of it ending; Milly's orange cake with what she said was a sauce to die for – vanilla, she thought, and deeply creamy – was eaten slowly and accompanied by quite a good deal more appreciative moaning which from Kevin's point of view (and particularly when she closed her eyes and slid the bowl of the spoon vertically down and around her lolling tongue) at times approached the frankly orgasmic.

And then – no kiss. Not so much as a peck. And certainly no hint of an invitation. Ah well: there was always Brighton. The bill had also been to die for (a funeral would have worked out maybe cheaper) but what with Emily's fifty and whatever else Kevin had managed to scrape together it had, at least, been covered. Tried hard to add twelve-and-a-half per cent but almost certainly messed it. Kevin thought of this now as he continued to amble aimlessly around streets he hardly knew. Did he underdo or overdo it? Didn't matter either way; the contempt he had earned from the staff was palpable, an all-embracing blanket of disdain, and either thing could well have done it.

But it was damn cold, wasn't it? It's not much fun walking around on your own on a fairly freezing night, so why didn't Kevin just pack himself off home and start sifting through the very best of the latest coloured batch of memory snapshots? Obvious, surely: Emily. She hadn't told him what time it was OK to come back, had she? I mean, OK, granted, it was now getting on for ten-thirty, but that was very likely to be too early, wasn't it? It would just be sheer hell if he got back too early, spoiling whatever it was she had intended to do. So – give it an hour, might as well.

Kevin shelved his rump on a short garden wall close to a streetlamp and hauled out from his coat two rolled-up copies of the current *Big Issue*. He had three more at home: always bought one from everyone who came at him and shouted 'Bee-Gishoo!' right into his face – sometimes through sheer intimidation, but more often because, well – you like to help out a bit, don't you? When you can.

He looked up into the white sodium glare of the streetlight and suddenly thought of Sophie, dear Sophie – I wonder where you are, I wonder just what it is you are doing right now during this actual moment of my life. Which has passed now: gone.

Behind quite a different garden wall – miles from the one Kevin is still perched upon (cold as you like and mooning at the moon) – Ben was busy being heftily sick over what might once have been nasturtiums while Adam was regularly beating him manfully on the back – didn't help Ben at all, this, was just about killing him as a matter of fact, but he was hardly in a position to say so, was he?

'Glah!' was the only noise Ben could make. 'Glah!'

It had been quite an evening that Adam and Ben could recollect and reinvent for years to come as a tumultuous and near-beatific rite of passage redolent of incipient manhood and beery glory; it had, naturally enough, been an absolute nightmare, if the truth be known – difficult to know which of the two had loathed it first or more energetically (until the other thing happened) but certainly after the first couple of pints with whisky chasers any gilt on this particular gingerbread was felt to be wearing decidedly thin.

They had started off in the Red Lion (Blue Lion? Some unlikely shade of lion) thoroughly enjoying being sucked into this too warm smog of forced and suppressed conviviality, their swagger betraying the secret weapon of their wealth as well as the fact that the evening had yet to begin!

'Ow ole dew?' intoned some boy behind the bar, looking, if anything, younger than either of them.

'Eighteen,' they both replied, dead in time, as if rehearsed (*was* rehearsed – on every single occasion they went out and into one of these places).

'Whop jew womp?'

'I'll have a pint of, dunno – what're you having, Ben? I think I'll have Theakston's, yeh, pint of Theakston's – what about you, Ben? Yeh – two pints of Theakston's, and a couple of Bell's – straight up, no ice.'

Yow! Adam just loved saying that. Robert Mitchum had said it first, but the spin that Adam put on it, he felt pretty confident, lent to it a certain something more.

'All I'm saying *is*,' said a man to Adam's left, darting his finger forward towards his mates rather as if doggedly prodding away at a long-distance number on a wall-mounted telephone, 'all I'm saying *is* is that of all the tarts in the programme, it's Pam you'd most like to give one to – that's all I'm saying, no more and no less.'

'Are you meant to drink the whisky now or after?' asked Ben. 'Are you sure about no water in it or Coke or anything?'

'If it's a *chaser*,' explained Adam with heavy patience, 'then you use it to *chase* the beer, right? Thicko.'

'*Granted*,' allowed the lusty debater, '*granted* they're all a bit of bloody more than all right – I mean, you're not gonna, are you, chuck any of them out of wossname, but it's *Pam*, with those tits on her – it's *Pam* you're really gonna give it to. Am I right?'

'I wish,' wished Ben, 'that I had a woman. I don't know if I'll *ever* have a woman.' He sorrowfully sucked at the Theakston's, which he detested.

'Maybe tonight!' laughed Adam.

Adam used to tell Ben that *he'd* had a woman, Christ yes – stacked like a shithouse – but then he'd gone too far and painted her as a cross between Mrs Robinson and Marilyn Monroe and then he had really compounded the felony by tacking on that she was only one of dozens, you'd better believe it, and that had well and truly blown it all right and Ben had bawled out with real scorn oh come *off* it, Adam, you're just full of *piss* and ever since then Adam had been forced to share in Ben's elegiac and mournful longings. Everyone *else* was getting it – you only had to look around – so what was so bloody wrong with Adam and Ben, then, hey? You just tell them *that*, if you can.

'Yeh of *course* I know they're bloody implants,' went on the man, still clearly fixated with the notion of making to Pam a donation. 'They've just goddabee – amazing how she bloody stands up – but *I* don't care, do I? Ay? I say *I* don't care, do I?'

'You want another of these?' offered Adam.

No, thought Ben. 'Yeh – great.'

Adam too looked pretty morose at this response but bravely chucked a smile across his face to cover all that and waved a fiver at the child behind the bar and then as avidly as he could manage swiftly dabbed his upper lip deep into another pint of bloody Theakston's.

'What I wanna know is,' roared the very same bloke at the bar – neither of the mummified men he was with had so much as uttered so far – save the odd hoarse chorus of sycophantic and God-aren't-we-the-boys harsh and braying laughter. 'I say what *I* wanna know is – where d'you buy 'em? Ay? These implant doo-dahs – can you just go in and buy a couple? Ay? *I* wouldn't mind buying a couple, I can tell you – lights out, one in each hand and you're away! Half a perfect woman straight off, no problem!'

Ben didn't dare accidentally spill any more beer – Adam was looking at him and his shoes were already soaked. He girded himself into the mental approximation of holding his nose and downed the rest of the filthy stuff in one and then threw down the whisky on top of it and felt worse than he had ever felt since first as a baby he had drawn breath on this earth. So *this* is the life, then, is it, he thought. And then – faraway at first – the discordant rumbling, the inaugural movement of the arousal of unease, just about quellable now, but later destined to make him say Glah and then Glah again as all his insides asserted their determination to be elsewhere entirely.

The Green Man next – Ben now looking rather as if he was auditioning for the part, among the very few intelligible things he said there being *I* wouldn't mind buying a couple of those things, those whatever-they're-called things – I wouldn't actually at all mind a couple of them. You think you see the way it's going, don't you? Do you think there's only ever one way evenings like this can go?

This looks a good place, Adam said later, hitching his thumb in the direction of the Old White Horse (Black Horse? Some really quite plausible shade of horse) and Ben just thought Looks the bloody same as all the other places, to me – and oh God I just don't think I can face any more of this dark and swilling bitter, can't I don't think stomach one more shot of this hot and punishing whisky: all this fun is killing me.

Maybe an hour later, could have been less, rather lost track of . . . anyway, some time on, in the . . . where was it? Rat and Something, needn't have been – or no, not that, that was the place with the fat lady in the corner and someone flushed with a gallon of ale was jeeringly threatening to drag down the citadel of pennies at the edge of the bar and the landlord had said you so much as touch that chummy and you are out of here so fast you won't *touch*, my son. But wherever it was – could've been that packed place and still they were chucking darts around (you wouldn't credit it, would you?) – there was a sudden and welcome air of hilarity, a moment when solid mahogany horseshoe bars briefly ceased to writhe like agitated spaghetti and looming ceilings knew their places and stuck to them; the lightness and gaiety swiftly engulfed both Adam and Ben and they were cackling and cuffing each other and then soon really cracked up into high-octane topmost gear with near hysterical *Julian* imitations, each one shrieking louder than the last their increasingly delirium-inducing bloody *Julian* imitations and just as Ben was yelling out well I'm very very very *sorry*, Adam, but I really truly really think that maybe drinking ten swimming pools worth of Theakston's and chasing it with a whole fucking case of *whisky* maybe just isn't so very very very wise a thing to *do* – then so did Adam bark out some hacking and to him rather odd, no (change that) very odd indeed sort of laughter and clutch hard at the table, then, thinking Woo, woopsy, nearly lost it, then – feel a bit, woof, oh now that's better, that's OK, feel quite fine again, now – and what about just one more for the gutter, then, Ben?

Which was, as is the way of things, where Ben soon found himself, kissing the kerb, and begging for oblivion. Adam had hauled him up somehow – fucking deadweight – and nearly had himself over in the process. Sort of more or less shoved him into this front garden and so sudden and lurching were Ben's last four or five flailing and rubbery movements that finally the revolt within him would know of no appeasement and a torrent of rebellion erupted from within him and took his bloody skull off while it was about it and if he'd seen this head of his hit a rooftop and clatter down to guttering before leaping to earth and bowling on down the road then it would not have surprised him in the least and he would surely have eyed it with no more than dispassion.

Adam, for reasons best known to himself, was now lying full-length on the garden path, the doorstep serving as a cruel but oddly comforting pillow, and from there it was the work of a moment to stuff his head right in through the catflap and what was this bloody cold hard thing now dangling in his face? It took ages, years, to understand, but here was a door-key, hanging on a string, and Adam wriggled back out and said Hey Ben, look – listen, Ben, listen – and Ben's last Glah was dying the death and he said any word at all in response to Adam's insistent urging and Christ he was tugging him now and pulling and OK yeah he did feel a bit fresher, well Christ he couldn't have felt any *staler*, could he, and what was it Adam was saying? What the hell was he on about a key for? What key? Huh? So there was a bloody key, big deal, so what?

'*So*,' came back Adam, 'we can pull it up through the thing, letter thing – box, flap thing – and then open the bloody door and we're *in*.'

Ben looked nearly at Adam.

'What do we want to . . . why do we want to . . .?'

'We can go on the *rob*, Ben. It'll be brill! I've always fucking wanted to do that!'

'Yeh?' checked Ben. Don't like this. Want to go now.

'Come on – come on, I'll get the key and you follow me in, OK?'

'I don't . . . no, Adam, no. Come on – let's fuck off out of here – I'm really pissed, man. Let's get the fuck out – I really need to crash out, Adam, I've bloody had it, I'm telling you.'

Adam flicked his hand into Ben's face and caught him on the nose – Ben didn't know whether he had intended to miss or flatten him.

'Well,' said Adam slowly, and with a determination that bloody surprised him, actually, '*you* bloody sod off if you want to. I'm gonna fucking *do* it.'

Gideon was still standing more or less in the doorway of his father's study, and still feeling very, um . . . sorry, what was that again? Say something? No no – you were just thinking, trying to articulate, what you are feeling. Was I? Was I really? Don't remember that. Why did you come up to Raymond's room, actually, Gideon? Do you remember *that*? Don't, as a matter of fact. It's been such a, God it's been *such* a very strange evening. Finding that woman here, you mean? Amanda? That *was* a bit odd, yes, now you come to mention it, what with the door – locked and all. Yes. But no – that's not it, not it at all. Anyway – she went, didn't she? Yes, she's gone. She went quite a while ago, actually. Said to tell Raymond something or other, I feel fairly sure; can't remember what, exactly: something.

No, I honestly *can't* remember why I came into this room, since you put me on the spot. Not to talk to *Raymond*, surely? Well no – not consciously, at least. Although earlier Raymond had, um, come up, if not exactly in conversation. Rather alarmingly, though. During that time – brief time, awful – he had spent with, er . . . oh God, I really don't think I can think about that; got to, though, really. Have to work it all out. What *am* I, exactly, hey? I mean: who *am* I? Maybe it's got to be faced. I have never in my life felt so many things within so short a . . . I mean *Christ* knows what I was expecting when I went round to Emily's – don't *ask* me. But I sure as hell didn't bargain for . . . oh God. Look, I'll tell you what – you go to your room, get out of Raymond's study (bit chilly up here anyway) and go and relax in your own room – bit of Chopin, maybe, and maybe also a drink? God don't even mention *drink* – I had so much brandy at Emily's I feel like I could practically –! OK, scrub the drink. Sit down, draw the curtains, close your eyes and think it all over – tell us what you felt at every stage of the game (not game – I don't mean game) – not for anyone else's vicarious enjoyment (do I even mean enjoyment?) but for yourself, Gideon, for your inner self – it really could do you some good.

Well – it started off OK (yes, things do) but all that normal sort of stuff didn't last long. What do you mean, exactly – *normal* stuff, Gideon? You're not making things very plain, are you? If you really want to disentangle all this in your mind (get a bit of peace) then you're really going to have to own up, you know. Aren't you?

Yes. OK. You're right, you're right: OK, then – here's the whole thing. I got there, right? I got there – bit late, about twenty minutes late, and that was deliberate, although I'm not really sure why. Anyway, there was Emily – looking just like Emily, nothing odd – although the quiet of the house was odd, it seemed strange that there was no one else there. So we sat down. Did I want a drink? Well – I did, to be honest: I was scared. Scared of what? Don't know. Everything. I was shit scared of everything. So – drank the drink, brandy, not Cognac, the other one – and then I had at least two more, I'm pretty sure, and Emily was next to me on the sofa and just looking at me in that way, not quite a new way, but the sort of way she always looked at me when she used to whisper *Ring* me, Gideon – *ring* me, why don't you? That sort of a way, but – more so, if you know what I mean. I have to say *I* don't really know what I mean, so God knows why anyone else should – but I can't really explain, can't really get any closer than that.

So? *So*: I was thinking, I was actually thinking this: when is she going to make her move? That's exactly how I felt – I felt, I don't know – maybe like a young *girl* feels when she's just sitting there, next to a predator, not really liking it, not entirely fearful either: almost like a victim awaiting an accident. Of course I don't *know* if that's how young girls feel – of course I don't – but I imagine, I mean I could well imagine . . . anyway, that is more or less how *I* was feeling. Certainly there was no question of *my* doing anything, not at all: I could have sat there chucking down the brandies till the cows came . . . *actually*, yes, this is it: I was waiting, waiting for a train, it was just like waiting for a train – a looming and juddering blur of thunder that would scoop me up and take me elsewhere. Except it wasn't like that at all: I seemed to have got it all wrong. I don't understand – I've never understood all the *psychology* of all this sort of, this sort of sexual stuff, but I suppose I naturally assumed that Emily – being Emily – would have just, well, told me what to do and then bloody well made sure that I did it.

But she didn't? No she bloody well didn't. She was wearing a sort of gown, silk I think, quite attractive, and that she let fall open – OK, no surprises there – but God you should have seen what she had on underneath! Heavy, was it? Let me guess – leather, the odd chain: fishnet? *No – no* this was just it! I mean *yes* – I suppose if I thought about, if I'd thought about it, I would have said all that sort of thing too, because she is, isn't she, Emily, she is a bloody bully – forever pushing everyone around, you only have to talk to Shelley about that (I must move on – can't think of Shelley) and I also suppose, now I'm being totally honest, that it was that, something on those lines I had been depending on. Look – I don't really want to get into all the ins and outs of my, oh God, *sex* life, if you want – but not everything lately

145

has been going entirely smoothly and I thought – I just thought Emily would more or less sort me out, there and then, once and for all – and then I could put behind me all the confusion and get *on* with my life, for what it's worth. *Normally*. Wasn't like that. What *was* it like, then? What was it like? I'll tell you what it was like: it was like *this*:

Emily smiling: lazily. 'You're not *shocked*, I hope, Gideon?'

Gideon gaping: wildly. 'No, of *course* – not shocked, I just.' And then, inanely, 'You're a very attractive woman, Emily.'

Which she *was*, of course – women are, aren't they? Pretty sure they are. But he wasn't thinking that, wasn't really thinking at all – just staring at Emily's underwear. *Well*? Right – here it is: dark blue woollen bloomers – right up to the waist, and not much short of her knees – and some sort of winceyette shirt-type thing, not winceyette, that stuff, what's that *stuff* – the stuff with the holes in: Aertex, I'm fairly sure, you see it on – well that's the bloody *point*, isn't it? You see it on schoolgirls playing netball in the playground with their incipient little breastlets barely making a dent and *Christ* OK she didn't have a battered straw hat stuck awry on her head and there was surely no sight of a hockey stick – but there was hardly any mistaking the *message*, was there? And now (you won't believe this, you won't – be honest: who would?) she was sucking her thumb (you heard right) and curling up into a little ball and cooing to Gideon in a small and very un-Emily voice Ooh you will protect me won't you, sir, you won't be beastly to me will you, sir? I'm a very innocent girl (promise – there's not much more of this) and I've never sat alone with a big strong man before. I know. Well just imagine how *Gideon* felt: hang on – maybe he'll tell us:

Galvanized. Good word (apart from the watering-can connection which is probably irrelevant) and one that held good for Gideon's lack of all impetus for, oh, I don't know – not long at all, really: seconds is all; because *no* – she *wasn't*,

146

was she? She couldn't be. She *was*, you know – she was expecting Gideon to *do* something: she was expecting Gideon (ha!) to be, oh God, *dominant*. Gideon: dominant. Well. No wonder he's in such a state; but what on earth did he *do*, for Christ's sake? How did he handle it? Make a bolt for the door? No. Thought of it, sure, but he lacked all ability to move.

Emily already seemed to be tiring of being a blushing and helpless virgin on the verge of pitiless violation – certainly that familiar glint was creeping back into her wide-as-you-like eyes.

'You *will* be kind to me, won't you, sir?' she tried, not sounding quite so goo-goo as formerly but at least working her eyelashes for all they were worth. 'You won't –' a bit more forward, this, not quite in keeping with the role '– you won't *touch* me or anything, will you, sir?'

And already by the end there was an unmistakable undertone in her voice that suggested that he pretty soon better bloody *had* touch her, buster, and quite a bit more besides, or else she would see his intestines drawn and twisted into an elastic clothes-line criss-crossing an alley spanning the privy-littered yards of an eternal terrace of pre-war urban slums.

So he touched her: had to, right? No great enthusiasm on show here, though. It wasn't that he didn't want her (did he want her? Yeh, of course. Sure? Yeh yeh: course) it was just that – well look, this was the problem he had with Shelley, wasn't it? Couldn't really get going. It was even worse than that, if the full truth be known (and it does appear to be the moment for full and frank confession), because even when Shelley, poor Shelley, more or less took over and tried just about everything a woman can be expected to try, it was still all utterly, utterly hopeless. What – Gideon and Shelley had never managed to, had what, not once ever . . .? No. Gideon could hang his head, he felt so bad – but no, you wanted the lot and now you've got it: no. Never had. Couldn't. Worrying, no? Yes indeed – the wrong side of complacency, certainly, but in the light of Gideon's present situation with Emily, positively life-threatening, I should have said. Could he save it? Well no, let's be clear here – it's not on the cards, is it? But he'd have a crack:

'Don't worry, little girl,' he croaked, feeling more than ever just like a little boy – quite apart from worried to the verge of derangement. 'I'll be gentle,' he assured both of them.

Gideon placed a hand, paw-like, on Emily's quite pink thigh – just between the jaws of her knickers and what he did believe were called ankle or knee socks, each one replete with the dinkiest garter you ever saw in your life. There things stood for a while, couple of years, and if Gideon was determined to be *that* gentle, then it was mental that Emily was going to go – yes, blown it now: couldn't keep this little lot going for even one second longer:

'*Look*, Gideon – you utter and total *cretin*, are you going to fucking well do it to me or *not*?!'

Not such a rhetorical question at all, as things turned out, the fact that Gideon was now up and running for the sweet cool safety of the sacred hall that led unto the heaven of away from here vividly illustrating to all parties concerned the irresistible conclusion that no, on balance, he was decidedly not.

'Stop!' screamed Emily, with all the sassy authority of a border patrol guard, this and her energetic loping in his very direction spurring on Gideon to unprecedented speeds as he scorched across the carpet, avoiding all the stuff.

'You just listen to *this* before you run away, you sad and pathetic little *girl*. You just bloody well listen to *this*!'

Gideon now had his hand on the front-door lock (safe!) and so felt he could afford to turn to hear with eyes as broad as soup plates whatever it might be that Emily wanted to say – but no: not saying, not speaking – Emily was making no attempt at talking at all. All she did was stoop down to the micro-system music centre hidden within a darkly carved Jacobean commode and depress a single button whereupon the only sound to reach Gideon's ears was a rhythmic thumping as if heels were being drummed on the floor, could well be, and then some ghoulish grunting and no more than a throaty wail or so and after a roar of might be agony a silence marred only by the fizzing of the tape and now quite suddenly broken by the unmistakable voice of Raymond saying Christ you cunt I deeply loathe you, Emily – what in hell is it that you do to me?

Gideon ran, telling himself all the way home that he didn't understand, didn't, couldn't get a hold on it – but knowing (of course he knew) knowing full well that he understood completely. He tried to put every sort of thought out of his mind, then (failed), and just as he turned into the garden of his house – his eagerness to be inside sending, oh, *dozens* of lichenous milk bottles skittering and cracking into every corner – it was only then at that moment that the thought of Richard flew into his mind, Richard from Marketing – why on earth now, I wonder? – and all he thought was well maybe I *should* call him up, as he keeps on urging me to do – why don't I, actually, when all is said and done, why don't I just finally give in to it? No clear reason, just at present – and just this tremor concerning work made Gideon almost shout out Oh thank you, God, thank you so much for making Mrs Milligan well again because I just don't think I ever again could have faced that trolley of hers – and please, God, while you're at it – could you help me go on thinking about simple things like that, stop me dwelling on all the stuff?

God it was dark; Adam was so buried by darkness that at once he was suffocating (his breath kicked out in gasps by a hammering heart) and yet he felt afloat within a deep and limitless void.

'*Jesus*, Adam,' wheezed Ben, damn near inaudibly. Adam for *Christ's* sake.' Ben was shaking badly – he felt cold and ill from the drink, sobered by such fear as to make his limbs uncontrollable.

'*Sh!*' hissed back Adam, nearly loving it all, scared as hell, excited beyond all measure and desperately needing to pee. 'Just follow – and for Jesus sake don't make any *noise*.' Then he walked into something heavy that made a sound like a detonating bomb – *wasn't* that loud, wasn't loud, no noise at all – any other time it would have seemed little more than barely disturbed silence – but Adam instinctively reached back to grab at Ben who was indeed very rapidly on his way out of here. The two stood still in the hall. Stood there a little longer, their combined and unsynchronized exhalations hitting Ben like the fiery roar of massed and furious dragons.

Adam led Ben down the hall. It wasn't getting lighter (couldn't be) but soon he was able to make out a doorway, door ajar, and beyond it a room made very slightly visible by maybe a streetlamp meanly filtered through gauzy curtains, lending only the dullest and yellowish glow of phosphorus. Right, thought Adam – more alive than ever he had been and determined to ignore the low moan (getting louder) from Ben right behind him. What did one do? What did one want? Anything, really – anything *good*. Adam discerned little as he waded across the room, his splayed and rigid fingers probing and patting air, his jacket tugged taut behind him by a could-be panicked Ben now fighting to breathe and close to fainting. It was, thought Adam now, a pretty crummy room (certainly it lacked his mother's touch) in what he imagined to be (just his luck) a pretty crummy house. Well – all the signs were there: catflap, bloody Yale key just hanging there on a string – vinyl, lino, something, Adam was pretty sure, all the way down the hall. What the hell could be worth nicking in *this* bloody dump?

Adam and – whether he liked it or not – Ben were close by the mantelpiece now (Adam could hear the ticking of some crap clock) and he gently ran his hands across its upper ledge as if studiously perusing Braille, and soon he encountered a tin. A tin – I ask you; in what sort of a living-room would you find a tin on the mantelpiece? Emily would have had a fit. Adam, certainly, was more used to architectural fragments, bronzes and maybe a globular tree stuck with dark red dried wild roses – certainly not a bloody tin. And then he remembered some programme – the whole scene he saw just now within a millisecond – some scene in some play, wasn't a film he felt sure, and yeh: there was this kid in the middle of burgling a house and there on the mantelpiece was some sort of tin and this kid, he unscrews the lid (the tin in this house had a pull-off lid, as Adam now knew because he was pulling it off while he remembered) and inside there had been this wodge of dosh and Christ it was all Adam could do to stop himself shrieking from the sheer lunatic thrill of fishing out of *his* tin this trussed up little bundle of notes, hard and heavy, and he had it tight within his fist, now, and couldn't tell Ben, Ben wouldn't get it, and so he turned and gestured towards Ben's arm as a signal to go and now they were padding and groping their way back towards the door and here was the hall and there was the front door, barely open, just as they had left it and then weren't they deafened and nearly killed on the spot by a fierce and nightmarish scream as some creature, maybe man, lunged out of the dark at Adam and had him by the hair and Adam was kicking out, connecting, kicking out again and Ben was pulling his arm nearly away from his body and braying in fear and caught tight between the onus of duty and the need to flee.

The man – *was* a man – he was now bleating with pain (Adam had hacked again and again at those buckling shins) and now the grip on his hair was relaxed and Adam turned to run and Ben was right in front of him and only then did Adam fall headlong, striking his head on the corner of something, a strangling grasp on his ankle holding him back and Adam now yelled out *kick* him, Ben, kick the bloody bastard's fucking *face* in and Ben half stepped on Adam and started kicking wildly and there were terrible noises of crunching amid all the howling and now Adam crawled away, staggered up to his feet and with his arms around Ben they both hobbled to the door, threw it aside and then flew back out into the night, the cold wind singing in their ears as their feet clattered down on shining tarmac and Adam's big and bursting heart first floating upwards before soaring in triumph towards the stars, borne aloft as it was on a blinding chariot of sheer and total fucking delight.

Raymond was driving his car, chewing on a handful of pills, and trying his hardest to make some sort of sense out of just about anything. What exactly was it that he imagined he was *doing*? He had just got over that brief and beastly little bout of fornication with the ever-lovely-Christ-I'd-love-to-*break*-her-damn-her-to-agony Emily, and now here he was well on his way to conducting that essential little chat with Amanda's father, vis-à-vis his coughing up half a million quid by way of his daughter's ransom. Yes *that* Amanda – the PA currently languishing in Raymond's study (wonder what she's doing?) and author of this quite unbelievable letter cobbled together from bits of newspapers and carefully folded into quarters to look as if it had been recently extracted from an envelope. Where was the envelope, then ? He'd be bound to ask all that. Well – where is it? Where's the envelope? Where was the letter posted? Good point, good point – I, uh, threw it away. You threw it *away*?! Good God, man, what in Christ's name were you *thinking* of? That's *evidence*, man – *evidence*. Yes. Oh God.

Raymond had swallowed his pills, so now he lit another cigarette, sucking as hard as might well a thirst-crazed child on a flat and sappy drinking straw. These pills: do we need to know about them? We maybe do – you never know, could be relevant later. Briefly, then – a month or so ago, Raymond had had his kind of annual BUPA check-up (for some reason beyond him he had authorized some corporate scheme for all the staff – cost a bloody fortune, didn't matter now) and most things had been sort of OK except for this: a gradual thickening of the arteries. What – gradual as in getting progressively worse, do you mean? That's what Raymond had wanted to know. M'yes, loosely, the doctor had replied. That's all you ever got, these days, wasn't it? That sort of an answer; well, what did you expect? Anyway, it wasn't a bypass job (not yet anyway, ha ha, said the doctor; ha ha, rejoined Raymond, gamely) but here was a good case for swallowing pills, apparently, and although there had been some sort of chit-chat on the general lines of suitable dosage, Raymond could not now remember any details and so he just chucked them down like Cheerios (whenever he remembered to take them at all – sometimes whole days and nights went by when he forgot about them altogether), reckoning vaguely that if just the one was good for him, twenty would render him immortal. Cigarette's finished, now – grind it out, grind it out, light a bloody nother one.

This was the roundabout, he was pretty sure, where he was supposed to take a right – not *sharp* right, Amanda had been explicit (take a sharp right and you get into that whole one-way thing) but more of a fork, if he knew what she meant. Right – managed that, done the fork, and now the house was really quite close on the left-hand side. Quite close, right – slow down, then, don't want to overshoot; don't know, though – why don't I just aim the car at that bloody wall over there and slam my foot to the ground? Could get me out of a lot of talking – maybe it's cheap at the price. This is the place: very grand. Right, said Raymond out loud (thinking Shall I bother with locking the car? No real point in the driveway, is there?), what you have to do now is *concentrate*. But even as he was ringing the doorbell, all he could wonder at was why on earth Emily had been wearing those extraordinary silly clothes and bloomer things under that sumptuous gown. Didn't matter, now. Not now it didn't. The trouble was, as far as Raymond could see, that *everything* mattered, but not *really*, it didn't: yes, that was half the trouble. Lights on in the hall – sudden very bright light above him in the porch had now put Raymond firmly on the spot. Clanking of a hundred locks. Oh Christ. Here we bloody go.

The first thing Raymond was aware of when he got back home was the loveliness of Chopin (Études? Think so) filling the corridors of the house: what a poignant contrast to all the mess around him and all the stuff within and without. So – Raymond is back at the ranch: how did everything go? Well? Badly? Neither thing? Look, if it's all the same to you, Raymond would very much prefer not to go into it all just at this juncture – was going to have to tell it all to Amanda anyway, wasn't he, and he could never stand going through the same thing twice; so, if we can all just bear with him while he tries to find a drink (tries to find a glass), smokes a packet or so of cigarettes – and, actually, gets Gideon to turn down that bloody awful music, because now it was really getting on his fucking nerves, if you want the truth, and despite all appearances to the contrary this *was* actually

Raymond's house (give or take the ninety-five per cent that belonged to a variety of banks) and surely to fucking goodness he held some sort of sway over the bloody *air* if over nothing bloody else: I simply cannot take in any more dirt and noise – dirt and noise I have had my fill of.

Raymond wandered into the kitchen, and groaned, as he always did, whenever he entered that terrible room. There might be a usable glass somewhere under all that, but tonight was not a night for tight-lipped and bile-suppressing excavations. Maybe in the room: try the room, and hope to God Maureen and bloody Rosie aren't plastered all over it.

But first he had to drag out of his coat some sort of greeny metal Chinese-y horse, which he had swiped from Emily's drinks table, and sling it into a gaping rubbish sack in the middle of the floor, seemingly brimming with the none-too-recent aftermath of a public disembowelling. Couldn't fucking *stand* that horsy thing: been driving him mental for ages.

We knew they'd both be in there, didn't we? Watching cartoons. The only videos Maureen and Rosie ever put on were tailored for mute and accepting five-year-olds: amazing either of them managed to keep up with the plots.

'Have you left any drink, Maureen?' sighed Raymond. The sole of his shoe had stuck to the glistening carpet: nothing unusual there. 'And maybe something to pour it into.'

'Raymond,' was all Maureen could manage. Christ she was really loaded tonight – legs splayed out before her, protruding like pallid and brittle sticks of Edinburgh rock from the grisly hem of something unspeakable. Raymond located a bottle of vodka with maybe an inch and a half in it and tipped up that to his lips. (You know, I don't think all this stuff with Amanda's father has gone at all well – he certainly seems to be in a bit of a state.) You can think what you like. For the moment, here's a diversion in the form of Rosie:

'D. H. Lawrence is a god!' is what she came up with this time, her crazy eyes daring Raymond to defy her. Then she turned back to Bugs Bunny who had just run over the top of a cliff and was loitering in mid-air right up until he grasped the implication, whereupon he plummeted like a meteor to earth. Why didn't bloody Rosie jump off a cliff? Solve a lot of problems. Raymond swilled into him the last of the vodka (looked around for another bottle, wasn't one – found a half-full litre of some red wine that gave off the air of petrol) and now he glanced balefully once at Maureen when the word 'Raymond' again fell out of her mouth; her lips were useless, and she seemed to be slipping off the sofa and on to the floor: let her. Rosie then started twitching rather oddly, a gleam of panic alighting in her eye – even cast a look of appeal towards Raymond, a hand now fluttering above her caved-in chest and then she started up the twitching with a vengeance: twitching all the time, now – jerking up and down. Let her. It was time to go and talk to Amanda. He lit another cigarette as he slowly mounted the staircase, pausing here and there (at least bloody Chopin had chucked it in), ruefully thinking back on the bad old days when he used to be a sixty-a-day-man; more like a bloody hundred, now.

Wait. What? Something wrong. What? Don't know. There's something wrong – can't put a finger on it, just know there's something wrong. Hang on, wait, be calm. Raymond has just one foot inside his study, his hand is clasping the doorknob, and suddenly he is as animatedly suspended as mid-air Bugs. What? What is it? What *is* it that is clammily clutching at whatever remains of the spirit that somehow keeps him going? *Zam*: he had it, oh God he had it: the door had not been locked. *Key* was there, granted, but Raymond had not had to turn it in order to gain entry into what he had come to think was his very own little makeshift Holloway, but it didn't now look like it, did it? It did not. But *surely* he had not forgotten to lock the door? *Priority*, locking the door: he *did* lock it, didn't he? He was *sure* he remembered locking it, remembered even *checking* he had locked it, so how . . . ? And does that mean . . . ? Oh Jesus Christ. Raymond opened wide the door and walked rather slowly into the silent room.

'Hello, Raymond,' sang out Amanda, gaily. 'You've been gone absolutely *ages*. How did everything go?'

Well quite: could hardly have put it better, nor more concisely. I mean, yes – that's what we all want to know, isn't it? But before all that, explain to me this little lot, if you can: what in fact has come as a mild surprise (all right all right – can't make head or tail of it) is how Amanda does actually come to be sitting there, and sounding pretty perky to boot. What go on? Quite simple, really: Amanda did leave, as we know, and then – for a number of reasons – came back. And it's no good pumping her – Amanda is, I think we have seen, not at all the sort of woman who takes to being pushed around: if she wants the reasons made known, then no one will be left in the slightest doubt; if not – not. That's the way it is with Amanda.

Raymond for his part was thinking hee hee hee – little does Amanda know that she has been quietly sitting here for hours and hours and all the time . . . hee hee, she didn't even think to try the door! Just imagine – at any time during the whole of the evening she could have upped and walked and what could Raymond have done *then*, then? Mind you, in the light of what he had to say . . . well, he really didn't know *what* would happen, what in the world was going to happen, now.

'Did Daddy go for the bait?' Amanda was eager to know. 'I bet he behaved exactly like I said he would.'

Well, yes and no, thought Raymond – halfway to placing a cigarette between his lips and finding one was already lodged there, burning away lazily, the blue coil of smoke damn near blinding him and he didn't even notice it. Right, then: here we bloody go.

'In a sense he did, Amanda – he was certainly very unemotional and businesslike. And he did say he wouldn't dream of saying a word to your mother . . .'

My God had he been businesslike! Christ – the first thing the man had said to Raymond, I mean after introductions and so forth had been made and received, the very first thing he said to Raymond after discovering that his beloved daughter had been shanghaied by in all probability a band of merciless hoodlums and cutthroats, the only bloody thing he had to say was this:

'Excuse me, Raymond is it? I'd really prefer it if you didn't smoke, if you don't mind.'

Raymond, of course, minded like hell, but never mind.

'Sorry, so sorry to, um, *spring* all this on you – but as soon as I received the letter, I thought I should –'

'Let me see the letter,' said Amanda's father, shortly. He read it, read it again, turned it over, held it up to the light and just about held himself back from tasting the bloody thing. 'Does anyone else know about this?'

'No, I – as I say, I came straight to you.'

'Hm. Well, much as I sympathize with Amanda's plight – perfectly stupid to allow oneself to be *purloined* in this manner, however, I have to say – any question of paying them the money is completely out of the question. We must hand the letter directly to the police and let them handle it. They have procedures, I am led to believe.'

Aargh! 'But the letter quite specifically states,' gabbled Raymond, 'that if the police are involved –'

'Yes well of course,' was Amanda's father's brusque reaction to that. 'They have to say all that, don't they? I mean it's perfectly standard, all that. No, our way is clear. The police. I think I should telephone them immediately.'

Aargh! 'The thing is, the thing is – they phoned me earlier, the gang – phoned me. Did I mention that?'

'You did not.'

No. That's because I've just made it up. Now I have to decide within the fraction of a moment it takes bloody old Hitler here to ask what it was they actually said, exactly what it might be that they actually said.

'They said they would be phoning me again tonight –'

'They phoned you to say they'd be phoning you?'

Aargh! 'Yes, yes – they said that tonight they would have a further message. That they'd put Amanda herself on the line – yes, that's good: *true*, I mean – Amanda herself, and she would tell us what it was she wanted us to do.'

Amanda herself's father seemed to be concentrating. Did Raymond dare chance another word? Thought he might:

'I really think we ought to keep it to ourselves till then, you know. I mean – if they get the slightest whiff of anything . . . I mean, we don't want to expose Amanda to any *danger*, do we?'

'I suppose . . . I suppose not. You may be right. Mm.'

Oh thank Christ for that.

'But –'

Aargh!

'– we wait only as long as tonight. If no message comes, or if they are still determined on demanding money with menaces, then the police must be informed immediately. Clear?'

Right: think I'll have to settle for that. Amanda herself can sort it all out: it's her bloody cackhanded idea anyway – it's her bloody *father*, after all. Oh Christ – I really wish I hadn't kidnapped her, now: it maybe wasn't brilliant. At least he didn't mention the envelope.

Raymond now watched Amanda as she digested all this:

159

so far, she had not interrupted, and nor had her face in any way betrayed whatever it was she was feeling. Raymond stubbed out his latest butt, stuck one more cigarette into his mouth and ritually set fire to it.

'*God*,' she now said with feeling. 'The mean old bloody *bastard*. I mean, Christ – I knew I wasn't exactly the centre of his universe but *Jesus*: he's just going to leave me to die! He won't even part with a few lousy quid to save the life of his only daughter! What if I'm tortured? What if I'm raped? What if I'm left to perish by the roadside?'

Gagging might be good for openers, thought Raymond; now he had to contend with histrionics on top of everything else, then, did he? Jesus, what a day: and I thought yesterday was bad.

'But you're *not* kidnapped, are you, Amanda? Hm? Not in that way, anyway. I mean – I'm not going to torture you, am I?'

Amanda smiled – she looked lovely when she smiled, thought Raymond. I mean, she was easy on the eye almost all of the time – not a bad-looking woman at all, Amanda – but it was when she smiled that Raymond felt all those murky stirrings that could, he knew, so easily unseat him.

'You can be so sweet, Raymond. That's why I love you.'

Raymond smirked: this was quite nice.

'Not going to leave you to perish by the *roadside*, am I?'

Amanda lightly touched his knee. 'Sweet,' she reaffirmed.

Might bloody rape you, though: coo, Christ – she really is quite a good-looking woman, Amanda, you know: just look at the way she's just *sitting* there, with her legs leading all the way up to her cunt, like that.

'So,' said Raymond. 'How are we going to play this?'

'You're sure,' checked Amanda, 'that there's absolutely no way that shit is going to pay up? Even maybe just *quarter* of a million?'

Raymond shook his head. One further thing that Amanda's

father had said was that if the kidnappers suffered the benefit of Amanda's company for too much longer it was they who would be offering large cash sums to anyone prepared to take her off their hands; but it didn't do to antagonize the girl, so best let that one lie. She was quite enough to handle as it was.

'Well in that case,' concluded Amanda, 'the whole damn thing's off, isn't it? I mean – if there's no cash, what's the point? They'll just have to let me go free.'

'*Who* will, Amanda? There is no "they", is there? *I* am the, if you like, kidnapper – and I *can't* let you go, can I? Because of what you'll do. But *now* if you don't suddenly turn up at work again and phone your father and tell him everything's hunky-dory, well – he *will*, you know, he'll have the cops running all over everything. Me, mainly. So what the hell are we going to *do*?'

Amanda shook her head: smiled quite impishly.

'The rules have changed, Raymond. I decided that I'm not going to do any of all that. Decided not to.'

Raymond stared at her: could this be something *good* about to happen? So damned unfamiliar, if it was – how could he be expected to recognize even its nature? Wasn't going to risk it by saying anything, though – just let Amanda enlarge, if she's a mind to: let her explain in her own time. It's always the best way with women: prod them, and they instinctively retreat like a snail into its shell; on the other hand, give off any sign that you are really quite careless as to whether or not they share with you their latest stratagem, and then they become quite unstoppable in their need to communicate. Raymond could tell even by the set of Amanda's face that this was quite how it was about to be – and yes, it was coming right now: now she had begun, and Raymond was eager to learn – it only concerned his whole *life*, after all.

'Look,' explained Amanda, 'you already know how I love you?'

Raymond nodded. He knew it in that he had heard her say it, but he surely knew nothing of the sort in any sane way that he could possibly relate to – but yeh, OK, she expected a nod, so nod for the woman, why don't you?

'Well,' she went on, 'I've decided that it *would* be silly to blacken your name – even sillier to bring down the company. Some of our accounts are going great guns, actually, Raymond – I think you could see off a lot of the debt fairly soon.'

'*Really*?' gasped Raymond, in a mood that could even be approaching happy, if only he could remember just how it went.

Amanda nodded. 'And it would be *doubly* silly if I'm going to be living with you, because who on earth wants it known that her partner is a bankrupt? Or an adulterer?'

Raymond's smile hovered now between the benignity of tolerance and the clustered freeze of outright horror. Time to talk? Utter something, should he? No, let her get it all out of her system so then we can all confront the full and vibrant extent of this new and invigorating twist on Raymond's existence on earth.

'Of course,' she went on in an offhand and somewhat authoritatively conversational style, quite as if they had been – erk – married for years, 'it goes without saying that Emily – I do believe that person is called Emily – is history. And Maureen obviously has to go – tomorrow for preference – and of course that unspeakable parent of hers. Then we can get the whole house fumigated, throw out almost everything, and then, Raymond, *then* –' and her eyes were aflame with the beckoning light of the future '– *then* we can be together, just as if none of this had ever happened. *Happy*, Raymond.'

Raymond dropped his eyes to the floor and wagged his head indulgently before bringing back up a face hung not too heavily with affectionate despair and avuncular kindness. But what he saw in Amanda's eyes bore no correlation to anything within himself: no irony, no wouldn't-it-be-luvverly wishful thinking, no trace of humour – not much sign of anything even *human*: what Raymond saw was a single-minded determination that teetered on the brim of lunacy, one foot jauntily dangling over the abyss and defying the slightest breeze to send so frail a cantilevered construction spinning off down into a fearful oblivion. And fearful is what Raymond was feeling now, because this woman, baby, was not joking; this woman meant it. This woman – and only now, as he shivered, could Raymond plainly see it – this woman was as close to crazy as made not one fucking bit of difference.

Shelley and Emily were hanging around the designer living-room, neither quite ready to go up to bed, both of them hugely disinclined to talk. Shelley – philosophical now about her third failed attempt to arouse the beast in pedagogic Julian – lit a Silk Cut and looked across the coffee table more or less in the direction of Emily (still more furious than she could say over the failure of Gideon – the child of dubious orientation – to have taken unfair advantage of her.) It was a sort of relief (a relief of sorts) when Kevin crept into the house (am I too early? Is anything going on? Oh please God don't let me be too early) and he too now had graduated to the living-room, unsure of whether he might be expected to speak and so in the end just standing there – Kevin, who had so recently failed to lay even so much as a finger on Milly (she who lived so close to Chez Nous, or whatever that horrendously overpriced and dispiriting establishment elected to call itself). But no one at all was going to speak, were they? And Kevin could never bear that – could never take the tension – and so he just had to come up with:

'Everyone have a good evening?'

Shelley looked up. 'Usual,' she said.

Emily nodded. 'Same.' And then, grudgingly, 'You?'

'Oh, very similar to yours, I expect. Just the usual. Anyway,' he buoyed up now, 'you're both looking very well on it.'

Well of course Emily would have laid into him for that – was aching for anything to go absolutely crackers about – but then the front door imploded thunderingly and the Adam that now stood before them was an Adam previously unseen, a totally alien Adam. His face – flushed with heat and health (Kevin could have told him how well he was looking) – now rent asunder by a smile that could have blinded.

'*Someone's* been having fun,' drawled Shelley.

'Yeh!' agreed Adam. 'And it was me! Brilliant!'

'What did you do?' went on Shelley, in her why-don't-you-just-drop-dead voice. 'Win the Lottery?'

Adam barked out that hoarse and coarse laugh that Shelley so very much loathed.

'Yeh I did!' he guffawed.

And then he was gone, pounding up the stairs as if he hated every tread and riser, slamming the door of his room in a way that anyone else would have done if they were very unhappy indeed and not – as Adam plainly was – euphoric.

Kevin jerked out his thumb in the direction of Adam's tumultuous departure as if to say blimey, get a load of that, but no one was looking at him so he packed it in.

Emily sat up abruptly and said accusingly to Kevin:

'Where's the T'ang?'

Kevin went from careless to boggling in one easy lesson. Where's the *what*? The tang? Some sort of relish, it it? Orange drink?

'The T'ang! The T'ang!' bawled Emily now, whose habit when not immediately understood was to repeat and repeat the very same thing increasingly loudly while the blood heat within her brain tore up to boiling point. 'The *horse* – the little T'ang *horse* on the drinks table! What have you *done* with it? Why are you always *moving* things? *I'm* the designer! *I* arrange things – not you!'

Kevin looked over at the drinks table: no T'ang horse; well, there wouldn't be, of course – the very point under discussion.

'I haven't moved it,' said Kevin, honestly. Actually unaware there had ever *been* a T'ang horse on the drinks table: it was true he wasn't over-observant.

'Well I'm going to have to have some pretty stern words with Lolita, that's all I can say,' warned Emily – making Kevin immediately think Christ I'm so happy that I'm not Lolita. 'She's been dusting around things again and she never hoovers all the way into the corners – but just too many things have gone missing lately and that's something else entirely. Is she *selling* them, do you think? There were the pyramids just the other day – and last week the Staffordshire dog. *That*, I imagine, she probably broke.'

No, actually: Raymond broke it – hurled it against his garden wall; *that* sure as hell knocked the smile off its fucking little face!

Emily went upstairs then ('Don't forget to do all the *lights*!') and Shelley drifted up soon after. Kevin went to lock and bolt the door, a job that made him feel warm: the master of the house, the keeper of the castle, hauling up the drawbridge when finally all the little ones, all his little innocents, were safely tucked up in their beds; there was a lot to be said for family life, you know – whatever the cynics might try to tell you.

'It's really just like that film,' Amanda was saying. 'That film with that actor who was in *Far From the Madding Crowd*, and he captures this girl he's obsessed with – keeps her locked away in his house.'

'Julie Christie?'

'No – *she* wasn't it in, no – it was some other woman, Samantha somebody.'

'But Julie Christie was in *Far From the* –'

'Yes well I know *that*, I know *that* – I meant the *man* who was in *Far From the* – Stamp, that's it: Jerry Stamp – Terry Stamp. He's pretty gorgeous, actually. Well, he was in *that* film, anyway.'

'But Amanda,' reasoned Raymond, gently – oh yes, very gently, very gently indeed. 'It's not really like the film, is it? Because I only kept you here in the first place because of the things you said you'd do –'

'And before I said I loved you.'

'*Yes*,' agreed Raymond, thinking Christ it *is* like a bloody film, isn't it? Fucking science fiction. 'But now you say you're happy to continue in the job and not *say* anything to anyone – well *now*, of course, you're free to go: of course you are.'

Amanda appeared dreamlike. 'Shame we didn't get the money,' she mused. '*The Collector*. Don't forget to phone Daddy later and tell him the kidnappers got cold feet and dumped me. We don't need the police. Not now. No – you don't *see* it, Raymond, do you?'

'Don't I?' responded Raymond, with something like alacrity. I *don't* see it, no, whatever 'it' might be – but if there's something I should be seeing then I surely don't want to miss it.

'You see, *now*, I don't *want* to go. In fact –' and she giggled, which Raymond found frankly terrifying '– in *fact*, I *refuse* to go. That's quite funny, really, isn't it, Raymond? When you think about it. Eggar. Samantha Eggar. Funny name.'

Oh dear, thought Raymond. Oh dear oh dear oh dear: what is it that I have got myself into? And why do I feel so cold?

'And what if I told you – what if I said you *had* to go?'

Amanda now wore the very sweetest smile.

'Ah well *then*, Raymond – *then* you've absolutely had it.'

Raymond nodded. Of course. The woman who just this very morning had damn near half-killed him in her attempt to get out of here was now point-blank refusing to leave the house ever. And if he made her go (and how, actually, would he set about such a thing?) well *then* we were back where we started, weren't we, with everything lying in ruins. It's neat, isn't it? Very neat.

It is easy, though, to share Raymond's puzzlement – if not what I imagine to be his deep unease at the insidious encroachment of a situation that could easily get (has already got?) well out of hand: after all, it's *his* life on the line, and no one else's. But the puzzle is twofold: Raymond can't work out why it is she should want to stay (even if they did give the whole house the treatment it so richly merits, it is doubtful that the deepest traces of malaise would ever quite leave it) or why she should be determined that Maureen and Rosie are out the back door (although precious little loss there, I should have thought). And what must Emily be? *History*, I think she said. Of course, Raymond must never lose sight of the fact that Amanda – and she keeps on saying it – *loves* him (but not in *that* way – not quite, it seems, in any way recognizable to man) and people do act oddly when afflicted, famous for it. What is *more* puzzling, however, is why – when finally she had secured her release via the shell-shocked, half-drunk and semi-demented Gideon – why on earth she had chosen to return. Not that Raymond of course, was ever aware of her having gone in the first place.

I think even Amanda herself would have had difficulty in utterly and totally explaining it all (*love*, she would have said) but a lot of it had to do with the fact that as soon as she was away, she – yes, sounds silly – missed him. And I *know* they were barely together, I am very well aware indeed of all that, but all the time she had spent in his study, fooling with his things, had somehow made her fonder than ever (in her way). *And*, she was fed up living alone, if she was being perfectly honest. *And*, she loved him (did she mention that?). *And*, although she could never love him in *that* way, she had just that afternoon glimpsed a fellow resident whom she thought she very much could (oh Gideon, oh Gideon – have you any idea, even an inkling, just what's coming your way next?). *And* most importantly, of course – she's nuts.

Anyway, Raymond was still sitting with her in his study, and still making spectacularly little headway in the twin fields of logic and sanity, while Amanda continued to prattle on airily about all her ideas for the house – all the stuff she wanted: carpets, curtains, you name it (no mention at all about where the money was supposed to come from – and no, don't even suggest to Raymond that he call in a certain interior designer of his acquaintance who might just agree to do the job at a knock-down price if only Raymond could persuade Gideon to serve as a nine-to-five concubine because, be fair, it's not really funny, is it? No it's not – it's cruel, not nice, and don't you maybe think Raymond has got about enough on his plate just at this time without his having to tolerate so-called jokes of this nature? Exactly. Well *think*, next time).

Actually, if Raymond was feeling anything right at this moment, it was heartily lustful. Yes, not an abnormal state for Raymond, agreed, but this particular and rather strenuous onslaught had been aggravated by Amanda suddenly deciding to lie full-length on the floor (her choice, as I say – perfectly filthy down there) and with her crossed hands behind her head serving as a bony pillow, she continued to rattle off a catalogue of all the things they would be buying and all the colours the walls would be, these little nuggets interspersed with bulletins about the limitless degree to which their mutual happiness would effortlessly extend. Raymond was thinking Don't do it, don't – she'll only go crazy. And then he was thinking Well Christ, what can she *do*? She's not going to *kill* him, is she? Is she? And then he was thinking Oh Jesus just *do* it, why don't you? Might not get such a good shot at it again – God she's a good-looking woman, Amanda, not a bad-looking woman at all, is young Amanda.

And then he just did it: within a jiffy he was lying right on top of her, all his hands sent out to skirmish. And hey – could it be possible that Amanda had suddenly seen the error of her ways? (Mm she was warm, I tell you – and soft to the touch.) Can it be that once she had taken it into her head to occupy and colonize Raymond's terrible homestead then maybe a part of this new and bewildering package was that now she could love him in *that* way? Certainly Raymond was warming to his task (what a thigh! What a thigh!) and although Amanda wasn't exactly crushing him into her then neither was she beating him to a pulp – actually appeared to be wriggling a hand around, which couldn't be a wholly bad thing from Raymond's perspective. Ah, but Raymond wasn't to know (how could he be expected to imagine?) that Amanda was reaching down to the top of her boot, and that as soon as Amanda had made contact with this part of her boot, she began to slickly extract a long and silver paper-knife and Raymond didn't see her clutch the shaft tightly in her hand, and Raymond was unaware that next she had raised it up high across the broad of his back, but he surely did register the fact that now she had brought down the blade hard into his shoulder and his initial reaction to this extraordinary sensation was to draw back his head and stare at Amanda for all the world as if she had just then imparted quite the most astonishing news, and only after did his face crease up into shock and a sort of sick consciousness of at least the nature of what had been done and then he rose quite stiffly to his feet and made for the door with the long, silver paper-knife jutting out of his shoulder like some totem from a recent and brutal session of titanic acupuncture and he stumped on downstairs feeling now a warm and steady trickle coursing across his inner elbow, rather as if his armpit had disgraced itself – and without at all having worked out why he should be determined on ambulation of any sort at all Raymond now found himself in the living-room and right at its centre was standing Thomas and Thomas was the family doctor which in the circumstances really was quite unbelievably handy.

Raymond now was more or less numb – didn't take in the sight of a newly sobered Maureen weeping away among the litter on the sofa, was unaware of Rosie stretched out on the carpet quite in the manner of Amanda, while thoroughly lacking the attendant allure. But nonetheless it must have been Raymond's own voice that he heard in the air around him saying Well hello, Thomas, what brings you round to this neck of the woods and then he registered Thomas saying that he had actually come to attend to Raymond's mother-in-law and then with a nod in the direction of Raymond's shoulder – do you want me to take a look at that? Raymond even managed a half-smirk, although he was aware he had begun to sway, and he came right back with yes, Thomas, I rather wish you would, actually – before tacking on I wouldn't bother about *Rosie*, though: she's well past saving, Thomas saying only How on earth did you manage to get this stuck in your back and actually you're quite right about Rosie, as it happens, because now the old lady is dead. Maureen set up an ugly wail – Raymond more or less heard it – and during the seconds before he passed out on the floor he just had the time and consciousness to think well well well – she finally died, fancy that, well there you are: *something* good had to come out of today.

CHAPTER SIX

Friday now – and finally, oh God *way* later than Kevin had planned, he was at last at the wheel of the Renault Espace with Milly sitting happily beside him – and Look, Kevin! Look! What? hazarded Kevin: what are you pointing at? (That's what I hate about driving – you have to be everywhere at once.) The first road sign to Brighton – that's what Milly was eager for Kevin not to miss: that proved they were really on their way – well *didn't* it? Exciting! Milly was squirming in her seat – Kevin hoped with pleasure, because they were miles from a garage, or anything and goodness, the muscles in her face seemed to be tugging her this way and that and she all but burst out singing (and maybe later on she would, who knew?).

And Kevin was excited too, of course he was (mingled in with all the lurking background terror that simply anything entailed) – but God, what with all the stuff he'd already been through today, Kevin was within an ace of becoming plumb tuckered out. Which actually is a phrase used a fair deal in TV Westerns during the Fifties, when Kevin was a lad, and for all these years it had lodged within him – though only very recently did he discover its meaning; he also had at the time very much enjoyed the thought of one day moseying on down to the corral and (amid clusters of cowpokes) chucking tin cups of caw-fee onto the snapping camp-fire, so far as Kevin could make out, the sole role of this murky brew. All of which is so much mish-mash, granted – but then again, maybe any little insight at all into the workings of Kevin is not altogether without its points of interest (within the really not at all grand scheme of things): what do you say?

171

Up at the crack of dawn, he'd been (nonsense, actually – who ever was? But early, anyway), and all Kevin had been thinking was never mind Milly, no good thinking of Milly *now* because first there are Things To Be Done, So he had driven like a rallyist down to The Works (Is this bloody great dresser affair actually going to fit in to the Espace – even with all the seats out? He was not at all sure) and got there in next to no time – traffic was a dream – but my God he almost laughed out loud when he caught a first sight of the thing and Jesus, thank the Lord *I'm* not Jim, is all Kevin could think, because if Jim thought for even one moment that Emily would forgive him for not having this blighted piece of furniture all thingme and Bristol fashion, ready as ordered, then our Jim did not know dear sweet Emily as well as Kevin did – that's all *he* could say.

'This just has to be a *joke*, Arnold,' Kevin was protesting to the long-haired pustule, rumoured to be living – actually more happy than he could express on account of being (a) not remotely responsible for this monumental mess-up and (b) for once actually talking to someone to whom even Kevin felt in no way inferior (and nor did he scare him, much). 'Where's Jim, Arnold? God Almighty, there'll be hell to pay for this little lot, matey.'

'E not ear,' replied Arnold, with a rueful shake of his curtains. 'Ad accidum.'

Not Latin – of course not (Kevin had worked out that in a flash) – but still a fairly startling thing for Arnold to come out with. I mean – *Jim*: fit as a fiddle, work is his life, never missed a day (rain or shine) – oh Christ, he could go on like that until the nerves in your teeth were close to screaming.

'Well I'm sorry to hear that, Arnold,' conciliated Kevin (thinking whatever sort of accident has befallen unlucky Jim, it is as nothing, believe me, compared with what he inevitably must soon encounter as the InterCity that is Emily ploughs through signals and churns up his buffers). 'But nonetheless, this really isn't on. Is it? Hm?' We-ell – not often he got the chance.

Arnold shrugged (think he shrugged – could have been fleas) and more in order to save precious time than any other thing Kevin issued Arnold with brief but explicit instructions as to just what to do with this ludicrous dresser – and pronto (oh yes – Kevin could be pithy, I'll have you know; Kevin was no stranger to the succinct, whenever push came to shove). And then he was out of there and on to Milly's: that shop of hers, what was it called? Bits N' Bobs, Odds N' Sods – something. (Wasn't Chez Nous, was it? No it's that other place that wasn't that; oh God – it's never easy, is it?)

Got there in the end: traffic had been – well, you wouldn't *believe* the traffic now: what a difference an hour makes. Kevin drove straight to the shop – had it off completely pat just what end of the blessed street it was – but of course there was nowhere to *park*, was there? So there he was, idling the Espace further and further down the Portobello Road until finally there was some nod in the direction of a space that he thought he might just about be able to sort of wedge into – and goodness, he wasn't much shy of the mark of where he usually found himself at times like these and it was one thing traipsing up the road and all the way back to – what was it? This N' *That* plain as day in big blue letters across the red-striped awning and just what *was* it, what in fact *was* it in Kevin that rendered even a name that was after all *designed* to be remembered instantly forgettable? And although we shall never truly find the answer to this (Kevin had given up trying) what is maybe more to the point is that Kevin had now lost the thread of what he was . . . couldn't quite connect with what he had . . . oh yes – *he* remembered, *he* remembered now: he was saying that it was one thing altogether walking *up* the road (remember now? Kevin did) but it was quite a different ball park – ball game? One of those – toiling all the way back again on God knows how many journeys under the weight of all manner of junk (the specifics of which were now well beyond recall) each lump of stuff soon to be arranged by Kevin the Master so as to come together into a whole so very profoundly *interesting* as to knock your bleeding eyes out.

'Oh now come on – be fair, Milly. I *didn't* buy the horse-collar, I couldn't have. We talked about it: *yes* I bought the diver's helmet and I do now recall the foot-binding wooden shoes – and I know I said OK to this brass-bound bucket affair . . . is it *really* for cooling wine? You'd need a hell of a lot of wine. But the collar – *no* I did not buy the collar.'

'I think the collar's the best thing. But if you don't want it, that's fine. Someone'll have it on Saturday. They're very big on things like that – Americans, mostly.'

'Yeh?' checked Kevin, flicking over eyes of doubt to Milly and fingering the thing.

Milly nodded. 'And Japs. But Americans mainly.'

Well he took the bloody collar, didn't he? Had to – leaving it behind could have been a *mistake* and mistakes were things that Kevin tried harder than most to steer clear of.

After the sixth and far from final trip to and from the car, Kevin seriously considered that on reflection he might well have been better off harnessing himself into the sodding great collar and hauling the rest of the muck behind him on some sort of sledge or trolley, and pursuing that line of thought almost gave in to adding to the pile a slender and wire-wheeled Victorian bassinet, if only to be able to sling into it assorted quite fascinating chamber-pots and sundry other fairly livid conversation pieces which Kevin for one had no doubt at all could given half the chance talk the hind legs off a donkey.

'I missed you yesterday,' said Milly, quietly, as a purple, stunned and glossy Kevin slumped against the wall, panting like a carthorse and exuding all the allure of a mid-bout Sumo wrestler.

'*Geh*!' responded Kevin, for all the world as if an unseen hand had closed down all of his orifices – no doubt as some sort of gag.

'How did the shopping go?' went on Milly. 'Get anything nice?'

'*Hoof*!' exhaled Kevin. '*Hoof*! Oh Jesus. Well you *know*, Milly, what I got – Christ I'm knackered – I got a *horse*-collar and I got a –'

'No, Silly – I mean yesterday!'

Yes, just the very second before Milly said 'yesterday', he had her meaning. On no account did he want to recall his clothes shopping trip of yesterday – it was raw, too raw in the memory; no doubt either Kevin or Emily will go into it at some stage in the future (maybe they both will, but if this proves to be the case, don't expect their respective foundations, blushers and shadowing to in any way blend into a seamless complexion) but the last thing Kevin could cope with at this very minute (three more journeys, he reckoned, taking into the equation the logistics of the stuffed impala's head) was even the thought of any of *that*. The thing to do, plainly, was to cart all this appalling lumber over to The Grange Hotel, conceal it from senior management lest one of the more sensitive suffers a seizure, and then high-tail it down to Brighton as fast as he and Milly could possibly go.

Which is, eventually, what happened – and now, as you can see, they're fairly bowling along. Kevin was of the opinion (not actually expressed in words) that everything now seemed to be going rather well. He was glancing sideways at Milly more often than he should (the reverberation of tyres on the hard shoulder was as if someone had taken to setting about the undercarriage with brief bursts of a chainsaw) but apart from the overt glee of a child on a spree, he was damned if he could read into her expression any sort of intent. Was there any sort of intent, do we think? Don't know. On the plus side, it is a well-known fact that

Londoners behave differently in Brighton: all to do with the ozone, see.

Emily was on her hands and knees, rubbing hard at the black and white travertine tiles of her ante-vestibule with a lint-free cloth so thoroughly saturated with methylated spirit that she could barely see straight any more. This was the only proper way to even begin to get a floor like this to glow, to radiate, and to share with us all the inherent beauty of its natural make-up (just try telling any of this to that little cunt Lolita!). When the cordless squawked, Emily very seriously considered allowing it to continue to do so, but responsible self-employed people simply didn't *do* that sort of thing and so she eased herself up from her hassock (actually a Timney Fowler classical print cushion, but one long since fallen prey to a Burgundy spillage) and announced her telephone number accusingly into the beige and rickety handset which Emily frankly loathed, while conceding its practicality.

'It's me. Kevin.'

'*Yes*, Kevin: I do know that.'

'You're sounding very well!'

'Where are you? Why aren't you back yet?'

'Yes well, that's just the thing. The car seems to have – that's to say, I've *done* everything – got the, you know, er –'

'Where *are* you, Kevin?'

'Stuff. Um – I'm in Brighton. In Brighton. Quite nice down here, actually – sun quite bright, but the wind's a bit –'

'Why are you still in Brighton, Kevin? Is the dresser in the flat? At least you did *that*, I hope. Did you get all the stuff all right?'

'You see this is the point. The car's – the car won't *start* is the fact of the matter, but the garage says it's not a big thing but they need a part and they can't get the part till the morning so it rather looks as if –'

'What *part*?'

'Hm? Oh – some oily part. The *dresser*, I have to say, wasn't ready at all – hang on, I've got to put some more money in. I really should buy phonecards but I never think of it.'

'I don't *believe* it! The dresser?! Jim promised me *faithfully*. I'll kill the little bastard. I've got to go down to the flat later – Fern has finished the lights, he says, and I was going to – oh *Christ* what is that bloody man thinking of? He's never let me down before!'

'Well there you are – I'm just the messenger. But look – I've got all the stuff you ordered from down here safely locked up in the car – no worries there – so I'll just, don't know – jolly inconvenient, actually – I'll just find some little room, cheap little room somewhere, and then shoot back some time in the morning. Depending on when they get the part.'

'Mm – well, all right, Kevin – it's just that – oh Christ, that means *I've* got to pick up your bloody suit, then – you'll never have time with all the rest, will you? Oh God – *this* on top of everything else. And the cleaning! The cleaning! I'm now doing all the cleaning! Lolita, the little bitch, has left us – walked out, gone. Can you *believe* it?!'

'Christ this thing really eats up the money . . . hang on . . . there, OK – that's my last fifty pee. Lolita? Really? Why?'

'You tell *me* why! I just told her to stop stealing things and breaking things and start cleaning things as they should be bloody cleaned and she gets up on her high horse and tells me she's *leaving*. I mean *Christ*.'

'Well look, Emily –'

'Just get back quickly tomorrow, Kevin – there's one hell of a lot to do.'

'Will do, natch. Just as soon as they've got the part. Look –

that's the pips, Emily. Bye, then. Um – anything I can bring you back? Rock, or anything?'

'Don't be such a fucking *prat*, Kevin,' spat Emily, just before the line cut dead.

Yes, thought Emily – bloody *Lolita* (just before thinking oh fuck the floor, I'll leave it) Can you imagine? Emily had perfectly rationally set out and then underlined the proportions of the girl's misdemeanours and was perfectly prepared to accept whatever craven repentance would surely flow – was even prepared for a round of ankle-kissing and pleas for forgiveness – but not a bit of it. This malevolent little chit of a domestic had merely narrowed her unnaturally black eyes (which, Emily could barely shrink from observing, contracted her thick and furry eyebrows into some large and querulous rodent) and said with venom just this – and straight into Emily's face:

'I not need diss. Why you no stick your job in your *bottom*?'

'I *beg* your pardon?!'

'I see you poach in hell, you bag of giblets.'

'*Look*, you little –'

'I go now. May you drown in urine.'

'Just clear off right *now*, Lolita – and don't bloody steal anything else or you'll have the police to contend with!'

'I steal only one thing – I steal your *soul*. I place curse on you and house. May your teeth fall into excrement.'

Whereupon Lolita made all sorts of gestures involving fingers, bad teeth, elbows and fists (some dimly remembered from a Desmond Morris programme) while Emily for her part flounced off to her room intoning with menace Twenty Minutes! Twenty Minutes, Lolita, to gather your things, and then you are out of here for good – understand? Ungrateful little *bitch*.

Precisely twenty minutes later – she had timed it to the second on that perfectly repellent and just barely tolerated little digital-radio-alarm-clock affair that Kevin had once bought from somewhere, proudly insisting that it was *cheap* (as if there was any doubt) – Emily descended with froideur together with a fair deal of hauteur as well, and although the silence proclaimed the emptiness of the house (at least she's *gone*, thank Christ) there was something else that Emily immediately perceived, something she didn't at all care for. The floor – the semi-buffed black and white travertine ante-vestibule was now overladen with a glossy patina of molten gold; why should this be? Because here is the natural result of pouring all over it one-and-a-half litres of Extra Virgin Sasso olive oil (proof, if ever there was, that maybe one is better off *without* the staff) and I don't know if you've ever tried to expunge all traces of any kind of oil from such a surface as travertine marble, but . . . well no: Emily hadn't either, but she had a pretty good idea that here was to be no one's idea of a fun day out and it wasn't often that Emily was prey to the sort of pang that made red the rim of the eyes, that darted salt into glistening and prickled eyes, but now she came so close as to be nearly there – *was* there now – and on impulse she phoned Raymond (who else could she call?) and ordered him to arrive *now*, *immediately*, and he had murmured, sounding strange, that he couldn't, not now, because he had just recently had a knife removed from his shoulder blade and was buggered if he was coming anywhere near such a mad bitch as Emily, no way, not the way he was feeling, and then he said OK, I will, might take a while, though – you fucking cow.

You're kidding. You're not really telling me that the day after Raymond was stabbed by the blithely spirited Amanda – you're not really saying that he's going to drag himself round to Emily's for a bout of ritual and ferocious mutual

179

abuse? Can this be true? We assume, then, that no lungs or other precious organs were cruelly punctured? The severance of nothing vital? No real worries about getting from A to B, in short. A clean wound they call that, don't they? Hmm, well Raymond – would demur about the 'clean' part (*wound*, certainly) if only for the fact that what with the bleeding during and the quite shocked retching afterwards his clothes were a complete write-off for starters (although neither effusion had any noticeably detrimental effect upon his environment, needless to record).

As to its being the day *after* this rather grisly event – Raymond really could not have told you. He was out cold for a goodly while, according to Thomas, and then as soon as he had woken he had screamed quite raucously so Thomas had tanked him up with some narcotic or other that had him hovering sweetly above a field of snowdrops for quite a time, although he well remembered too swooping and pitching between the branches of trees with all the grace of a starling.

Come to think of it, it *couldn't* have been yesterday, last night, all of that, because now he really felt as fine as you can while woozy with drugs and dead down one side. Didn't stop him smoking, though, oh Lord no: the ash in and around the various saucers and plates and saucepans massed across the table and floor could well have passed muster as all you have to show for it after a hard day's work at a small crematorium.

So what's Amanda up to, then? Still dippy, is she? Or has this spot of attempted murder brought her closer to what we may or may not feel comfortable in referring to as her (don't laugh) senses? And Maureen. Grieving, yes? Or too far gone to feel? No point asking about Rosie, I suppose? In the circumstances. No, that's one thing gone: put to rest, if you will. Well all right, since you ask – let's take it one at a time: Amanda, first. Hang on: just stub out this fag, gulp a handful of heart pills (haven't eaten for ages: starving) and now just quickly light up another fag and we're off.

Amanda, yes. Oh God – I mean, all very well but where does one actually begin with a woman like this? If you looked at her now (and Raymond was – he was looking at her now as he lay on that sofa-bed that he had practically ruptured himself by carting in in an attempt to make Amanda more comfortable during her erstwhile captivity, while she in force had fallen upon him rather in the manner of – it no doubt would have occurred to her – that film *Zulu*); yes, if you looked at her now, you would think you had imagined the whole damn thing. Or else that some warped mind had made it all up. She was alternating between itemizing all the lovely new things they were going to get for the house (yes, she was very much still latched on to all that side of things, though more sanely, maybe – saying it all as if, well, as if she really *did* live there: hm, not so sanely, then) and this time Raymond *had*, he *had* brought up the money thing. Who exactly, Amanda, he had queried, who is it that you imagine is going to pay for all this stuff? Oh, don't worry about any of that, Raymond, she had replied quite airily – *I'll* pay for it, no trouble there. Alternating between that and chatting about arranging things with the PR accounts that in her opinion were going to prove to be real money in the bank, no problem, and those that, frankly Raymond, I think we have rather outgrown: dead in the water. I see, yes, Raymond had said several times, while not once having the vaguest idea of even the nature of the businesses on whose behalf his company allegedly related to the public. He also said this:

'Why did you stab me, Amanda?'

'We need to get the computers really up to par, though, Raymond. It's not that our system can't handle the work-load – it's just that the opposition are forever updating the software and we simply have to be there too: the clients expect it, nowadays.'

'Amanda? Why did you stab me, in point of fact?'

'And in return for my input, by the way, I'll expect a partnership. Stab you? I didn't *stab* you, Raymond!'

'Oh no I promise you *did*, Amanda,' protested Raymond.

Amanda looked at him cold and hard. '*Understand*, Raymond: I could not have stabbed you because the only way I would have done such a thing is if you had assaulted me and you did not assault me is that *plain* Raymond? I hope it is plain because I really do not wish to allude to this ever again. It is not a question of forgetting: *it simply did not happen.*'

So that's the first question answered: yes, still dippy as you like. It seems as if that last statement of hers simply didn't happen either because now she was happily babbling about PR again:

'I actually just landed two new accounts for us, Raymond – would have told you but the last few days have been a little odd.'

A little odd, thought Raymond: yes.

'One is a sort of tonic wine – I didn't think they actually made that sort of thing any more, it's so Fifties – like Beechams Powders, and things. Anyway they *do* – and they want us to sort of sex up the image. And some muesli. Some new muesli that's determined to shake up the major players So what I've done is I've got them both into a promotion advertorial in *GQ* – it's going to be brilliant because Marriott hotels and Jaguar are in on it too and, I think, Doulton, or one of those big china people.'

Raymond nodded, not knowing what in buggery she was talking about, but feeling sure that she would tell him. Just as she started up again he shuddered with no pain from a non-existent twinge from the un-wound in his shoulder.

'What they are is, um, these promotions, is six or eight colour pages right at the heart of the magazine and they get these really super-looking models – guy and a girl, usually – to sort of pose with all the products, and then some copywriter ties it all together with a little storyline. I've suggested one, actually – it'll be brilliant if they take it on because what'll happen is that this really cool guy and drop-dead gorgeous babe, they turn up at a Marriott hotel in their Jag, right, and the first thing they do when they check into their luxury suite is order up a bottle of Elixir Tonic Wine – that's the name, that's what it's called, pretty good I think – and a couple of Doulton or whatever bowls of Nutri-Good muesli. Then there's a shot of them wolfing that lot down and then it's off in the Jag again to some other Marriott hotel – more muesli and tonic wine before dinner, and then back in the Jag to another Marriott hotel with a nightclub and the final shot, pretty sexy, is of them about to get into bed – moon shining away outside the window, the girl in some-thing slinky – and they're toasting each other with a nice big Doulton mug of tonic wine and this time they tuck into a fucking great mountain of muesli all on the same huge Doulton plate, which I reckon is pretty romantic, actually. What do you think? Winner, right?'

'Right,' agreed a partially mesmerized Raymond. 'Win-ner.' Christ, he thought – she said 'fucking' again.

'*And*,' added on Amanda – quite as if this had anything at all to do with either tonic wine *or* muesli – 'you've got to tell Maureen. Not about that, but about the other thing – her leaving, me staying. Do it today.'

'Her mother's just died,' said Raymond.

'Yeah?' checked Amanda, quite unconcerned. 'I don't actually see the connection.'

Odd that Maureen should have half fallen into the room just at that very moment – God she was absolutely like latex with drink, but what was strange was the slash of what could well be happiness splattered all over her face. Too boozed to have any control or understanding of whatever it was her features were up to? Could be, Raymond supposed: could well be.

'Tell her now,' said Amanda.

And Raymond didn't know – maybe it was the drugs alternating between zigzagging marathons and rapid diagonal sprints across the whole of his mind, maybe it was because he just couldn't imagine that anything at all he could say would render this situation any farther from reality than he already felt it to be – or maybe it was just easier, these days, to do what people told you to do, when they told you to do it. Whatever the reason – and it won't have been any of these in seclusion, of course not, it never is – he just wheeled round in an arc from his position on the sofa-bed and intoned to Maureen:

'Hello, Maureen. You're leaving this house.'

'Today,' put in Amanda.

'Today,' reiterated Raymond, 'and Amanda is moving in.'

'Permanently,' added on Amanda.

'Permanently,' corroborated Raymond.

Maureen tried to rein in one or two of the wilder elements of her forehead and cheeks, which entailed a fair deal of contortion, but eventually tamed most of it down into some sort of composure.

'That is sad,' she said, reasonably steadily. Then her face brightened up, rather surprisingly, and she came up with something that was considerably more surprising than that:

'I've got good news about Mummy!'

Amanda looked at Raymond with a *looking* sort of a look that said I thought you said . . . ? And Raymond mugged back another look that replied I *did*, I *did* – but also coursing across his brain was oh Christ great: now Maureen's gone the way of Rosie and here I am in what was once a perfectly innocuous if outright filthy little study, reduced to merely the luncheon meat sandwiched in between two thick slices of fucking nutcase.

'What *news*?' asked Raymond – gently, was his intention, though fear was probably the spur.

'She might be coming home tomorrow,' slurred Maureen brightly.

Alarm – that's the only word for the strong white gleam that sprang into Raymond's eye (and Amanda was looking none too happy either, it has to be said: loonies never register their own home-grown lunacy – only the lunacy farmed out by all the others). 'Maureen,' tried Raymond, as patiently as he could, well aware of the quake in his voice that the presence of crazies always provoked, 'your mother isn't coming home tomorrow. Is she? Hm?'

'Nor are *you*!' cracked out Amanda, which Raymond adjudged a little unnecessary.

'Oh but she *is*, she *is*!' insisted Maureen. And then her voice dropped down into intimate disclosure. 'Well – maybe not.'

Thank God, thought Raymond. 'Exactly,' he said.

Maureen's eyes popped back up as they fixed on some point quite close to Raymond's direction.

'Maybe the day after,' she qualified.

'She's *dead*, you stupid bitch,' sang out Amanda – and Raymond was amazed to see Maureen's face swing round now to where she imagined might have been the source and become lit by what to his eye was indeed happiness, plain as day.

'But that's just it, do you see – she's *not*. She's not at all. She *twitched*.'

Raymond blinked. 'She did bloody *what*?'

'*Twitched*, she *twitched*,' shrilled Maureen, urging Raymond to become a part of this new insight into wonder. 'In the mortuary – on that awful slab thing. *Twitched*.'

Raymond felt this churning in his mind, rather like a shovelful of gravel and cement in the drum of a rusty and encrusted mixer.

'She *twitched*?'

Maureen nodded until she nearly fell over, then sent out a

185

hand to find her head. '*Twitched*.' she confirmed. 'She's alive. Recovering. She's going to be *all right!*'

Oh *fuck,* thought Raymond: why is it that only good things ever unravel? Bad things never do. Well that says a lot for Thomas's unerring skill as a medical practitioner, I must say. Christ – he doesn't even know when someone's alive and when they're fucking dead! So what the hell had he injected into Raymond, then? Maybe it was Raymond next for the slab – and you can bet your (oh Christ) *life*: there'd be no twitching then, would there? Raymond never ever got a second chance.

Amanda heard the doorbell, Raymond didn't – and Maureen staggered off in the direction of the landing and fondled her way around the study door. Seizing the hand-rail, she began her unsteady descent downstairs, leaving behind her a throbbing trail of clatter as her knees rhythmically strummed each of the spindles in turn, a sigh of pain escaping her only at the final clonking collision with the newel post in the hallway.

Raymond looked at Amanda and said dully:

'Her mother *hasn't* just died.'

Amanda shook her head. 'I still don't see the connection.'

Raymond lit a cigarette: funny smell, couldn't draw on it. Lit the wrong end, hadn't he? Chucked it away, lit another one. Maureen was back pretty quickly.

'There's some policemen, 'she said.

And Christ that sent Raymond goggling back at Amanda again and some of those oh-my-God-you-*did*-didn't-you looks were exchanged with of-course-I-fucking-didn't ones in return because he hadn't, had he? What with being stabbed in the back and being as high as a cloud on whatever form of cyanide fucking Hippocrates had filled him up with, he hadn't, had he, got around to telling Amanda's father that Al Capone and friends had dropped all plans to pursue the half-million – hadn't got round to

186

telling him at all. And you know what he said he'd do.

'Well,' he said softly to Maureen (thinking go on God – keep it coming, keep it coming), 'you'd better show them up.'

And while he waited, he wasn't going to look at Amanda: he wasn't concocting a plan, no, he was just thinking about Rosie's death; Christ, he was thinking (get a load of this): *it simply did not happen.*

'Oh God *no*,' muttered Shelley, with real bitterness 'Not *them*, of all people.'

'Who?' said Gideon. 'What?' And then he let out a laugh – Christ knows why.

They were sitting on not at all comfortable stools up at the bar of the pub more or less just around the corner from Kevin and Emily – early evening, loads of people: who could Shelley be talking about? Gideon craned his head around in a fairly useless manner, not knowing who he was searching for or maybe avoiding.

'Bloody *Ben*,' said Shelley, with true disgust.

Yes, it was Ben, Adam's chum – and he looked like he'd downed quite a few already that evening. His father was with him, too – Shelley had noticed this (of course she had) but had chosen not to focus on his presence: Ben alone was bad enough without bloody Julian as well.

'At least bloody Adam isn't with them,' went on Shelley – any relief she might really have felt from that single negative blessing now instantly evaporating because of *course* Ben was coming right over, wasn't he? Grinning his bovine grin and flapping around loads of money (*that's* a first, for a start) and Julian was following, as Julian did – reluctantly maybe, but following all the same.

Gideon for his part was pretty relieved. He had thought

that he and Shelley had just been popping round the corner for a drink or two – he hadn't been aware that it was her intention to start talking about their (oh God) *future*. Gideon didn't have a past, on the whole pretty much tolerated the present and now he was expected to face this *future* thing. Well – he *says* he didn't have a past: true right up until just last night. He had hugged the beauty of the memory to him tighter and tighter – wasn't, in truth, listening too hard to any of Shelley's hopes for the future; she had said that if there were now any things to be arranged, then maybe now was the time for arranging them, but Gideon had affected blankness on that one: didn't care for the sound of it. Shelley, to give her her due, didn't push it – didn't seem to be too bothered one way or the other. At least, she had said, at least we're not falling over each other *laughing* any more – at least now we can actually talk. Yeh, thought Gideon, it's true – they hadn't been laughing: nothing really to laugh about. Never had been, in truth (Raymond had been right about that, Gideon allowed, even if he was right about nothing else), but there had certainly in the old days been a lot to cover up. Particularly when it came to the sex. Or not. Laughter was the best medicine – when things wouldn't come together: when they refused to fuse.

And then last night, just last night – Gideon's very first non-solo orgasm: he had no words for the joy of the experience – the tingling was still all over him And the warmth afterwards – the holding of a warm and contented body after so much hard and vicious invasion and blessed peace – the thought of now living without such a thing was unbearable. The shock when he came home and discovered that his grandmother was dead jarred so utterly with the wash of hot discovery that was running right through him that he felt he might fragment: bucked up a good deal when later he learned that in fact she wasn't dead at all: oh good, he remembered thinking.

'Wanna drink, Shell?' offered a flush–faced Ben – managing to make it sound (well certainly to Shelley's ears) like the grafting of an in-your-face insult to a taunting jibe.

'I have one, thank you, Ben.' Prim voice.

'Oh go on – ave a drink. I want everybody to ave a drink. Christ – I've even got my *father* to ave a bloody drink!'

'I have to say, Ben, that one drink is all well and good – no one wishes to be a puritan in these matters –' (Julian? Yeh, Julian) '– but I should say your intake this evening has erred on the side of excess – I'm sorry, but I do think so.'

'Excess, yeah,' agreed Ben, quite readily. 'Oh go *on*, Shell – ave a drink – and your bloke. Sorry mate – can't remember your name.'

'Gideon,' said Gideon.

'Yeh?' checked Ben.

Gideon nodded. 'Yes,' he confirmed.

'OK then, Gideon – ave a drink. Go on – I got plenty of money, ave a drink.'

'Rob a bank, Ben?' asked Shelley, sweetly.

'Yeh – machine-guns, the lot!' wheezed back Ben, before coughing, going mauve, and glugging down the last of his pint.

'I think it would be very unwise to have another one, Ben,' cautioned good old guess-who.

'Oh just one more, Dad! I'm celebrating!'

'What's the great occasion?' enquired Shelley. 'Learned to tie your shoe-laces?'

'It would appear,' said Julian – not looking at Shelley, didn't feel he quite wanted to – 'Ben was lucky with the Lottery – some hundreds of pounds, I gather. I personally don't buy tickets – I'm not saying it's *wrong*, in moderation, but I personally –'

'Yeh right,' interjected Shelley. 'Got you.'

Ben, meanwhile, was buying drinks wholesale: a Guinness for Gideon, a lager for Shelley ('I told you, Ben – I've *got* one'), a small dry sherry for Julian ('I'm not at all sure it's wise, but I suppose this is after all something of a special day') and anything else at all for anyone around. For himself there was another pint of the bitter he loathed, and a slily bought large whisky, which he had now decided he liked very much, downed in one in the corner bar – couldn't use it as a chaser because the Sermon On the Mount that *that* would have incurred could well have kept Julian going till Christmas.

'We have to go,' said Shelley sternly, right into Gideon's left eyeball.

'I've just got a drink!' protested Gideon. Mildly.

'We're going,' Shelley made clear.

Eager to be alone with him, is she? Understandable in the light of what we've heard. No not that, not that at all. Quite the reverse, in point of fact. She was just looking at them all, just looking at one face and then another: the leering, drooling, ape-like Ben, the perfectly helpless Julian (his eyelashes beating away behind those stupid glasses like those of a child, promised a surprise), and then Gideon – the original lost cause. Did real men *exist* any more? Whoa, back a bit – lost cause? Not now, one wouldn't have said. *Before*, maybe – but not after last night, surely? Last night? Ah no – last night was when Gideon had given himself up to those brief but rapturous hours with Richard from Marketing. What's wrong? Hadn't he made that clear?

'Right,' exhaled Kevin, that one syllable chock-full of the-die-is-truly-cast-and-Christ-haven't-I-just-crossed-the-Rubicon undertones, overtones – any sorts of tones you fancy, really. 'Done it.'

'What did you *say*?' Milly was eager to know. 'What did you tell her?'

'I said it was some *part*,' replied Kevin, simply. 'Some part on the car I couldn't, um, get hold of till tomorrow.'

'And she went for it? What part?'

'Oh God don't you start up too, now, Milly – I don't *know* what part – I'm no good at all on cars, what makes them go. I just said some *part*. But yes,' continued Kevin, more slowly, 'yes – she did go for it.' Yes, she had appeared to; other things on her mind, of course – but then, in the circumstances, what else could she have done but go for it? One of those things, right?

This is another side of Kevin we're seeing here, though, isn't it? This is the fellow who hadn't actually thought of building Milly in to this little joyride down to the coast, and now here he was making a fully-fledged tryst of the thing, replete with no-holds-barred and cold-blooded lies to (yipes!) no less than Emily – who at least had been a hundred miles away at the time: he could never have looked her in the eye and done it, no fear. So to what do we attribute this new and lusty daring? You're not trying to suggest it's all down to *ozone*, I hope, whatever intangible this might be. No no – it's Milly again, isn't it? Milly is what it's all down to; she doesn't say much, this girl, but when she does speak, Kevin surely listens.

'It's such a lovely day,' is what she kicked off with. 'Just look at the *sea*.'

And Kevin did; well, when you're on the promenade thing with your back to the hotels, there's not a lot of option.

' 'Tis nice,' he said. Well: 'Twas.

'It seems a pity to go back,' ruminated the ingénue that is Milly. 'Back to all the traffic. Work.'

'Mm,' murmured Kevin, investing in that little noise if not outright negativity, then certainly a good and healthy portion of non-committal. Yes of *course* he knew what she was driving at – it excited the hell out of him, if you force him to be honest – but it was this age-old thing of yes, but what if he was *wrong*? What if Milly was in her way simply banging on about the sea and the London traffic without any sort of ulterior intention in her mind? And *if* this was the case and Kevin took it a different way and brought up the word 'hotel' (following the utterance of which, no such idle conversation can ever be the same again) and *then* if Milly were to turn to him a shocked and maidenly face, then Kevin could see no alternative but to wade right on into that squinting sea and stubbornly stay there until gingerly removed several days later by seen-it-all-before lifeboat men, beige and bloated and with all life's juices (coursing around him now like red-hot skunks) well and truly sapped.

'Could we not,' Milly ventured now – maybe sensing that if it was Kevin's initiative she was waiting for, then night could well fall – 'possibly go back in the morning?'

Kevin almost burst with relief: it was as if he hadn't breathed in for simply hours: oh bless her, bless her, for making it *plain*.

'Yes,' was all that emerged from his happy, happy face. *'Yes.'*

What an afternoon! What a blissful afternoon! For as long as he lived, young Kevin (and he couldn't judge for others, couldn't speak for others, but just going by the zingy and fresh-faced look of her, then by God Milly too) would never ever forget this day, each clear and utterly innocent bit of it. They had picked up all the antique-or-so bits and bobs from the shops that Emily had specified – not in The Lanes (of course not, Kevin, she had said quite sternly – that is where the *tourists* go) but in a really rather attractive bit of the town, in a slummy sort of a way, quite close to the station and known as Kensington.

'Different from *our* Kensington,' Milly had commented.

Kevin nodded. 'Nicer,' he said.

But the actual nature of the stuff had given him pause; it was all really rather nice, and actually pretty normal. A bronze bust of some maybe Victorian general (moustache and medals) and a lovely military drum in bright lacquered colours with a gently faded skin: a black Wedgwood urn – Jasper, the man in the shop had said, though Christ knew who *he* was. It was just maybe that Kevin had got the wrong end of the stick in Milly's little shop (which was called . . . which was called . . . no, gone, leave it) because he was under the impression that to be *interesting* objects had to be out-and-out weird – but apparently not. Christ alone could tell how on earth all the lumber on which he had lavished a fortune (Emily's fortune) was expected to sit with all these rather lovely things: joys to come. Anyway, he locked it all away into the Espace, and now – now could the fun begin? I think it should, don't you, Kevin? If I were you, Kevin, I should let it rip.

'What sort of hotel shall we, um, get? Milly?'

I know. But then Kevin had never made a secret of the fact that if ever in his life he was confronted with a bull, it was not its horns he would take to so much as his heels; and Shelley would any day have witheringly conceded that as far as 'manhood' went, her father was a prime and typical specimen. But there was a woman here, thank God – Milly would see that things got properly arranged (just you watch her go).

'The Grand is too grand,' she opined. Too right, thought Kevin – and too damn pricey; he was still smarting from the drubbing he had received at the place that wasn't Chez Nous at all – Christ, it wasn't so long ago that in return for such a sum one could have reasonably expected a share in the freehold.

The Old Ship was full; well, I say full – they did have a twin-bedded room (with a good sea view) but Milly – bold as blazes – made it so plain as to render Kevin aubergine that this was not at all the sort of thing they had in mind. Yipes! Got a nice little room in a much smaller place around the corner: little L-shaped room (Kevin had seen that film – not read the book, but he surely remembered the film: just as well it wasn't Amanda here or they'd both be up all night putting a name to the director); but they were all L-shaped, these days – all down to the boxy bathrooms built in to the corner, complete with peachy bath half the length of a child and brimming with sachets of things that humans never used like bath caps and shoe rags as well as the stuff people rather liked – foam, lotions and oil (bring them home, use them later, was the usual idea, but more likely throw them out a hell of a while after, when they began to ooze).

The woman now leaving them could well have been the owner – too proud and old to be a maid – and while Kevin had mentally logged the business of operating the very strange door-lock as being very much Milly's department (you slid in plastic) he was much impressed by the presence of a video recorder beneath the television, and clearly the woman who could well have been the owner was very proud of this not-yet-mandatory amenity because she alluded to it time and again and moreover pronounced it vid-*ay*-o – and although no doubt this was possibly correct, Kevin nonetheless had to suppress a very silly fit of the giggles whenever the woman came out with this vid-*ay*-o because each time he had a vision of her launching into a swift bout of limbo dancing before leading off into some jaunty calypso. And do you know, among the films on offer was *The L-Shaped Room*? Coincidence or what? Life, thought Kevin, was funny like that.

They didn't stay in the room, though: Milly's decision. Not a formal decision (no manifesto or timetable of events was at any time referred to) but the way she opened the door and stood in the corridor and said Hey let's go left Kevin in

194

little doubt that even the kiss he had been summoning up since the woman who could well have been the owner had finally left them (the muscles in his lips by now quite flexy) was clearly not on the agenda so he happily decanted himself into the corridor thinking Ooh great – an afternoon in Brighton with Milly Milly Milly! And then there's later, later.

They went to English's, a small and naughty fish restaurant hard by The Lanes (Kevin rather liked all the intercommunicating alleys, jammed with antique shops jammed with antiques – even if it was just for tourists; but then, what was Kevin if not a tourist for the day? Yes sirree – Kevin was tripping). Even with the tall stools, the oyster bar seemed terribly high – so much so that Kevin found it difficult to prop up his elbows without assuming an attitude of fervent prayer; he dropped his hands to his knees at one point but not holding on to anything at all made him feel decidedly vertiginous so in the end he just gripped the bar's marble edge and hung there.

'We'll have a bottle of champagne,' announced Milly, and Kevin nodded as eagerly as he could while thinking a couple or things, namely champagne always goes to my head and yipes, oh lumme – thirty-five quid.

'And a dozen Natives.'

Calypso time again! No, not really – Kevin knew what Natives were. Didn't care for them, it has to be said; wasn't anything to do with once having had a bad one, no, although he did recall that just getting the slimy little thing into his mouth had been trouble enough because all the wet sort of stuff in the shell had been dribbling down the corner of his mouth and so when he swivelled his head to catch the drip (not reckoning that when he moved his head his head would come too) he missed the egress of the oyster altogether and it had slavered across his chin and plopped into his lap and he had parted his legs in order to let it drop to the floor and of course it had ended up on his shoe which was suede and it was still there an hour later in the street because no-one had felt inclined to mention it.

'If you're not too keen on oysters,' said Milly – maybe it was just the way he was looking at the things – 'you can cover them with pepper and Lea & Perrins and Tabasco and then you bite them just once before they go down the hatch and they're absolutely delicious like that.'

So naturally enough Kevin had scraped pepper over his oyster and dabbed on Lea & Perrins and Milly had added a whoosh of Tabasco and off the little thing went into Kevin's none-too-eager gullet (having been bitten on just the once) and then it was that Kevin's eyeballs hit the mirror behind the bar with slapping force before rebounding like a googly back into his face just as his mouth dropped open into a mime of Pavarotti in full and final throttle.

'Nice?' urged Milly.

Kevin wept silently for a bit, before coming back with the fairly wheezily expressed opinion that on balance he didn't really reckon that at base he was truly very much of an oyster *man*.

'They say,' said Milly, downing her fourth, 'they say they're an aphrodisiac. That's what,' clarified Milly – dispatching a fifth – 'they say.'

'Really?' commented Kevin.

Yes – *wanted* to say something slily suggestive. nearly laughed out loud at the thought of winking, toyed with the impossibility of appearing in any way raffish – but 'really' is all he finally said. He rather thought that he would leave Milly to deal with the oysters (she appeared to be having little difficulty) while he made goodly inroads into the champagne. That too was meant to be an aphrodisiac, wasn't it? Or was it the other thing? Couldn't have told you. Anyway, between the two of them they made quite short work of it (a bottle went nowhere once you had the bit between your teeth) and it was the work of but a moment for Milly to order in another. It hadn't got to Kevin's head yet, so he didn't mind too much and he was now quite decided that he wasn't going to think about money any more, he wasn't; well it was *silly*: this is the *essence* of life, all this – quaffing champagne with Milly in Brighton, *that's* the stuff of memories: *that's* what it's all about (and you can stuff the hokey-cokey). What – on his death-bed, Kevin would be grateful for the *money* he had saved, would he? I think not. So to hell with the expense – let the expense be hanged! This is the *life*, I tell you! Blimey, though: thirty-five quid.

'Shall we get more oysters?' piped up Milly.

Kevin shook his head. He was still using champagne to put out the fire. 'Unless *you* want more,' he offered.

Milly too shook her head. 'It'll spoil dinner. I thought maybe room service would be nice.'

Kevin thought room service would be very nice too, Milly's adeptness and, let's face it, forthright attitude only slightly spoiled for him by the glancing and why is it so painful thought of gosh she's so terribly good at all this she must have done it before – of *course* she's done it before, probably dozens of times, well not dozens, maybe, but more than once or twice. And why *shouldn't* she have done it before, actually? She was an adult person, was she not? She was, she was, of course she was – dismiss the thought, cast it out. Kevin did that, as near as dammit: only a residual sliver of pain hanging around, now – hardly anything at all.

Milly was looking at him; what she did was, she swigged a hefty mouthful of fizz, billowed out her cheeks before letting them subside and then still with the flute at her lips she cast over a long and maybe could be meaningful look right into one of Kevin's eyes (which lost no time in becoming acrobatic – a bit of excitement, loads of alarm) and there was Kevin now goggling back with the best of them but oh Jesus wouldn't the champagne now choose to hit him between the eyes (you'd better believe it) and goodness he hoped that Milly interpreted that sway in her direction as no more than a bit of body language intended to convey the need for closer proximity – it would be good if she did, because if she had seen it for what it truly was (an involuntary lurch, a jerky spasm triggered by the prickling thought of wooze I feel woopsy or should it be woops I feel woozy doesn't matter because gah I nearly bloody fell off the stool, didn't I?) well then in that case she wasn't going to be over-impressed with him now, was she?

Kevin smiled, but packed it in when he saw she was drinking deep again and hadn't yet got around to the looking at him bit. To synchronize all this was clearly going to require a fair deal of work, not least because they were sitting side by side, you see – and he was getting the most terrible crick in the neck on top of everything else and he surely would have loved to abseil down from the apex of this accursed stool that he didn't trust for a single second and clamber into one of those clarety and plush banquette affairs but to do so would appear too gauche, would it not? It would hardly signal style. Too late he thought to hell with style – for now he was pitching forward right into Milly (couldn't arrest the lurch, not this time he couldn't) and Milly's champagne spluttered up into her nose and all that spluttered down from it was a laugh of pure joy and as Kevin took this into him and delighted in the big brass band that was her eyes and her mouth and her sweet – how sweet they are, her little teeth, then Kevin lurched again in another way altogether and it was all busy happening within him and although the feeling was a sort of pining and lonely sickness, almost like a slow and reluctant semi-orgasm followed by queasiness, he well recognized it for what it was because he had felt it once, felt it before – he had known it with Sophie, and now he was knowing it again.

Well, I suppose it was inevitable, Kevin falling like that – and it is not the topple from the stool that is being referred to here, as well you know. Milly a party to it, is she? That's what Kevin was hoping he would soon find out, because they were back at the hotel, now – not hotfoot from English's, as it happens, that would have been fine by Kevin, but Milly really did seem intent upon milking all the goodness from this sun-kissed jaunt to the seaside. They had to, she said, go on the pier. Right, Kevin had said – while not, in truth, sharing the compulsion. He changed a ten pound note into fifty pences, and when they lost that lot, he changed another. When there was just one pound of it left (and Kevin if not Milly had grown truly weary of sending money into clattering oblivion) Milly suggested they each have a go on that little chromium crane that threatens to grab up cuddly toys and send them whooshing down a chute into eager arms attached to a pair of excitedly hunched up shoulders (lurking beneath an open mouth and the widest of eyes) before thinking better of it at the very last moment and groping at air, the claws yawning over the abyss with no more than that on offer. Kevin knew that's how it went because half their money had gone on this thing (Milly kept coming back to it, and Kevin thought he knew why: she wanted a little cuddly toy to have and to hold, a part of the day to cling on to – and so much more fun, so immediate, if it was a casually acquired but potent trophy: buying it would not be the same; Kevin sort of understood all that).

Milly went first, and missed everything altogether: there wasn't even so much as a tantalizing moment. Kevin was wearing about his tenth smile of commiseration as he spun the little wheel, not really looking, and it was only Milly's squeal that alerted him to the truth that oh gosh look – those little silver talons were fast closing in on a little black and white stuffed kitten and he had it now, looked quite firm, and it was when the crane swung over the hole affair that you usually lost it, that's when Kevin thought he would lose it, but it hadn't slipped yet, the little black and white stuffed kitten, and Milly was cramming knuckles-a-plenty in between her teeth right now because there was hardly any distance and here we go, here we go, it's nearly over the chute and Kevin's eyes were ablaze despite himself and he just loved it when Milly said the little black and white stuffed kitten was just *adorable* and it was then that the fucking thing dropped back down to all its fluffy mates and Milly may well have looked bereaved but Kevin was on the point of bursting into tears because it's funny how this sort of silly thing can really get a hold of you, you know. Later, Kevin bought her a little black and white stuffed kitten from a gloating vendor on the promenade: ten more quid.

And then Milly dragged him on to the beach – just had to paddle, didn't she? It was at this point that Kevin wondered whether she might be overdoing it all; it was almost as if she was screen-testing for the role of blissful gamine with goofy guy at loose on the glittering coast, but she seemed genuine enough, in truth. He held her shoes and he held her waist and the sea rushed up towards them and that was fine for her but Kevin's shoes, naturally enough, were still laced up around his feet and *yes* they were the old suede ones which had been sulking anyway since the oyster incident (no great loss – pleased to see the back of them) but it wasn't the best time in the world to be writing them off for the simple reason that he had nothing else to wear and if you've never actually had the sea coursing into your brogues there is little point in trying to convey the sensation but I can say this: what is worse, far worse, than the attendant squelch which of course you would expect, is the firm conviction that whatever it is, amok and oleaginous around your soles, it is

200

surely something worse, far worse, than water. You don't even want to think about it. He bought some truly disgraceful grey slip-on sort of moccasin things somewhere seriously cheap and slung the soggy suede numbers onto a municipal tip.

They shared a cloud of Cartland pink and sticky candy floss – like so much loft insulation, to Kevin's way of thinking – and there was plenty of rock in the shop (bright and blinding cylinders, tactile in cellophane) and if Kevin is honest then he did momentarily contemplate buying a stick for Emily. As a joke. That's when he decided not to: they didn't do jokes, Kevin and Emily – and just think how he'd feel when she cracked it round the side of his skull.

Finally Milly allowed the two of them back to the hotel – though she was still mourning the loss of a large, round pebble that Kevin had handed to her as she was paddling. She had dropped it, and then decided that it was the most precious thing on earth and actually had Kevin groping around in the hissing surf *looking* for the thing (only I, thought Kevin – as his cuffs became comical – could be detailed to hunt for a stone on a shingled shoreline). And his gag about there being plenty more pebbles on the beach? Forget it: this wasn't just *any* old pebble, apparently. Women did this sort of thing, Kevin knew, might be a good sign, though. Might be good for later – that on top of the little black and white stuffed kitten – and no, he hadn't forgotten any of that touch of aphrodisia chatter in English's.

So: back at the hotel. Did Milly have any spot of bother with the funny little lock? She did not; Kevin could have been meddling with it for half the night, as well he knew, so he was grateful to be in (wanted a shower – Christ this room is absolutely *baking*: how do you turn this damn thing down?). Milly was on the phone in a jiffy and ordering steaks and chips and salads and ooh look crèmes brulées and champagne, of course champagne, but natch.

Kevin was absolutely sure he was looking forward to all this. Wasn't he? Of course he was: what could be sweeter? But even by denying fear, he knew he was summoning it up. It wasn't a question of being afraid or not being afraid – he had found out that much in the past; no, it was the very word fear itself – as soon as it entered the head, didn't matter in what context, didn't matter if you spent ages doing all the Fear? Fear? I know not the meaning of the word type stuff, didn't matter at all. Once the worm of the word was embedded within, it would feed and gnaw and rise up and throttle the bleeding life out of you, no questions asked, and so although Kevin was ostensibly thinking to himself hm, steak and chips, that'll be nice, better go easy on the champagne, though (Fear! Too much booze and you'll be useless), and Christ it really *is* hot in here (Fear! How can I do it if I'm panting with the heat?) and yes I really think I'll feel better after a nice cool shower (Fear! What if I test out my body part and it doesn't bloody work?) – yes, although all this was ambling casually through the brain, the simple word called Fear (as I think we have seen) had clearly done with lurking and had now begun to pounce.

The water coursed over him as he pointed up his chin to the shower head: never knew why he did that as he hated getting the spray into any facial orifice and so to make sure that never happened he had to snap on a tight and grimly determined smile of tacit acceptance (bravely making the best of a bad job, sort of style) as well as shut down his eyelids and thus he was when Milly darted in an arm in order to slap his little buttock and so utterly startled and instinctively modest was our Kevin that he shrieked once first and then hauled around him the slimy shower curtain whereupon all the little fasteners at the top of the rail went plop plop plop plop as the entire bloody thing caved in all around him and Milly was laughing her head off and not just because Kevin was wetly batting at the curtain as if fending off a footpad but also because Oh God look! You know those little plastic shower caps that we all assumed no human being could ever wear? Meet the one who does!

All right: joke over, shut the bathroom door, give the lad a bit of privacy. Good. Kevin was dry now, warm as toast (warm as a bloody foundry, in point of fact), the steaks had been munched and most of the champagne was gone again: champagne had this amazing habit of *going*. And now all that he had yearned for could not be put off another minute. That's how he saw it. You see the way the worm was worming?

Milly had taken off all her clothes and she was standing before him and his eyes travelled up from the gentle tangle between her legs to a slim but rounded belly and nipples not much smaller than the breasts they advertised. Her eyes were alight and she said Kevin and Kevin said Milly which was fine and dandy as far as it went but not much mustard could ever be cut if this went on for too much longer and it was Milly now who was moving towards the queen-size bed (would be, would be) and Kevin followed her, of course he did, and Milly was in between the sheets by now and Kevin was shall we say barely behind her. And I know it sounds impossible, given the circumstances (though maybe not, given the bloke), that the very first thing to shoot into Kevin's mind the second he was alongside her was blimey O'Reilly there must be four blankets minimum on this sodding bed, at least one of them cellular, and then they go and put this bloody great quilted eiderdown on the top of it all and the room's already like an oast-house doing the business and Christ I'll pass out before I even touch base – impossible, maybe, but this *is*, I have to say, the fact of the matter – and OK, now Milly was reaching for him with long pale arms so his mind was well on the way to relegating the matter of heat to some back burner but now the very thought that not only was he far from physically aroused but that whatever manhood he had once possessed was now cowering amid shelters he knew not existed (and quite likely whimpering badly into the bargain) filled him with such straight, pure uncut white Fear as to make every other part of his body stiffen as if starched which can only, he philosophized (oh – so much later), be God's idea of some sort of a gag.

Milly was so sweet. Milly was so tender. Milly was so bloody determined that Kevin did not think he could stand it. The more women did all these sorts of things ('at times like these' – aargh!) that the more in-your-face magazines told them to do, the more the pressure on types like Kevin became intolerable. The worm had invaded all of his intestines and was making its way round to his throat. True there was a vague sort of tingling thing dancing almost in tune with down there where it mattered, but if ever a body was subject to a wildcat, right lads (down tools) anarchic striking work-to-rule go-slow then surely it was here and now – and so because of all that there could, alas, be no forming of a union.

Milly said it didn't matter (Did!); Milly said it happened a lot (Didn't!); Milly said he was overtired (Wasn't!); Milly said it would be different in the morning. Oh God: she said what? She said it didn't matter, happened a lot – no no, got all that: the last bit, the last bit – what was that last bit she said? She said it would be different in the morning. That's what I thought you said she said; oh God well that's that, then. Fear! Fear! Fear! Fear! *Calm*, Kevin *calm*: look, she's drifting off to sleep now. It's OK now – yes, I think she's asleep. What about a bit of that for yourself? It has been quite a day. Yes, thought Kevin, it has. It has, really. Yes.

He lay like an ironing board intent upon the ceiling, just one sheet across him, Milly near indecipherable under all the rest. Couldn't see the ceiling – too dark. He wanted to become excited, now the threat had passed, determined to wake up Milly pronto because you couldn't just whistle up this sort of thing to order, you know, as I believe has been sadly demonstrated. But no – nothing. Soon he thought he rather could make out vestiges of the ceiling: yes, hours had drifted by, and now the dense and none-too-comforting shawl of a night with a stranger on alien ground might just have begun to be teasingly tweaked away from him, admitting a shadowy and colder other world of only dimly perceived and round-shouldered potential. The night had all but passed, and now Kevin was making out the nameless forms of unfamiliar things. Milly, whom he loved, is still asleep beside him – unaware that yesterday was gone, and that new and awful thing that followed it is here again. There's the wardrobe, there's the dressing-table: look at that chair, with all our clothes nearly piled up on it And there's the vid-*ay*-o.

Daylight come, but I don't wanna go home.

Everything about the morning had been just terrible: the I-suppose-we'd-better-get-up routine (get up out of bed, that is, because contrary to Milly's assurance that come the raw day things would be different, things quite naturally were not at all) and then all the little smiles of shared consolation that Milly kept darting across to him throughout a dispirit-ing breakfast. She *should* have been looking at him long and smoulderingly, liquid eyes swimming darkly amid pools of luscious memory, and it was his fault she couldn't, Kevin well acknowledged that. But his feelings for Milly were now maybe even more intense than they were before, because the awfulness of the endless night, just lying next to Milly and sensing her warmth, had bonded her to him in a way he did not fully understand, and although he was quite sure Milly was feeling not one jot of any of this, there was always a chance (there was, wasn't there, always a chance?) that maybe she might feel *something*, anyway. Apart from let down. And during the long drive back to London, Kevin was doing his best to find out:

'Milly, I'd really like you to know a bit of what I feel,' said Kevin – but Milly made no reply, not even of the non-committal 'would you?' or 'really?' variety, and certainly several miles away from anything encouraging; vexing, actually, because it had taken about two silent sheets of motorway since that last roundabout back there for Kevin to formulate in his head even this one opening sentence and he surely wasn't prepared to let fly with another although he well knew too that this journey, this journey back, could well be it, one way or another. So he was astounded to hear himself cutting to the quick:

'I *love* you, Milly,' is what he said next. 'I really, really *love* you.' He sighed, before tacking on, 'Sorry.'

Milly was looking at him now, and he surely felt it: would have loved to turn and face her so as to at least have some hope of reading whatever if anything there was for him there, but any larks of that order would have the Espace in a ditch in no time with Emily's antiques strewn across Sussex and maybe even Kevin and Milly sweetly dead together, and possibly smiling. Oh but *please* don't let her say what Sophie had said – please don't do this to Kevin, not after last night, please don't do it. If Milly came out with anything on the lines of her being very *fond* of Kevin, if there was even a hint of affectionate hopelessness within her wide and honest eyes, then truly Kevin could not bear it – this would really be more than Kevin could handle the second time around and really I do feel sure that any such response on Milly's part would surely break even more than Kevin's heart.

'What did you say?!' barked out Kevin now: he thought he had heard, kind of did hear what she said, but by God he had to be sure of it in order to get even a part of his mind around this because, let's face it, his mind was among the things currently on the line.

'I said,' repeated Milly with tender patience, 'that I love you too.'

Emily had absolutely and utterly had it: nothing to do with all this Lolita business, God no – in the light of this terrible, terrible thing that had, God, so recently happened any thoughts of Lolita stood no chance at all. Nor was she still spitting and fuming over the fact that fucking Kevin had apparently instructed Arnold to spray-paint the bloody dresser after Jim had spent days and days distressing the pale blue paintwork to resemble eighteenth-century French farmhouse style and can you believe that Kevin had thought it looked *scruffy*, didn't seem to understand that that was how it was *meant* to look the fucking dolt and now it was obliterated under two coats of bleeding Dulux fucking brilliant bloody white and although that had sent Emily spiralling into orbit she had thought that any blood vessels not already bulging magenta would surely erupt into a fountain of lava when on top of this she had seen the *lighting*, the *lighting* at the flat and she just simply couldn't, couldn't *believe* it: in the living-room there were about thirty bloody picture lights – it looked like an installation of picture lights in a go-ahead gallery – and didn't Kevin understand the *size* of Piranesi etchings for the love of Christ?! So more than half of those would have to go and that meant the bloody walls were consigned to buggery but never mind *that*, never mind *that* – the bedrooms looked like a provincial b & b with their stupid little central pendants and the rest of the flat was lit like a fucking underground car-park and hadn't Raymond then rung up and said in fact he *wasn't* coming over (he didn't mention that the police had

207

just been) and Emily had just said *good* – and she didn't mention either that the police had just been, but they *had*, they *had*, and this is what was so terrible and now she had just *told* Kevin this, Kevin who had at last seen fit to return from his little seaside holiday, and Kevin – instead of *doing* something, instead of just *doing* something, he had bloody stood there and said:

'You're joking!'

And that was that. That was just the end of it for Emily and she flew at him screaming – had to knock Shelley out of the bloody way first because Shelley had perceived the true danger before Kevin had even had time to duck but even a wilful and determined Shelley was no sort of obstacle to a wild and demented Emily and Kevin was simply knocked to pieces before he even hit the ground and now her fists were pummelling into his face and it was blood that he was tasting, blood, and even his forearms thrown up in protection were bruised and flagging from this numbing assault and the salt of his tears was stinging into a cut open mouth and only now was Shelley managing to drag Emily from the thrashed and flailing form of her battered father and although Emily was content now to be away from the affray she was still twitching and sputtering and yes she was crying too but it was in deep and physical pain that Kevin was now moaning because he had never been so much hurt before in his life, and his eyes were alive only with horror.

It took ages for everyone to act as if they had more or less calmed down, but even after well over an hour, Kevin was feeling he might take the rest of his life to *heal*. The truth was plain, though – what had happened, this thing with the police, was so deeply serious (seemed deeply serious to Kevin, Emily and Shelley, anyway), that even this very harrowing domestic incident (and if Kevin was not still one pulsating and livid wound he would not have believed it could have happened), even this was quite secondary to the fact that Adam was as we speak in police custody, very probably facing charges of theft and whatever the name was of the Detective Sergeant had implied (Emily had stuck his card somewhere) maybe more: even *worse*, was the message that Emily had received, but no one would elaborate.

'But why can't we *see* him?' asked Kevin for the second or third time. Even talking hurt.

'I *told* you, I've *told* you,' came back Emily, now sounding more weary than anything. 'He's got some lawyer there, apparently, probably no damn good, and – oh God – they're *interviewing* him, can you believe it? I mean this is our *Adam*, we're talking about, Kevin, for God's sake. Adam!'

Kevin nodded: was indeed.

'And Ben's there too, did I say that?' went on Emily. 'Christ – Julian'll have a fit.' A sardonic twist of the mouth came and went. 'Separate rooms. Christ alone knows what *Ben* will say to them.'

'But surely there's nothing for either of them *to* say,' protested Kevin, holding his ribs as undemonstratively as possible. 'I mean it seems perfectly reasonable to me – why *shouldn't* they have won the money on the Lottery? Lots of people *do*.'

Emily sighed. 'I know, I know – that's what I kept *telling* them, but they went on about all these muggings and burglaries and God knows what else and most of them are committed by young boys, usually – but Jesus, what has that got to do with *Adam*? I mean, what – are they going to arrest every young boy in the country just because he's got money on him? It's *absurd*. We've got to *do* something, Kevin. Got to.'

Yes, Kevin was aware of that – but *what* to do, that was the question. Always was.

'Well,' he started up, 'until they've decided whether or not to press *charges* . . .'

Shelley spoke now: Shelley was still there, not saying anything until now. She had been just looking at Kevin and Emily, one and then the other: first her father, and then her mother. Just looking at them.

'How long can they keep him?' she threw in. 'I mean, without charging him.'

Emily shook her head 'I'm not sure of the legal . . . I tried phoning Partington but he's on a *golfing* holiday, would you believe. I mean, the only time you *need* a bloody solicitor and he's buggered off somewhere playing bloody *golf.* And no one else there seems to know anything. But the police person, detective person, said that tomorrow morning – oh God that means Adam's going to be in that dreadful place all *night*, Kevin, oh God. Tomorrow *morning*,' she forced herself to resume. 'they'll either be letting him go, or . . . and they said something about going through *evidence* and there could be *witnesses* . . . oh Jesus it was all like some ghastly TV programme. *You*, of course, weren't even here,' she accused Kevin. 'You were busy having fun at the bloody *seaside*.'

'Dad didn't know,' muttered Shelley.

'Could've left a number,' said Emily equally quietly; it didn't really matter now – it was only conversation. They were all just saying things in the wake of shock; some people made endless pots of tea, they made idle conversation. It filled the air.

It seemed to Kevin that there was nothing to do but wait, but it was always he who eventually had to draw these negative conclusions and so he thought possibly if I keep quiet someone else might say it. Well no one did, but maybe each of them had more or less independently reached a similar conclusion: talk of action withered away.

'And what on earth did Adam imagine he was *doing* in

that awful little knocking shop?' Emily wanted to know. 'You'd have thought he would've had more sense – walking in there and flashing his money around all those bloody little tarts. How did he even *find* such a place?'

Not difficult: he and Ben had been drinking again, lusting after girls, and some older bloke had said tell you what, buy us in a couple of rounds and I'll take you to a place where there are girls who'll do *anything* and Adam had said Yeah? Great, OK, yeah and Ben had said Oh I don't know, Adam, are you sure? And Adam had done that lightish cuff on his face again and said *Course* I'm sure – come on. And it was true: in that dank little basement just off Goodge Street, aswirl with decades old bedroom carpet, there were girls upon whom dark red lamps shed a kindly light who would have done anything at all for the hundreds of pounds that Adam and Ben were each waving around (nearly a ton had already been blown on Spumante) but a windy management put them back out into the street because Christ Almighty they were only bloody *kids* and it didn't do to upset the comfy relationship with the local Bill and a phone call later they were nicked in the nearby alley and Emily has more or less told you all the rest.

Shelley put two bottles of the rather good red on the table (Emily thought she had been saving them for something, but she couldn't remember what, now) and it was amazing – maybe not – how quickly they went down. Shelley was thinking of it as something of a Last Supper without the food, because although she had mentioned it to neither Kevin nor Emily (what would have been the point? Even less point now) she was finally set to move into her rather super place in Belsize Park. The fumblings with Julian had finally tipped the financial balance – though whether the deal would hold good in the light of his son Ben in all probability spending the rest of his days breaking asunder rocks in Alcatraz would have to remain to be seen. Would it make a difference? Shelley couldn't see why it should. So. Leaving. Moving out. Bliss. And maybe even tomorrow. Yes, in spite of all this, maybe even tomorrow.

Emily looked sideways at Kevin from time to time, sipping wine, saying nothing, maybe wanting to catch his eye; Kevin was aware, but determined to keep his eye on the loose. He knew that a momentary fusion of glances would constitute all he would ever get in the way of apology, but he didn't wish to be a party to any of that. The terrible aching in his body, the tightness of his lacerated mouth, they all amounted to the battle honours of the moral victor, and they would brook no hint of dilution. And had his injuries played a part in his decision? His *decision*, did you say? His *decision*? Yes indeed – his decision: *Kevin's* decision (good, isn't it?). Could be – don't know. So tell me, the nature of this decision being . . .? Oh big: he's leaving Emily. For Milly. And maybe even tomorrow. Yes, in spite of all this, maybe even tomorrow.

CHAPTER SEVEN

Raymond was in his study, trying to reason with Amanda. I know; uphill struggles aren't even in it. Easier to reason with a horde of marauding dingos, I should have said, but he just *had* to, didn't he, make her see the awful insanity of what she truly did appear to regard as an utterly workable game plan – the dumping of Maureen in the street with a suitcase, with similar treatment meted out to Rosie immediately on her return from the dead – or maybe just smother her with a pillow if only to satisfy any vestiges of curiosity over whether or not the woman is actually killable (could be the first of a new breed of crackpot immortals) – *and* somehow manage all that without directly calling to attention the fact that Amanda herself was seriously unhinged because he was not at all sure he could cope again with any of her Norman Bates impersonations (and he certainly wasn't about to allude to *that* or they'd be spending the next week deciding who the actor was who played the private investigator who goes up the stairs so slowly in that horrible and creepy house and all you hear are the creaks on the treads and then there's that screechy scary music and down comes the knife in tune with the basso effect and his eyes bulge out and he could be dead now, think he is – the actor, I mean).

'Godsake, Amanda – be *reasonable*.'

That's what he was reduced to, now, after – oh God, *ages* and *ages* of pointless chat. There she was, rattling on about eviction and maybe murder (why not? Could get to like it) and then turning the house into one of Emily's designered set pieces and following that the blissful cohabitation of a

213

man on the brink and a truly dippy woman who *loved* him, do you see (but not in that way). And this was on top of all the *police* business – that endless and terrifying little interview with the police. Oh God oh God – at one point he thought he was *finished*. OK, granted, it was all quite neutral and concerned at the beginning – but it was terribly important, the more senior of them kept on stressing, that they subject the ransom letter to every conceivable analysis; ah yes – the ransom letter.

'The letter, no: don't have it, I'm afraid.'

God – they had looked so *stern*.

'No,' banged on Raymond. 'Left it with Amanda's father, I seem to recall. Yes, pretty sure of that.'

'The gentlemum remembers otherwoys,' said DS Someone; he could pronounce all his vowels all right, but chose to put them into all the wrong words. And what a suit – just look at it. 'He is toutally convinced otherwoys, in point of fack.'

'Really? Well there you go. Anyway – I'm quite sure I don't have it. Are you *positive* he hasn't got it?'

Oh God – it was in Raymond's inside pocket, the bloody letter, and Raymond even as he daringly spoke was willing it to be absorbed through his skin, blood and ribcage and embed itself into his lower intestine.

'Maybe he or I have, um, mislaid it?'

Well no, OK – neither policeman actually repeated the words 'mis*laid* it' in tandem and replete with an exclamation mark as if on cue as the chorus in a pantomime, but the mingled horror and disbelief was perfectly plain for anyone to see – and Christ, you should have seen their bloody faces when Amanda popped up from behind the sofa and dropped her particular bombshell – did I tell you that Amanda was still hanging around? Well she was (just as bloody well as things turned out) and this is what she said:

'It doesn't actually matter any more, the letter, because I'm back. As you can see.'

Not a single penny was dropping, though: not quite yet.

'And who my chew be, Miss?'

'Amanda. I am Amanda. I was the one –'

'*You're* the one who –?!'

'*If* you would let me finish,' interjected Amanda with acid (oh Christ please don't let her have a machete about her person, prayed Raymond now, or else these two young coppers are so much meaty history). 'I am, as you now have gathered, the Amanda who was kidnapped. Yes. And now I'm back.'

That was the only thing Raymond and Amanda had briskly thrashed out during the time it had taken the policeman to climb the stairs (rather faster than that *Psycho* actor, the one with the eyes, you know the one I mean).

'I can say it was a *joke*,' Amanda had said. 'A practical joke on Daddy.'

'No,' insisted Raymond, '*no*! I'm the bloody one who played the fucking so-called practical joke, aren't I? They'll slam me away. Your father will sue me. Kill me. No – It *can't* be a joke, policemen don't *get* jokes. Christ.'

'OK,' conceded Amanda. 'Then I'll just say I'm back.'

'Sow,' said the policeman slowly – a slightly nervous glance in the direction of his colleague, who had his mouth so wide open you would think he was in training to suck a doorknob. 'You're back. They release chew, then, did thy? Can you give us descriptions? Now where they hell jew?'

'Round the waist,' replied Amanda. 'But only the once.'

The policeman fair goggled at Amanda now, a palsied tic to the left of one eye possibly no more than just a visible suspicion that maybe someone could be taking the rise, putting on the wind-up, extracting the Michael – that style of thing?

'Oy mean,' he intoned with heavy patience, 'what oy mean is do you have any inform-eye-tion on where you were kept jawring your ordeal? How long did they keep you, in point of fack?'

Hm – what a lot of questions. Raymond was as pleased as anything that he wasn't the one who had to answer them. Though he might chuck this in, though, for what it was worth:

'I'm so relieved you're back, Amanda. So very happy.'

'Yeah – quiet, Raymond. No, I'm afraid I don't think I can give you any real leads. What – catching them, you mean? Before they strike again. Yes. But you see I was snatched in the dark and I had a black bag over my head – not *before* I was snatched, of course, no, that would be silly – *they* put it over me, you see? The black bag. At least I *think* it was black – couldn't actually see, you see.'

This is, has to be, the policeman was thinking. This just had to be a wind-up, right?

'What about sands?' he went on doggedly.

'Sand? No – no sand,' replied Amanda. *Sand?* What's the silly fucker talking about *sand* for?

'Sow, you didn't actually hear anything. No sands?'

'Oh no, I see: no I didn't hear anything at all – no sounds. They plugged my ears.'

'They plugged your ears,' echoed the policeman.

Amanda nodded. 'With earplugs,' she clarified.

'Was it a long journey to wherever thy took you, would you sigh? Or nop.'

'Oh God yes it was *hours*,' supplied Amanda readily. 'Oh God yes. I mean at one point I thought God, we'll drive off the edge of the British Isles at this rate! Maybe we did – maybe we went in the tunnel to France. I do recall a faint smell of onions.'

Raymond nearly had a seizure. A faint smell of onions!

'You smelt,' said the policeman, in his now-let's-just-get-this-absolutely-right voice, 'onions.'

Amanda nodded, her eyes wide with you'd-better-believe-it. 'They didn't plug my nose, you see. Just my ears. Maybe could have been shallots.'

'But you can't have had this bag on all the toym.'

'Did. They kept it on me.'

'What abaht wem you ite?'

'Except when I ate,' allowed Amanda. 'But then it was in a completely dark room: no windows. Not nice food, either,' rattled on Amanda, quite getting into the stride of the thing. 'Some sort of gruelly soup.' And Raymond thought oh Christ *steady*, Amanda, *steady*, just before she tacked on, 'maybe that was the smell of onions.'

The policeman sighed (as well he might).

'Did jew get the impression there was more than one mam? More than two? Big people, were they?'

'Two at least,' decided Amanda, after a bit of a pause (yeah let's have two, why not?), 'because there was a bit of frog-marching at the outset. Big? I don't know about that. Averagely big, I suppose.' And then, with such a livid grin of inspiration, '*Raymond's* sort of size, I would say at a guess.'

Raymond grinned weakly; he'd just stubbed out his very last cigarette so he groped in his jacket (no, not *that* pocket) for his bottle of pills and crammed half a handful of those into his mouth instead. First thing, first thing as soon as these bloody coppers have gone (they *would* go some time, wouldn't they? Before Raymond died of old age or anxiety, whichever hijacked him the soonest), first thing was to drive just anywhere and buy some corner shop's entire bloody stock of cigarettes; maybe even get the screwball Amanda to pie for them – *pay* for them, he meant: Christ this bloody policeman was *invading* him and why wouldn't he just conclude that here was a case that simply would not be cracked because let's face it the perpetrator of this erstwhile kidnapping *wasn't* going to strike again, was he? No – but he wouldn't bloody mind being kidnapped himself, wouldn't mind at all: I wish, thought Raymond, I wish someone would plug *my* ears and put a black bag over my head (or any colour, really) but OK, I confess, I'm not too keen on the onion gruel side of things and do you know I think the time has come when I think I might finally be losing my *mind*?!

Oh great. Cop number one was clicking shut his biro, and cop number two was clicking shut his gob, so intent was he on excavating the inside of a hirsute and unsavoury ear prior to taking his leave (couldn't do two things at once). Cop number one was thinking. Not even worth logging on to the computer but bloody *have* to, of course. Nah. Maybe I'll hit lucky and walk into a couple of blokes in le bleeding Shuttle with a bagful of earplugs and chewing on an onion (or could maybe have been a shallot). Anyway – at least the bitch was back. Can't actually imagine anyone *wanting* her back: stuck-up bloody bitch. Wouldn't mind giving her one, though: bet she's a little wriggler (no, as a matter of fact, Raymond could have contradicted him: more of a back-stabber, actually).

They left ('If any other detile comes to moynd, down't hesitite to give us a caw') and Amanda said Silly fucking plonkers when the door was shut behind them and Raymond said nothing – he was just so relieved to see the back of them – but he was thinking Christ Almighty I'll never get used to this girl saying fucking, like that.

Emily was sitting at the kitchen table feeling absolutely wretched; tea was cold. A blend of Lapsang and something else, something she couldn't remember, and the cups were Royal Worcester: she had bought four, with their saucers – where now? *God* I feel so utterly, utterly . . . oh *why* did all this have to happen? Why wouldn't they *call*? All night Emily had been upstairs, downstairs, prowling, dreading thinking, incapable of stopping even for a second. Nearly the whole morning was gone now and they hadn't called;

they *said* they'd call but they hadn't. *She* had called, of course she had – from dawn onwards at half-hour intervals until the desk sergeant had really got quite tetchy and made it plain that the minute there was any news to impart she would be contacted and not, please, to phone again. A fair in Stratford, I think it was, those four Worcester cups – probably about 1820: not the *fair*, she even briefly smirked (although Christ I feel even older than that); no – the cups: she had verified it in Cushion's book of marks. But there *were* only about twenty minutes of the morning left because everyone knew that mornings ended at twelve but people are so *loose*, these days, aren't they? So loose about things like that. When she had got the Rayburn delivered – she remembered this quite clearly – they had said a.m. delivery and she had said right, then: before twelve and they had said no, an a.m. delivery can be any time up to two-thirty; it had come at gone three. God, Emily had been furious (you can well imagine) but it was a beautiful cooker, the Rayburn – very dark lakeland green. Reconditioned. Emily was a great one for reconditioning. And then *another* four cups had turned up (would you believe it?) in a little shop not a hundred yards away from her own front door – it wasn't often you could make up eight of these, that's really very rare. Down to seven now (it caused Emily physical pain to ponder this: she would never find more, not again – no one was going to be *that* lucky). Had Raymond known the upset he would cause when he pocketed the cup and saucer during whichever terrible afternoon he had felt impelled to do so, could he have seen into her features when she knew they were gone (at least she was spared the sight of his reversing the car over them – took three goes to align the wheels) then maybe he wouldn't have; maybe he would have, he might have even still: who ever knows?

Can't make any more tea, can't: don't want to drink it. Why don't they *phone*? Kevin will be back soon; even Kevin would be something, today – but it was, it was – it was Emily's fault that he was out: he hadn't wanted to be, had wanted to stay, but Emily had decided No – we've got to try and preserve *some* sort of normality, we can't just let everything slide away. So Kevin was dispatched to arrange the lounge and cocktail bar in The Grange Hotel: great, he thought – I have decided to leave my wife for (gosh, have I really?) Milly Milly Milly and my son is in the hands of the police and I am now on my way to hang up a bloody horse-collar in a cocktail bar. What about the ball, then? What about the ball tonight, Kevin had said, just before leaving. Emily passed a hand – shaky hand (no sleep, you see) – over her bulbous eyes and they stung her and she shivered just slightly and said Don't, don't – I can't even think about it: please just don't.

Well she simply couldn't wait a moment longer: it was just coming up to twelve and they *said*, they promised they'd ring and God this is the *police*, Christ help us: you were meant to be able to *trust* the police but then hey look if they're going to go around locking up innocent little kids just because they've struck lucky on the Lottery what hope is there left for the rest of us? Just you answer her that. I'll give it, decided Emily, just five more minutes; five minutes, and then that's that. And then she thought oh God oh God I need something simple to console me. Would a brandy be terrible? Can't, can't do that. I'll have a chocolatey-coffee drink, very vulgar; she took out a mug (no one, but no one, had ever seen any of *this* before) and she boiled up the kettle and she spooned into the really very silly mug (it had that cat, is it Garfield, that cat? Heaven knows where that had come from – maybe some old and jokey Easter egg, maybe) two quite large and rounded mounds of Charbonnel et Walker chocolate powder and then a much smaller sprink-ling of Nescafé (which must be ancient) and actually quite enjoyed gurgling in the boiling water – but not too high up, because milk was next and yes, a spoonful of double cream and finally two teaspoonfuls of sugar and oh my goodness I deserve this and just put it to your lips, Emily, and suck it in while it's hot hot hot and she did, she did, she sank half her mouth into it with gratitude and gingerly, just as one would one's whole aching body beneath the sweet foam of a Badedas bath after a long day's weeding – but then the contortion to which her lower face was now subject injected her brain with a jerking surprise and she spat out and recoiled from her great big friendly warm mug of help while snatching up the sugar bowl and the hit of it was enough to have her crying out *Salt*! Fucking salt! I'll fucking kill that Lolita, if I ever see her again.

Emily hurtled the whole mess into the sink – yes, mug and all – with tears itching the back of her eyes and *now* she was going to ring those bloody officious policemen you bet your bloody life she was because it was her *son*, actually – it's my *son* you've got there, holding there, my Adam – and you've no right, no right, because he's mine, he's mine – he's not bloody yours, he's mine! And she dialled the number and it was engaged and she dialled it again and it was *still* fucking engaged and so should she maybe go down there, should she? Sort it all out in person. What's bloody Partington have to be doing in Spain playing bloody *golf* when he was for the first time in his useless bloody life needed here and now?! Emily dialled the number again and exhaled hissingly at the bloody engaged tone but hey that was a key in the front door now and of course it's going to be Kevin saying can't do it, couldn't do it, Emily, *please* come and do the arrangement, Emily, but at least he was *back* the hopeless cretin so we had the car now and maybe if we *both* go down we can knock some sense into these bloody people – but it wasn't Kevin (wouldn't be) – but then it wouldn't be Adam either, would it? But it bloody was, you know – you just ask Emily about it later, the way her legs felt they were going and her face was wet all over from the one great tear that had been longing for so long to be shed, or else seep back inside her.

It took Emily just slightly longer than usual to suppress her immediate impulse – to rush up to Adam and take him in her arms, as it happens, and yes she was surprised to be charged by the urge, but the flicker was gone now because she had snuffed it out.

'So,' she said – quite like Emily. 'You're back.'

'Hi, Mum,' said Adam, looking if anything happier than ever.

'You had us worried half to death. What did they do to you there? Christ Almighty, if they think they're going to get away with this – just keeping you, just keeping you like that . . . what did they say? What *happened*, Adam?'

'Any chance of a cup of tea?'

'Make it if you want it. Answer me, Adam: what happened?'

Adam clattered around with the kettle (yuk – what a disgusting mess in the sink: never seen a mess in the sink before) and he was thinking Yeh, good question – what *did* happen, actually, cos I was shit-scared and I really thought I'd had it and I was thinking Christ knows what fucking Ben would be doing – weeping, probably – but Jesus what with all the tests and the samples . . . *that's* what was worrying Adam, late last night: that's what was making him nearly piss himself. He'd twigged quite early on that just the *money* was nothing: it wasn't thousands, after all – only a few hundred. Could they check out the Lottery story? It was such a crap explanation. Just stick with it – have to, now: what can they prove?

'So – Adam, is it? Yeh – Adam. What sweet old lady did you nick this little lot off, then – ay?'

'I never nicked anything. I *told* you.'

'I *know* you told me – I *know* you told me, my son, and

quite frankly me and my friend here are getting very tired of hearing it. That right, Frank? Yeh, that's right – Frank agrees with me, see. So what it is, what it is is time to change the record, isn't it my son, and tell us where you *really* got the money. We'll understand, won't we, Frank? Course we will. I mean – not the end of the world, is it? Young lad – wants a bit of action, no loot, still at school – well, almost natural, in't it? Purse, handbag – nip in a back door. Not the end of the *world*, is it? Tell us, son. You can't shock us – we've heard it all, mate. Right, Frank? You just tell us, ay? Then we can all have a nice cup of tea.'

'I *told* you –'

'Oh dear. Oh dear. Oh dear oh dear oh dear. I think we've got one here who's hard of thinking, Frank. What chummy here don't get is that we already *know* where you got the money, see? But if we don't have it from your own sweet lips then believe me, it's going to go very badly against you. Don't think I'm telling porkies, neither.'

Adam had hesitated. Did they know? Had Ben blurted? Earlier – an hour earlier, just after fingerprinting – they'd told him to take off all his gear and there he was standing on a circle of white paper and some sort of doctor geezer was combing at his skin and taking a brush to all his clumps of hair and paring his fingernails and generally collecting a regular sandstorm of what even Adam plainly saw as one whole bucket of evidence. He remembered his hair tearing in the old man's grasp; remembered the livid scratch on his arm as the bloody old man had gripped him tight while Adam was kicking the legs from under him. Ben would probably be all right: he just kicked the bastard a dozen times in the face; Ben would have noticed if there'd been blood on his Docs. Ben was very particular about those DMs of his. But they'd asked about the scratch, course they had, and Adam had said Scratch? Oh that – hadn't even noticed: just a scratch – and one of them had repeated that: just a scratch, he'd said, and Adam's mouth had maybe trembled just a bit but all he had said was Yeah.

And then later – when all the fake avuncular and wide-faced questions were still coming at him, Adam felt a good deal better: bluffing, right? Course they were bloody bluffing: if they'd matched any of his, Christ – I don't know, hairs, skin bits, whatever – to the bloke he robbed and beat the hell out of, then they'd be kicking him around right now, making formal charges and telling him he wouldn't be back on the streets till he was old and grey and Mummy and Daddy are going to be none too pleased with you are they, chum (should have thought of that before) – and you've heard, have you? Maybe you haven't. Have you heard about these young offenders places? You haven't? Then believe me, son, you don't wanna know, you really don't wanna know. But they weren't – they weren't doing any of all that: they wanted to frighten him into confessing to anything at all, really – at least then the bloody paperwork wouldn't be a complete fucking write-off – and it was then that Adam determined to say nothing at all. He knew that Ben could blow it any minute, of course, but he couldn't do anything about Ben, could he? Had to try and look after himself.

So he was only half surprised the following morning (*this* morning – ha! I'm *out*, you stupid bastards!) when one or other of these dozy morons had sloped in and said Sling it, go on – sling it. But don't get cocky, son, because we're looking at you so close it's like a telescope up your bloody arse; go on – sling it. And Adam had thought well Jesus Aitch Christ – so much for all their forensic and their computers and their bloody testing – Christ, if they can't put this little lot together then you could be Jack the bloody Ripper and you wouldn't have a fear or a care in the world.

But the truth is there *were* no samples and bodily detritus to match with those of Adam, and nor was his oppportunis-

224

tic and, as it turned out, pretty bloody violent robbery even
under investigation – for the simple reason that their victim
was still – even now, as Adam was swaggering home – lying
in the hall of his house in exactly the same position as he had
been when Adam had crashed home the door behind him,
near asphyxiated by the greatest high that had so far
wooshed into his life.

Adam answered Emily's question like this:

'They didn't do anything to me, Mum. Nothing happened
because I didn't *do* anything. Winning the Lottery's not
against the law, is it? They should've believed me in the first
place.'

No, thought Emily, no it's not – but there's no way on
God's earth that you won a penny of that money, no there
isn't – and you just let me tell you this: I didn't believe a
word of any of *that* crap, not for a single bloody second.

Emily got Adam to ring Kevin at the hotel and tell him the
news – and also (tell him) that the ball is now very much on
– you bet it is – and so (tell him) to make sure he's back in
plenty of time. And *you're* coming tonight as well, Adam –
no buts! I said *no* – no argument; you can wear your father's
old suit – on you it might even look good. I don't *care*
whether you want to go or not, Adam – when you're
eighteen you can do as you please. I can't *explain* what I
mean, Adam, and frankly I'm getting very bored: you're
coming and that's the end of it: I just want you somewhere
where I can see you.

Well Kevin was very relieved by the Adam side of things
(how could they ever have suspected Adam of any such
thing?) and also, if they *hadn't* released him, what was it that
Kevin had been expected to do? He'd been racking his
brains all night – sleep was a no-no, what with Emily's

stalking and tea-making – and by morning he'd come up with nothing, absolutely zero. So, we can forget about Adam, then (phew) so – what about Milly? There was only one down side to this Milly caper, so far as Kevin could see: *yes*, she had said she loved him . . . oooh, sorry, sorry to do this – but for Kevin, just for Kevin's sake: shall we run that by just one more time? *Yes*, she had said she loved him (yipes!) but his plan actually to decamp with her this very day possibly erred on the side of the impetuously optimistic in that he hadn't, it must be said, actually, um, *put* it to her, not as yet. So anyway, here's how Kevin's future plans Mark 2 are currently looking: *go* to the ball (at least *she'll* be there) and then maybe tomorrow when Emily's got it all out of her system, then maybe tomorrow is the time to – well, make the break. But where would he and Milly go? But what would he and Milly live on? But when would – oh stop, don't, *don't*: you *know* he hasn't thought through any of this – the man's been in a state of trauma: let him just enjoy the moment, because you never know with moments – sometimes they last next to no time. And another thing: his ribs and his face and his arms were absolutely killing him because let me tell you, that ferocious assault on his wellbeing might just have slipped the minds of some, but as he stooped down now to heft up the diver's helmet (ah yes, the diver's helmet – now it was *in situ*, as it were, Kevin was none too sure) let me underline to you it was very much to the fore of his.

He put it down again. He sat on a chair. It was a nice chair – one of a pair; not one of *his* purchases, of course – they were, as I say, nice: ebonied and leggy, touch of Chinese fretwork, yellow silk pads (*très chic, non?*). Emily had said to use them imaginatively (what – hang them on a hook?) and maybe incorporate them into a subtly lit (yes – that again) oasis of style. Now look – was it just him or *what*? He simply couldn't get his mind round *any* of this; I mean, look – the walls were lovely (Emily had attended to them – self-stripe silk, looked like slabs of slippery underwear) and the carpet was lovely (Emily had attended to that: charcoal, deep as you like) and then sitting in the most godawful heap in the middle of it were side-tables and little shelf affairs and lamps and pictures and ornaments (all courtesy of Emily Taste plc) in addition to the contents of Steptoe's cart, as thoughtfully provided by Kevin; all that was missing was the bleeding horse. Had the collar, though.

Kevin had already hung on the wall a couple of rather strange mirrors: couldn't for a minute see the point of them. The actual reflective surface was convex, so as to render your face globular and leprous, while the frame was in the form of a gilded and epileptic sunburst, and for some reason quite beyond Kevin each of these surely misconceived and showy things was surmounted by a gold and aggressive eagle, wings akimbo – maybe they had once belonged to an American president? Who knew? Who knew why designers came up with mirrors you couldn't look into? So why not bung an eagle on top? What's to lose?

And hanging them had been far from a pushover. Kevin had decided that one each side of the fireplace would be as lovesome as anywhere (did toy with hanging them right next to each other, side by side, almost touching – the sort of thing Emily might do, but in the end he simply lacked the courage) and so he banged in one of those flat brass hook affairs with blue steel nails angled through the little holes and that went suspiciously well – the wall was penetratable, nothing snapped – and heigh ho, here we go, up it comes: here – a bloody silly golden hubcap (replete with eagle) was now quite firmly in its allocated designer-place. But could he get the other bleeder at exactly the same height? He could not; he could not even, until six goes and twelve holes in the wall had come and gone, get it at the *approximate* height – and then he did, yeah, that's sort of right if you close down one eye, but it's not *really* right, is it? I mean, there's a good couple of inches leeway there, isn't there? And you can hear Emily. You can hear the sort of thing she'd say: 'If you lack the imagination for anything but *symmetry*, Kevin, then precisely symmetrical is what it has to be. So take it down and do it *properly*, you insufferable little man.' Yeah, OK – Kevin obeyed the inner voice and took the bloody thing down and the silk wall behind looked like the backboard in a rifle range by this stage of the game but if he didn't bang in the next hook too far down all the holes would be covered (please!) so it shouldn't be too bad but no, no – *that* wasn't right either – it was too bloody *high* now and so Kevin went over to the first mirror and raised it but it was still too low and Kevin just looked at the pair of abominations squinting back at him lopsidedly from either side of the fireplace and he thought why, in fact, am I doing this? What exactly am I *doing* this for? It's not me – it's just not me, all this sort of thing.

Eventually he hit upon the ruse of bending upwards one of the hooks and wrapping a lump of paper around it and that more or less did the trick although the fixing, it had to be said, was now none too secure but it should be all right if no one entering the cocktail bar and lounge took it into their heads to breathe, or anything. Now then – what's next? These classy little black chairs – what about them? How about one each side of the fireplace, under the loony mirrors? Can't be bad. Wouldn't recommend that anyone sit in the one on the right-hand side, though, because if he raised his voice he could suffer a severe and concussive crack on the head due to the descent of said large and stupid mirror – but look, so long as he just spread everything around a bit, used it all up, that's all that could be reasonably expected of him, yes?

So he stuck the chairs there (tiptoeing with the one on the right-hand side) and then put up a selection of botanical prints on a few of the other walls (no, Emily, they're not *meant* to be aligned – I thought that if I staggered them then it would be infinitely more *interesting*) before turning his attention to various little coffee tables and a few more chairs and quite a lot of the junk from Milly's little shop, whatever it was called (the diver's helmet he stuck in the fireplace; what when they want to light the fire? Can't think about that now – heave the bloody thing out again, I suppose) and apart from the fact the chairs ended up miles away from the tables and even taking in to account that despite all his tweaking and fine tuning most of the stuff bore the haphazard air of being just *en passant* and awaiting collection, Kevin really thought the whole thing had gone as well as could feasibly be expected. There was, of course, still the little matter of the horse-collar; shame there weren't two, because then he could have bunged one on each side of the fireplace – propped up in readiness for the next pair of Staffordshire Punches who happened to idle through in quest of a dry martini. Oh Christ – what could he *do* with the thing? In the end he stuck it in the grate: under the diver's helmet. Well look – it was *different*, right?

Kevin was getting out of here: not much more horror left – that was the way to look at things (bright side, always think bright side) because as soon as this awful ball thing tonight was over all he had to do was, um, leave. Just go. Walk.

Yipes!

It really could be true, though (might well be), that by this time tomorrow, Kevin could be living quite a different life in quite a different place (where? Sh!) with (you bet) quite a different person: it was all a matter of arranging things. Just get tonight out of the way, and everything else will be fine and dandy. I wonder if Emily has collected my suit?

Yes she has: just hung it up to try and get rid of the creases –
God, you'd think these bloody people could at least have
given the thing a bit of a pressing. The trousers had had to
be shortened, while the sleeves, of course, needed to be
nearly an inch-and-a-half longer: why couldn't Kevin be
even remotely *normal*? God – the number of suits she had
ordered him to try on before she could pronounce one of
them even *vaguely* satisfactory: Emily had found the entire
business wholly exhausting, but then she had well appre-
ciated that here was going to be no fun day out – with Kevin,
it never was. And before they had even got to the tedium of
trying to find a halfway-OK dinner-suit, Emily had had to
undergo a severely long session of Kevin's customary
bovine oafishness and utter incomprehension which he
would wave like a standard whenever confronted with
style: it was so perfectly obvious what did and didn't suit the
man, so why was he so totally incapable of *seeing* it? And
(even more infuriating, if you can believe it) why – when
Emily simply *knew* what was right for him – did Kevin
always feel obliged to put up his token and feeble little male-
type arguments?

'I really don't think that's *me*, Emily, you know – I mean,
the check is so big, and the blue is really very –'

'It's *gingham*, Kevin – *gingham*. It's a classic pattern – it has
freshness, it has *ton*.'

'What about this one? This is a better blue – it's not so –'

'Kevin, that is a perfectly reprehensible, not to say shitty
little shirt. It is a middle-management-season-ticket-to-
Dorking of a shirt. The collar curls.'

'Well I don't see that . . .'

'No. You don't. Obviously. Now, Kevin – try on this jacket.
We're having the knitted ties.'

'Why *knitted* ties, Emily? Christ – have you seen the *price*
of this jacket? *Can't* be right. Four hundred quid for a
jacket?'

'You have to *pay* to get anything good. Mind you – I didn't see it was *that* much: I'm fucked if I'm paying that much for a jacket for *you*. Put it back.'

'Not sure I even *like* knitted ties . . .'

'No, Kevin – you favour the sort of tie that looks as if someone has spilt motor oil down it. Don't *argue*, blast you, Kevin – just be grateful I'm here to do the choosing for you. And the paying.'

'I quite like these trousers.'

'No you don't.'

'Right.'

'Anyway – you don't need trousers: we're not here for trousers. It was shirts and ties you needed – sick of seeing you walk around like a tramp – and maybe a jacket, but if they're all that sort of price you can forget it: make do with the ones you've got. But the *main* thing is –'

'I don't *mind* the ones I've got: I'm perfectly happy with the ones I've –'

'Don't bloody interrupt, Kevin! You're forever bloody *interrupting*, aren't you, you contemptible little creep? Hm? Now everyone's *looking* now – can't you see everyone looking? *As* I was saying, the main thing is the dinner-suit, so let's pay for these – or can we take them with us? Pay all at once. I'll ask the man. Anyway, let's get the bloody suit bought because I really need to get home and lie down. I really sometimes do not know why I even bother with you.'

'Are you *sure* I need another suit, Emily? I mean, it seems so silly when I've got one already. I mean, it's not as if I often have to wear a –'

'Kevin, we've been into all this. You've said all this and I have answered you. I am not buying the suit for my own selfish pleasure, Kevin: I do not enjoy forking out large amounts of my extremely hard-earned money on people like you, you know. It is simply – as I *think* I have already explained, though quite possibly one or two of the longer words may have confused you – the simple fact is that if I *have* to be seen with you, then I should prefer that you do not resemble a walking advertisement for a rummage sale – clear? I am not doing this for you – I am doing it for me.'

'*Is* for your own selfish pleasure, then.'

'Being facetious hardly becomes you, Kevin.'

'Right.'

'Are you coming or not?'

'Am, yes. Right.'

'Well come bloody *on*, then – Christ, I don't know what's *wrong* with you. Not *that* way, Kevin! It's not *that* way, is it? It says quite clearly that's the way to Beach & Leisurewear – God, the bloody sign is big enough. Don't think we're going to get a dinner-suit in Beach & Leisurewear, are we, Kevin? I mean we can *try*, by all means . . .'

'No, OK. Which way, then?'

'I mean, if you'd *like* to go to Beach & Leisurewear and see whether maybe they think dinner-suits are suitable for snorkelling . . .?'

'Yes, all right Emily: point made. Which way do we go, then?'

'Oh God, Kevin – you really are the last bloody word. You annoy me so bloody *much*. Just *follow* me, Kevin. I sometimes wonder whether I can put up with you for even another *day*.'

'Maybe you won't have to.'

'What did you say, Kevin? You're mumbling.'

'Nothing. I didn't say anything.'

'Well it *sounded* as if you did. Must be *extremely* interesting if you can't even remember what it was you said.'

'It was nothing. I didn't say anything. Let's just get this suit if we're going to, shall we?'

'You're a very strange man, Kevin.'

'I daresay. The suit. Let's get the suit and then just get out of here, shall we?'

So they found the department and Kevin tried on about a

dozen suits, avoiding the salesman's eyes as Emily barked out comments. Eventually she settled upon what she resignedly accepted as being the sort of best of a very bad job; when it became clear that the trousers were far too long she called him a short-arse, and her reaction upon learning of the necessary lengthening of the sleeves was to compare him to a gibbon. God, Kevin was never more relieved than when finally they did, they actually did get out of that place.

'Well?' challenged Emily.

'I'm sorry,' hazarded Kevin. What now? What now?

'What do we say?'

'What do we *say*?! What on earth are you talking about now, Emily? What do we *say*?!'

'I should have thought that a small word of thanks might be in order, Kevin, no? Have you any idea how much I have just spent on you?'

'No, I. Thank you, Emily. *Thank* you.'

Emily smiled with her mouth. 'Quite all right,' she said.

Yeah – thank you, thought Kevin. Thank you and *goodnight*.

Maureen, tottering only slightly, was rubbing hard at the borders of Raymond's desk with a pair of Raymond's underpants: old ones, grey now – weren't always grey, white once, but grey now and getting greyer by the second because Raymond's desk (in common with absolutely everything) had not been the subject of an attempted cleaning for very possibly years and so quite soon these erstwhile underpinnings came to be richly coated with an abundance of the sort of ashen and fibrous silt more commonly associated with the guts of a Hoover. A lot of the muck was hurled up into the air, of course, which had everyone retching briefly and forced into smelling deep-down bad things. Everyone? Well – Amanda was there, staring at Maureen as if she was some remote and greeny-blue planetary being, recently fallen to earth, while Raymond had not long ago switched his look from one of incredulity to irritation, and now it was shifting again (always on the move) – concern, I think this one is: concern over the fact that Maureen was still nagging away at that same little piece of desk and this was the sort of thing compulsives, obsessives did (you saw it on documentaries all the time) but any concern there might have been on Maureen's behalf was now fully eclipsed by the new and rather more intense expression which surely denoted alarm because now he saw his position as underlined in bold – alone in a room with not one but two women who were both without a trace of a doubt certifiable and as the only place he was intending to go had Emily all over it (wall-to-wall), to Raymond's way of thinking the imminent and short-term future was decidedly shaping up as really anything but rosy.

'Why are you doing this, Maureen? What actually is it that you think you are doing?'

'She's nuts,' grunted Amanda.

'I don't think,' said Maureen – stopping the rubbing momentarily, started up again now (harder than ever) – 'that your new little friend is very polite.'

'Not a question of polite,' asserted Amanda. 'You're nuts – it's as plain as day. It's a fact. You're nuts, and that's the end of it. And I'd also like to know why you're still here. I made it perfectly clear to you that you're leaving – *didn't* you, Raymond? So why are you still here?'

'Amanda –' tried Raymond.

'That,' beamed Maureen, rub-rub-rubbing away (Christ, she'll be down to the chipboard underneath the veneer at this rate), 'was just silly talk. Raymond knows that, don't you Raymond?'

'Maureen –' tried Raymond.

'I've seen the light!' trumpeted Maureen now, quite as if she'd, well – seen the light, really. 'I *did* let things go a little round here,' she conceded (Raymond chucked up both eyes to the ceiling, fielded them in time to catch a glimpse of Amanda apparently in the midst of the initial stages of heaving). 'But from now on things are going to be –'

'Don't tell me,' intoned Amanda – and yes, sardonic was there in bundles, '*different.*'

Maureen nodded as eagerly as a greedy child bolstering her assurance that she has indeed been a good girl today. 'Different, yes. The very same. Oh, and Raymond?'

'Maureen –' tried Raymond.

'I'm going to *cook* for you!' said Maureen delightedly. Would've clapped her hands together, but one was mighty busy eroding the desktop. 'Yes really – all your favourite things.'

'Look!' barked Amanda now. 'You're just not getting it, are you? You're *leaving*. You're out of here. Here is where you *used* to live. No longer. Raymond doesn't *want* you any more, do you understand? Can you get that one single fact into your bloody head? He wants *me* – he can't even stand the sight of you, you mad old drunken bitch!'

'Amanda –' tried Raymond.

'That's just where you're wrong!' announced Maureen in triumph. 'It's *you* he can't stand. It's *you* he hates because it's *you* who's mad, not me. And Raymond also hates you because he hates it if you put knives into him –'

'Maureen –' tried Raymond.

'– And *also*,' went on Maureen, quite implacably, her wide eyes now full on Amanda's face, 'because you won't let him fuck you, like Emily does.'

Raymond nearly fell over. Actually felt for his heart – connected with his pill bottle, poured out about seven (staring at Maureen, just staring at Maureen), swallowed a

235

few, crunched up the rest, fumbled for a fag, lit the bloody thing (staring at Maureen, still staring at Maureen), inhaled a gulf stream of smoke as far down as the soles of his feet and then just went on staring at Maureen.

'I don't love him in that *way*!' bawled Amanda. 'And nor do you – you don't either!'

'I don't love him in *any* way!' shouted back Maureen. 'You silly, silly little girl – you really don't know *anything*, do you? But Raymond knows, don't you, dear? Raymond knows exactly what I mean. He hates Emily too, of course. Even more than he hates you.'

'Maureen –' tried Raymond.

'You totally mad fucking crazy bitch!' screamed Amanda. 'I really would love to *kill* you, you know that?'

This jolted Raymond out of the grip of whatever it was that still had him goggling at Maureen (and now Amanda had said fucking again – it was all too much, that, on top of all that stuff that Maureen had just come out with – and *she'd* used the word too, and Raymond was sure she never had done before, not in nearly twenty fucking – oh Christ – years). When Amanda talked of killing, though, you took notice, right? This was no expression pre-heated to intensity by the passing moment, as Raymond well knew to his cost. I mean, that knife, that knife – and how had Maureen known that Amanda had stuck it into him? Process of deduction, I reckon – no one else left (Rosie dead but not really) and a hell of an angle for him to have achieved himself, even had such a desire at the time assailed him. But that knife (seemed sort of familiar – rather like an old letter-opener he used to have), where had it suddenly appeared from, ay? Raymond certainly didn't see it coming, that went without saying, so it had surely been, as they say (don't they say this?), about her person. So who's to say what on God's earth might be about her deeply psycho person this time around? Flame-thrower? Bazooka? It didn't do to tangle – didn't do to find out the hard way: gentle intervention, that's the key, swiftly followed up by subtle diversion.

'Amanda –' tried Raymond.

No – no good at all: Amanda wasn't taking a blind bit of notice of Raymond – too intent on ramming home message after message to this unbelievable *Maureen* woman.

'I'm *not* going to kill you,' she began.

'Of course you're not – silly girl.'

'Maureen –' tried Raymond.

'I'm not a silly *girl*!' raved Amanda. 'Not a *girl* and not *silly*!'

'Mad, then,' allowed Maureen.

'It's you! It's you! What in Christ's name is wrong with you at all? It's you who's the mad one! *You!*'

'Not polite. Raymond, your little friend is not polite.'

'Just get this, bloody Maureen! This is the last time I'm saying it. First thing in the morning, you walk. Understand? Clear? You walk. Take what you like and go. Got it?'

'Mummy's coming home tomorrow,' said Maureen – quite wistfully. 'I think I should like a drink.'

'She's not! She's not! "Mummy" is not coming home tomorrow, Maureen, because this isn't bloody "Mummy's" home any more – you can both go off and rent a skip if you want – but one thing is absolutely certain: you are out, your fucking mother can go and die again – and Emily, I don't know if you care, is also out of the picture. Gone. History.'

'Amanda –' tried Raymond.

'Anyway,' chatted on Maureen, 'I've got to go and cook a lovely dinner for Raymond now. Will you excuse me?'

'Raymond won't be here for dinner, Maureen – he's going to tell Emily goodbye forever. Right, Raymond?'

'Amanda –' tried Raymond.

'Oh he'll eat it,' smiled Maureen. 'When he sees what I've got for him, he'll eat it all right.'

'It's not a question of – Christ Almighty I have never in

my life met anyone so terminally *stupid*. He Won't Be Here! He's going out. Out. Know the meaning of the word? Out. Won't be here – dig?'

'I'll just nip across to the shops,' said Maureen.

'Yeah,' agreed Amanda. 'Another crate of booze.'

'And food,' insisted Maureen. 'Food for Raymond's dinner tonight.'

'Maureen –' tried Raymond.

'Oh leave her, for Christ's sake,' hissed Amanda. 'Just leave her. Let her do what she likes. She can do whatever she fucking well likes, but tomorrow morning, believe me, she leaves.'

Yes, Raymond had heard – and *yes*, it once more gave him the strangest feeling: couldn't explain it. Maureen had clattered downstairs now, muttering words like fish, eggs, potatoes, melon, and Raymond was left looking at Amanda, wondering what in the world she might say now. Here it comes:

'Lock me in.'

'I'm sorry?'

'When you go. When you go to see Emily. Lock me in.'

'Why, Amanda? We're not doing that any more, remember? We've done the kidnapping game – it's over, that particular game. We're now playing the I'm-not-bloody-going-but-everybody-else-bloody-is game, aren't we? So why should I lock you in?'

'Because it's a masterful thing to do,' explained Amanda, quite sweetly. 'You could tie me up too, if you want to.'

There was only one reason on earth why Raymond would want to do a thing like that (felt quite lustful just turning it over), or maybe, yeah, maybe two – the other being that it would make it a damn sight easier if she were trussed up like a carpet to chuck her into a nearby canal.

'I'll lock you in, but I don't think I'll tie you up,' said Raymond.

No, on balance, not. Because if I did, if I did tie you up (and I can't bloody stop thinking of it now, God damn you), if I did that thing to you, tie you up (mind you, it's good in a way, isn't it, that you quite care for the thought because that means when the time comes – as it surely will, it's wholly inevitable – you won't be too put out by the intimate constraints of a straitjacket) – but that aside, if I did actually take you up on this bizarre, yes bizarre, and I must say quite unexpected offer to tie you up – that is, if I am reading it right, to lay you down on the ground, and tie together your very sweet wrists and raise your arms above your head so as to add the sort of solid fullness to your really very encouraging and not at all too gentle breasts, both of them, and then maybe bind each ankle separately – attached to two quite distinct and heavy pieces of furniture, conceivably, this causing a quite unavoidable and V-shaped gap between your sturdy thighs – if, as I say, I were to do any of this as you lay, passively allowing, maybe smiling just slightly in a secret way – if I were, in fact, to follow this through, well then I would, wouldn't I, fuck you swift and violently whereupon I simply know I would experience quite the most charged and clotted, short, thick orgasm of my entire life on earth and then, in the fullness of time, you would – I know you would – quite as you promised to do, kill me.

And so no, on balance, not. But it won't be easy, for here is what assails me: scent of cunt (turns men's minds).

'They're all out – they've all gone, Raymond. It's that awful ball thing, tonight.'

She explained all this fairly brusquely because, as Raymond could see, the floor of the living-room was covered in stuff – Shelley's stuff, looked like – and a good deal more was spilling out into the hall. Shelley had actually completely forgotten about the ball (so had Raymond – hardly surprising – but now he remembered) and could barely believe her luck. The whole house empty for the entire evening: she could get all her stuff packed and out of here before they came back. Phone her mother tomorrow – explain the situation. And if Emily didn't like it, then to hell with her. Shelley would phone tomorrow. Her phone. From her flat. Great.

'Even Adam's gone,' went on Shelley, now kneeling on the floor in front of a suitcase, stacking into it chunky pullovers and what looked to Raymond like about half a dozen little dolls dressed in various national costumes. 'He looked such a geek in Dad's old suit! He really didn't want to go, but Mum was absolutely determined, in the light of everything.'

The light of everything? Raymond raised an eyebrow, registered mild surprise, but no, don't go into it – don't even ask. Don't really want to know, do I? So why ask? Got enough, don't you think? Yeh I do: quite enough, thank you. Raymond too was quite relieved that no one was here; had not the slightest intention of conveying to Emily the message that Amanda had practically spelled out for him (literally) and he was never too keen to encounter Kevin (nice enough fellow, yes – all things being equal – but he was so, I mean he really could be a bit of a – oh, look: you know Kevin). So what was Shelley up to, then? God, just look at her legs – tight in denim: will you just take one bloody look at those legs. So what's she up to, then, hey? Holiday? Looks like she's going for a year, with all this stuff. Wonder what little Shelley – little Shelley, over whom my bloody shit-useless son Gideon's baby-soft hands have exploringly roamed – wonder what little Shelley (oh God the mouth, the mouth), wonder what little Shelley is up to, then. Ask her, shall I? Yeh – ask her, why not. Is there an ashtray round here?

'I'll go soon,' said Raymond. Yes but where to? Where to?

'Probably in the way. Is there an ashtray round here? Can I do something? Help in some sort of way? Holiday, Shelley? Somewhere nice?'

'Better than any holiday,' laughed back Shelley – hadn't planned to laugh, but now she heard it she knew again how happy she felt : out of here, out of here for good: great. 'there's an ashtray over there, but I don't know if it's one for using. I've finally got a little place of my own – not so little, actually, hell of a lot more space than I've ever had here. My own bathroom! Can you believe? Can you imagine? A bathroom just for me – all clean and shiny every day of the week. Can you imagine?'

No, thought Raymond. And nor can I remember. But how wonderful – a place of one's own. I wish *I* had a place of my own. You see, the thing is, I don't actually care if Maureen, Rosie and Amanda stay or don't stay in that big old stinking filthy house – they can please their bloody selves. All I have to do is go – just leave the lot of them to it. What about money? What about the company? What about what Amanda will do? Yeah. Unreal, isn't it? But how wonderful – a place of one's own. Shelley's going to have a place of her very own. Can I come, Shelley? Can I? No. No of course not. Because then she wouldn't be on her own, would she? No. And nor would I. Don't want to be on my own: she does – I don't. But just think: a clean little flat (not so little, actually), a clean bathroom, and a young fresh girl (clean, no doubt) just sitting there before me, complete with legs, mouth – the mouth! – and all the places I crave that she carries (about her person) constantly.

'Course,' went on Shelley, 'I can't *afford* it, or anything. Haven't got any *money*, or anything.'

No, thought Raymond: nor have I. But at least you have a place of your own; I haven't got a place of my own. You may have no money, but you do, Shelley, have a place of your own. Whereas I . . . I . . . Oh dear oh dear, I feel so cold, yes I do – chilled right through, because all I have is nothing.

Shelley, on the other hand, was thinking this: well, it had been a bit of a long shot. Worth a go, though, because everyone knew that Raymond was loaded (that's what Mum said, anyway) and as to the looks he gave her! Christ, Shelley had often thought that Raymond should be chained up: you could almost see – Jesus, you could almost *feel* – the progression of lewd and flagrant images flicking beneath the surface of his eyes. Which surely was not passed down to his son. And equally certainly, very little of that sort of thing ever swaggered across Julian's mind – oh God, look: don't even *talk* about Julian, OK? Shelley had absolutely had it up to here with that bloody little rat *Julian*. She had been quite right about him, fucking little weasel. Christ, you should have heard him on the phone:

'Shelley, so glad to have caught you. It is Julian speaking – Julian here. Look, um – that is to say, um: are you well?'

'What's the deal, Julian?'

'What expressions you do come out with! Um. Shelley. No, in point of fact – and I do fully realize that in view of my prior undertakings you have every right to take gross exception to what it is I am about to say, but I truly do feel in all conscience that what with Ben and everything else – his mother, I need hardly say, was quite beside herself, which I do concede was a wholly comprehensible reaction though quite untypical of her psychological make-up, I have to say –'

'No deal, then, Julian?'

'Shelley, I really do very much feel that I am duty-bound to take the whole family on some sort of vacation so that we might gel once more as a unit, if you follow, and having searched my soul, Shelley – for I am not one to enter anything, or indeed, extricate myself from anything without a considerable degree of thought and I really think that any other risk of any sort of, well – *scandal* is just possibly overstating the case, but I am sure you are well able to pick up on the undertone of my subtext here, Shelley – and then the expense in the light of this quite untoward and wholly unexpected –'

'Yeh, OK – got you, Julian. Have a good trip.'

'That is most understanding of you, Shelley, and I must say –'

'Julian?'

'Yes, Shelley?'

'Just fuck off, yeah?'

You know the moment that phone call came? Just as Shelley was hauling down all the suitcases, her fingers tingling; just as she had laid out the cardboard boxes and the black plastic sacks, her lips tugged back with excitement. Well no one was going to spoil it: she had the flat, the deposit was paid and so was the first month's rent and listen – she was *going* (make no mistake). And the next month's rent? More than she earned at the shop. So what to do? Don't know. Just get there, enjoy it – revel in it – and then maybe something, haven't got a clue, have I, exactly *what* – might just turn up. And she supposes if she is honest that that is why Shelley – intensely irritated at first by the advent of bloody Raymond – hadn't more or less shut the door in his face. Look – there's no room for *ethics*, here, it's too late for all of that. If she could suffer those awful, awful bouts in the back of Julian's Volvo – well Christ, surely anything has got to be a step up from that. And Raymond didn't seem – despite what he said – to be seriously planning to leave, and even with her back to him Shelley could feel his eyes like a laser-warm web being spun all over her. So feel, Shelley. Feel your way, but gently: you know how it's done.

'Could you hand over that pile, Raymond? The one there – nearest to you. No, yes – that one, yes.'

Raymond had been flicking a finger between several piles, any of which might have been the one, but now he had the go-ahead, he picked up the pile of – oh goodness, most of the pile seemed to be made up of all sorts of rather frilly things – crunkly in parts, icy smooth elsewhere – and it was silly, wasn't it, silly that such inanimate little bits of stuff (I mean, they're all stacked up in shops in mountains and you wouldn't even give them a second . . . yes, but it was different, yes it was different when before you squatted on its haunches the body they had clung to; different when such fingers reach out to take from you this charged and fragile cargo) . . . but silly, nonetheless – not *explicable*, not wholly – why just the touch of such things could make a man tremble.

Shelley smiled warmly. Warmly? Not too sure about warmly – she smiled in some sort of a way, though, that Raymond had never before noticed sailing in his direction – and he would have, he would have noticed, and he surely would have remembered: would have smiled back, as he was doing now; might even have acted on it. Acted on it? What do you mean? Not quite sure, not quite sure yet: wait a bit and I'll tell you.

'I'm a sucker for all this sort of stuff,' said Shelley, now. 'I just love underwear – this sort of thing. The really feminine stuff.'

'Do?' checked Raymond; hadn't planned to say 'Do?' – hadn't even heard himself say 'Do?' because whatever his mouth was up to, his mind was up to something else: hovering with hot feet, hopping between possibilities, tiptoeing around implications. What's this, now? What's all this, then? Hey?

'But it's all so *expensive*,' went on Shelley. 'The good stuff is – terribly expensive. That's the trouble with me,' she sighed, holding up a black and lacy could be for wearing at night, sort of thing – barely cover anything and would keep you far from cosy. 'I just have *such* expensive tastes. And now with this *flat* and everything – well, I just don't know.'

She laughed – quite ringingly, and quite as if this novel and throwaway and very preposterous little thoughtlet had just this second floated into her wacky and womanly head: 'I need a sponsor, I think! They did that with artists once, didn't they? Patrons. You just got on with whatever you did, whatever it was you had to offer, what you were good at – and somebody else paid the bills. I'd love that. Of course, it's only fair that the patron takes a share in all the good things.'

Now look: Raymond was no idiot, as well we know – but he was picking all this up wrong, right? I don't know, though – look at the way she's looking, holding his gaze. And gazing is maybe too light a word for the total transfixion that had now taken a rigid grip on Raymond's features. But he could be wrong. Can't be wrong – *look* at her. But he *could* be wrong – *could*. Yeah – could, I suppose – but I don't know, though – look at the way she's looking, holding his gaze. Say something. Say what? Don't know, don't know – no, I don't know because I could be wrong; *can't* be wrong, can I? When was the last time I was right? Don't know, don't know. Is she still looking? Is she still – yes she is, she is: *well*, then – not wrong, *can't* be wrong – say something. Say what? What does she want? Money. Haven't got any. She doesn't know that. Say something. Say what? Say this:

'I wish just a lack of money was *my* problem. Money means very little to me,' went on Raymond, somehow avoiding bursting into tears. 'It's the other things in life that are important: the tender things.'

(This is balls, right? Yes, right. Absolutely.)

Great, thought Shelley – oh great.

'But there must be scores of people – women, anyway, Raymond – who would just adore to look after you. Life at home not that good, then, Raymond?'

No, he thought – not that good. Got a mad secretary, you see, locked into my filthy study at her own request; got a mad wife who drinks and has to leave home because my mad secretary says so – and so does my mother-in-law who is (did I mention?) mad. So not that good, no. Christ, Shelley, if it wasn't for periodically banging your fucking mother, whom I loathe, I wouldn't get by at all. And she's mad too, but you probably know that.

'No,' he said. 'Not that good.'

'Maybe,' suggested Shelley – and yes, just the fingers of one hand, gently resting on Raymond's near-hysterical knee – 'maybe I could help you. Now I've got my own place.'

Great, thought Raymond – oh great. Not that great. Why not? Because now you're supposed to make the counter-offer, right? Money. Haven't got any. She doesn't know that. Offer. Can't deliver. Offer: *she'll* deliver – what do you care? Bit of a dirty trick. Bit of a dirty mind – so what? Yeah. I will offer. Got to. Look at her mouth. Look at her legs. Oh Christ you're right, you're right – I've just got to fuck this bloody woman: I'll offer her anything at all in the whole wide world.

See? Scent of cunt: turns men's minds.

Raymond was now leaning against the wall – actually sitting on the floor of Emily's hateful drawing-room (and Christ it was in a mess – Christ what a mess of it Raymond and Shelley had made: how wonderful, how absolutely wonderful) with his back against the wall, his eyes twisting up towards Shelley, who was dressing, one of them stinging from the hit of blue smoke from another cigarette jammed into the corner of his mouth. He adored to watch a woman dress: more compelling, much, than when she merely took off her clothes. It was, Raymond thought – needn't be true – the steadily increased confinement of her; first the snugness of the panties – just that brief tightness amid so much soft and pink – then the enveloping snap of tights (I know – but just you tell him who wore stockings nowadays; just you point him in the direction); it was lovely the way they adjusted the bra: women truly thought of what they were doing when they made sure the grasp was right – they thought of nothing else as they looked on down (drawing in the chin, dropping the mouth ajar, the better to see just how all this coaxing was going). Thin-ribbed sweaters were favourite, then – but you could by no means rely on that: belts were quite magical, broad ones particularly. The fluffing of hair, a touch of lipstick – all whole again, but with all that wonder still knowingly and glowingly intact beneath, and the smell of the romp all around.

Shelley had seemed genuinely thrilled by the way Raymond had come into her – like a bloody express train (and who can blame him?) – because Christ let's face it, what with Gideon and Julian, this was nothing if not a novelty. But her disappointment at the brevity of the encounter was palpable in the air even before – as the young and dissatisfied will – she put it into words of one syllable:

'Christ that was short.'

'Short? God I can hardly *breathe*, Christ Shelley. Where are my bloody cigarettes? What do you mean, *short*?'

'I mean about thirty bloody seconds short – it's called *premature*, Raymond. *Premature*.'

'Well of course it's premature!' snapped back Raymond. 'It's fucking *sperm*, isn't it?'

Shelley looked at him. 'Are you kidding? Is that a joke?'

Raymond glanced away. 'It might be,' he said.

Shelley smoked too: she'd run out of Silk Cut, so she took one of his.

'You know what I did yesterday?' she asked.

Women did this, Raymond knew. And then they just waited for you to say no – so he did that, and now she was telling him:

'I asked Gideon to marry me.'

Just as well Raymond was sitting or he would have nearly fallen over again; as it was, the cigarette dropped out of his mouth and he was batting around in his lap and broke the bloody thing but the tip was still burning so he ground that out into some maybe Chinese rug affair which happened to be cream, unfortunately: ho bloody ho.

'Is *that* a joke?' he managed to get out.

Shelley shrugged. 'It might as well have been. He just sort of shuffled around and said he didn't know.'

'Doesn't know bloody *anything*, that's the trouble – that's half the trouble. But Jesus, Shelley – you don't really want to marry bloody *Gideon*, do you? You *can't* do.'

She shook her head, inhaled smoke. 'I don't. I couldn't bear it. I just asked him because – oh, I don't know why I asked him – because I knew he'd say no, I think. And that I wouldn't know why.'

'Did he say no? He said no, did he?'

'He went further, really. He said nothing. Not a single word. That's always mega-no, isn't it?'

Raymond nodded slowly – might have been thinking about it (doubt it). 'Yes,' he said. 'Yes, I think that means no. Thank God he didn't say yes – bloody fool, not saying yes: *I* would've said yes – I would've. But thank Christ he didn't; what would you have done if he'd said yes?'

Shelley smiled. 'Changed my mind. Or married him. Don't know.'

Raymond looked up. Hang on, hang on – this wasn't the start of mad talk, was it? I mean, it can't *really* be endemic to the entire fucking gender, can it? No, on balance – no. It's just the way dreamy girls sometimes go: paradoxes spare you commitment. Maybe that's it.

Then they thrashed out the details. Raymond would really like the flat, Shelley had said, and Raymond (thinking jeepers don't these weird things happen quickly) replied rather politely that he was sure that she was right. The rent was twelve hundred a month (joke, right? I mean, if Raymond had been asked for even twelve hundred a year he'd have to steal it from Amanda). Amanda. Ah yes, Amanda. What shall we do about that little thing? Don't know – can't care. And if truth is particularly in fashion this Saturday night, then Raymond – now that he'd done what he'd done – didn't much care about Shelley either, and her attitude towards him – now that she had secured a financial agreement which, dear soul, she actually maybe imagined might even be honoured – was, it would be fair to say, cooler. But Raymond would rally round again, when the lust thing freshly assailed him, and no doubt Shelley would be reminded of all his boundless charms whenever rent day next wound itself around: such is union.

'I never did it with him, you know. You probably don't. With Gideon. I never did it with him.'

Raymond chewed a thoughtful heart pill, while dragging on a fag.

'Joking,' he said.

'Not. Not joking. Never did it.'

'Don't blame you,' grunted Raymond – and yes, he allowed his soul to give full throttle to the song it was yearning to sing. But Christ – all that wasted jealousy, and he'd never even done it; jealousy on Raymond's scale really takes it out of you, you know.

'Is it, was it because you couldn't stand the bloody sight of him? I could understand that – that you couldn't.'

'I wouldn't have minded. Quite wanted it, sometimes. No – it was him. Couldn't.'

Too much ecstasy, surely, for just one Raymond to bear? Was this really true? That Gideon was as utterly and totally useless as Raymond had always told him he was? Well if *that's* the bloody case, young Miss Shelley, don't come the premature with me! Premature is a whole lot better than bloody two years late. Anyway – I quite favour premature: frees your time for other things.

In the light of this fresh and invigorating news, Raymond managed to push away his larger problems (stacked them ten deep and densely as a wall) but he had just one regret – no, not really: not, actually, a regret so much as an if-only. The if-only goes like this: Wouldn't it have been absolutely out-of-this-world fantastic if only, during those thunderous thirty seconds when Raymond dreamed of dying within the trench-hot sweetness of Shelley, wouldn't it have been quite the most thrilling thing if the door had opened and there had stood his spastic son alongside Shelley's hopeless father with (just has to be) her evil, crazy mother? I mean – just to have all of them there so that come the shuddering end to his wonderful attack on Shelley he could really know that he had finally let them *have* it.

You should have seen Maureen: Gideon could scarcely believe it – couldn't remember the last time he had witnessed his mother attempting anything even vaguely domestic – and goodness, the energy she was putting into it all: shoving and clattering around the kitchen, pulling out drawers with such unaccustomed vigour that out they came all the way, banging down on to Maureen's shins (twice this happened – what with that and the drink she could barely stand up any more), and there was the cutlery all over the floor, along with ages-old packets of stuff best left alone (one of them looked like milky jelly – needn't have been). And she did leave them alone, of course, because actually picking up things was never a priority at the best of times, but if Maureen was to prepare for Raymond (because the light she had seen was glistening still) the best meal of his entire married life, then it was the culinary side, surely, that deserved her full attention; anyway, she was good at stepping over things, around things (lifetime's practice) and sometimes a good part of the afternoon would pass and she wouldn't fall over at all!

'Can you cut the melon, Gideon? I don't trust myself.'

Gideon smiled. 'First time I've seen any fruit in this house that wasn't sprouting strange blue growths.'

'Unkind, Gideon. Not kind. It's all going to be different from now on. Give the place a good clean-out tomorrow. Just cut it into quarters. Oh God – there aren't any spoons; there used to be so many spoons.'

Gideon shook his head in a mild and affectionate sort of wonder, as he set about the melon. Give the place a good clean-out! God, the poor old thing (and not yet fifty) was so far gone she didn't even see it any more: it would take a brace of excavators and a gang of navvies several months to even crack the surface of the filth and disorder in this quite unbelievable house. What did Maureen imagine she was going to achieve tomorrow? Gideon closed his eyes to the too touching and utterly ludicrous vision of his half-cut mother flitting about with a yellow feather duster. Dismissed the thought, then: Gideon had so many other things to think about, now. His life had (yes) taken a turn, and much as he yearned for someone else (anyone else) to make the decisions for him, there seemed to be no getting away from it all.

In a way, it was his job that concerned him most. His *job* – really? That is rather a surprise, I have to say: Raymond more or less had it right about Gideon's rather non-job, from what we have seen – I mean all that *trolley* stuff with so-called editors squabbling over bloody chocolate éclairs, was it? Not exactly the cutting edge, I should have said. Surely what should be exercising Gideon rather more is this – well, *is* it a relationship with the Richard person? Because the odd one-off encounter in this sort of world is all part of the general, um, cut and thrust. Or is it something different?

Little to tell, is the truth: Gideon was only just beginning to work it out himself, so really there has been nothing of substance to say until now – and even *now* there is to be no great revelation, no life-changing decisions. As I say, Gideon is turning it all over in his mind right now, while slicing the melon and dodging his vodka-glugging mother's wilder gestures and journeys to and fro the cupboards; maybe if we were party to those thoughts, we might be able to glean something more, latch on to something concrete, maybe. But surely it isn't the *job* side of things that consumes him? That can't be right. And didn't the lovely Shelley actually propose marriage to the lad? That must have knocked him for six: no wonder he just stood there and didn't say a word – most men in his rather singular situation would, I imagine; well look – what's to say?

Well there's this to say: Gideon actually rather liked the idea of marrying Shelley. Yes. But he hadn't believed she had meant it: Gideon just *knew* that Shelley didn't want to be married to him. Shelley was bored – he thought he meant bored, wasn't quite bored, but there was a secret side to Shelley that he had given up all hope of penetrating, something she needed that he simply knew he could never supply. Just sometimes, the way she looked at him when she thought he hadn't noticed – a shiver of contempt, to Gideon's mind. Also hurt – it was hurt, earlier on, because all they'd do is laugh themselves silly for hours on end about absolutely nothing at all, go to a pub – drink a bit – go to a cinema (see a film), go to bed – and nothing. Christ, if he'd had to apologize just one more time he would have taken the easier option and killed himself. So they stopped going to bed (seemed easier) and then the laughter petered out, and they didn't even go to the cinema, now. So maybe her asking him to marry her was some form of test, some way whereby he could sum up what, if anything, Shelley any longer meant to him. And he had said nothing – nothing at all. Didn't smirk, didn't weep, did nothing extravagantly committal or otherwise with any of his limbs. And what was she supposed to make of that?

So, in the light of this – and, lest we forget, that really rather awful little scene with Emily (don't – try not to, Gideon, think of that) – we may safely assume that Gideon has accepted that his erotic interests lie fairly and squarely in another camp, yes? Almost yes. The idea of being married, as I say, rather appealed – and why not Shelley, then? I mean, he *knew* her – they were mates. I'll tell you why – because within days, Shelley would have become Emily and Gideon couldn't blame her, not a bit, and he well knew too how easily he could assume the mantle of Kevin, and then after that his broken-backed future.

'Is corn oil the same as olive oil? It's not, is it?'

The sound of Maureen's voice startled him – he hadn't even been hearing her wrecking the room. Lost the thread, now: damned annoying, actually.

'They're different,' he said. 'They're different.'

Yes. So where was I? Oh yes, I know: Shelley would become Thing and Gideon, yeah. But it still wasn't plain, because although Richard (yes it is a relationship, it is: that's what Gideon meant about the job thing: couldn't stick the bloody job, but the thought of not seeing Richard every single day, now, he simply couldn't bear) – so although Richard surely did excite him (it frightened him how much, frightened him badly) Gideon still did find the prospect of women a welcome one (he thought). Not maybe Shelley any more, no – not Emily (no!) but – well, take that secretary, assistant of Dad's: there was something really very attractive about her, don't you think? A mutual attraction, unless he had imagined it – and OK, yes, he didn't know her, or anything, but she didn't seem domineering and plain bloody scary like Shelley could be and like Emily was as a permanent state. She was probably quite sane and perfectly sweet. And it's no good even glancing off anyone else's view of such a conclusion, because here is something I think young Gideon might have to find out for himself. The hard way? Could be: who can tell?

And there's something else; yes, there's something else – and that something is called Raymond. If Gideon lays himself completely bare, then he must acknowledge that one of the driving reasons why Gideon might one day force himself to live as normally as it is possible to live with a fully-fledged woman (not very, granted) would be to shut Raymond up and then turn him green. Because unlike many lusty and gutsy fathers, Raymond – and Gideon knew this, he had understood this little lot since way back – would be absolutely beside himself with joy if ever Gideon were to betray just one tinge of sexual ambivalence. All the taunts (all the jeers) over all the years would finally bind into a tumultuous chorus that would deafen and render him blind for the remainder of his days.

'I haven't done this for so long,' said Maureen – actually drinking vodka while she spluttered it out – 'I can't remember times and temperatures and things.'

Richard had asked Gideon to move in with him.

'Mum – you know Dad's not coming back for dinner – he said it, he said it twice just before he left. Why not leave it? Just leave it, hey?'

'That's where you're wrong. He'll eat it – when he sees what I've got for him, he'll eat it.'

Oh God. Mum's going the way of Gran: maybe it's just this house. And Gran's coming back tomorrow: feels great, apparently (amazing), except that now she thinks her name is Sally.

'Come on, Mum – turn the gas off, and everything, and I'll take us out for a pizza or something, OK?'

'Can't disappoint your father, Gideon. Can't.'

Can, you know: I've been doing it all my life, and so have you. It's a nice flat, Richard's. Quiet and comfortable.

Gideon was aware first of a gleam of quite bright light, and then came a clatter and a yelp soon followed by shrieking and Maureen's mouth was horribly agape as this panicked braying ripped out of her and at him and now a plume of flame was streaking up from the blazing pan and now the noise and terrifyingly dazzling firelight rendered Gideon tense and loose, tense and loose – though he was moving before he knew it and beating at the sleeve of his mother's housecoat while she wailed hysterically and batted her arms all around her and Gideon saw the vodka bottle just as it was going over and he threw his mother onto the floor and dragged her screaming across the lino just before the alcohol burst into a burning ball that now was hotly insinuating itself around the sides of the cupboards, licking at tea towels and devouring rubbish and sending up the stench of burning terror and how could Gideon get his mother out of the door? *Had* her out of the door, now – the door shut behind them – left Maureen whimpering in the corner, her eyes raking the room and beseeching him – and now he was dialling – his fingers, his fingers, his useless bloody fingers – though when the door blew open again and the sheer wall of fire invaded the next room, Gideon hauled his mother to her feet and they fled through the front door with the heat at their backs and already from the coldness of outside the whole ground floor was glowing and Gideon was barking at a startled neighbour (he sounded like a dog, now – sweaty and barking) and stiff and quite frantic signals sent the man scurrying inside and help would come, of course it would come, but help took time and Gideon now just stared at the house as the fire took hold while Maureen buried her wild and soaking face deep into his shoulder, flinching badly when the first window cracked and splintered outwards, raining the garden with a tinkling of glass as the greedy fire sent out bursts of lusting tongues to make good their escape, then thickened and tightened its red-hot grip on the very guts of the stunned and roaring building.

And when a shocked-white Raymond was told the news, all he could think was: Amanda.

CHAPTER EIGHT

The hubbub in a ballroom brimming with quite so many interior decorators, designers, conceptualists, stylists, life-style consultants and whatever else they chose to call themselves (each one a peddler of stuff) is something you rarely encounter elsewhere, and although Emily became almost transparent while visibly blossoming as she gave herself up to being sucked on into it all, she still felt irritation (quite intense) at the undeniable truth that Kevin had already high-tailed it off to the Gents before they had even come within grasping distance of that inaugural and coolly welcome glass of champagne – and while it is true that even in normal (!) circumstances Kevin would have delayed his first escape for not very much longer, on this occasion his need was pressing and authentic because just three steps from the hotel's I suppose imposing entrance – no distance at all from where the taxi had dropped them – Kevin had espied a shiny and nice Victorian street bench with 'Wet Paint' roughly scrawled and slung by string around its curlicues and so of course he had to touch *that* and now his hand had become an embarrassment of Thames green gloss and so a quick rinse, a warm towel and words of encourage-ment from a soft-spoken and kind-hearted attendant were all sorely needed – and better, surely, better to abandon Emily immediately than witness or experience whatever she might say or do to him as a result of Kevin's lurid fingerprints appearing upon glassware or (don't even *frighten* me by thinking this thought!) the rear and graceful panel of Emily's cream and perfectly plain shantung, full-length sheath dress.

Kevin didn't linger as long as he might usually have done, because if the truth be told the attendants down there weren't as friendly as he remembered them, but this could be at least part due to the fact that the guests had only just begun to arrive and here now was a not-two-minutes-ago twinkling white basin besmirched with what could well be sewage and it took not one but four little towels to even begin to rid Kevin's palm of the bulk of it (and still there were traces: the residue lurked) and of *course* it was very vexing to Kevin that the towels were linen (of course it was) because paper would easily have done but there you have it: posh is as posh does in these impossible places and what was Kevin of all people to do about it? Even less than precious little; just get back to the throng, find somewhere to hide – dodge Emily, look out for Milly, pray that no one else approaches him and hope to God to get by somehow.

How was Kevin looking? I mean, we've more or less got how he's feeling (not too many surprises there) but how was the new suit hanging on him? How were the injuries shaping up? The injuries, yes: Kevin hadn't forgotten them, either. Not as bad as he had feared (at one point he had gazed with real woe at his face in the mirror, and Christ, what he saw reminded him of his reflection in one of those foolish eagle-topped gaudy efforts that he'd banged up on the wall in The Grange – one of which could well still be hanging – because all he saw there was distortion). He had thought no, here is not a case where even plastic surgery might intervene – just get a new head and be done with it. But things had simmered down – a darkened eye socket, it was true (just a hint of Chinese designer-yellow loitering at the edge), one cheekbone maybe more protuberant than the other (who would notice? The whole bloody world) and then there was just the cut lip which Kevin was sucking, couldn't stop sucking. It won't *heal* if you do that, Emily had hissed in the taxi, which Kevin had thought a bit rich –

wouldn't *need* to heal, would it, if you hadn't gone to war? Didn't say anything, though – best keep quiet. The suit? Well, the suit was OK – yeah, I suppose it was sort of OK; they'd overdone the trouser shortening a tinge, though, and so it suddenly mattered that his socks were grey and not black – or so guess-who had a field day telling him: didn't matter to Kevin – not two hoots.

He strode across the foyer (quite well) towards double doors flanked by men with trays. Kevin thought Oh God, champagne always goes to my head (thought of the last time he had drunk it, useless he was, beside a warm and gloriously naked Milly) so maybe I'll just have Buck's Fizz, no I won't, waiter'll think I'm a – oh God my fingers have been dithering between the two of them for so long now he already thinks I'm a – oh what the hell I'll have the, yeah, I'll have the champagne, yes here it is, God it's full, better give it a slurp before I try walking with it – my hand, my hand is shaking – yes it would, wouldn't it, and now the champagne's down the side (sticky fingers, sticky base) and I'll feel guilty about setting the glass down anywhere now – and I *know* that in hotels people don't mind, don't think like that, but *I* do, *I* do: I just do, that's all.

Oh but here's a bit of luck – there, just over there beside the – behind that man, is it a man? With the extraordinary hair and a, God, white suit (looks like Liberace) – behind him, that's Jim, isn't it? Old Jim from The Works? Think so, yeh 'tis – and goodness, talk about *Kevin's* injuries: just take a look at poor old Jim! Has he been in the wars or what? What on earth could have happened to poor old Jim? No one was talking to him (isn't, usually) so Kevin lost no time in cutting through the rustling colours and conflicting scents (some of them really got up your nose) and the snatches of dialogue ('we're not all like *you*, you know' . . . 'well speak for yourself!'') and putting the question to him directly:

'Don't ask,' responded Jim with – could this be bitterness?

259

Yes indeed: here was gall. 'Don't even ask about it. I just don't know if I can talk about it, Kevin. If it hadn't been this here ball, I wouldn't be out at all. I haven't been, since.'

'Since –?'

'I just can't bring myself to get *into* it. Christ if I ever lay my hands on those little bleeders I'll fucking crush the life out of them, so I will. You don't know what happened, do you?'

'No, I –'

'No – well I'll bloody tell you what fucking happened. Walking home one night, quite the thing – I *hate* this bloody fizzy stuff, that's the thing I can always never abide about this do, there's never any *proper* drink, just this bloody fizzy stuff – minding my own fucking business, right? Bit tired, quite tired, long day – wasn't late, or anything – still light – and suddenly there's this bloody great shove from the back, bloody great shove – I felt like I'd been hit by a bleeding bus – and then there was this bastard on my back –'

'No!'

'I'm *telling* you, son – on my back, on my bleeding back he was and I'm telling you I didn't know whether I was coming or –'

'But that's terrible!'

'Too fucking right it's terrible, son – but you ain't heard the half of it: now this other bloody sambo's kneeling in front of me – I'm flat on the fucking pavement, right? And this bloody coon – can't have been more than a kid – he's kneeling in front of me and going through my pockets like he's lost something – cool as you like – and of course I start struggling then because I had quite a lot of cash on me – that's where I was going, I was on my way to the bloody bank, can you credit it? Well he gets it, of course – over a grand, more than a fucking grand – and all this time this other bastard's on my back and it's normally quite busy, that road, but no one come along, there was no one and I thought you bloody black *bastard*, I thought, just you let me up and I'll fucking kill you.'

'I don't *believe* it,' said Kevin, sounding exhausted: and it was true, he didn't; I mean OK, you hear about this sort of thing all the time, but when it happens to someone you –

'*Believe* it. Then they started bouncing my fucking face off the bloody pavement, don't they, the fucking bastards. And the kicking they give me! I tell you, son, I don't know how I got home, I don't know how I got there. Phoned the thing, wossname, hospital – they come pretty quick, to give them their due, and here I am – just about able to tell the tale. Two cracked ribs, bust-up nose – and all these other bloody bits. Christ, I'll never forget it, the little bastards. Haven't *caught* them, course – you don't expect it, not nowadays you don't. You don't look too bright yourself, Kevin – something of the sort happened to you? I wonder if I could get a Scotch; I don't know how people can drink this stuff.'

Some woman in purple jostled Kevin from the rear – he spilt a bit more champagne (which he had forgotten he had been holding) and turned to apologize to her, but it didn't look as if she heard him because now she was busy saying in imperious tones to the man who was her accessory, 'Well what if there *is* another war? It's not as if it's the end of the *world*, is it?'

'Me?' checked Kevin, rhetorically – smidgen of a throw-away smirk – 'no no, not me, thank God. But God, Jim, that's just awful – thank Christ it wasn't worse.'

'Could've been, could well've been – here, waiter! Waiter! Yeh – any chance of a Scotch, at all? Yeh? Oh great – make it a large one, could you? If you bring a bottle it could save you time. Good lad. No, Kevin – could've been the end, finito – over and out, mate. They wanted me dead, no doubt about it. Couple of cars come by – didn't bleeding stop, though, did they? I think that sort of frightened them off: *bastards*. And they *had* the bloody money, too! They just wanted me dead. So what happened to you, then, Kevin? One too many? Walk into a door?'

'Ha ha. Something like that. Had a fall. Landing light packed up, you know how it is – whoosh! Straight down. Not fun, I can tell you.'

Get off that subject.

'But Jim, it's funny you should say all this – well, not funny, I didn't mean *funny*, obviously – but all this mugging business, it must be really on the up because – you won't believe this – *Adam* was picked up by the police yesterday, just yesterday – just because he had a few quid on him, that he'd won on the Lottery! Can you believe it!'

Jim narrowed his eyes, and then widened them again, maybe because it hurt.

'What – *Emily's* Adam? Young Adam?'

Kevin nodded. 'My Adam too, Jim. But yes – Adam.'

'Kidding me.'

Kevin shook his head. 'They held him at the station all night long.'

The waiter returned with a silver tray, and Jim's face broadened at the sight of a whole bottle of Famous Grouse – together with a bucket of ice, and all the other things like water and soda that he wouldn't require.

'With the compliments of the Committee,' explained the waiter, as proud as if he had just this second laid an egg. 'Hoping you recover soon.'

'Nice,' smiled Jim. 'Nice of them – hey, Kevin?'

But even as he drank deep into a very large Scotch, something was troubling Jim, now – yes, you could tell; something itching away at the back of his mind: could take a while to work itself forward.

'Didn't Emily tell you about all this, then?' he said now. 'Mention anything about it? I was under the impression that young Arnold had filled her in.'

'Could've done,' fenced Kevin. 'Been away, matter of fact

262

– just back. And what with all this Adam business . . .'

'Yes,' said Jim.

Why was Jim looking at Kevin, now? That's what Kevin was wondering. I mean, yes – the two of them had been looking at each other on and off throughout the – God, why didn't people look where they were *going*? Why did people keep bashing into Kevin? They didn't seem to be bashing into anyone else – yes, um, as I say: looking at one another from time to time, making the faces match the words, but now it seemed to Kevin that Jim was damn close to eyeing him. Why should Jim be eyeing him, then? The nuances of expression involved the sort of facial contortions that now actually hurt both Kevin and Jim (each of them, bruised) but they would go on with it, they would indeed – because didn't one do this, pain or not?

'Yes,' continued Jim, more slowly, 'yes, I can quite see that coming back to all that . . . so they let him go, eventually, did they? Police? Let him go, then.'

'Oh God yes – *eventually*. I mean – Christ: outrage in the first place, wasn't it? Can they do that, actually? I mean – are they allowed to just pick up anyone they like and just hold them like that? That can't be right, can it?'

'Course it's bloody *right*!' came back Jim with force – bulbous eyes and his wet mouth wetter. 'Too right it's bloody *right* – they want to break their bloody legs, the most of them. Look what happened to *me*!'

'Yes I know, Jim, I know,' conciliated Kevin, thinking oh Christ, oh Christ, one of his legendary and belligerent tempers – and the whisky wasn't helping: shouldn't have brought up this Adam thing (saw that now – Emily'll kill me), too late to do anything about it, so better just start agreeing with anything else that Jim might think of. A lot, as it happens:

'That's the whole trouble with this country, this bloody country – never used to be like this, did it? Did it? You remember a time when it was safe to walk about, don't you? Don't you? Course you bloody do. Well it's not *like* that any more – there's so much bloody *stuff* going on you wouldn't believe. How many times I done that walk to the bank? Ay? How many times? I'll fucking *tell* you how many times – more times than I can bloody remember, *that's* how many bloody times. Now – now, you walk down the bloody street –'

'What's Jim so het up about?' asked Emily: Emily had arrived – must have just recently glided along.

'Emily,' said Kevin, quietly; not too sure if this is a good thing or not: soon find out.

'– You walk down the bloody *street*, I say, and what happens? Two of these young bloody bastards that you think are so *precious*, Kevin, so bloody *untouchable* –'

'I didn't say –' attempted Kevin, thinking hopeless, hopeless, you'll never stop him now; Kevin actually ceased to try even before he was talked through:

'– So bloody *untouchable* – oh dear oh dear: what a poor little *boy*, can't pick him up for nearly beating a man senseless, can we? Can't do that. Can't break his fucking legs for him, can we? Oh dear no –'

'What on earth are you *talking* about, Jim? asked Emily in her why-shouldn't-I-be-good-humoured-I'm-at-a-party-after-all sort of voice. 'Are they coming round with the champagne, Kevin? Can you see?'

'I'll tell you, I'll tell you what I'm *talking* – I'll tell you exactly what I'm *talking* about, Emily,' charged on Jim, voice loud enough to attract the odd glance now – indulgent, mostly (people here well knew how Jim could be), and he was stabbing not just the air with one aggressive forefinger, but very much Emily's airspace, which in any circumstances was never wise.

'Pipe down, Jim,' said Emily, curtly. 'What's happened to your face?'

Ah, thought Kevin: could be a bad move, that. Yes – Jim had slugged back the last of another whisky – was half turning to bang down the glass – but even before Emily had finished throwing one of her looks towards Kevin (equal measures of What's he on about and Christ he's bats) Jim was back, oh yes – Jim was back, all right – lips that were permanently wet and slackened now pulled back tautly to bare his teeth as his eyes went on gleaming with zeal:

'What happened to my *face*, Emily, is that it was smashed into the bloody ground by a couple of black little bastards that Kevin here thinks are so *wonderful* –'

(Should Kevin come up with his 'I didn't say –'? Nah – best leave it: no point, is there?)

'– so bloody *wonderful* that they should be left to do exactly as they please. You wanna take my money? Here, son – have it: hope it's enough. You wanna kick me half to death? Fine, lad, fine – I'll just lie down so's you can do a good job. Is that right? Is that right? I say is that bloody *right*?'

'Of course it's not right,' said Emily, one hand batting down the noise, eyes flicking to the left and right of her.

'Of course not,' was Kevin's twopenceworth.

'Oh *course* it's not bloody right!' roared out Jim, 'so why are you fucking *arguing*?'

'I think, Jim, we'll maybe talk later,' said Emily, quite primly, 'when you've simmered down a bit. Have another drink.'

'I fully *intend* to have another drink,' grumbled Jim, at least more quietly. 'Fully *intend*.'

'Can you *see* anyone with champagne, Kevin?' Emily did a bit of stage neck-craning. 'Are they coming round or not?'

Kevin hadn't heard that. Kevin had just seen Milly. She was talking to someone, which in normal circumstances would have been quite enough to keep Kevin skulking behind a pillar for however long it took until whoever it was had safely sloped away, but now he found himself approaching anyway. He was aware of the receding sound of his name repeatedly barking out of Emily, but he did not flinch, felt no wavering of resolve. Milly and Milly alone was the sole point here, and now he was beside her – suddenly not so much consumed by something solid as invaded by it, his chest and all the organs within full and pulsating – but still he managed to speak, just after hoping that whatever he said would convey at least something of the hugeness of what he was feeling.

'You're looking very well, Milly!'

Oh dear. Never mind: at least he was talking. Well – I *say* talking: wasn't *now*, of course, because Milly had swung round to face him (the face! Just will you look at the face – quite alight) and now it was *she* who was saying:

'Kevin! Hullo! I looked out for you earlier – couldn't see you anywhere.'

And the dress: her long, white neck sweetly slid into shoulders and the creamiest plateau, brought up abruptly by breasts betrayed by the most soft cleft and caught by jet-black, sparkling and alive with crusty silver-white, just like a sugary pastille. Kevin had opened his mouth to say something or other but Milly was talking again so he closed his mouth on the something or other and was busy being all agog at whatever it was that Milly had to tell him right up until the moment she did:

'I don't think,' is what she said – turning towards the man standing just beside her (oh look – there's a man standing just beside her) – 'that you have met my husband, Kevin. Kevin, this is Matt; Matt – Kevin.'

Matt had his arm outstretched towards Kevin and Kevin must surely have taken this hand – must have done that, because he was grasping it now – and he didn't quite wish to meet the eyes in the head of the man who was Matt – oh: there they were – blue as blue – and now Kevin thought that

Matt was saying *well*, Kevin – that's what it sounded like: *well*, Kevin, is how it was coming across – so presumably that is precisely the fact of the matter and for some reason or other (no doubt coming) Matt, Matt – Matt (which is a paint finish oft specified by Emily – although eggshell too was not to be sneezed at – whenever maybe Kevin would instinctively have plumped for gloss – as with the dresser, the dresser which you recall, or, indeed the shiny and nice Victorian street bench – not that gloss was always shunned – no, of course not, but then it tended to be referred to as lacquer, as Kevin well remembered from the last time Emily had attempted to din into him this one simple fact) – so Matt, Matt was indeed saying *well*, Kevin – seemed to Kevin that he had been standing here now for what? Fifty years? Something of that order, and here was an eternal Matt, his big warm hand had latched on to Kevin's (and could it be Milly just shimmering alongside?), saying unto him *well*, Kevin: *well* is what he was saying, so why not take the lead from that? That's what I'll do: I'll take my lead from that (why don't I?) – form my mouth into the semblance of words, and if any emerge I'll know that I haven't quite yet died, not quite: I'll know that I'm breathing still.

'You're looking very well, Matt,' is all that came. 'And,' he added to Milly, turning upon her eyes above the hurt so roundly brave as to spear into anyone who felt like caring (think not of the heart, whimpering now and diving for cover), 'I must say so are you.'

'Do anything? Can I? Is there anything I can do? Call someone?'

Shelley had said this, this sort of thing, many times now. Raymond appeared not to hear: she had heard of shock, and here it was, then – had to be shock, right? Well – under-

267

standable, understandable. I mean, one minute he was briefly fucking her, and the next he had learned that his house had just burned to the ground. Well, *not* – not *actually* burned to the ground (the walls were still there, still just about holding up) but the police person had left no doubt in the minds of anyone that here had been no mere flash in the pan: we were talking conflagration – mega. But Gideon was OK, thank God – and he had got Maureen out safely and Rosie was still in the hospital so it wasn't as if it was . . . you know, *fatal*, or anything; and Christ, there was nothing, surely, that Raymond could actually have cared for in that dank and malodorous house: anything that might once have mattered had long ago become veiled by something far deeper than dirt, had taken root with the abandonment of the surrounding jungle, becoming just another thick and humid part of it. But Raymond's expression (wasn't glazed – not shock, then? He seemed more seriously appalled) had barely altered – give or take a flicker or so – since first they had hit him with the lowdown:

'But what . . . Christ, I can't *believe* . . . I'd better get there – see what I . . . but how did it *happen*?'

'Too early to say, sir,' said the young policeman (it was his turn to break bad news: thank fuck there weren't any bodies involved). 'Fire Inspector did say that the seat of the blaze – hottest point, flashpoint, I think they say – was in the area of the kitchen. They often start in the kitchen, but we don't yet know this. I wouldn't actually bother going, sir, if I was you, just yet – fire people are still there, there's nothing you could actually do. Maybe you'd like to see a doctor? Your son is coming over shortly – he's quite OK, as I say, and so is your wife. Lucky escape. I think your wife might be staying overnight at the hospital – bit shocked – but your son said he'd be over directly.'

But all Raymond could think was: *Amanda*. She wasn't tied up (no) but she was locked in (yes). How could this have happened? How could Amanda from the office be locked into his study as his house had gone up like a torch in hell? How do these things happen? How does it all come to pass? How come we bother about all sorts of stupid stuff, little stuff, while the real stuff (the big stuff) creeps up behind us, swift as you like and as silent as the air, with rehearsed-to-within-an-inch and merciless fully choreographed disasters that change one's life forever? How's all this *work*, then? Don't know: couldn't tell you. Last person in the world.

'I'll leave the door on the latch, I think,' Shelley was saying now (doesn't matter much what I say, Raymond can't be listening: wasn't even smoking). 'Do you want tea, or anything? Sometimes I don't hear the bell in here and it would be awful if Gideon came and . . . maybe a drink, Raymond? There's wine – or I think Mum's got some Armagnac, somewhere. No? Oh Raymond – please talk: say something, Raymond. You can't go on just *looking* like that. Do you *want* to go to the house? Would it make you *feel* better? I think he was right, though, the policeman – there *isn't* much point, is there? But just think of the *insurance* you'll collect, Raymond. All that lovely money.'

Raymond turned to face her: he had heard that last bit – look at the look on Shelley's face. She was busy thinking about all that lovely money, but all Raymond could think was: *Amanda.* How long before they . . .? Oh God, oh God. And why hadn't he told the police that there had been (had been!) someone else in the house? He hadn't said a word: they'd remember that, of course they would. They'd remember that for sure.

'I'd like to fuck you again, Shelley,' said Raymond.

'Yeah?' checked Shelley. 'OK, then.'

Didn't want tea, no to the Armagnac – but wouldn't turn down a fuck: OK – what the hell? Just think of all that lovely money. Anyway, one had to be kind: poor old Raymond – he's had a hell of a day, *non*?

Shelley used her hands to good effect (at least it's not me, she thought, at least it isn't me) and now Raymond was behind her, as Shelley bent over the table (and now she was gripping the rim). Soon, soon, soon I'll be done – I feel the sweet dream rising, I know that deep-down ripple is imminent – so fuck her, *fuck* her – yes, just do it: and now that Gideon had entered the room, his face held hard as if just struck, Raymond fucked as if he meant it – *now* it brimmed, now the thudding pleasure overcame him, though all excitement fountained up out of the mad delight of finally letting one of them *have* it – and it was only when Raymond saw now Amanda before him that he screamed out once and then he clutched his heart.

Old man – then he had said 'old man'. This Kevin had registered, for some reason or another. But the fact that Adam was now pushing past various bodies – two glasses of wine held high – and fast approaching Kevin presumably means that he had at some point left Kevin's side – was this right? Yes, think that's right – it's just that I can't quite get the sequence of events, um, fixed in my . . . fixed in my . . . Um. Mind. Fixed in my mind, yes. I think I am traumatized. I think I must be. If this is trauma, then trauma I know you. Why was he thinking like this, now? Why these odd constructions? Kevin didn't talk like this, did he? No – so why was this now the structure (and the content? Yes – the content too) of what we shall call for the moment his thoughts? Possibly because he is traumatized.

Adam had – oh yes, now I sort of remember: putting it together, now – Adam had come up to Kevin when Kevin was still (or maybe not) talking to, sort of to, Matt; Matt, who was (Milly did not think they had met) her husband. They had indeed not met, not before, but now they had met most surely. Matt was married to Milly; he was her husband. Together they formed a married couple: she was not Kevin's Milly Milly Milly! No. She was Matt's. Oh – and then things got worse: things became bizarre and truly disturbing, then, because Adam got chatting to Milly (they seemed to get on – seemed to, as far as Kevin was any judge – although it is fair to say that Kevin could barely recall his own name by this, er, stage of the game) and the two of them sort of drifted off, then, did they? Think so: Adam said something about another drink and he and Milly faded back into the crowd and that left Matt and Kevin, Kevin and Matt (Matt being – they had now met – Milly's husband, do you see? Making Milly his wife, of course – by marriage), and maybe or maybe not Kevin could have assimilated a good deal of all this (buried big chunks of hurt, with an X to mark the spot) but Matt was talking, Matt was laughing now in an indulgent, all-lads-together sort of a way. Why was Matt doing such a thing? Don't know – will know soon, though, because what he was saying was:

'Sounds like the two of you had quite a time in Brighton.'

Kevin almost certainly said 'Brighton?' – the best and most non-committal comment, in the circumstances, but here was no gamesmanship, no show of diplomacy, no – it was just the word that came, while thousands of others stampeded within.

'Millicent told me all about it,' went on Matt. And then he added: 'Don't worry.'

Which bit? Which bit can Kevin get a part of his mind around? Subdue the clamour, damp it down – first say 'Really?': Really's good. Have I said it? Is it out? Think I've said it, think it's done – so now I can quickly think think think before Matt speaks again, which I suppose I really want him to do, now, although I fear and dread each word: but I have to *know*, now, don't I? Don't *want* to know, not really (though deep down I do), but it must be done, now, must it not? I think I am traumatized. I think I must be. But 'all about it' – she can't have told him all about it, surely? That she *went*, maybe – OK, yes, I can just about take that on board, but not that we . . . (but we didn't, did we? No I know, but we nearly did, could've done – *would've* done if I hadn't been so fucking – right word? – useless) . . . and why should I not worry? What was he telling me not to worry about? Hey? And then the big non-thought that annihilated the rest: *Millicent!*

'You mustn't,' continued Matt, 'think badly of her. She does this sort of thing, you see. I can't pretend I like it – but it seems to be just the way she is. She didn't say she *loved* you, did she? I always think it rather cruel when she goes that far.'

'She did,' whispered back Kevin, failing to field his soul as it fell to the floor. 'She did, yes. As a matter of fact.'

Matt shook his head, maybe conspiratorially. He touched Kevin on the shoulder, a soft and decidedly conciliatory touch.

'Sorry,' he said. 'Sorry about that.'

Kevin can't have replied 'Quite all right', can he? Think so – just came out; stuff does that – just comes out.

'Can I get you a drink or anything, old man?'

And Matt must have left, and now Adam was here – Adam was back, wrapping Kevin's fingers around a glass of wine (yes, yes – and then he had said 'old man'), and Adam was now talking in a rush, careless of how Kevin looked, mindless of how Kevin was behaving.

'Christ, bloody hell, Dad – what a bloody gorgeous woman! I think I'm in with a chance there, all right. You know her, or anything? Christ, she's gorgeous.'

'Who?' said Kevin.

'The woman. Millicent. The woman you were talking to – she's well up for it, I can tell you.'

Millicent! Kevin turned slowly and dashed his wine into

Adam's face – chalk-white, mouth agape – and stared into him for two full seconds before bringing the palm of his hand hard across the side of Adam's face. A circle of space formed around them as laughter cut dead and whispers abounded while the farther edges of the ballroom continued to throb and bray. Emily was here now, hissing into Kevin's ear What in bloody Christ's name do you think you're *doing*? And Adam – hand to his face, hard wet eyes – would maybe now have spoken, but he fell as if demolished from the collision of Jim's attack as he wrestled him to the ground and started punching him hard in the stomach.

'It was *you* – I know it was you, you black bastard! Your bloody father – covering for you! It was you who done this to me – *and* to your bloody father, you –!'

'Jim! Jim!' shrieked Emily. 'Get off – get *off* him – you're crazy! You're mad!'

Three men were now hauling Jim to his feet, pinioning his arms.

'You!' came the guttural roar as he struggled with fury. 'You! You black bastard! Kill you for this!'

'Come on – you're out of here,' grunted one of the men. 'He *isn't* black, is he? You mad cunt.'

'This boy!' screamed Jim, as he was hustled towards the nearest door. 'Listen, everyone! Listen to me! This boy – this bastard – get *off* me, you sods, let go of my – this boy *Adam* – you know him, you know who I mean – Emily's boy: he's a *mugger*! He's a *thief*! He beat up his father and he done this to me! He done it! It was him who done this to me!'

Oh Christ, screamed out the insides of Emily, would they never get him *out* of here – kill him, why don't they just *kill* him? Just stop, stop him talking – I can't bear it, I can't bear the things he's saying – he's demented, he's drunk – he doesn't know what he's saying – I've got to get out of here, got to leave – Adam can hardly stand – *Kevin's* no bloody use for anything: look at him – he's still there, he's still just

273

standing there – it was he who had started the whole thing! What did he think he was *doing* – hitting Adam across the face in the middle of the Interior Decorators' Annual Ball? And Jim – what on earth did he *imagine* –? Adam's not *black*, is he? You only had to look at him to tell *that* much (Christ I think I'm going mad) and I've got to get out of here, got to go now – gather up Adam, gather up Kevin, out into the air, and surely out for good – because whatever it was that Jim had inflicted on Adam, he had surely done for Emily in the most absolute manner because the sea of eyes that burned her, the mass of eyes that stuck her with pain, was not filled with pity, no, and Emily knew that she and Adam were not perceived as the blameless victims of a mad old drunk and she well knew too that it did not do to get on the wrong side of Jim because Jim was vital, vital to all of them – and maybe too there was just something about Adam, an air about him, that suggested to people that no, he was not black, of course not, so he couldn't have been one of the two who robbed and beat up old Jim – but I wouldn't put the possibility past him, it's not beyond the realms of consideration: if he didn't do it to Jim, he sure as hell did it to someone else – and all that talk that Jim had been spreading all evening: the police had Adam down the local nick all night long – had it from the lips of his father. And you know what they say about smoke, don't you? We've all heard what they say about *smoke* – and here was smoke, all right: and look at Adam, yeah just look at him – here's the smoke and Adam's bleeding blazing.

On fire. It was the thought of the house actually on fire that Raymond couldn't . . . visualize. I wonder what love is like? That is another thing I find it hard to see. (Where was he? Where was he, actually? In bed. Yes. Not in his own bed, no.

This one smelt clean.) Do I know this room? I do not. Why should I be in a bed, then, in a room I do not know? I do not know. No good asking me: last person in the world.

When I say I find it hard to see what love is like, I do not mean to imply that I have never known this thing. I have known it. I have known it once. Just the once. And it was beautiful, deeply beautiful. And I killed it. The most beautiful thing I have ever had. And I killed it.

I know why I am not in my own house: my house no longer exists. Burned down, you know. Just this evening, I'm pretty sure – think it was just this evening. So it would be silly, wouldn't it, very silly indeed, to be propped up in bed in the midst of charred ruins? Yes. These thoughts, these thoughts I'm having, are rather similar in nature, don't you think, to dreams. They are fragmentary. And quite dippy. Like dreams. I think this must be Emily's house, you know. That's where I was when . . . *got* to be Emily's house: look at the swagged border along the I think they call it dado. Yes, this is where I was when . . .

I loved that woman. And she loved me. Beautiful girl, beautiful. Very elegant: great style. Mad and bubbly light red hair, pale blue eyes that made me dissolve. I loved her more than I even loved me, which had never happened before. We talked, we laughed, we talked, we laughed, we loved, we loved, we loved. I thought I would know her for ever, which is why I bought her forever things: I give nothing to anyone, now.

Oh yes . . . and then Gideon came, just as I did – oh *yes*, I remember – just as I was fucking young, um . . . good Lord, do you know I've forgotten her, um . . . name. Amanda. Not Amanda – the other one. Shelley. Of course.

She was married. And so was I. She was married to quite a decent fellow. They were contented, she told me, contented. They still sort of made love – maybe once a month, maybe less: no big thing, no great joy. She said she did it to be kind. He's a nice man, she explained, and I do it to be kind. At first I didn't mind this; it felt good to be the one man in the world chosen by her to be a fine and ardent lover (she had never been unfaithful before: she told me this, and I believed her. And I *was* ardent, I was – I was always excited by her, always: every time we made love – three, four times a week, maybe – far more often when we got away for the weekend: non-stop, then – all I wanted in the world was to do it again – and sometimes, she was that exciting, I did just that. And then she said you're wonderful: what a man – a real man, and God – so *passionate*. I was. I was on fire for her).

My orgasm came just as Shelley looked up and saw Gideon. I hosed into her just as her eyes looked into his. There will be no so fine an orgasm ever again in my life. But Amanda! Not dead, then, Amanda. She was there too. She loves me. But not in that way. Shelley doesn't love me. I don't care.

I have had a heart attack: I remember now. Just after the orgasm came the heart attack. So like life. *Is* life, of course: *is*. Didn't kill me, then. No – I'd know if I was dead. It's rather like being in a novel where no one dies – the author wants immortality for not just himself but for all of his characters. Rosie was dead in a mortuary, but apparently not. Amanda was burned alive in a locked attic room but wasn't, clearly. And now me – clutching my heart, falling away from Shelley and on to the floor, chest close to crushing me . . . and here I am, chatting. I remember the doctor, vaguely. There was a questing face hung above me for quite a time. I think I feel like this because of drugs: he gave me something.

And then it wasn't so fine, she and her husband sort of making love maybe once a month, maybe less. Not so fine at all. I saw her less because she was busy at work – and it was true, that – she was; she did see me whenever she could, and often when she really shouldn't – God knows how she fitted everything in. I became jealous, jealous of everything and everybody. She wanted to set up her own business and she was meeting all sorts of people. I didn't mind. And then I did.

What must Gideon have been thinking? Was he tempted to let his father die on the floor? Who phoned the doctor? Gideon? Amanda? Or Shelley? It would be interesting to know. I wonder whether Kevin and Emily are home yet. Where did they go? Oh, the ball. The annual ball. Emily always enjoyed that: at least Emily will have had a good time.

I asked her to leave her husband, and I would leave my wife. But she said no. It would be too disruptive. And anyway – I love it just the way it is. Also, she said: I'm pregnant.

What will become of all of us now? Can't throw out Maureen and Rosie, as Amanda has been telling me to do: no house to throw them out of. I wonder if Amanda still loves me – in any way at all. That's two women she's seen me fucking, now. Mother and daughter.

She said she thought it would be a little girl. I said: is it mine? (We never used anything.) She said, It's ironic, but for the first time in a long time, it maybe just isn't, but somehow she felt sure that it was: ninety-five per cent certain. So I said (but that five per cent was already killing me) Why won't you live with me, then? and she said that her husband – who was older than she, I recall, quite a bit older – had always wanted a child and I already had one and admit it, Raymond, admit it – you don't want to go through all that again (but I did, with her I did) and anyway, we're much too alike to be together all the time: we'd constantly be at each other's throats.

Shelley thinks I'm going to pay for her flat. Shelley thinks the blackened stub of my house is going to yield up a

277

fortune. The building was covered – all bound in with the various mortgages – but I own only about five per cent of it. And even that five per cent was killing me. And the dirt inside, that wasn't insured.

My love for the woman was by now ferocious. I hated all her business contacts – and her husband (decent bloke, apparently – a nice, kind man): I hated him more than anyone. Every night she was in the same bed with him. Even if, as she said, they rarely touched. For the first three months of her pregnancy, we saw each other maybe once a week, and then less often. Lunch. Dinner. She didn't want sex. It's not *you*, she said: not you. If I felt I wanted it, it's you I'd want: I just don't. Will you be patient? I said I will. I wasn't. I felt she didn't want me. Nothing of what she said any longer included me. I spoiled the lunches, ruined the dinners. And then I did the big, bad thing.

Why do I fuck and hate Emily quite so much? Well, she's very fuckable and utterly loathsome, I suppose is it. Will it go on? Will anything now be the same? God, there's been so much stuff, just lately.

I telephoned her husband – and he did, he did sound a decent bloke, a nice, kind man – and I told him everything. I had dates, places, *proof* – I blew her every alibi. I told him I was the father of the coming child – one hundred per cent, totally (because the five per cent just went on killing me). She did not believe me when I told her I had done it: I barely believed it myself. She would not see me again: I'll never forget the look. Her husband stayed with her. It was a little girl. She's two in two days' time. The five per cent? It kills me still.

So I have known this thing. I have known it once. Just the once. And it was beautiful, deeply beautiful. And I killed it. The most beautiful thing I have ever had. And I killed it.

CHAPTER NINE

'My hero,' Amanda had grinned.

'I wouldn't say *that*,' qualified Gideon – and despite the fact that he had only just deposited his mother in an ambulance (the family home was still as they stood there a riot of flame, fizzing and popping up into the night air) he found himself grinning as well.

Amanda had smelt the burning, but not the danger. Christ, she remembered thinking, Maureen's bloody cooking: it's a miracle she doesn't burn the whole house down. Then the fumes became something else altogether, and Amanda reached for her bag, took out a key, unlocked the study door and walked into a wall of smoke and not even pausing to think she crashed on down the stairs and Christ it was hard to see – but now on the ground floor the light and the heat were fierce, and it was as she hesitated between two doors that Gideon had caught sight of her from the garden and he had run to the side-door, the door that was nearest – the fire had not yet taken hold here and he shouted out and she came to him and he grasped her wrist and they ran from that reeking and scalding place and tipped over each other into the cool of the grass and Amanda was completely unharmed and not even grubby and she laughed and pushed a hand roughly through her floppy hair and said to Gideon that he was her hero.

And are we to know about the key? Here was no locked-room mystery then, apparently – so how come she had the key? Well, obvious really: obvious to Amanda, anyway. When she had left the house the first time (when Gideon had unlocked the door that time – yes? Not knowing he was freeing a kidnap victim) she had had the wits to take the key with her: she didn't mind being locked in (quite liked it, actually) so long as she had the means to get out. So she had a couple cut (it would be awful if she lost the one and only) and before voluntarily returning to her den of capture (by then Amanda had decided to give the sucker an even break – save him, shall I? Chuck out everything and everyone and start again) she had picked up one or two other things that her very strange and duplicitous mind had suggested to her: a pocket tape-recorder, most notably. Raymond did not yet know of the tape-recorder. Raymond, of course, was unaware she had ever left the room. Just as well about the key, though: otherwise Amanda would by now resemble the fragments of Maureen's last attempt at toast.

They both got tired of watching the house burn down after a while, so hey – why don't we go and have a drink, said Amanda. Like to, I'd like to do that, agreed Gideon, but first I've just got to pop in on the hospital to check that Mum's OK – I'm sure she is, but Christ she's had a hell of a shock; you should have seen her face when the pan went up – it frightened the life out of her; thank God I was there. Do you want to come along? Or shall I maybe meet you somewhere? The policeman I was talking to said they'd send someone to tell Dad – it's just as well I knew where he was. Then I'll get round there too – he'll want to know everything. Christ, what a thing. What a bloody thing, ay?

They went to the hospital together and Maureen was as fine as Maureen ever gets: kept on babbling about Raymond – you must tell your father, your father must know. Of *course* I'll tell him, course I will, Gideon assured her – it's his house, after all. No, not about the *house*, Maureen said urgently, the *meal* – the *dinner* I promised him – tell him I'll do a wonderful dinner for him *next* time and I hope he isn't hungry because he would've eaten it, you know – when he saw what I had for him, he would've eaten it, all right. And

Gideon – you couldn't slip out and get me a little, well not *too* little, bottle of vodka, could you? They said it would be all right. Mummy's coming home tomorrow, you know, Gideon – but she can't really, now, can she? Where will we all go? Where will we all stay? Don't know, Mum. Early days. Don't know yet.

'They'll chuck you out of here for sure,' said Amanda. 'In no time. Face it, Maureen – you're just the sort of person who gets chucked out of everywhere. It's what you're for.'

Later, on the way to the pub (it can only be quick, though – I've really got to talk to Dad because these police people aren't very subtle, you know, and he could be feeling terrible), Gideon said You don't like my Mum, do you? And Amanda had replied No, no I don't; I love your Dad, though – and do you know what, Gideon? I think I love you too – but in a different way. I could never love you the way I love your father – which, believe me, is better for you, although you can't know this yet. And Gideon had thought I have no idea what this woman is talking about (how on earth could she possibly love Dad? How could anyone?) but I like her, I really do – *love* her? No, course not – don't love her (all that's just talk) – but you know, I do actually find her quite exciting: more so than any other woman, anyway. Which may or may not be interesting.

'It's like that film where the skyscraper went up in flames,' Amanda was saying now. They didn't have any champagne at the pub, so she was drinking Mâcon. Mâcon's fine for me too, said Gideon. (What's Mâcon?)

'Skyscraper? I'm not very up on films.'

Amanda nodded. 'The fire chief, he knew that the building was an accident just waiting to happen – Steve McQueen, pretty sure – and it had loads of stars doing little bits and it did, it did catch fire and there was some posh party on the very top floor so *they'd* had it for a start and there was a – have you really not seen this film?'

'No. Don't think so. I don't really, you know – *do* films, much. What's it called? I *might've* seen it.'

'Can't remember – but there's this outside lift, they say elevator, and that breaks away – God, it's *awful*, that bit – Towering something – and it's odd, actually, that watching a skyscraper burn down can be so much fun, but it is. More fun than watching *your* house go up, anyway.'

'That's maybe because Steve McQueen didn't show.'

'Was that a joke, Gideon? I quite like jokes. Yes it *was* a joke, wasn't it? Because Steve McQueen's dead.'

'Ye-es,' agreed Gideon, shakily: wouldn't have been likely either way, would it? She's a funny girl, this Amanda – rather odd, in many ways.

'D'you know I think even Fred Astaire had a small part in it. He's a dancer. Dead now.'

'Let's go and tell Dad about the house.'

'Inferno.'

'Yes – I suppose it was.'

'No – that's the name of the film: *Towering Inferno*. And Paul Newman – yeah, he was in it. I like him. Eyes. He's not dead.'

'And nor are we, thank God.'

'I know. Good, isn't it?'

So they went round to Kevin and Emily's and rang and rang on the bell but no one was answering and Gideon said well that's odd because *somebody's* got to be here but Shelley actually often doesn't hear the bell, it's true – oh and look, the door's on the latch all the time – she must have done that for me so right, let's go in then, shall we? So they went into the hall and on into the living-room where they stopped and stared quite briefly at Raymond undergoing what might well be termed his fucking heart attack.

❧

'Oh *God*, what an evening! What an evening! What a terrible, terrible evening!'

Emily was saying this as she unlocked her front door. She had been saying this and things like this all the way home in the taxi, sometimes flushing hot from some memory of a part of it. Kevin had sat there, in silence, ignoring all of Adam's pained enquiry.

'Why did you *hit* me, Dad?' asked Adam, again and again – and it hurt Kevin, this, because he knew from the voice that Adam really did want to know. He could not tell him. How could he tell him? I hit you, Adam, because you talked lewdly of a person known to me as Milly and others as Millicent (who never kissed me) with whom I had fallen in love, and further with whom – following my failure to fornicate with her in a hotel in Brighton – I was planning to spend the rest of my life, abandoning you and your mother, but it turns out she is married to Matt (who is her husband) who tells me Sorry, sorry about that, but that's the way she is; as, Adam, you found out. So I hit you, I hit you, Adam, because I needed to kill myself: OK?

'You never hit me before,' said Adam.

True; it was true – Kevin had never done this before. Emily had – Emily had clouted both Adam and Shelley (and Kevin) countless times in the past, but this one act of violence from Kevin, he knew, would wipe out all of that.

'Why did he hit me, Mum? D'you know?'

'Because he's a bloody lunatic,' replied Emily. 'How should I know why he hit you? Why did Jim attack you? Christ, *I* don't know. What an evening! Oh Christ what an evening. This evening has been the worst evening of my entire life.'

Poor Emily – did she really think it was over? Not, I'm afraid – oh no, not by a long chalk: the next bit was under way as soon as she had the front door shut behind her.

'What's all this stuff doing in the hall? Kevin – do you

know anything about this mess? Christ – there's *stuff* – stuff all over the bloody place.'

'Shelley's stuff,' said Adam. 'This is all Shelley's stuff. Maybe she's moving out. Great – I can have her room.'

'Of *course* she's not moving out,' snapped Emily. 'Don't you think I'd know if she was moving out? She's probably just – well I don't much *care* what she's – but this mess is going to be cleared up right this minute, that's for sure. Shelley! Shelley – where are you?!'

'In here, Mum,' called Shelley from the living-room. 'Come on in and join the party.'

'What does *that* mean?' Emily muttered to Kevin. 'There's no one here, is there? No one was coming over this evening, were they?'

Kevin didn't even shrug: *he* wasn't here, certainly.

'Oh it's *you*, Gideon,' said Emily as she strode into the room, Adam shambling in behind her and Kevin, quite like a Dalek, taking up the rear. Now Emily was training her and-who-might-you-be look fully on Amanda.

'This is Amanda,' said Gideon. 'Dad's assistant.'

'I see,' said Emily, glowering at Amanda's expansive smile. Why is Raymond's assistant all over my living-room? Why have I returned from an evening in hell to find my beautiful house looking like a jumble sale with perfect strangers littering the corners?

'Dad's upstairs,' went on Gideon. 'In bed. You see –'

'Did I hear you correctly, Gideon? Raymond? Upstairs? What – *these* stairs? *My* stairs?'

'You OK, Dad?' said Shelley.

'No he's not,' put in Adam. 'He hit me.'

'*Why* is Raymond upstairs, Gideon?' pursued Emily. 'In bed.'

'Good for him,' said Shelley. 'Three cheers for Dad.'

'Be *quiet*, Shelley,' insisted Emily. 'I am trying to make sense of this – and what do you mean by strewing all your

284

things all over the hall – and in *here* too – my *God*, what a mess.'

'There are a few things you might as well know,' said Shelley, quite impishly.

'Excuse me, *Amanda*, is it?' interjected Emily. 'One hates to appear rude, of course, but would you mind explaining to me why you are here? It has been a very trying evening and if there are things to be said concerning my friends and family, then I rather think –'

'*Look*,' cut in Amanda.

'You interrupted me,' said Emily – and you certainly knew icy when you heard it.

'Just *listen*,' banged on Amanda. 'I was in Raymond's house with Gideon and bloody Maureen when it burned to the ground and we came to tell Raymond – who seemed to be getting on awfully well with your daughter, I have to say: we might have a chat about that, later. Getting on quite as well as he gets on with you, in point of fact: you might not have seen me before, Emily, but I have seen you. She is – your daughter, that is – moving out, she's got a flat – *and*, she has just been telling me – is this right, Shelley?'

Shelley nodded. 'Yeah,' she said.

'Shelley,' said Emily, with wonder. 'What is this woman telling me?'

'There's more,' grunted Shelley.

'There is,' Amanda agreed. 'I gather that the plan is for Raymond to move in with Shelley. I have not been consulted about this, but needless to say I shan't allow it. You might have views yourself.'

'Shelley,' said Emily, quietly, 'this is a joke, yes? Kevin – *say* something for Christ's sake! Are you *hearing* this?'

'But the reason we can't actually have it out with Raymond right now,' continued Amanda, 'is that since his heart attack an hour or two ago, the pressure might kill him. And we don't want that, do we? We want him *alive*.'

285

Emily sat down heavily (oh God – one of Jim's bergère chairs).

'This is a joke. This has *got* to be a joke.' She turned up truly weary eyes to Shelley. 'Shelley, please – tell me that all this is just a joke.'

'In a way it is,' said Shelley. 'Quite a lot of it's pretty funny. But it's all *true*, if that's what you mean. What did you mean, Amanda – when you said all that stuff about me and Mum? What was all that about? I don't care if Mum knows what was going on here – I'm not a kid any more, I can do as I like. And anyway, by tomorrow I'm gone.'

Emily looked distraught. She rubbed a hand all over her face and screwed her eyes up tight. 'I'm confused,' she said. 'I'm so confused.' Yes, she thought, and I want to cry. I do not understand all of this, do not care for the odour, but I surely have enough to know that here are grounds for tears. I yearn to be weak, I yearn to let others take the pain – but I have never been allowed to be vulnerable, never had the leeway to be cared for. It was all the fault of the tragic men: tell me – into whose arms could I swoon? All of them, all of them would let me fall: I need a man I can look not at or into but up to – and there is no such thing; no such thing exists.

'How bad is Raymond?' asked Kevin.

'Oh you *are* still alive, then, are you, Kevin?' snorted Emily.

'He's OK, I think,' said Shelley. 'The doctor said it was more of a sort of heart spasm than a real sort of, what do they call them? Coronary thing.'

'I just simply don't believe any of this is happening,' whispered Emily – and it was true, she did feel now as if she was dreaming it all.

'Christ,' said Kevin. 'No wonder it happened, though – I mean – hearing your *house* has burned down! How did it happen?'

'I don't think it was *that* that did it,' smiled Amanda. 'Do you, Gideon?'

Gideon's legs were wide and his hands were slung into a cat's cradle across his knees; his head hung low not far above.

'No,' he said. 'No.'

'And *you* can still talk, then, Gideon, can you?' hooted Emily, who was thinking this is all I can do, now – this is what I do, but I need to cry, and then to be consoled.

'No,' chimed in Amanda. 'We think what did it – quite apart from the million cigarettes he smoked every day of his life – was seeing me alive: that's a bit of a long story – and also maybe the strain of – can I be frank, Shelley?'

Shelley shrugged. 'Say what you like. Doesn't matter, now.'

Amanda nodded. 'The strain of fucking Shelley, and standing up to do it.'

Emily's whole face was set up for the ultimate exclamation, but not one sound emerged.

Kevin said, 'I think I'll see how Raymond is.'

Emily swivelled a quite white face towards him.

'Is that – is that all you have to say?'

Kevin nodded in misery. 'Yes,' he said.

'*Please*, Shelley,' tried Emily once more, her voice now faded to a shadow. 'Please tell me, Shelley, that all this isn't true.'

Shelley looked up at the ceiling. 'Believe what you like. Think whatever you want to think.' But now she faced her mother: 'What do *you* care, anyway? You never cared what I did, who I was with. When did *you* last care about anything to do with me? You don't care – and I don't either.'

Adam shouted out, '*Slag*! You're a right little *slag*, you are, Shelley,' and so barked and sudden was it that it completely obliterated Emily saying softly I do, I do care: I *do*.

'Look!' shouted Shelley. 'I don't *need* this – I don't have to *take* this. I'm going to bed and tomorrow I'm out of here for good and I can't bloody *wait* – OK?!'

Shelley flounced out, and a moment later Adam went in quest of his mother's brandy. Emily turned to look at Gideon.

'Gideon,' she said. 'What are you going to *do*?'

Gideon closed his eyes. 'I'm so tired,' he said.

Maybe, thought Emily, he doesn't care about the woman because he's a woman himself; this Amanda certainly seems man enough for him. Maybe that's what I should have been.

'I mean,' pursued Emily, 'you and Shelley . . . Raymond, your *father*, I mean – *God*, Gideon?'

Gideon wagged his head rigidly from side to side as if denying all temptations.

'I'm not going to do anything,' he said. 'Shelley and I – *aren't*, any more. And it's not really anything to do with Dad, not really.'

'He's mine, now,' said Amanda, with pride.

Emily sighed. 'Take the other spare room, Gideon. There are sheets and things in the cupboard.'

'I could sleep *anywhere*,' yawned Gideon, extravagantly.

When there was just Amanda and Emily in the room, Amanda leaned across as if to confide a secret at a sorority.

'You're not going to let Raymond get *away* with this, are you? I mean, I know about your, shall we say, *relationship* with Raymond – and now *this*. You're not just going to let him get away with it, are you?'

Emily sighed again: God, I keep on sighing. Do you know, I probably *am* going to? Let him get away with it. I'm just so exhausted – all these things going on, all this stuff. Could there still be futures?

Amanda correctly interpreted the silence.

'Well *you* might,' she said. 'But *I'm* not. No bloody way.'

Raymond was propped up in bed smoking a cigarette when Kevin tiptoed into the room – now, in view of the scene, assuming a more straightforward gait. Quite a few butts in a Dresden bonbon dish that Emily wouldn't be very pleased about – or maybe now she wouldn't care: hard to say.

'I think,' said Raymond, 'that these must be your pyjamas – someone, Shelley I suppose, said to put them on.'

'How are you feeling, Raymond? I've heard about – well, just about everything.'

'What happened to your *face*, Kevin? Emily again?'

Kevin nodded. 'Yup. Emily again.'

Raymond shook his head in that I've-told-you-before-but-you-won't-be-told sort of way he had.

'So,' prompted Kevin. 'Not feeling too bad?'

'I feel fine, rather oddly,' said Raymond. 'Thought I'd had it at the time, though – but even that didn't make me feel too bad, if you can believe it. I didn't panic, or anything – didn't feel scared. When the doctor bloke came I just let him give me whatever – I'm still a bit high, I think – because I couldn't actually *move* and I thought oh Christ: this is a bloody *stroke*, that's what this is – and I didn't at all care for the thought of being a wheelchair case, I can tell you. But it seems OK – just a scare. *Warning*, of course. The next one will get me. So bloody what?'

'The fags don't help,' said Kevin.

Raymond exhaled with a hiss. 'They help *me*,' he said.

'I'm sorry about the house.'

'Yeah, the house. I haven't actually seen it, yet, but from what I've heard it's a complete and utter write-off. Well – has been for years, really.'

'Any idea how it happened?'

Raymond shrugged. 'How do these things happen? With Maureen it was only a question of time. Christ – all the lumber, all the *stuff* in that house – must have gone up like a bomb.' Raymond smirked, briefly. 'What with one thing and another, I think it's safe to say that you had a rather more pleasant evening than I did. How was it?'

Kevin smiled sadly, and slowly shook his head. 'Not good,' he said.

'No? Well – never mind, at least your bloody house didn't burn down.'

'No,' agreed Kevin. 'But quite a lot else seems to have been going on.'

'Yes-es,' said Raymond, with caution. 'Shelley – has she –?'

'Told us? Which part? The moving out part?'

'Moving out, yes . . .'

'And you moving in with her. I should be shocked – I have been trying to summon up all sorts of feelings Raymond, but I can't. I can't.'

Raymond nodded. 'I think I know. What you mean. I tell you, Kevin – if it really does bother you, I'll back off – I mean, I don't actually *care* either way. I'm sorry if that sounds, I don't know, rather –'

'No no. I know what you mean. It's a bit like what you were saying about the dying thing. If it was going to happen, fine; if not, not.'

'That's it! That's it! It's terrible, really, but you know lately I just don't give a fuck about anything. Do you know what I mean?'

'I do. I do.'

'And if some lovely girl comes along – sorry, Kevin, but *you* know what I mean – well then: why not?'

'Yes,' said Kevin. 'Why not indeed?'

'Do you know, Kevin, in all the years we've known each other, this is the very first time we've actually *talked*? You know – *communicated*. Maybe it needs stuff like this to – you know – make you think.'

Kevin nodded. 'Or stop you thinking.'

'Yes. I have this theory about women, you know: they're almost a disease one keeps on catching. It's the scent of *cunt*, Kevin: turns men's minds. Agree?'

'Yes,' said Kevin. 'Despite what you might think of me, I do. Yes. Stay here, Raymond, for a day or two – probably better than going off straight away. Where is this flat of Shelley's, by the way?'

'Belsize Park, I gather: don't know the area.'

'I don't. Never been there.'

'Quite nice, by all accounts. But Christ I'm in no hurry. What's going to happen to bloody Maureen, that's the point. And her bloody mother Lazarus is due out of the hospital tomorrow. Did I tell you about her? Didn't, did I? She died. And then she didn't. It's not been a good week, one way and the other.'

'They can stay here,' said Kevin. 'Probably best. Till everyone decides what they're all going to do.'

'And what about you, Kevin? Same old thing? Still going on with it all?'

'It rather looks that way. There was a possibility – well, I *thought* it was a possibility that there might be some sort of change, but no – not now. No.'

'You know, one day Emily will go completely over the top and bloody kill you, Kevin. You do know that she's quite capable of it, don't you? There's nothing Emily wouldn't do. Like Amanda.'

'I know you know a lot about her. Emily, I mean.'

'I can't stand her, Kevin, if you want the God's honest truth. I can't bloody *stand* the woman.'

'Except for sex.'

'Christ. You know about that, do you?'

'Not really – I don't really *know*: it was just something I . . . something I thought might well be happening. Why else would you know her? I don't actually mind that either – I don't actually care either way.'

'No. Nor do I. Nor do I.'

So it wasn't ever a question of letting Kevin have it, because Kevin, poor bastard – he had it all the time.

A drink, maybe. Kevin didn't really want the drink as such (wasn't really much of an alcohol man) but it was the sort of evening, surely, when a drink was called for if only as a prop: a large drink in a squat tumbler – the sort of drink with which one could sit down heavily in a big, deep armchair – maybe even wheeze on impact – and then balloon one's cheeks while full of whisky (brandy? Don't know what Emily's got, whatever Adam's left) and then sigh like a put-upon man in tune with the swallow. Yes. Something like that would be good. A bit of silence to think. Or to stop one thinking.

Too late he saw Emily alone in the living-room – too late to veer, too late to swerve, for already her eyes had alighted upon him with something approaching eagerness, but all hint of attack had now deserted her. Kevin noted this; Kevin had learned, over the years, how to read the signs – knew precisely just what level of panic was appropriate.

What Emily said was, to Kevin, the most terrifying thing she had ever uttered.

'Kevin,' is how it went: 'I'm frightened.'

Well if Emily was frightened, Kevin was paralysed: always, always, Emily had been never anything less than Superman; even Superman she rendered as insipid as his journalistic alter ego, so what was all this *frightened* stuff? Frightened for herself – frightened for others? One of those nameless fears you read about? We'll all know more, Kevin included, when Emily takes it that little bit farther.

'All this stuff with Jim, Kevin – it's not good. Not good.'

Jim. Kevin had assumed that Shelley would be first under the microscope, but no: it's going to be Jim.

'He was drunk,' said Kevin. 'Drunk nearly a whole bottle of Scotch.'

Emily shook her head impatiently. 'Doesn't matter.

Doesn't *matter*. The point is now he won't do any work for us – he's got it into his lunatic head that we're all murderers and villains and I'm telling you, Kevin, by tomorrow my name's absolutely *mud*. This simply couldn't have come at a worse time. What with that *disaster* at the flat – the lighting, Kevin, the *lighting*. It took me an hour on the phone to calm him down. I'd promised the flat would be ready at the weekend and now there's at least four more days' work, could even be a week – and all that's coming out of my pocket.'

'Sorry. I'm sorry, Emily, but I *told* you –'

'And the hotel! The hotel! The Grange. The manager rang just before we left for the – oh God, the bloody *ball*, oh Christ oh *Christ* what an evening – and he seemed to think that what you'd done there was some sort of practical joke. Your English sense of humour, yes? He kept saying that – he's French or Dutch or something. So *that* I'll have to sort out tomorrow, but the point is we're never going to get another commission, are we? Not once bloody Jim's started shooting off his bloody mouth. And even if we *did* – even if we *did*, we can't do anything without The Works, can we? Without Jim, we're finished – and he's the one who's doing the finishing! It's all too *ghastly*, everything, but just this one thing is bad enough – I mean this is our *livelihood*, we're talking about here. I can't *do* anything else – and you, *you* can't do anything, full stop.'

Kevin nodded. 'I know. Is there anything to drink?'

'And look what's happening – look what's happened to everyone around us! Never mind about drink, just *listen*, Kevin. I mean – Shelley. *Shelley*, for God's sake, Kevin!'

Shelley's turn. 'What about her?'

'What *about* –? What *about* her? You *heard*, didn't you? You were sitting there, weren't you? She's talking about living with Raymond. With *Raymond*. And God – from what that weird Amanda person was saying, they were – they were

293

actually making love! In the living-room. In *this* room – oh my God I can't *bear* it.'

'Why?' asked Kevin, still thinking am I going to say this, even though he had started now. 'Is it not good making love to Raymond? Have you not done so in here?'

Emily stared at Kevin. Didn't blink. Kevin thought he knew all of Emily's expressions, but there was nothing here for him: he could read nothing at all there, nothing at all.

'Kevin,' she said. 'Do you not think we could start – everything – all over again? Make it new?'

Kevin's face twisted into a smile that wasn't funny.

'No, Emily, I don't. I don't think so, not at all.'

Emily nodded as if she had anticipated such a reaction, but had thought the motion worth going through anyway.

'I've had an idea, Kevin. It's a crazy idea, I suppose it is – but it would help, it would help us all, Kevin – Adam, us, Shelley – even Raymond. Everyone.'

'This sounds very unlike you, Emily. You're reacting in strange ways to all of this. Just let things settle down: it's the only way.'

'*Not* the only way,' said Emily petulantly. 'Not not *not*. If we let it all settle down, it'll all settle down *wrong*, I just know it will. We've got to all try to be the way we *used* to be, and maybe then everything will untangle.'

'It just doesn't *happen* like that, Emily. That's just not the way it works. You're going to tell everyone to do what you want them to do, and they're just going to say no. Everyone now is doing what they like. Almost everyone is.'

'But just listen to my *idea*, Kevin – please!'

Kevin had never before seen pleading in Emily's eyes, and he was touched by it; this would pass – of course it would – but for now he would hear about Emily's idea, and whatever it was he wanted it to happen: here was unfamiliar ground.

'What I want to do,' said Emily, her eyes now wide with

urgency. 'What my idea is is to bring forward my birthday to tomorrow.'

Kevin just looked at her. To bring her birthday forward to tomorrow. Is that right? Is that what she said? She wants to bring her birthday forward to tomorrow.

'Don't you *see*? We can do everything we always do on my birthday, and everyone will be happy – they always are.'

They never are. Happy? On Emily's birthday? We touched on this earlier: Kevin's most dreaded thing after the Annual Interior Decorators' Ball, and here was Emily proposing the one the very day after the other. And all through this, his heart was so heavy with Milly. Milly Milly. Oh, Milly . . . Milly . . . Milly . . .

'And *that* means,' rushed on Emily, 'that Shelley won't be dashing off to this so-called flat of hers – it must be vile, on what she earns – and Raymond's already here, and Adam's here, and Gideon's here, and *you're* here –'

'And there'll be a few more by tomorrow. I said to Raymond that Maureen and her mother could stay for a few days. Until something's sorted out.'

Can you imagine how the Emily of old might have greeted this nugget of information? All the Birthday Girl had to say was:

'Well that's fine! A real house party – everyone'll be here and it'll be *marvellous*.'

'Emily,' said Kevin quietly, with as much indulgence as he could muster (I'm tired now – I'm really tired). 'You saw Shelley – you heard her. Nothing on earth would stop her going to that flat tomorrow. Even if it was your *real* birthday, she'd be off like a shot. And you don't like Maureen, you know you don't – you're always saying that. Her mother you've never met, but you know how Raymond goes on about her – she's completely bats. As to Gideon – well, what with this Shelley situation, well . . . and if Gideon's here then that Amanda will be here too, because she's never going to let him out of her sights, I can tell you that.'

'But it's a *party*, Kevin – a *party*. Everyone comes to a party.'

Kevin shook his head. What language would she like it in?

'And,' went on Emily, 'I can ask Sophie. It was lovely seeing her again tonight – the only thing that was. Remember Sophie? She always used to love my birthday parties. And I might need her, the way things are going – she might have to give *me* a job: that'd be funny, wouldn't it? But it could easily come to that.'

Sophie. Do you know, what with all this – what with all this *madness*, Kevin could have sworn . . . you know it just goes to show the turmoil he was in, because now the vision of his love, real love, was dancing before his eyes because he could have sworn that Emily had just said –

'Sophie now has a very successful business of her own, she was telling me. Actually, if I'm honest, I *knew* that – she's been taking out colour ads in *The World of Interiors* and *House & Garden* – they cost a fortune, those. Anyway, she employs about ten people, so maybe there's a lifeline there. She's even got a kid, now – God knows how she manages – but the marriage was a disaster, apparently. She's on her own, now. She sent her love. Anyway, we'll ask her – we'll ask everybody, and everybody will come. Yes, Kevin?'

'Yes,' said Kevin. 'Yes. I think it's a marvellous idea. I'll make sure that everyone comes, if that's the way you want it. Will it be just like your real birthday, Emily? Is that the way you want it?'

'Oh I *think* so, don't you? The cake. Monopoly, but of course. It wouldn't be anything without the Monopoly, would it?'

'OK, Emily – fine. And you'll phone Sophie, will you?

'Yup – first thing. First thing tomorrow. It'll be *lovely*, Kevin.'

Kevin smiled. 'I know it will.'

He went up to his room, because he had to be on his own, now. The marriage was a disaster, apparently. She's on her own, now. She sent her love.

CHAPTER TEN

Shelley was yawning in the hall quite early the following morning (no one else seemed to be up: no one was around, anyway) and sliding out of a jaggedly torn-open envelope a shiny postcard featuring a great deal of very blue sea and sky. It was from Julian (for who else would seal up a picture postcard into a pre-gummed and wallet-sized business envelope? Who but Julian?) and in the quite black copperplate more usually associated with a wedding invitation, he had written the following:

Dear Shelley, I hope this finds you quite well. We are, as you may see, in Majorca – not, I hasten to add, the Majorca of which you may have heard tell, but the nicer part, more elevated. The sun is rather too hot, I have to say – you really do need to wear a hat. No doubt we shall speak again. Fond regards – your friend, Julian.

'Prat,' said Shelley, quietly, picking up from the mat another postcard (naked), this one addressed to Adam: 'It is *skill* here, man – totally wicked. See ya! Ben.' Shelley flipped over the card: the torso of a deep-brown woman (naked) with a glistening glass of ale in each fist.

'Bloody *prats*,' hissed Shelley, before whispering to herself Right, then: let's do it. Out of here.

'You're up early, Shelley,' said Kevin, suddenly beside her. Of course she was, but naturally: out of here, right?

'Hi, Dad. Yeah – I'm just stuffing all this lot into carrier bags and ordering a taxi. Might get it all in – otherwise a couple of journeys, maybe.'

Kevin opened his mouth to say something just as the

phone started to ring so he closed his mouth on whatever (nothing much, shouldn't have thought) and was on his way to the phone when the doorbell rang and so Kevin glanced across at Shelley and they each darted out a forefinger in differing directions as both bells went on ringing (because whoever it was at the door had rung again already – some people have absolutely no patience at all) and then Shelley swung wide the door more or less at the instant that Kevin picked up the receiver and while he was saying to some man at the other end Yes, I see, oh dear, well she's just here, actually, I think you'd better speak to her yourself – Shelley, at the door, was saying to some man who stood there Yeah, I'll take it, thanks – do you want me to sign anything or anything? And then they were saying to each other more or less as simultaneously as you ever really get: it's for you. And now Shelley had the receiver to her ear, just as Kevin lifted the lid from the shoebox addressed to him that Shelley had placed in his hands. There was a note on top of something in tissue.

'Oh shit no – you can't *mean* it,' Shelley was saying – quite exasperated, pleading with the man to please not *mean* it.

The note said: 'I think maybe now that you should have this.'

'But Christ it can't be *that* bad, can it? How bad is it?'

And after this message there was an X.

'But I can't *wait* a bloody week! I've paid the rent – I've paid the rent from *today* – I don't want to wait a bloody week!'

Just an X. No more.

'Well I'm just totally pissed off – I just don't know what to *do*, now. No it's not just the rent – it's just – yes. OK. Yes – oh all right. No, I *know* it's not your fault, it's just –'

And inside the tissue was a little black and white stuffed kitten.

'Yeah, OK. OK. Well, phone me whenever, yeh?'

And Milly was wrong, because it was still she who should now have this, because this was all she ever did have of me: that's all I ever gave her.

'Great! Just great! You won't *believe* this, Dad – did you get all that? The bloody ceiling's come down in the flat! Some bloody shithead let the bath overflow or something and now the ceiling's got to be . . . and the carpet's *completely* buggered. Oh *Jesus*. Christ. What's in the box?'

'Nothing. Just something. It's good you hadn't already moved in all your stuff, though, Shelley,' said Kevin. I won't tell her about Emily's plan for the evening: she'll find out soon enough.

'They say it'll take a week – I just don't know if *I* can take a week, not here, in this place. Oh *Christ*, I don't believe it. Why did this have to happen?'

'It's only a week,' said Kevin. 'A week's nothing.' No, he thought – in the light of the time I've been serving, a week is nothing at all. Oh Sophie. Oh Sophie. I do hope you come. Because although I suppose, Sophie, you cannot really be a hope, you are to me – my one and only.

Shelley had been wrong to assume that no one else was up. Raymond was surely fast asleep (Shelley had crept in to see him, praying he hadn't died or something – but no, there he was, making a droning noise, unshaven and ugly). Why have I asked *this* to come and live with me? The thought crossed her mind. And then she chastened herself by thinking Hey, wise up, girl – why do you *think*? Money. What else? Dimbo. And Gideon was as dead as the living can be – Adam his usual vile and smelly self, snorting like a train, now, underneath a rag pile. But Emily was gone. Emily was long gone: things to do – busy busy busy. Got to make things as right as they can be – and by tonight (who knew?) everything might even be better. Surely everything could maybe come right? Come together? I mean it was a *party* we were talking about here – right? And that's what parties are all about: coming together (as everyone knows).

First thing she did (as she said she would) was telephone Sophie; a bit *too* first thing, as it happened, because Sophie was still asleep. She had sort of rallied round but you could tell, though, you could tell by her voice, that she had been a witness to that awful Jim business last evening (who hadn't?) but Emily must now bury her shame because she badly needed an ally. She was prepared to trade on anything: old times' sake, obligation – pity: anything it took. She had to use them all: it took the bloody lot. Sophie already had an engagement that evening, she was sorry (and Emily was left in no doubt at all that Sophie had an engagement *every* evening), and why hadn't Emily given her a bit of notice? Because it was all planned last night – I know it sounds crazy but I do, don't I? I do do crazy things. But it's *not* your birthday, is it? I thought your birthday was in – No no, it's not, but we're all going to *pretend*. Keep talking, keep talking – she already thinks I've lost my mind (wouldn't mind losing it, actually, but I can't, I can't – it keeps on turning up) so just keep pushing, keep pushing – has to say yes because I need her, I need her, and if she doesn't help me, then I'm finished and I can't say that now but I can say it when she's here because you can say anything at a party, anything at all. She said yes, after a hell of a while, and Emily put down the receiver thinking thank Christ – although I suppose, Sophie, you cannot really be a hope, you are to me – my one and only.

Next stop was The Grange – and of course it became plain at once that the manager hadn't at all (not for a minute) considered Kevin's handiwork some form of *jeu d'esprit* – the lighthearted frivolity of a typical Englishman? I don't think so. No – the manager (French, as it turned out; maybe

Belgian) well knew ineptitude when it hit him in the face, and Emily had now to endure the tacit though no less impending threat of one last chance or else. But he was happy, he was happy enough by the time she left: Emily rearranged everything (everything) with as sure an instinct as she had ever possessed. She always just *knew* where everything should go – couldn't understand how people couldn't see it. The horse-collar she sent down a chute that led to the garbage disposal unit, deep in the basement. Beyond belief that he paid money for that.

But Emily was aware that there were many other rooms in the hotel that needed redesign, that required refurbishment, and the manager's silence on that score had struck her hard: the manager was saying nothing. A wrong had (kind of) been (sort of) put right, and the account had been settled in full. There was no more: no more *work*, certainly. That was for sure. Oh dear me.

The first thing Kevin said to Emily when she got back home (before even she had the door shut behind her) was Is She Coming? Did You Phone Her? Is Sophie Coming To The Thing? And Emily had dropped her keys into the Indian incense-burner in the hall and said She's coming, I phoned her, she's coming – and have you told everyone else about it? And when is Shelley going to see her way clear to getting rid of all her stuff? And have you got the food, yet? Have you done the food? Why are you so interested in Sophie, all of a sudden? How's Raymond, this morning? Not that I really mind that much – but he won't, will he? I mean, there's no danger of his actually *dying*, is there? That would be just too awful, if he did that here.

'He's all right – he seems just about the same as ever. *Can't* have been a heart attack, can it? Not a real one. He's on the phone – trying to get some sense out of his insurance company about the house business. I'm not suddenly *interested* – I just wondered whether or not she's coming,

that's all. Shelley *will* be here this evening, by the way –
some sort of hold-up with this flat of hers, apparently.
Ceiling. Something. And I'm pretty sure you can count on
everyone else. Nowhere else to go. Of course, Shelley could
decide to go out – I've no idea what she'll do, really. You
might have a word with her. She'll put all this stuff back into
her room, now, I should think. Speak to her. So she definitely
is coming, then, is she?'

'I *told* you, Kevin – I *told* you. She says she's coming – I
told you. I don't know what all this interest in Sophie is all
about – you didn't give two hoots for her when she was
here. It's *I* who need her now, not you. Christ what a bloody
mess you made at The Grange, Kevin; couldn't believe it. So
Raymond's still upstairs, is he?'

'Yes,' said Kevin (you're wrong, Emily, you're wrong – I
did give two hoots: I gave all the hoots going – and my need
for Sophie is so far greater than yours, you could not even
begin to imagine). 'He's still upstairs.'

Yes, he was still upstairs. Banged down the phone after his
third non-conversation with a non-person in the insurance
company. So what happens now, he had asked him. My
house and everything in it has gone up in smoke – what are
you going to do about it?

'I see. Most unfortunate. Do you have the policy number
on you?'

'No. My house and everything in it has gone up in smoke.'

'Were you yourself harmed during the incident?'

'Not in the way you mean. I was having a heart attack
somewhere else.'

'Not fatal, however.'

A joke? Was this some sort of a sickish joke from the non-
person in the insurance company? Don't know – couldn't
tell you. You can never tell with these sorts, can you?
Raymond gave him the address, which the computer
eventually coped with, and the drone was now saying

would your first name be Raymond and Raymond had replied that it would, in fact – yes, it would.

'Hm. Three interested parties in this particular property – collectively, to quite a sizeable, not to say overwhelming degree. Would you have the names of the lenders? Your contacts there?'

'No. My house and everything in it has gone up in smoke.'

'Hm. You see, *bicycly*, the way forward rests with the lenders. They may not wish to proceed with a rebuilding programme. They might insist on their moneys.'

'Got no moneys.'

'Well no – but that would be forthcoming, as soon as we are assured of the circumstance of the incident – that would be forthcoming from ourselves.'

'What – you mean, they take their whack and chuck me the fiver left over?'

'Oh I think you'd find there would be more than *that*. Though on these figures, I have to say, there wouldn't be much.'

'And where shall I live then? What happens then?'

'Well they *might* rebuild. Or they might offer a new mortgage on an alternative property.'

'And they might not.'

'M'yes. Bicycly. Of course, your *contents* are quite another matter. Would you have the details of your contents policy, at all? Ah no – because your house and everything in it –'

'– has gone up in smoke, quite. Anyway, there isn't one – didn't have a contents policy.'

A pause. 'Are you saying that your contents were not insured by ourselves?'

'Not insured by anybody. No contents insurance.'

'Oh dear. Oh dear me. Not really your day, is it?'

Another joke? Another one? Couldn't tell you; not a clue. He said he'd phone the banks. And the police, and so forth – familiarize himself with the lay of the land, bicycly.

Raymond just said good and banged down the phone – just couldn't bear *listening* to the man any more. He wasn't convinced that any of it really even mattered one way or the other. I mean – he'd live *somewhere*, presumably. Shelley, initially (until the next rent was due), and then who knows? Council, maybe. And Maureen and Rosie? Colney Hatch; Camden Town Recycling Plant. What the hell did it matter anyway?

The doctor dropped in later on – pronounced Raymond pretty OK, considering; cigarettes aren't too clever, though, he had cautioned. I know, said Raymond, lighting another.

Shelley and Gideon had had a sort of arrangement to go out that evening, but that had been kind of agreed on one or two days ago, when they still each knew one another, and before all the stuff had changed their lives.

Bit of an awkward moment in the hall – well, bit awkward for Gideon, anyway: he had felt slightly funny about it because he had to inch his way around her protruding bottom in order to get over to the door because she seemed to be gazing at her reflection in a fingerplate and brushing upwards the lashes of an eye. Sorry, he had said – can I just squeeze past? Shelley had not replied, and nor had she moved. Women said and meant all sorts of stuff when they did absolutely nothing, Gideon rather thought. Though quite *what* was something else, of course. Women did all sorts of funny things that men didn't do – making up in front of a door, say; walking down the street with their arms tightly crossed in front of their bosom; crossing the left leg over the right; kicking out their calves, Charleston-like, while running; rendering a newspaper an unreadable mass of waste; holding their noses whenever they laughed; tossing their heads; disclosing other people's secrets – things like that: you know the sorts of things: lots of things.

Gideon was on his way to collect his mother and his grandmother from their respective institutions (have a look at what's left of the house – shouldn't think there's anything to salvage; he only missed his CDs, if he was honest – nothing else, really). Amanda came in just as he was leaving (he was unaware that she had ever gone – thought she was upstairs, somewhere, in some room or another).

'The police tracked me down here this morning,' she said. 'Said they thought they might have picked up the two men who kidnapped me and would I go down to identify them.'

'*Kidnapped* you, Amanda? When were you kidnapped? I never knew you'd been kidnapped.'

'Oh yes,' Amanda said airily. 'Didn't Raymond tell you? No, I suppose he wouldn't have. It was quite an ordeal, as you might imagine. I had a bag over my head throughout.'

'Good God – I had no idea. And was it them? These two men?'

'Hm? Oh yes – it was them, all right. No doubt about it. Just once I'd managed to sneak a look at them – they didn't know, of course, or they never would have let me go. I would've been dead in a ditch. So I said Yeah – that's them, all right – that's them for sure. They had denied everything, of course, but the cops believed me. You could tell. I hope they go to prison forever and die there. I'm going to fuck you, Gideon, later on.'

Gideon drove to the hospital in his father's car and Maureen said to him how nice of you to come and see me and Gideon said I haven't come to *see* you, Mum – I've come to take you (not home) away. In the car on the way to the other hospital Maureen said Where are we going? And can we stop on the way to wherever we're going to buy a small, not too small, bottle of vodka? Gran, Mum – *Gran*: we're on our way to pick up Gran. Oh *Mummy*, of course – I'd forgotten, said Maureen; and then we're going back home after, are we? No, Mum, no – we're not going back home, we're all going to stay with Kevin and Emily for a bit and Maureen had said Why on earth should we be doing that? Why can't we go home and I can cook your father a really nice dinner? The *fire*, Mum, the *fire* – the house burned down last night, yes? You, in the kitchen, fire – yes? Remember? The *house* burned down? Really? Last night? Oh yes, of *course*: now I remember. And where did you say we're going? *Gran*, Mum, Gran – we're going to pick up Gran. Oh *Mummy*! Oh yes, oh yes: I remember now. Of course. And who did you say we are staying with? I don't see why we can't go back to our own house, cook your father a really nice dinner.

Rosie eased herself into the front seat and said What took you so long? I've been in that place for twenty-seven years, come August Bank Holiday. Even Gideon was moved to whisper Oh Christ. Mummy, said Maureen, we're going to stay with some people, can't quite remember who, because, um, because – sorry, Gideon, why are we in fact going to be staying with these people? Gran, said Gideon, we've got some bad news: last night the house burned down, completely burned out. I'm afraid you've lost all your things – I'm terribly sorry. But no one was hurt. All my things? All my things? I've lost all my things, do you say? I'm afraid so, Gran, yes; we all have. What – my photos? I've lost all my photos? Yes, Gran, yes: sorry, but yes. Even the photos of Brian? Who is Brian, Maureen wanted to know. Brian is your father, replied Rosie. Really? Is he really? Brian is my father – *really*? Not *now*, he isn't – he's dead. But before he died he was your father, yes – and now we haven't even got any photos. I'll never remember what on earth he looked like if I haven't even got any photos. I've lost all my photos. How careless. I cannot imagine how I could have done such a thing. And why are you both calling me Mummy and Gran when you know perfectly well that my name is Sally?

And just before he had left, Kevin had told Gideon that they were all invited to Emily's famous birthday party that evening and Gideon had said Oh, I didn't know it was Emily's birthday. I thought Emily's birthday was in – It is, it is, cut in Kevin, but for the sake of argument, right, it's today. Gideon now in his mind tried the thing for size: for the sake of argument, right, it's today. Well, OK – seemed about as sane as everything else did, didn't it?

Vol-au-vents are what Emily liked. Vol-au-vents and those little sausages on sticks and tiny Scotch eggs – all the old-fashioned stuff, the traditional stuff that she'd always had. The formula for the party was forever the same, and that's why (according to Emily) it always worked so well. They were just the *snacky* things, of course: the *real* meal was turkey – turkey, yes turkey, with (guess what?) – yup! All the trimmings. This was one of the things that most maddened everyone, because Emily's birthday – not this impromptu hey-gang-let's-do-the-show-right-here-yeh-why-don't-we type birthday, but the real McCoy, the thing from which Kevin cringed within – was only a week, barely a week after Christmas and, well – you know, don't have to spell it out: coming out of your ears, right? Sick of the bloody sight of the stuff. Duck's nice, Kevin had said one year; or how about a roast? Emily replied that he was right – duck *is* nice, and roasts too (she was not denying) certainly had their place in the larger scheme of things – but *turkey*, Kevin, is what we are having because we *always* do: clear? Clear, said Kevin: right.

So Kevin had put the turkey on early (that was another thing – Kevin was in charge of all the cooking, all the food and all the drink); well look – he could open a few bottles and stick things on a plate, fair enough, but God alone knew that he was no *cook*: cooking was yet one more of these things that he would freely admit to anyone that he simply could not do. Of course, if Emily had ever been within earshot, she would come out with her mandatory And What Exactly *Can* You Do, Kevin, that's what we'd all like to know. What exactly *is* it that you can do, Kevin? Tell us, please. Or is it a secret?

'Can I do anything?' asked Raymond, who wandered in.

'It doesn't seem likely, does it?' replied Emily. 'Certainly there's no precedent.'

See? A woman of few ideas, do we think? Few words, uses them incessantly? With the odd twist, the odd dive (but no duck, got it? It's *turkey* we're having).

'Did she say what time she's coming?' asked Kevin. 'Sophie?'

'She said seven,' said Emily. I said come earlier – come at six for vol-au-vents and sausages and a drink of something but she said no, seven – I really can't possibly get away till way after six. Very grand. Anyway – seven is what she said.'

Seven, thought Kevin. That's only a couple of hours. In a couple of hours I'll be with Sophie and I haven't even seen her for more than a couple of years. And what had she been doing during those more than two long years that seem like nothing, now? For the first of them, and for a good time into the second, Kevin had hugged himself and hidden from all the incursive pain, flinched away from the sting of it.

'So,' said Raymond. 'There's nothing I can do?'

Maybe he still felt a little frail? Playing right into her hands, wasn't he? But Emily too seems to have lost the edge: just listen.

'I don't really think so, Raymond,' is what she said. 'Go next door and have a drink.'

Hm. Well if things don't liven up pretty soon, this is going to be one hell of a dreary evening, it seems to me: even by Emily's birthday standards.

Raymond did as he was told: he went into the living-room in search of a drink. What – didn't he even want to throw Emily onto the ground and fuck her blind for a second or so? Oh yeah – he always wanted that, but Shelley, he had to say, had been something of a revelation: much tighter fit altogether. Trouble was, fuck Shelley and you could end up dead on the floor – particularly if mirages of those presumed already well dead come wafting into the room. Oh and look – here's the very undead person now: Amanda, lying on a sofa, looking upwards into the bowl of a glass of white wine, a fingernail tracing rivulets in the cool and bubbly wet outside.

'Hi, Raymond,' she said. 'Not dead yet? So where are you really going to live now that your horrible old house is gone? Did you think of me burning alive, Raymond? Joan of Arc? I bet you thought Oh Christ – now who's going to run the business.'

The business. Raymond hadn't given a single thought to the business for at least a thousand years; forgotten he even *had* a business. *Did* he have a business? Don't know – couldn't tell you: last person in the world. Depends on Amanda. And when anything depended on Amanda, then it was decidedly rickety at the outset. The funny thing was, it didn't matter any more – not to Raymond. When Amanda had threatened all those things, it had mattered terribly – but now, Raymond couldn't even remember why he had thought it could *possibly* matter, why he was driven to – oh God, he could almost laugh out loud – *kidnap* the girl. He didn't, did he? He did, you know.

'They got the kidnappers,' said Amanda. 'The police.'

'Funny, Amanda,' sighed Raymond. 'Oh-so-funny. Is there any red wine? Or is it only white?'

Amanda sat up and widened her eyes.

'No I mean it, Raymond. They really got them. They

arrested them at Folkestone. Apparently they were hanging around some young girl, the bloody perverts, and they arrested them on suspicion and of *course* they denied everything but the minute I saw them I just knew it was them, no question about it. I've just come back from there, actually. At least they won't do it to anyone else, anyway. I wouldn't want to think of anyone having to go through what I went through. They'll keep them banged up for about a year before the trial is even close, apparently. So the whoever-he-was was saying, anyway.'

Raymond sat in an armchair, with a glass of white wine. There was red, but it would've meant opening it and Raymond felt far too knackered to even think of doing anything like that.

'Very droll, Amanda. Highly amusing. Most inventive. Ever thought of writing a novel? Bestseller material, I should have said.'

'You're very *thick*, Raymond,' riposted Amanda, sitting forward now. 'Why can't you get this one simple fact into your head? They've *caught* them, they've got the men who fucking kidnapped me. Christ – I thought you'd be *pleased*. Sometimes I wonder just why it is I love you.'

Raymond looked into her eyes. Raymond looked into her eyes for just a tad longer. Oh Christ. Oh dear oh dear. She meant it. She really meant it. The psycho has landed. And she just said fucking again. Oh look – here comes Emily now with a plate of vol-au-vents, and close behind my son Gideon – together with Maureen and the wreck that is her bloody Mummy. It would appear that the party has begun – so welcome to my world, then: won't you come on in?

Adam didn't want to be there – of course he didn't – but at least there's plenty of booze and anyway with Ben fucked

311

off to Spain with that bleeding cunt of a father of his, there was really no one else he could be with: wasn't as if there was a *girl*, or anything. Hadn't even thought to get the number of that Millicent woman – she'd be good, once she was well tanked-up; bit old, though.

Christ what a bloody row in here – look at them all, stuffing their faces. Better have another glass of this pisspoor wine, I suppose; Dad didn't lay in any beer (typical) and all of Mum's brandy's gone and yeah, OK – there is a bottle of vodka on the table but there's no way Gideon's cracked old mother is ever going to let go of it, is there?

Do you know the one thing that really got on Adam's tits? The thing that was really bloody getting to him? I think you maybe do: Jim, right? Yeah – Jim. The fact that that drunk old crazy nutter had got *away* with it. What Adam had been going to do, right, what he had it all worked out in his mind he was going to do, right, was get himself round to Jim 's house (oh yes – he knew where he lived, all right: looked it up, hadn't he?) and kick the fucking shit out of the boozy old bastard. But then Adam got wise, didn't he? Even if he got him from behind, Jim'd be sure to tell the law it was him – and the law, don't forget, had Adam's dabs, had Adam's hair, skin and blood – amazing they hadn't held on to one of his fucking legs. So it'd be a right wide-open trap, right? So Adam didn't do it, wouldn't do it, no – but it was really eating him up, you know? The fact that the bastard had got *away* with it. The bastard.

'You're very *thoughtful*, Adam,' hailed Kevin from way over the other side of the table: had to shout.

'This bloody turkey's half raw,' said Adam – Kevin didn't hear (was cocking an ear, mouthing Say again? Say again?) but Shelley heard him, she did, and she said so bloody *what* – why don't you just eat the cooked bits and shut your bloody stupid mouth. And she closed her ears to all his crap about *can't* eat the cooked bits if I've got my fucking mouth shut *can* I Miss-Bloody-Know-It-All because Raymond was talking to her now and she supposed she had better listen to what he had to say as it was he who was going to be bankrolling her way clean out of this bloody madhouse and Christ there were all the bloody *games* to get through, yet.

'Is there somewhere we can go?' said Raymond.

'Go where you like, Raymond. What do you mean, 'go'?'

'I mean – you know: *go*,' stressed Raymond, jerking a thumb, narrowing the eyes, lifting an eyebrow, pursing the lip – Christ, what was it going to take to make the dumb girl *get* it?

'Oh, *that*,' twigged Shelley. Christ – if only he wasn't so bloody *old*; why were the ones with money always so bloody *old*? 'Maybe later, Raymond. I'm eating. This bloody thing's only half cooked – what's yours like?'

'Untouched, is what mine's like. It's terrible.'

'I've lost all my photos!' wailed Rosie. 'Do I know you? My name is Sally. I came over with the Normans.'

'Christ Almighty,' whispered Raymond.

'Of course,' conceded Rosie, 'I'm going back a bit, now.'

'Maureen,' pleaded Raymond, 'why didn't you leave her wherever she bloody was? Christ, she's worse than ever.'

'D'you know,' drawled Maureen, 'I could've made you a much nicer dinner than this – it's barely cooked. I would've cooked it *properly* for you, Raymond.'

'Yeah,' said Raymond, 'and burn down another house in the bloody process. Where would we all go then, Maureen – the lot of us crammed into Kevin's car? And then you'd probably let the hand-brake off and kill us all.'

'Car?' checked Maureen. 'Are we going on a trip?'

'Oh *Christ*,' moaned Raymond: it was really wrung from him.

'Where are we going?' demanded Rosie now. 'We've only just arrived. I think Clark Gable looked much better without his moustache.'

'That one,' said Amanda to Gideon, 'is absolutely as cracked as they come. I'm going to fuck you, Gideon. Later on.'

'Yeh?' said Gideon, as throwaway as he could. Actually, I quite like that idea: Amanda is quite an exciting woman – more exciting than all of the others, anyway. Maybe he *would* get fucked by Amanda, maybe he could: but he knew he'd have to think of Richard (some things you just have to face).

'Not eating, Gideon?' said Kevin, turning immediately away from Gideon's I'm-really-not-all-that-hungry-as-a-matter-of-fact and hissing now with just-checked desperation into Emily's ear, 'She's terribly *late* – it's nearly eight o'clock. You do think she's *coming*, don't you?'

'Why couldn't you have cooked this bloody turkey *properly*, Kevin?' came back Emily. 'It's all horrible and red in the middle. You don't *have* rare turkey – no one has rare *turkey*. Do you want stuffing?'

'Where *is* she, Emily?' Where do you think she can *be*?'

'*Look*,' said Emily, placing down her knife and fork in a way that suggested that boxing gloves could be next on the agenda. 'I've *told* you I've *told* you I've *told* you – all I can do is tell you what she *said*. She said she'd be here at seven – she's terribly busy and there's something she had to cancel and she'd try to be here at seven. I'm desperate about it *too*, Kevin – I'm finished if she doesn't help me. And so are you – at least you realize.'

'What's the book?' asked Kevin, nodding towards a paperback to the left of Emily's place (oh I *do* realize, I *do*!).

'Do you know,' piped up Rosie, 'I do believe this is the place I was billeted during the war: changed a bit since I was a girl.'

'This?' queried Emily – ignoring Rosie, but naturally. 'That strange girl Amanda's sense of humour, I think. It's some novel called *Poor Souls* that she bought me as a non-birthday present because the title, and I quote, "somehow seemed appropriate". I ask you.'

'I haven't been here,' went on Rosie, 'since the battle of Crécy.'

'Anyway,' continued Emily. 'I hate novels, as well you know. Not *real*, are they? I mean – the things in them: didn't *happen*, did they? Just some person's fantasy. You do think she'll *come*, don't you, Kevin?'

'Marmite soldiers,' Rosie was crowing, 'often desert their posts.'

'I don't know,' said Kevin to Emily. 'I sincerely hope so.'

'This,' concluded Rosie, 'is known.'

'Rosie,' sighed out Raymond, 'why didn't you die? Hm? I mean – you *almost* did, you *nearly* got there: why couldn't you have just seen it through?'

'You've never called me Rosie before.'

'Let's go next door, everyone!' announced Emily – on her feet now and hitting the side of a glass with a fork; no surprise to Kevin when it shattered – she doesn't know her own strength, Emily – *I* do, of course: I know it well. (Damn, thought Emily – that was Waterford, one of six.) 'It's Games Time, children! I'll bring through the cake.'

Amid the scraping back of chair legs, Rosie was talking to Raymond again:

'It's a silly thing to do, actually, because my name is Sally. Were you ever one of my children, Raymond? Or am I confusing you with Romulus, Remus and that rather amusing Popeye person?'

Raymond was close to tears: he felt like crying, and then crying out through all the madness.

'Come on – come on!' he was now chivvying anyone around. 'It's Games Time! Games Time, kiddies! Let's all play Kill The Fucking Crackpot! Plenty to go round – prizes for all!'

'Raymond,' said Maureen, softly, 'do you think you could

hold me up because otherwise I think I might embarrass you.'

'Gideon,' whispered Amanda, 'shall I fuck you now?'

'Er – I don't think they're quite the sort of games Emily had in mind.'

'Well I tell you *what*,' roared Adam, now (this shit wine actually really got to you if you put your laughing gear around enough of the stuff), 'I'll say this *now* and I'll say it *once* – if we're playing Monopoly I want to be the car – and if we're doing teams I'm not going to be with bloody *Shelley*.'

'I wouldn't be in *your* team,' ranted back Shelley, 'if you were the last human being on the entire bloody – Raymond, stop *tugging* at me, stop pulling at my *shirt*.'

'It's just,' babbled Raymond, darkly, 'it's just I wondered if there's somewhere we could, you know – *go*, or anything.'

'Raymond,' came Maureen's voice (fainter now), 'I rather do feel as if I'm going to be –'

'Oh *Jesus*,' wailed Raymond, half carrying her to the door, 'let's get you to the bloody – oh *Christ*, Maureen, why do you always have to *drink* so much all the bloody time?'

'She always did,' snapped Rosie. 'And I have the tits to prove it.'

'You get them all in, Emily,' said Kevin, 'and I'll sort of clear up a bit in here. She's not coming, is she?'

'Dad!' called across Shelley. 'What is it if you spill red wine? Is it salt or white wine or what?'

'Well OK Gideon,' said Amanda (quite sternly), 'we'll play just one of these stupid games, whatever they are, and then we just might see about getting you fucked.'

'Sounds reasonable,' said Gideon (well, what did one *say*?).

'What,' screamed over Emily, 'in God's name have you spilt it on? It's white wine, I think – or is it just water?'

'*I* didn't spill it,' countered Shelley, 'it was bloody flatfooted *Adam*, wasn't it?'

'Doncaster,' explained Rosie, 'is a perfectly nice town for a visit, though I shouldn't at all care to live there.'

'I hate it when things get spilled,' worried Emily. 'I don't know, Kevin, I don't know – it really doesn't look as if she *will* come, now: at least she could have phoned. Come on, everyone – let's all go in and play a game and try to *enjoy* ourselves. What on earth –? Oh God this tastes . . . oh Christ – I'm *sorry*, everyone, but the cake's going to be rather dry and boring because there's Fairy Liquid in the whipping cream – Jesus, Kevin, if ever I lay eyes on her again, I'll kill that fucking Lolita.'

'*Look!*' roared out Adam, 'this is absolutely *useless* – it's always like this with so many people. We've been playing and playing and playing and none of the teams has even got a *set*, yet. I mean, look – me and Dad have got Fleet Street and Strand but there's no way bloody Shelley's going to sell us Trafalgar Square, is there? She just *won't*.'

'No I won't,' agreed Shelley.

'Does anyone want a chocolate?' offered Emily. 'No one's bought Old Kent Road yet, Adam, and you've got White-chapel –'

'I *know* we've got Whitechapel, I know that – but even if we get it – and Christ, *no one's* landed on it yet and we've been round about a million times –'

'I'd quite like a chocolate,' said Maureen. 'Are there any soft ones left?'

'You'll be sick,' said Raymond. 'Again. You've eaten half the bloody box. And try to remember to ask for the bloody two hundred for passing Go next time, you stupid woman.'

'– Even if we *get* Old Kent Road, Mum – you can't ever win a game with just the *brown* ones, everyone knows that.'

'Have all *our* properties,' offered Amanda. 'Me and

317

Gideon have had just about enough of this, haven't we, Gideon?'

'Well,' said Kevin quietly. 'Ten o'clock. She certainly can't be coming now. Anyone want a drink?'

'You can't just *give* them away,' objected Shelley. 'If you give Dad and Adam all of your stuff they'll make up the blue set *and* the orange set and that's a whole *side*.'

'These are good chocolates,' pronounced Maureen. 'Does anyone want to buy my Get Out Of Jail Free card? I never seem to go to jail. Why don't *you* ask for the two hundred if you're so clever, Raymond?'

'Well I want a drink, anyway,' said Kevin. 'I'll just open a few bottles and whoever wants takes, shall I? I seem to have spent half the game in jail. Whose go is it?'

'Ours,' said Adam. 'It's our go.'

'You've just *had* your go!' squawked Shelley. 'You're such a *cheat*, Adam. I'll have some wine if you're getting it, Dad. White, please. Stop *touching* me, Raymond.'

'Sorry,' husked Raymond. '*Sorry*, for God's sake. You know, I'm rather with Amanda on this, everyone – maybe we should just call it a day. Christ – we seem to have been playing since Thatcher was in power – I've had enough, quite frankly.'

'The trouble is,' said Rosie, 'I seem to have lost all my photos and I don't know where to look for them.'

'Oh *Gran*,' moaned Gideon. 'I've *explained* about the photos – you haven't *lost* them, lost them – they went up in the *fire*, yes? Look, folks – I think Amanda and me *will* retire from this, if that's OK with everyone. Have a bit of a breather.'

'Cruel to burn my photos,' muttered Rosie. 'Has Ringo Starr been told?'

'Come on, then, Gideon,' said Amanda. 'Let's go off for a bit.'

'I wouldn't mind,' said Adam softly, 'going off for a bit.'

318

'Oh look!' piped up Emily. 'It Is Your Birthday – Collect Ten Pounds From Each Player – that's really rather funny, isn't it?'

'Not really,' grunted Raymond, 'on account of it *isn't* your bloody birthday, is it? Anyway, I don't know about anyone else, but I'm out of the game. What about that drink, Kevin?'

'Yes,' said Emily. 'Let's everyone have a drink and try to *enjoy* ourselves, shall we? This is a *party*, after all.'

'Come on, Gideon – come *on*: what's the matter with you? What's wrong? Would it be better if we lay down?'

'Sorry, Amanda, sorry – it might be better if we . . . yes. Standing up's a bit . . . isn't it?'

They were in a bathroom, for some reason (Amanda's choice), and Amanda had decided too that leaning against a wall and he oh-so-urgently ramming up her like a warhorse would amount to the grooviest quickie ever on record (you know, she might have been better off with Raymond after all – who knew no other way – but did she mention that she could not love him in that way?). But Gideon – not, by nature, one of life's most urgent rammers – was now close to panic because if he failed again, if this was to be yet another humiliating write-off . . . The devil of it was he *did* find Amanda a pretty sexy proposition but only (how could he put it) up to a point. She had pulled his hand right up tight between her legs and that was warm and friendly enough, as far as it went, but from Gideon's point of view there wasn't in truth very much to get hold of.

But they were lying down now (bit of a tight squeeze – it wasn't a large room, or anything) and bathroom carpets have a smell all of their own, don't you find? A sort of nylon newness, overlaid with the sprinkle of recent talcum. Amanda's hands were all over Gideon and Gideon was

319

concentrating hard – eyes screwed tight and summoning images. His body began to react just as he knew Amanda was losing patience and could well have reached out for that lavatory brush and summarily brained him. And suddenly it was OK! Gideon beamed with the pleasure he was suddenly feeling and the knowledge that it would get much better really soon – and now it did, and as he tensed right up before the final relaxation he gasped out Rich! Rich! Rich! before slumping down on top of an at least now vaguely appeased Amanda. That, she said, was a lovely thing to say, and then – maybe planning other and more protracted sessions during which she too might at least feel *something* – Amanda added on But it can be richer, you know, even richer, my sweet man.

While Gideon worked away at his teeth with a forefinger – spitting out Colgate, rinsing well – Amanda was tugging herself back into shape; now she touched him lightly on his hunched-up shoulder and this is what she said:

'Let's get out of here, Gideon – right now. I can't stand this house any longer. Let's just go.'

'Nowhere *to* go,' said Gideon, through a towel.

'Wrong,' said Amanda. 'What everyone seems to have forgotten during all this farce is that I in fact *do* have a place of my own. An extremely nice flat, as it happens. I haven't been there since before I was kidnapped – seems a long while, but it hasn't been, really. Nice to see it again, though. So come and stay with me there – and tomorrow, Monday, first thing – we can get you all togged up with brand-new stuff, because it maybe hasn't quite yet dawned on you, Gideon, but you have nothing, absolutely nothing at all.'

Gideon listened to the words until they faded and then he said OK.

'Christ, Raymond,' said Amanda. 'What are you going to *do* about her? I mean – look at her.'

Raymond looked at Maureen, face down on the carpet, one hand twitching, the noise 'blur' from time to time emerging from her twisted lips. He shook his head.

'You tell me. Gideon used to tend to her, mainly. If it wasn't for Gideon, she'd be dead.'

'Maybe better.'

'Maybe. And now you're taking Gideon away. Good idea, Amanda? You don't know him. He's useless.'

But, thought Raymond, I don't really mind too much, because what *he* doesn't know is that you, Amanda, are a class-A raving maniac but he *will* find out, he will find out soon, and I find that thought not at all disagreeable. For myself (not that you ask) – well, it looks like the rest of the week here, at best a month or so with Shelley (who of course despises me, but at least some fucking is on the menu) and then who knows? As to the blackened heap of bricks that used to be my vast and heaving dungeon (and yours too, briefly) – well, the way forward rests with the principal lenders, bicycly. Maureen? Dunno. She might die of alcohol poisoning or choke on her own vomit or walk under a bus or – more likely – live for another hundred years and join forces with her eternal mother to form an archaic consortium of insanity able to drive everyone else within radius to the point of distraction, while retaining an air of gaga detachment.

'But *you*, Raymond – you will never be free of me, which is good and bad, I'd say. I think I *will* go on running the company – I might even let you stay with that absurd young Shelley person, for a bit – but whenever I am in the mood, I shall threaten your destruction.'

'My destruction.'

'Correct, Raymond. There are several ways. You don't know about the tape-recordings, I think. All those talks we had about the kidnapping business? All on tape. Police wouldn't be happy, Raymond – police wouldn't like it at all.'

Did Raymond mind about this? He did and he didn't. Meaning? Meaning, one: he hasn't quite decided, and two: he's had a lot to drink and when Amanda has fully finished (clearly hasn't done so yet) then he will confront the texture of all of this and then he will decide whether or not any of this is really worth minding about.

'So,' he said, 'you *don't* actually believe you were kidnapped by two men in Folkestone? You do actually recall that all that was nonsense cobbled up between the two of us?'

'What I think about that is my own business. There is no doubt in my mind that they did it: you could see it in their eyes.'

Raymond couldn't resist a secret smile: oh Gideon, oh Gideon – have you any idea what on earth you have taken on here?

'Plus,' went on Amanda, 'I still have that long and silver knife that I stabbed you with –'

'Oh you *did* stab me, then, did you? I was under the firm impression that this simply did not happen.'

'– and one day, Raymond, one day – maybe when you are sweetly asleep with this little Shelley girl, you will find me standing over you with that long and silver knife and do you know what? It'll be just like that *film*.'

'*Psycho*, presumably: for once you've got it right.'

'Not *Psycho*, no – *Fatal Attraction*. Michael Douglas. And the woman, you remember?'

'There was another film that did all that much better – I can't remember the name of it.'

'Oh *I* know the one you mean – yes, that *was* good, that one. Paul Newman, wasn't it?'

'You think Paul Newman's in every film ever made. It wasn't Paul Newman, it was . . . someone else. Oh yes – I know, it was Clint Eastwood.'

'Oh yeh, yeh – Play Something For Me, yeah – and he

didn't know what he was dealing with – he thought he could just go on fucking her and then go back to his girlfriend, but she wasn't having any of that – and nor was the woman in *Fatal Attraction*. Was it Faye Dunaway?'

'Oh I see, I see – you see these women as the *heroes*, do you? Avenging angels.' She said fucking again: never get used to it.

'Yeh. Yeh. I do. Sorting the men.'

'But they were *mad*, Amanda. You do see they were mad?'

'Maybe *they* were – but I'm not.'

'You're *joking* – you're madder than both of them put together. You're completely *screwed*, Amanda.'

'Glenn Close, it was. Can't remember the wife. So anyway, Raymond – I just wanted you to know that wherever you are and whatever you're doing, you will never ever be free of *threat*, and of *danger*. OK, Raymond? Misty. Play Misty.'

Raymond has decided now. Now as he watched this woman leave the house with his son in tow, he has decided that it probably is worth minding about, because threat (I think another drink would be nice) is never easy to live with. If Amanda had stuck the knife into his heart, he wouldn't have minded much; if she had told him the company was history, he could have lived with it; had she informed him that the police already knew the truth about all that kidnapping stuff he would have thought oh well, there you have it. But Amanda was far more cruel: she had suspended menace above every new day of his future existence, and he minded; yes, on balance, he minded a lot. Did she mean it? Did she *mean* it? What do you think?

'Where's Shelley?' asked Emily. Haven't seen Shelley for a while, she was thinking: thought she might have helped with the coffee.

'Not sure,' replied Kevin (but I've got a good idea. Odd that I really don't mind: Emily, though, I feel would). 'Do you think Maureen's all right, face-down on the floor like that? She's making some very odd noises. And Adam doesn't look too bright.'

'Turn her, do you think?' said Emily, idly. 'Gideon's gone, I know. Gideon, I said, it's really a bit early to break up the party, but he took that Amanda with him so it's probably to the good. You just can't relax with people in the house you don't really know. She's a strange one. I think Adam's rather overdone the wine – he's not used to it. And where's Raymond?'

Rosie sat up in her chair (it was easy to forget about Rosie, when she was quiet).

'I saw him quite recently,' she said.

'Yes?' said Emily. 'Where?'

'On the Suez Canal. The dear old Queen was with him.'

'Christ,' said Emily, quietly. 'It must be awful to be like that.'

Nothing to do with what she was thinking, though. She was thinking Shelley's not here and Raymond's not here and so where, in fact, are they? And although she knew it could not be the right thing to do (she was risking pain, a pain quite indefinable) she got up anyway and moved to the staircase and said to Kevin (who did think, fleetingly, should I stop her? Before deciding no – best go on seeing Emily as altogether unstoppable) I'm just going upstairs, Kevin, just popping upstairs – and it was true: she was nearly halfway up already.

It would be stupid to open that bedroom door. Why on earth should Emily do this to herself? There could be no doubt, so why redouble the – oh God, I'm not even sure it *is* something so simple as pain, though certainly there is wounding there. The sound was unmistakable – how many times had she heard it? There could be only three or four more seconds, now, so why not turn away and leave it alone? Couldn't, could she? Just couldn't. She opened the door at the moment when Raymond's livid mouth was thrust open by the charge of just having had that damn little child Shelley again and Emily (quickly shutting the door on all of that) would be forever struck by the gleaming eyes amid his sweat-soaked face that let her know as surely as if he had impaled her on a spear that this time and at last he was rejoicing in finally having let her *have* it.

It was the doorbell that jerked Emily away from whatever it was that had this grip on her, and she quickened her step on the staircase thinking well *Jesus*, Sophie, what a time to arrive – it must be gone – God, it's nearly – but I'm glad you have, whatever the time – and look at Kevin, watch him go, agitatedly crossing the hall with purpose in his eyes, and he had the door open just as Emily reached the foot of the stairs and God, the force behind the door that now struck Kevin full in the face was something that came from somewhere bad and now that Jim was finally in – legs way apart and swinging above his head some terrible tool intended for Christ knows – all else seemed to cease until the wild man's hoarse and vicious voice began to cleave through indecision as he bayed for the blood of Adam.

The impact from the door had Kevin staggering but not yet falling and he made a blind and too late grab at Jim as Emily screamed and rushed at him from the rear but the strength in this crazy man reeking of drink and determination was coming from something other and the massive hunk of serrated metal was scything the air and as the whimpering of Adam in the living-room rose to a near hysterical pitch now a white-faced Shelley clattered down the stairs and Kevin – reeling badly – called out to her *No, Shelley, go back,* Shelley and for God's sake call the *police,* and then quite suddenly a policeman was there at his side – yes? Holding him up – and now here were two more, one of them kneeling square atop Jim's chest – but this can't be right because no one had called them, but it *was* right, it must be – yes, it was *true* – the hall was full of policemen and Jim was now out of it, all nerve cut dead, and Kevin was sagging to his knees as Emily clutched at the rough dark blue of the nearest policeman and *thank* you, she said, oh *thank* you, she whispered – the madman was out to get my Adam and another policeman – I suppose a policeman, no dark blue but presumably with them – was now saying that's why we're here too, in fact, and the perplexity on Emily's face found a soulmate in Kevin's and by way of quelling the rush of questions that cluttered the air the policeman explained (and now they had Adam) that a charge was to be preferred (and Emily – Adam's slim young wrists are encased in steel!) on account of an old and battered man had recently been found and in his house and on his body was so much forensic as to do for young Adam for the rest of his natural – and cold and still the old man was, and so the charge is murder.

Emily had gone – Shelley had taken her – but still the shrieks she left behind hung all over the house like the frayed and shredded colours from old and bloody battles that no one will forget. She had fought, Emily – she had fought as fiercely as ever she had, and two of the policemen were injured before they decided to get a bit tougher. She was even threatened with arrest herself, but maybe they wouldn't have done it. Adam had been hustled out none too gently, his eyes near doubled in size amid the pool of dismal light that now made up his face. A near-unconscious Jim was taken away to sleep it off. Shelley and a detective held Emily down on the sofa until the ambulance came; she was shaking as if electrically shocked. Shelley conveyed by means of a string of unconnected monosyllables that she would accompany her mother. And Kevin? Kevin stood stock-still. Should he, could he, go, come, to wherever it was they were taking him? (Adam. My son.) Not at this moment in time, sir. You may consult a brief (the undertone being either you sure as hell will need one, or else I really wouldn't trouble, sir, if I were in your shoes). A brief, yes. Partington. Golfing in Spain. No hurry, sir (we're looking at all the time in the world). But Emily had been screaming, Kevin felt sure, because deep down she believed that Adam had done it. Had they picked up Ben yet?

'Christ,' said Raymond. 'Christ, Kevin – I don't know what to say. I mean – drink? Get you a drink of something, yes?'

'My father said,' said Kevin – wasn't really focusing, wasn't looking at Raymond, anyway – 'Do you know what my father always said? He said, Men Grow Up To Be With Men, And Women Do So Too.'

'Yeah?' said Raymond. Talked as much shite as you do, then, ay? Runs in the bloody family. Can't say that, can't say that – got to say something but I can't say that – so what shall I say, then? This fag is burning my fingers so I'll light another off it and that'll fill a bit of time.

'Everything is fine,' said Rosie – oh Christ, Rosie's still alive – 'right up until the moment it isn't.'

Raymond found himself nodding at this – a thing he had never before done when Rosie had uttered.

'That's true – that's true, that. It's another way of saying – well, that you just never know what's coming. What's around the corner. Why are you suddenly talking sense, then, Rosie?'

Rosie smiled. 'Because, Raymond, it is no longer necessary to be mad. There's no room for it, now.'

Maureen stirred on the floor, spitting a bit; what with everything, no one ever did turn her over: could have died; *didn't*, predictably. The only person to have died is someone unknown to us all.

'I was wondering how all this would end,' said Raymond, after a while. 'I knew there had to *be* an ending, but I wondered just how it would be. Didn't expect anything like this, of course. Well – who would?'

It's peaceful at the moment, he was thinking, but you just wait till the press get hold of it. I envy Adam: there's a point to him, now.

'You're wrong,' said Kevin. 'this isn't ended. Things don't end, they never do. That's one reason why Emily has no time for TV series and novels and stuff like that: they always come out so pat in the end, but things just don't – she's right when you think about it because really there can *be* no end. Not in that way.'

'Maybe not even in death,' said Rosie, wistfully. 'It's funny.'

'Killing,' grunted Raymond. 'Oh Christ – sorry, Kevin.'

'Although in many ways,' continued Kevin, 'this has been something of a Last Supper. Everything's different, now. It's a shame Sophie never came. Or maybe not.'

'Where is everybody?' Maureen wanted to know. She was sitting up and ruffling her hair. 'Someone should've woken me up – I must have dozed off. Have I missed anything?'

'Maureen,' said her mother, 'you're a fool.'

'Not polite, Mummy. Not. I'm rather hungry.'

'All the food is back in the kitchen,' said Kevin, quite automatically. 'Have what you want. Raymond – please take drink, or whatever. You know where it all is. Actually, although it might seem odd, I think I'll go up to bed, if that's all right with everyone. I don't suppose I'll ever see her again, not now.'

Maureen lurched away in her quest for food while Rosie

settled back into the sofa and closed her eyes. Kevin went upstairs ('if someone could maybe do the lights . . . ?') and soon afterwards, Raymond followed him up. He found him, as he had expected to, sitting on the edge of his bed and staring nowhere much. But he had obviously registered Raymond's presence because now he was saying (sounding very far away):

'It's rather odd, Raymond. There are some strange little whitish things at the bottom of the lavatory.'

Raymond cleared his throat. 'Oh yes – those. Yes. They're just a few of Emily's infuriating little Japanese ivories, but I couldn't seem to flush them away. Most of all this "interiors" stuff drives me absolutely mental, if you want the truth.'

Kevin nodded. 'Maybe the only interiors we should consider are our own.'

'Do you know, Kevin – that's the first of your turgid little homilies that has ever made an ounce of sense?'

Kevin looked quite blank.

'It wasn't one. It wasn't one of those. The thought just occurred to me. I don't suppose anyone put away the Monopoly, did they?'

Raymond sighed. 'Who's this Sophie you were talking about?'

'Hm? Oh. Just someone.'

'You don't mean Sophie who used to work for Emily? Christ I *loved* that woman – the only one I ever did: the only one who wasn't crazy. You know what? I've never told anyone this before: I'm ninety-five per cent certain that I have a little girl who is two years old tomorrow. Don't know her name.'

There was a silence between them before Kevin said: 'Maybe, actually, Raymond, this *has* ended, at last. There can hardly be more. God, though – it's all so *ragged*. Can an ending be said to be ragged?'

'Christ, Kevin – *I* don't know: all a bit philosophical for me – last person in the world. I shouldn't have said so, though – if it's ragged, it can't be said to be finished, can it? God – I don't know. Look, Kevin – you get yourself into bed – tomorrow could be a long one. I'll see to all the lights and locks and stuff – Rosie'll be fast asleep on the sofa by now, and Christ alone knows what Maureen's up to in the kitchen.'

Kevin nodded. Trials come to an end and sentences are passed – but finally, still, there can be no finale? And then his nose began to twitch.

'Do I smell burning?' he asked – just as Raymond caught a whiff of it too.